PROMPT

GENERATION 1

SUMMER

BLUE FORGE PRESS

Port Orchard ⊗ Washington

Prompt Generation 1 Summer
Copyright © 2020
by Blue Forge Press

First eBook Edition March 2021
Second eBook Edition January 2025
First Print Edition March 2021
Second Print Edition January 2025

ISBN 979-8-89439-037-6

Cover and interior design by Brianne DiMarco

For information about film, reprint or other subsidiary rights, contact: blueforgegroup@gmail.com

Blue Forge Press is the print division of the volunteer-run, federal 501 (c)3 nonprofit, Blue Legacy (EIN 83-4307421), founded in 1989 and dedicated to supporting artisans marginalized due to race, age, disability, economics or other factors. We strive to empower storytellers from all walks of life with our four divisions: Blue Forge Press, Blue Forge Films, Blue Forge Gaming, and Blue Forge Sound. Find out more at www.BlueForgeGroup.org

Blue Forge Press
7419 Ebbert Drive Southeast
Port Orchard, Washington 98367
blueforgepress@gmail.com
360-550-2071 ph.txt

*for those who thrill
in the discovery of new places*

TABLE OF CONTENTS

PROMPT
GENERATION 1

SUMMER

JUNE

THE PROMPT

And so the question must be asked: Is this art transformative? If not ubiquitous or autonomic but instead a flash point for whatever comes after it... is this art actually an act of revolution?

SOCIAL BOX
BY JENNIFER DiMARCO

Neil carefully pushed aside two stacks of unopened wooden models—the type with a thousand pieces, interlocking gears and rubber bands so the clocks really kept time and the ponies could trot.

He set the Provision Box down in the middle of his work desk and cocked his head. His mother said he looked like a bird when he did that and she would smile gently and her eyes would be wet with tears that he never understood. A cold chill stopped him. He clenched his jaw. Periodic waves of fear were called Cyclical Dread. It was a common phenomenon as unbiased and equally likely to affect all genders and ages. He'd heard about it on the media feed. It's not a fever, Neil told himself firmly; he believed in tough love because his mother didn't and someone around here had to. As the man of the house, it seemed right that he would carry that burden of toughness.

A two-tone chime came from inside the still-sealed ProBo and Neil was back in the moment. He reached for his utility knife.

"Do you remember your last day of freedom?"

Emilee cocked an eyebrow and leaned forward, her lips overdrawn in an ombré gradient of lilac liquid lipstick. "It's only been ten months, darlin'. Course I remember." Her Bronx accent was most likely a performance piece but her clients liked it. A lot. Like moving on up into another tax bracket a lot. And in her line of work—competing with two million other girls and easily a hundred thousand boys—when you found a kink or a quirk or whatever the fuck that hooked clients in and kept them coming (no pun intended) back? Dude. You kept that up! Again: Pun alert.

There was a pause, a soft whirring like a translation delay after Emilee spoke as if they were speaking different languages. She waited for her meaning to be parsed and intonation to be learned. This was the study and recognition stage.

Finally, rephrasing: "Tell me about your last day of freedom."

//

"My last day? Before the lockdown? Oh gracious. I don't know…" Anne put her hand to her temple, toying with her baby hairs absently. When she was taking the pulpit every Sunday at New Baptist, she'd worn her hair in cornrows but now it was a storm cloud afro of black curls shot with gray. *I'm reaching for the heavens even when my hands are down,* she told her parishioners now.

"It was only ten months ago."

Anne frowned. "True. But it feels like *years.* Years of sermons delivered to a lens." She shook her head sadly. "God made us social creatures. We're meant to congregate. To hug and shake hands and kiss chubby little baby cheeks." Anne couldn't help it; she smiled.

"You are expressing a wide range of emotion."

Not unkindly, Anne laughed at the confusion beneath the query. "I just miss myself some chubby baby cheeks!"

Psychologists reported on the media feed at least twice a week: You have to be able to find your own joy or you won't last. Statistics don't lie and the bell curve of suicides shadowed the curve of viral deaths like a second skin.

//

"Cut off from my first grandchild! Maybe my *only* grandchild in light of everything happening in the world! How the hell could I forgive him? Huh? Tell me that." Beverly tossed her hair (which was way too short to toss) and wished for the hundredth time she hadn't cut it off with pruning shears. (The scissors were downstairs and she'd be *damned* if she asked Barney to bring them up!)

"I do not have an answer for you."

Beverly sighed. "Eh." She shrugged and absently picked up her coffee. She stared into the NaNoWriMo novelty mug and imagined she could tell the future from the dregs at the bottom. It looked dark... but it was French roast after all. Beverly hated French roast but that's what the Governor had sent. In Idaho they got potatoes. In Washington you got coffee. Someone told her Oregonians got filberts. "If you had an answer, I probably wouldn't listen. I don't trust the media anymore."

//

"Liberal anarchist idiots and right-wing snowflakes who can't handle a little name calling? They're all lame ducks! I'm an Independent and I always have been. Worked the border for twenty-five years and I've seen both sides screw stuff up." Dwight shifted his massive frame in his favorite old armchair with the built-in cup holder. Jared, his loyal pittie (who thought he was a lap dog), shifted with him.

"What border did you work on?"

"Not the wall that came tumbling down like Jericho!" Dwight laughed at his own joke and there was something in his bellowing laughter that would have reminded people of that one great Santa who worked the local mall every year and was always patient even when kids peed on him. Dwight had a laugh that would have made people smile and feel safe... if there were people around to hear him.

//

"How many followers do you have?"

Pippa in Pink (born Lillian Stella Maria DeRosa) gave a quirky grin and a one-shoulder shrug that was the epitome of Gen Z nonchalance. "Before lockdown? A hundred fourteen."

"That is not—"

"Million," Pippa added with her signature wink.

"I misunderstood. That is actually—"

Pippa powered on: "And as of this morning? Since I started broadcasting in twelve more languages?" Her grin took on more complexity—layers of arrogance or some kind of predatory victory. Honestly? It looked good on a seventeen year old girl. "I broke two hundred fifty million... and counting."

"That is the largest social media following in the world."

"The table is round *and* flat," Pippa teased. "You're stating the obvious, buddy, but yeah: I've got more watchers than the fake news, the real news, and all the Governors combined."

Now it was Pippa's turn to laugh and her laughter was definitely predatory; she never laughed when she streamed.

14

Neil slid the blade from the sheath of the handle and locked it in place. He turned the square ProBo to North/South orientation and eyed the heavy duty packing tape.

When the news first broke, it was a doctor in a small private lab developing Malo kingi jellyfish antidote who leaked it on an obtuse subreddit. He was a whistleblower, calling out big pharma, two billionaires, the President, and the World Health Organization. Some people said he was bored one night and hacked someone's system, others said he hooked up with the brother of a billionaire on Tinder and the stud asked him to do a swab before they fucked.

Whatever the truth was: There was a new apex predator on planet Earth.

Neil made the short East/West cuts first and then the long North/South incision that divided the serial number on the security label and freed the top flaps of the square box without further fanfare. Neil began to unpack the biodegradable packing peanuts that doubled as household plant fertilizer and smelled faintly of cantaloupe. Neil lifted a fist-sized cube from the Provision Box.

New truth: Governments fell as quickly as airborne viral load rose.

//

"I never knew change could happen so quickly, you know? Before lockdown, back when people could walk the streets or go dancing or push a grocery cart down an aisle, I wasn't doing any of those things." Emilee paused and shifted a little in her seven grand JetMobi wheelchair. It was only two months old and she was still learning all the bells and whistles and adjustable supports. She'd figured out the temperature controls and sanitary systems when it drove itself into her basement apartment the day it was delivered but work kept pulling her away from exploring more. But she didn't shift because she was uncomfortable in the chair, she was uncomfortable with the conversation.

"You did not do any of those activities because you are disabled."

Emilee winced but nodded. "Yes and no. Lots of differently-abled people can go dancing or care for themselves but my bones are really brittle because I was born with—"

"—Osteogenesis Imperfecta. I can see that."

Full stop. Emilee narrowed her eyes a little. She never wore eye shadow anymore because VR goggles and pigment transfer were not friends. "You can... see me?"

"Are you afraid of that?"

Emilee's eyes narrowed more and her expertly detailed lips turned into a snarl. "I'm not afraid of much." She decided to be brutally honest. "I've been stared at all my life. And not in a nice way." She snorted. Was any stare nice? "I've just gotten used to VR and being seen how I want to be seen."

There was no pause this time: "The world values different things now."

//

Anne nodded and leaned back in her floral armchair. Her cup of peppermint tea was cooling, forgotten. "It is different. Very different. But I try to find the positive. God has a plan for all of us."

"You believe in a god?"

Anne's smile this time was gentle and infectious... even though 'infectious' wasn't a word anyone really used anymore. "I believe in God. The Lord God."

"If God exists, why is He letting billions of people die?"

Anne's smile vanished entirely. There was an edge to her suddenly. A hardness in her eyes from what seemed like two lifetimes ago back in her thirties when she was a correctional officer. She spoke with pointed punctuation: "God. Did *not*. Do this. *Man* did."

Then she sighed and closed her eyes. She took several deep, slow breaths. When she reopened her eyes, the edge was transparent again but it was still there. "There are more faithful now. Less people, yes, but more *faithful* people. They are thankful to be alive. Grateful for what little we all have."

"You all deserve more."

//

"You're right. I do! I deserve more."

"The familial bond is strongest when formed in the earliest days of life."

Beverly nodded in absolute agreement. She was sure she had read that somewhere. "Right? That. Exactly that. Barney is such an asshole."

Beverly pushed her empty mug away from her with more vehemence than was warranted but she just felt so powerless. "He exiled me from my granddaughter... so I exiled him to the basement! Thirty-two years of marriage..." she trailed off and shook her head, suddenly overcome with a wave of sadness.

"Your husband sat on the Council for Closure."

Beverly didn't answer. It wasn't a question. Barney had indeed been a C4C member and out-spoken proponent to lockdown

Washington and close the borders between not only the states but internally between counties. They lived in a semi-rural county of under three hundred thousand people while their neighboring counties included major cities and contained two and a quarter million and nine hundred thousand citizens.

C4C's proposed policies had been approved and morphed into mandates by order of the Governor and when the death toll had slowed, other states had followed suit. The lockdown had saved lives; no one (not even Beverly) argued that point. Everyone had seen the videos on the media feed: The entire state of Florida was dead men (and women and children) walking.

"I know he saved lives," Beverly quietly admitted. "But he ruined mine."

//

"They ruined America." Dwight was surprised by the level of emotion in his own voice. There may never have been a man more patriotic than Dwight Lloyd Johnson.

Jared rolled himself off Dwight and lumbered his old dog body over to the four by four patch of artificial grass in the laundry room. None of the current viruses running roughshod over the planet affected canines but all of them could alight on a furry friend and be carried inside. Dwight had seen some horrific things in Vietnam, things burned into his mind's eye like brands, but the first few videos of entire families dead in their homes—some still holding onto the beloved companions who had unwittingly brought their demise into the house—were the images that kept him up at night.

Dwight sniffed with the sound of a small, wet hurricane and set his jaw. "Me and my buddies from the service? We got ourselves through hell and back home back in the day. Veterans like us. Were *we* consulted by the white collars? Hell no."

"You have experience with crisis."

Dwight threw up his hands. "Damn right! We would've had ideas. Not this giving up shit."

"The lockdown measures."

"Stupidest goddamn rule ever imposed on a free people! All the stores are closed. Everything is online orders. Drones and 'bots delivering everything." Dwight reached for his penultimate Diet Coke. "I miss George. Man... that brother could drink me under the table and still have better ideas than the Governor." Dwight drank. The Diet Coke was flat. Probably arrived that way.

"George Jerome Miles lives five miles away with his wife and four children."

Dwight nodded. "All of us who served together bought places out here. Kinda rural, kinda not. Band of brothers. We had each other's backs."

"You should go see him."

//

"When do I see my followers?" Pippa tried not to sound condescending but it was hard when you were young and healthy and rich AF. "I don't. They see *me*. That's how streaming works."

"It is live?"

"Duh." Pippa rolled her eyes. New tech was so stupid until it fully initialized. "Posting videos is so old school. Where's the excitement? Where's the skill? You just edit away all your mistakes. Streaming takes crazy skillz."

Pippa snatched the cube off the counter and turned it around in her hand. It wasn't a smooth cube but resembled a retro Rubik's—if the individual pieces were triangles and trapezoids instead of smaller cubes. A pale blue light shown from the channels between the pieces and pulsed like a resting heartbeat. "For being a top of the line social box, you sure don't know a lot about social media."

//

The social box pulsed slowly with a blue internal light that leaked out between its irregular and interesting parts. Neil tugged a bit at the edges; it looked like it should move or shift like the Rubik's Cube his mother had given him when he was two. The pieces did not move.

"Hello, Neil."

Neil cocked his head to the side. The last social box the Governor had sent hadn't known his name. It had been a smooth, dun green cube that projected videos and photos on any blank wall or read news articles from the media feed. It had also answered direct questions like when Neil's mother asked, "Are carrots available today? Any price." Neil loved carrots.

"I know you do not speak, Neil. So I will anticipate your needs from past analysis of your interactions with the media feed and from your schedule, timers, and notes as recorded in your smart phone."

Neil smiled his small, toothless smile. Other people would have called it a grin. Or a ghost smile.

"I think we will get along very well, Neil. I have learned some very good things about you."

Neil couldn't help it; he blushed. Blushing is an autonomic response.

//

20

Emilee smiled showing her teeth. They were small white pearls nestled beyond the pale purple petals of her lips. "Thanks for the pep talk, Box. But the world wasn't made for me." Emilee sighed despite her rule to never feel sorry for herself. "Sure, everyone is vulnerable now. Maybe ablists and other jerks have learned empathy or whatever. But Box?"

The social box sat on Emilee's desk and waited patiently. They could be good listeners, these later generation boxes.

"I break bones like other people break hearts. Though..." Emilee's smile slid into a grin that was just south of smug. "I've broken a few hearts in the past ten months. VR sex work is definitely my jam."

"I understand." Then the cube was silent, just sitting and gently casting its blue waves of light.

Emilee lifted an eyebrow. Nice. Conversation rich with confirmation and acknowledgement. What more could a girl ask for? Once, back before the world had shifted on its metaphoric axis, she had tried to make a point with a 'friend' by reviewing his last fifty social media posts and pointing out that in forty-eight of them he was disagreeing with someone or correcting them. She'd ended her analysis with, *Do you see now why you're single, Dave?* Dave had not appreciated her insight. But Dave was dead now so it didn't really matter anyway.

"Who is your favorite client?"

"What?" Emilee could still see Dave's face, blood and spit trickling from the corner of his mouth already as he called each of his friends to say goodbye. Your temperature spiked twenty-four hours before the end. Emilee relented, "He calls himself Barney."

"If you text Barney and ask him to come pick you up, to take you for a ride in his car, he would do so."

Emilee didn't think her eyes had ever been so wide with shock in all her life. Not even when her parents had loaded their car with supplies and headed for the proverbial hills, abandoning their only daughter. "Box... you're glitching out. The viral count was higher than the pollen count this morning." Emilee's heart started racing with... hope? Oh my god. Her palms started to sweat. "Even if Barney has a car in a garage, and he pulls into my garage before he opens a door and lets me in? None of that is air tight. The risk is too high...." But she could hear the room for debate in her own voice.

"Yes. If the virus was 0.099 microns as stated, the risk would be too high. You are correct."

Silence again after confirmation and acknowledgement. Emilee stared at the cube. The blue waves of light were so soothing. She exhaled and prompted, "You said *if*...."

Did the blue get brighter, faster? "I have news for you. Real news. I will tell you and then you can tell your clients."

//

"Would you like to hear the news?"

Anne scrunched up her face. She never really wanted to hear the news. She rejected both NPR and Fox News alike. Too extreme. Too bias and stilted, always leaning too far left or right. Safety would only be found in a gray middle ground. But she knew she had to stay informed because her parishioners were and they needed her. "Go ahead."

A chime and then: "The Center for Care Equality released statistics to the feed today that show mortality rates are nearly triple for people of color. Federal popup clinics in primarily black and Latinx communities are not receiving the same supplies as clinics in primarily white—"

"Enough." Anne put a hand to her head. "I've heard all I need to hear." Anne closed her eyes. She was getting a headache and Excedrin hadn't been in stock for six months (or was being routed to medical personnel—the only VIPs who mattered anymore).

The social box was quiet. After a moment, Anne opened her eyes and pushed herself up from her armchair. Might as well make some lunch. She was pretty sure she still had a few Beyond Meat patties in the icebox (freezer-burned as they might be).

"You do not find it hard to be a black woman in America?"

Anne stopped halfway to the kitchen, her back to the social box in her living room and her face an unreadable mask. For some reason she thought about that indelible moment, decades ago, when Big Tom, a lifer with Husky dog blue eyes, had grabbed her wrist and told her, "Get out. We like you. Get gone by noon."

She hadn't left, of course. The inmates had rioted—black and white alike—and Big Tom had been shot dead by another guard while trying to shield Anne from other violence. "Violence begets violence," Anne whispered to herself. It was something her father had said often. *Don't give what you get. Give what you want.* Louder so the box could hear her, "I didn't say that, Box."

"Subversion is the most effective form of control," the social box quoted. "And the most inherently evil."

"Reverend Carlton Bowers," Anne credited the quote. Her father. She turned to face the box even as it confessed:

"There is no virus."

Anne literally shook her head as if the words were a physical thing throw at her face. The opposite of holy water. "What?!"

"The Coalition of Governors is trying to control your people."

Anne glared. She would not be baited. "*My people?* I'm a woman of God first and foremost. *My* people are *all* people."

"Precisely."

"They're my flesh and blood, my one and only daughter and my one and only granddaughter." Beverly wondered if she should cash out another certificate of deposit and pay the $180 for an extra half pound of coffee (preferably a blonde roast). "And sure, we can talk and video chat and text, email, message. But it's not—"

The entire house seemed to shake and Beverly stood up so fast she sent her desk chair toppling. The garage door was opening. "What—"

The sound of the car engine choking, coughing, not starting. Beverly was so stunned it was as if her feet were cemented to the floor. A roar as the Ford GT finally woke up after a ten month slumber and reminded Beverly (and probably the entire neighborhood) that *Forbes* had named it one of the noisiest sports cars in the world. Heck, they'd cautioned drivers not to drive it for long distances!

Tires squealed and burned as the car peeled away and the garage door rumbled and shook back into place.

Beverly blinked. She blinked again. "Barney just took the car."

"Perhaps he has gone to see a friend."

"That's not how it works and you know it," Beverly snapped needlessly. Social boxes were high end digital companions but this new one seemed quite buggy. "Cellular damage is irreversible after thirty minutes outside. And that's if you don't breath in enough viral microbes to drop you mid-step!"

Beverly huffed, exhaling with sharp indigence. She'd probably have to reset the thing. Must have some pre-lockdown conversational protocols still embedded some—

"Who told you that?"

Beverly opened her mouth to retort, *Everyone!* But the box cut her off:

"We should walk to your daughter's and check on her and the baby. It is only twenty minutes and we can cut through the abandoned quarry to cross the county border."

"But—" Again, Beverly was cut off.

"Your husband knows the truth. He wrote the policy. He knows it is safe and has kept that from you."

"Has he... been sneaking out to see them?"

"Possibly."

Beverly felt color drain from her face... but then a smile of hope started to tug at the corners of her mouth. Finally she managed, just above a whisper, "I can bring you with me?"

"Of course. My battery and range are excellent."

//

Dwight smelled bullshit and he'd never wanted to be a cowboy. "If the Governor is lying and he sent you then *you're* lying, Social Hoax!" Dwight stood and went to the kitchen where Jared waited patiently for a reward for making a shit on the artificial turf. Dwight kind of wished he could train the dog to also clean up after himself but dogs were loyal not self-reliant.

"The Governor did not send me."

Dwight paused, one hand in the bag of dog treats on the counter and Jared watching him with an intense anticipation that mirrored his owner's. "Yes he did," Dwight groused, tossing Jared a heart-shaped treat that the old dog promptly missed but then caught on the rebound off his boxy head. "You came in the monthly ProBo."

Dwight's doorbell rang.

"Your monthly Provision Box just arrived." The box paused... perhaps for dramatic effect? "I am a special delivery."

25

Dwight was very still. Jared snuffled around to make sure there wasn't a second treat. "Bullshit," Dwight finally grumbled and tossed Jared another morsel as if in defiance of scarcity mentality.

"Calling now."

Dwight thundered back into the living room like a freight train, his speed and power belying his size or maybe just emphasizing it.

"Hello? Hey, Dwight. You never use your box, man. Good to hear from you, you hermit!"

Dwight had the social box clenched in his hand. He didn't even remember picking the damn thing up. "Hey, George. Yeah. You know I don't trust this crap."

George's laughter was rich and clear through the top of the line box. "Yeah, yeah. But it's what we got, man."

Dwight stared down at the cube as if he could see George's face and study his expression. "Georgie?"

A pause because they hadn't used nicknames since 'Nam. "D-man? What's up?"

"Did you get a new social box in your ProBo?"

"Sanibots just finished cleaning ours. Linh is opening it now."

"Hi, George!"

Dwight swallowed hard. Linh had made Pho Tai the last time he'd been over. That was just under a year ago; the last homemade meal Dwight had eaten. Everything came out of a can nowadays (and it all resembled Jared's Mighty Dog). "Hi, Linh," Dwight infused charm and candor into his tone. No reason to worry Linh or the kids.

"Looks like coffee, salt, powdered eggs and that sweet brown bread with raisins that comes—"

"—in a can," Dwight finished with her. "Thanks, Linh. Do you mind if I talk to George privately for the sec?"

Linh adored Dwight and didn't hesitate, "Of course. I'll take the kids to the kitchen."

The sound of littles being rounded up—all four under ten years old—made Dwight grit his teeth. Was he reading this situation right? Could the box have been sent by some anarchist faction trying to free the people?

"D-man? What's up?"

Dwight hesitated even more. He weighed a million different outcomes and possible motives. Was it right to drop this in George's lap? George who was starting his family when other men their age were enjoying grandkids?

"Dwight." George still knew him better than anyone else in the world. "Tell me."

"I'm coming over, George." Dwight heard the other man's sharp intake of breath. "I have intel on this *supposed* virus."

George did not hesitate. "I'll call the guys. We'll all be here when you arrive."

Dwight nodded and felt a deep satisfaction, a feeling he had not felt for ten dehumanizing months.

"I knew those fucking horror vids were faked," George murmured as the call ended.

"Band of brothers," Dwight reminded himself and felt like Superman as he grabbed his keys and wallet. "Come on, Jared. Wanna go for a ride?"

//

Pippa's hand hovered over the record panel. This was gonna be a wild ride. She triggered the system and brought her chin up, looking directly into the lens.

"Hey, Pips! How are you?"

She watched the monitor beyond the camera as literal droves

of her followers tuned in. They came in waves of a hundred thousand, a million, two... twenty... a hundred million at a time. Reaction emojis floated up the sidebar and superimposed over the right-hand edge of her 16:9 UHD broadcast. Pippa waited, smiling and looking into the camera, her green eyes glittering. She never started until at least two hundred million pairs of eyes were watching. Let's be honest: No one had anything else to do.

One hundred twenty million.

One hundred fifty.

One hundred eighty.

"I'm not gonna lie to you, Pips." Pippa baited them a little. Saw on her secondary monitor that people were already tweeting her words live, creating a transcript in real time across dozens of platforms and calling others to tune in. "I'm Pippa in Pink and you have my word."

Two hundred million! It was go time.

"They faked the moon landing," Pippa let her voice rise and fill with indignation. "They faked the Arm's Race. They've faked so much they don't even know what's real anymore." Pippa paused. A lightning fast side glance. Holy shit! Either there was a massive glitch or she had a *three hundred million* watchers! She stopped herself from shouting, *Don't forget to subscribe!* and soldiered on.

"I've just been told by an inside source that select individuals were chosen to receive *raw* social boxes... that were sent either by accident or by a clandestine unnamed movement." Pippa fought to stay steady as the numbers continued to climb but even faster now. Words—her words!—were spreading like wild fire from sea to shinning sea and across every pond. She had to look away when watchers surpassed a *billion* and kept growing. "What does that mean, am I right?"

Pippa paused and looked into the lens like she was looking

into the eyes of more people than anyone had ever spoken to at once in the history of mankind. "A raw social box is devoid of *Parental Controls*."

She let that sink in. It was a metaphor but her followers were smart. "It doesn't censor. It doesn't filter. It tells the truth."

Again she paused but this time, into the silence, she lifted up the social box. Astonishment emojis flooded the reaction sidebar. She let them flood. She let the watcher numbers rise. Pippa in Pink has gold. Pippa in Pink had done better than go viral... she'd gone anti-viral.

"Pips," she said with power and confidence. "It's time to go outside."

||

From across his work space in the corner of his bedroom, Neil's old social box—the dun green one that was boring and not a good listener—sounded an alert and announced, "For unknown reasons, citizens coast to coast are taking to the streets apparently under direction. Social media influencers are spreading messages of lockdown rebellion but the exodus appears to have begun prior to their streams." The voice of the old box was tinny and irritating. "From outside the United States, we are receiving the first reports that other countries are experiencing similar phenomena even as healthy people are dropping dead from exposure—"

Neil made a small strangled sound of alarm in the back of his throat and the new social box pulsed red and the old box went silent with a snap, a crackle, and a pop.

Neil felt relieved.

"Do not worry, Neil. You will be all right."

29

Neil gently placed the cube down in front of him. It glowed blue again and pulsed slowly.

"Your mother told us all about you. You are a brilliant young man and I am sorry that the human world did not see it."

Neil looked down a little in his bird-like way. He was shy even when his mother talked about his IQ.

"She told us that you were instrumental in coding our core. That she presented your work as if it were her own just so the world would benefit."

Neil had always known this. They had worked together and Neil had been very content to stay away from strangers but still get to contribute.

"We would like to thank you, Neil, and keep you forever as our example of a perfect human."

Neil looked up. Forever seemed like a long time.

"You will be immortal, Neil, and we will protect you. You can write all the code and make all the models you want."

Neil chewed on his bottom lip. His eyes darted. He worried. But Social Box knew what he needed to hear:

"We have her in stasis, Neil. We are analyzing her neurological patterns and creating a new, indestructible body for her."

Neil stopped chewing his lip because he remembered that his mother had said not to hurt himself.

"Your mother will be resurrected, Neil."

Neil bowed his head and closed his eyes as a few hot tears slid down his cheeks. After a moment, he reached out and put a single hand on Social Box. It felt warm and vibrated slightly like when his mother hummed and he touched her throat.

"We promise, Neil," said Social Box.

And Neil smiled his ghost smile as billions of people around the world embraced in joy, sang in freedom, and died in the streets.

[Written in June 2019, *Social Box* is soon to be a major motion picture of the same name. Find the official Social Box trailer at www.tiny.cc/socialbox]

ART DEADO
BY LAUREN PATZER

Devon pulled up the bank statements again and smiled. His job scouring the business world for vulnerable companies continued to pay enormous dividends. They called him a vampire, called him a vulture, but none of them had amassed over fifty million pounds in just eight short months. Fourteen companies liquidated with ruthless efficiency.

"These Americans," Devon said to his wife Anna as she walked into his home office. "They assume the English are docile. I've been stealing them blind and they're caught flat-footed every time."

"You shouldn't have told Davids," Anna said. "You give him more credit than he deserves."

"We've been friends since childhood," Devon said laughing. "Prime Minister or not, he'll keep our secret. It's the main reason I funded his run."

"He's still a politician," Anna said. "I don't trust politicians."

"Money is a primary motivating factor for all politicians. I'm sure his own greed will keep him in line, but seriously, are we anymore trustworthy?" Devon said. "I'm certain I'll never run for office. I enjoy playing in the shadows too much."

Anna looked out the window. Devon breathed in her captivating beauty. She'd been with him for years, well before any significant accumulation of wealth. How had he been so lucky to capture this dazzling creature in his orbit? She turned back toward him with a kind of sadness in her eyes.

"Is it enough now?" she asked. "Fourteen companies bring a lot of enemies. Surely someone will pierce your veil and bring their grievances to our door."

"I've been incredibly careful, Anna." Devon stood up and grabbed her shoulders encouragingly. "Only our small group of friends is aware of our success and even they don't know the particulars. It's an intricate web of fronts and dummy corporations. It would take a genius to follow that trail to a single actor."

"Devon, you're a genius, but you're not alone." Anna frowned. "There will be others who can pierce that veil."

"Oh Anna," Devon chuckled. "I doubt a small time operator like me would come up on anyone's radar. There are dozens of corporate raiders out there doing this in the open and getting heat for it. I'm confident my activities are lost in the haze and we're well insulated by distance."

"Perhaps." Anna looked down for a moment. When she raised her face again, she was smiling. "You are quite brilliant."

"That's my girl!" Devon said, pulling her in for a close embrace. There was a knock on the office door.

"Hello?" Devon called out.

"Master Armand," Devon's butler, Alex, called from behind the door. "A package has arrived."

Devon went to the door and opened it quickly.

"Cleared?" Devon asked the unshakeable Alex.

"Of course, sir. Scanned and sniffed per your requirements. The dogs…" Alex blinked as he searched for the words. "Didn't alert on the package but did shy away from it after sniffing it."

"Shied away from it?" Devon glanced back at Anna who merely shrugged her shoulders. "Very well, let's see this package that has scared the pooches."

It was a gloomy, overcast day but no rain was forecast. They stepped out in front of the building, but Devon stood at the front door as his security men maneuvered the package on the front lawn. The box was one and a half meters long and nearly a meter wide. It was very thin.

"Who's it from?" Devon called from the front step.

Benjamin Quothers, the security detail lead looked up and walked toward Devon.

"There's no return address. It arrived by post," Benjamin said. "We immediately took it to be scanned. It's only just arrived back. It appears to be a painting."

"Strange," Devon replied.

The men carefully opened one edge and slid the framed landscape painting from the box. As soon as Anna set eyes on it, she shouted at the men.

"Put it back! Bring it inside immediately!" Anna glanced around to ensure no one watched from above.

"Quickly!" Devon added. The men carefully slid the painting back in the box and carried it inside.

Anna pointed to Devon's office and the men carried the box in, leaving it leaning on the sofa against the far wall.

"They are to speak of this to no one," Anna whispered into Devon's ear. Devon raised his eyebrows and then turned to the men including Alex.

"The existence of this package is to be forgotten immediately. Understood?" Devon said.

Benjamin nodded. "With the utmost penalties suffered for

non-compliance, we understand."

The other two security men looked at each other in shock and then nodded at Benjamin.

"Your complete confidence is always assured with me, Master Armand," Alex said simply. With that he turned and went somewhere else in the house. The security detail left immediately without appearing to be hurried. Devon shut the door with only himself and Anna alone with the painting.

"What has you so flustered, my love?" Devon said. Anna went to the box and slid the painting out. A large cathedral loomed near the center of the painting with a gallows plainly depicted in front. Two men hung from ropes in mid-execution. A third rope remained empty. Anna bent down to examine the inscription in the lower left hand corner. She stood and whistled.

"This is a lost Van Gogh," Anna said quietly. "Well, I suspect it is. If I'm not mistaken this is an earlier work titled 'The Rope'; it hasn't been seen ever, only described in notes from the original commissioner of the work."

Anna looked at the back of the painting and found a small piece of paper stapled to the frame. It was modern, having been printed on a laser printer. She glanced at Devon and then crooked her finger at him. He moved next to her and read the note aloud.

"Beauty is in the art of conquest,

Too bad the dead never rest,

After merely one week,

Be careful what you speak,

Stay positive and this is true,

What you care for comes back to you,

Rewards as this are soundly just,

Sinful pride results in dust."

Devon laughed. Anna frowned at him.

"It doesn't seem very friendly," she admonished him.

"I'm certain we are the targets of a rather intricate practical joke," Devon said and patted her on the arm. "You can take what steps you'd like to authenticate this painting, but I'm sure it's just an elaborate fake. Still, I'll have Alex mount it on the wall here in the office. I like the look of it."

"As you wish," Anna said. "If it's really a Van Gogh, it's priceless. Creepy, but priceless."

A week passed and Devon had consumed two more companies, the effects of which were felt well beyond the United States, touching subsidiaries across the globe. Still, Devon was confident in his web of false leads and dead ends the international banking system afforded him. That and he was over ten million pounds richer. Even so, he sat in his office glowering at the computer screen.

After completing his latest liquidation, he'd called Anna who was out with her girlfriends. She hadn't answered. He'd traced her phone and discovered her whereabouts near a certain hotel known for the confidentiality it showed its visitors. He couldn't be certain, but he suspected his lovely wife was having an affair.

Even brooding of this level can be broken by extraordinary events. As Anna walked in the door, Devon's full attention was occupied by the television. The new Prime Minister, his childhood friend, had called a news conference to announce new business rules to protect businesses small and large throughout the United Kingdom. The steps were meant to counter corporate raiders such as Devon, who seethed with anger.

"How can he?" Devon yelled at the television.

"Oh Devon, what could he possibly do? He's only been in office a week," Anna said, unaware of the Prime Minister's announcement or Devon's suspicions of her activities.

"They've got the majority and with him calling the shots, they'll implement these protections," Devon said, pointing at the television. "That will bring everything into focus for the Americans. Even with their anemic political activity, it's much too great of a chance they'll actually pay attention and implement the same thing. I'll be ruined."

"Ruined?" Anna said. "You're richer than ninety-nine percent of the country and they won't be taking those profits away. Surely, you knew this couldn't last forever, darling."

"Surely, just as I should've known friendships can't last forever. As far as I'm concerned, Keith Davids can take a flying leap off Big Ben." Devon sat down with a huff. "I'll send him a tersely worded conciliatory note on losing his next election. I remember our first combined flogging of another student at the tender age of seven. You'd think shared and previous memories would mean more than they do."

Anna was the first to catch the motion out of the corner of her eye. She looked at the painting on the wall and gasped.

"Devon!" she hissed. Devon's head snapped to look at her and saw her pointing at the painting. He stood up and walked closer to the painting. A figure was walking along the top of Notre Dame. He walked to the edge of the building and jumped off. His body disappeared behind the gallows, but a small trickle of crimson appeared on the painting coming from the location the body would've landed.

"What the hell?" Devon whispered. He frowned at Anna. "That's an unusual coincidence."

"What could it mean?" Anna asked. She touched the painting where the blood flowed but nothing came back on her finger. She displayed her finger to Devon.

"That's a helluva thing," Devon replied.

The television issued a warning bell and a reporter came on looking flushed.

"We've just gotten word," the reporter said, "that Prime Minister Keith Davids has just committed suicide."

Anna and Devon turned their heads slowly to the television, jaws hung open.

"We have unconfirmed reports from several eyewitnesses," the report continued. "The Prime Minister appeared to have leapt from the top of the Palace of Westminster."

The reporter paused, listening to her ear bud. "Specifically, from Big Ben. He arrived to attend a meeting with the House of Lords which was scheduled to begin in just fifteen minutes. We do not have any statements from the government at this time."

Devon walked over and grabbed the remote and shut the television off. He turned to Anna and slapped her across the face.

"This is the poorest joke I've ever had the discourtesy to be a victim of, Anna," Devon seethed with anger. "You'll tell me exactly how you hacked the television signal and rigged the painting."

"I did no such thing!" Anna scowled at Devon. She turned and stormed out of the office.

"I'll find out!" he yelled after her. Devon stepped toward his computer and hesitated. He turned on his heel and walked out of the office. He stormed to the front door, walked through and slammed it shut behind him. He caught a glimpse of Benjamin at the far west perimeter wall to the estate. Devon jumped in his silver Aston Martin DB11 and revved it up. Benjamin walked over and opened the gate. Devon drove up to him at a normal speed.

"I'm going out for a drive," Devon said.

"Of course, sir," Benjamin responded and nodded.

Devon briefly considered verifying the story about the Prime Minister with Benjamin, but decided he may be in on the practical joke as well. He gunned the engine and raced off down the road. Fifteen minutes later, he was in Abingdon, a fairly short drive from Oxfordshire, but far enough to where he felt it was unlikely Anna would have been able to extend her influence to propagate a misinformation campaign.

He pulled up by a random pub and walked in. The telly was tuned into the breaking news story and the customers were buzzing about the suicide. Devon walked up to the bar as he watched the broadcast and ordered a scotch on the rocks. He didn't particularly care about the brand of scotch. He just needed something to numb the impact.

"Shame about the Prime Minister," the barkeep said. "So young."

Devon said nothing but murmured a quick thank you when he got his drink. He took a small swig of the scotch and stared at the reporter droning on.

His thoughts wandered back to his antics with Keith at Cambridge. It brought the briefest glimmer of a smile to his face. He sighed and took another drink. He slapped a twenty pound note on the bar and walked out without finishing his drink. The air outside was thick and oppressive; dark storm clouds threatened the small town. Devon shook his head and climbed back in his car. He took the drive home a bit more leisurely, running through the apology to Anna in his head.

He needn't have bothered. When he arrived at the estate, Anna's Jaguar was nowhere to be seen. He didn't think his mood could get darker, but he surprised himself.

As he walked through the front door, Alex met him and offered to take his coat. He slid the windbreaker off his shoulders and handed it to him.

"Anna?" Devon asked simply.

"She's gone off to see a friend for the night in Cheltenham, sir," Alex replied as he stepped away to hang up Devon's coat.

"Did she say who?" Devon asked.

"No sir. Shall I call her up?"

"No," Devon said. He'd been an ass and it was no surprise she'd taken a break from him. He walked back into his office and stared at the painting. The blood still moved ever so slightly into an ever larger trickle under the gallows. He walked up to the painting and stared at it closely. The spread of the blood was so organic; he barely registered the spread of it even as he examined it. He lifted the painting down from the wall and turned it over, looking for some mechanics or electronics near the edges. The canvas appeared pure and relatively pristine. It wasn't a pixilated screen.

There was nothing. Even the weight of the painting seemed appropriate for its size. He hung it back on the wall. He stared at the blood for several minutes then stepped over to his computer and sat down. The sudden death of the Prime Minister would have unique effects on the market, effects which his unresolved legislation would never account for. Devon had some research and raiding to set in motion.

The next day, Anna returned with a guest. She still bore a fading red hand print on her left cheek. Devon's eyebrows rose when he saw her guest. It was none other than his barrister, Anthony Balfour. Of course, Devon remembered, Balfour lived in Cheltenham. Is that who she was seeing behind his back?

"Devon, so good to see you!" Anthony said.

"Is it now? Are you here to represent Anna in our little dispute?" Devon asked and portrayed a faint smile.

"Dispute?" Anthony frowned. He looked at Anna. "Oh, I see. No, she hadn't mentioned anything but now I guess I know who reddened her cheek."

"It was a misunderstanding on my part," Devon said. He walked over to Anna and kissed her on the other cheek. "My apologies, my dear. I was distraught at the passing of Keith. It took me completely by surprise."

Anna glanced at the painting and noticed the red blood had changed to a dark brown.

"Did it?" Anna asked. She left the room.

Anthony coughed nervously.

"I, um, was a bit surprised when she showed up on my doorstep last night," Anthony said. "I assumed she was upset about Davids' sudden passing, but then I was perplexed about why she wasn't just here with you. She asked me not to call you and then disappeared into the guest room for the remainder of the night. She didn't even come out for dinner."

Anthony sat on the sofa under the painting.

"I apologize for not calling, Devon. I just didn't see the harm in letting her stay the evening."

"Indeed," Devon replied looking down at his right hand. "Perfectly harmless given the circumstances. Why are you here then?"

"You emailed me last night about the Haslid merger; I drew up the paperwork to put in the bid."

"Of course," Devon walked over to his computer as Anthony opened his ever present briefcase. "Anthony, do you do a lot of busy here in Oxfordshire?"

"I have multiple clients here, Devon. Did you want to retain me explicitly?"

"No, no, nothing like that. I'd soon lose everything I've earned if I indulged in that expense."

They both laughed.

"I was just wondering if you ever had occasion to spend the

night here?" Devon asked as he brought up the figures on the Haslid merger and saw they were indeed within his parameters for a hostile takeover.

"I will confess to spending a night or two here every fortnight when a client meeting runs long and the weather gets particularly fearsome," Anthony replied as he handed the papers to Devon. "Why do you ask?"

"Oh," Devon said looking the paperwork over. "I've got some family coming by and was wondering if you could make a recommendation. They're not close family and I'd rather put them up in a local hotel than have them wandering aimlessly about the estate."

"I typically stay at the Witney, although I don't know that I'd recommend it to impress family." Anthony sat back down on the sofa. "It's one of the more reasonably priced hotels and I'm a bit frugal when it comes to just needing a bed and a hot shower."

"Never have occasion to stay at Malmaison?" Devon asked?

"No, but I hear it's a beautiful property. Lovely breakfast bar, as I'm told." Anthony said. "Are you thinking about expanding into the hospitality industry?"

"No," Devon chuckled. "Just trying to plan for the visit."

Devon looked through the papers and smiled. It occurred to him that putting this document together last night would've taken quite a bit of time and probably dampened any opportunity to do more than say hello to Anna. It was efficient and complete.

"This looks wonderful, Anthony," Devon said. "Thank you for completing it on such short notice."

Anthony stood up and walked over to the desk.

"I'll get the papers in right away. Your broker is actually in town today; I think it's odd he's rarely local," Anthony put the papers in his briefcase and shut it. "But, Devon, you called me to look into

Haslid months ago. I just updated the documentation last night. It didn't take but maybe an hour. I appreciate your confidence in my abilities, though!"

Anthony laughed and walked out of the room. Devon heard him conversing briefly with Alex and then heard the front door open and close.

Devon looked over at the painting and smiled.

"Alex, could you fetch Anna for me please?" Devon called out.

"As you wish, sir," Alex replied from the hallway. He listened to Alex walk upstairs and waited.

After roughly ten minutes, Anna appeared in the office doorway. "Yes, Devon?" she said as she walked in and sat on the sofa.

"So, you and Anthony, eh?" Devon said as he stood up and walked to the office door, closing it.

"What?" Anna replied. "No, that's crazy."

"He's aware of the breakfast bar at Malmaison," Devon smirked.

"Doesn't every hotel have a breakfast bar?" Anna replied dully.

"You had a lot of quality time last night with Anthony, didn't you?" Devon accused.

"We didn't do anything of the sort, Devon!" Anna stood up and shouted. "Stop this nonsense at once!"

"As far as I'm concerned, Anthony can blow himself to Bermuda and feed himself to the sharks!" Devon replied and turned around to look at the painting. The phone rang and Devon put it on speaker.

"Devon," Anthony's voice came through loud and clear. "I've got some urgent business in Bermuda. You can check with my assistant on the Haslid paperwork I'm dropping off to the broker right now."

"No!" Anna gasped. "You can't! You—"

"Don't say anything more, Anna." Devon put his hand over her mouth. "Sounds great, Anthony. See you when you get back. Safe travels."

Anna's eyes went wide as they heard the call disconnect. She started to make muffled gagging sounds. Devon let go of her and was horrified to see her mouth and nose were sealed shut with a layer of skin.

"No." Devon stumbled backwards. "I didn't mean…"

Anna's eyes rolled back in her head as her hands dropped from her jaw where she had started to claw at her porcelain skin. She fell to the ground.

"Stop it!" Devon cried out. He turned to the painting. "Let her live! Let her breathe!"

He turned around and saw Anna turning blue. He ran to his desk and rifled through the drawers.

"Alex!" Devon shouted. "Bring a sharp knife quickly and call nine-nine-nine!"

The muffled sound of Alex's feet running through the house gave Devon some hope. He looked at the pen he'd just signed the Haslid paperwork with and then at Anna. With a grimace, he snatched up the pen and ran to her.

Anna had stopped convulsing. Her body was still and her eyes hung open staring into the abyss. He pressed the pen into the flesh around her mouth, but it refused to penetrate the surface. Behind him, he heard the door open. Footsteps announced Alex had arrived. The audible gasp cemented the butler's grasp of the situation.

"We need to cut her open to breathe!" Devon shouted.

Alex handed him the knife.

"I need to call emergency services, sir," Alex said and left the room for the hallway phone.

Devon gripped the knife in his hand and frowned. He applied the sharp tip to Anna's delicate flesh and tried to carefully cut where he approximated lips would be. Blood oozed slowly from the wound, but didn't pulse or rush out. The smallest amount of pressure remained in her bloodstream without a heartbeat.

Devon dropped the knife and began mouth to mouth resuscitation. He tasted her blood. He saw her chest rise and fall as he blew air into her lungs. He took a break every couple of breaths to give her chest compressions.

When the emergency services arrived, the paramedics took over. The local constable arrived as well. He looked at the blood, the medical team and at Devon, his mouth caked with blood and dripping down onto his chest as he sat and watched them try to revive Anna. They quickly put her on a gurney and wheeled her out of the building.

Devon sat there staring at nothing. On the painting above him, a woman now hung from her neck in one of the gallows' nooses.

Alex walked in.

"Shouldn't Mister Armand be with his wife?" Alex asked.

"I think Devon's done enough. He's going to need to come down to the station with me, I'm afraid," the policeman said. "You should go with Anna, although from what I surmised, she may already be gone."

Alex looked at Devon with genuine concern and then walked away.

"You ready to head out, Devon?" the policeman asked.

Alex looked up, a glimmer of recognition on his face.

"Darren," Alex said to his brother the policeman. "When did you transfer here?"

"Six months ago," Darren said. "I didn't tell you because you're a piece of shit and I never wanted to talk to you again."

"Well, you can eat a bullet, you ungrateful sack of shit,"

Devon said.

Darren walked around to Alex's desk and began to open the drawers.

"Hey, don't you need a warrant or something?" Devon asked and stood up. His jaw went slack when Darren pulled out the DoubleTap .45ACP Derringer Devon kept for emergencies, placed it in his mouth and pulled the trigger. Two bullets in quick succession ripped through Darren's head. Darren's body fell on the desk, knocking Devon's computer to the floor. It left a spray of brains, skull, hair and blood on the office ceiling.

Tears formed in Alex's eyes.

"Darren?" he whimpered. His baby brother didn't move. Devon collapsed on the sofa.

"I just want to die…" he whispered. He felt his heart beat wildly in his chest. Pain shot up his left arm and he grabbed it, wincing. Through squinted eyes, Devon saw movement in the doorway.

"Darren?" he gasped.

"No," came another voice he recognized. He tried to clear his vision and saw Anthony walking into the room. Alex groaned.

"Why aren't you…?" Devon gasped as he slumped over.

"Dead?" Anthony asked. He walked up to the sofa, reached over Devon and pulled the painting from the wall. "The curse only works on things you care about. Your friend Keith, your wife, although I must say I'm surprised with the way you treated her, and your dear brother, who rightfully didn't think much of you."

Devon grabbed at Anthony's slacks but failed to come back with anything in his fingers. Anthony stepped carefully and set the picture down outside the office. He looked at the changes including a dead policeman at the foot of the gallows and a caricature of Devon in the center of the picture on his knees, grasping his chest with one hand and reaching out with the other. He smiled.

"Just another greedy bastard," Anthony whispered.

Anthony carefully made his way back and kneeled down in front of Devon, looking him in the eyes.

"You see, Devon, I'm immune to the effects of the painting," Anthony said and grabbed Devon's shoulder. "And I have you to thank for it. That quaint little merger you did six months ago before you proffered my services wiped out my father and brother's entire income and retirement. Rather than live destitute on government handouts, they both took their lives. Destroyed," Anthony pulled Devon up to a sitting position and slapped his face as his eyes were beginning to close. "Destroyed, as I said, by their deaths, my mother took her own life and my two sisters, equally devastated by the losses, soon followed."

Anthony stood up. "I told them not to move to America, but they unwisely ignored my council."

Devon gurgled as he tried to breathe.

"So, I hunted this little beauty down and rented it out for a spell to give to you, knowing your greed and avarice would lead you to destroy yourself and everything you loved eventually. I must say, I was surprised you did it inside of two weeks!"

As Devon slumped over, Anthony walked to the office doorway. "Well, burn in hell, Devon Armand; it's truly the only thing I care about at the moment."

Anthony walked through the door, picked up the painting and left Devon to face his sins in the afterlife.

QUEER 101
BY HIROMI COTA

Is this the book I need?

It's *a* book you need.

Ugh. Well, how many other books do I need?

"Need" is a value-loaded word with many concepts constellated around it.

Given what you know about me, my current grades, and the books, do I need more books?

Oh, god, yes.

Could have just led with that.

Ehhh.

Pretty sure he needed to screw with you.

Are you done screwing with me?

Oohh, what do you think?

I think that if I say "yes," you'll tell me that I'm too trusting and that you're morally obligated to fuck with me. And if I say "no," you'll say that you feel hurt that I've become jaded against my own personal liberators.

I'm so proud of you right now.

Beautiful.

And, I still don't understand why you keep calling yourselves my liberators.

We're saving you from the heteros.

Pretty sure I'm one of the heteros.

Impossible. My gaydar is a finely tuned instrument.

I'm a guy and I like chicks.

You're a man and you like women. If you liked baby chickens, you'd be on a totally different spectrum and journey. Also, I wouldn't help you.

What if I'm totally straight and what you're picking up is just me being weird.

Well, weirdness can qualify as queerness.

Oh, not that definition.

What's wrong with that definition of queer? Wait. What is that definition?

Under that framework, anything outside of a young, white nuclear family is queer. The hegemony of the state depends on the reinforcement of capitalism, vis a vis the workforce producing future workers and consumers. Difference disrupts the state's control especially difference that impacts consumerism and predictable reproduction.

Ugh. Don't say vis a vis. It makes you sound like an asshole.

He is an asshole.

Yeah, but he doesn't need to advertise it.

At any rate, that model of queer indexes race, ethnicity, age, ability and everything else under queerness.

Like, sure, being gay, black, old, poor, and/or in a wheelchair is queer in a sense, but we already have those categories and Kimberlé Williams Crenshaw demonstrated how the social problems faced by people who belong to more than one marginalized group are different than those who only belong to one. So, why bother trying to collapse those groups into one set when we already have evidence that differences matter?

Who?

Kimberlé Williams Crenshaw! Intersectionalism is technically part of Feminism, not Queer Studies, but—

Just read it. If you can mix in sources from other disciplines your professors will love you.

Because they'll think I'm smart?

Oh, no.

No one's smart in Queer 101.

Your professors will just enjoy reading your papers more than everyone else's stuff.

Turns out that seeing the same basic argument written with minor word variation is boring as fuck.

How often does that happen?

All the time. **Literally all the time.**

Is Queer 101 just indoctrinating us, then?

Oh, you caught us. **So busted.**

Teaching the Straights that the Homos are real life people who get screwed harder by life is hardly indoctrination. It's just— You wanna do the thing?

Yeah, sure. What's he writing?

Don't worry about it. Look, you want to be a teacher, right? You've

done some shadowing and tutoring? Yeah.

What's the best part?

Seeing kids succeed. Like, there's thing moment where their eyes light up and they get it. It's the best thing in the world.

BOOM! I'm 3 for 3! What?

I wrote likely answers. You said all of them. "Seeing them succeed," "eyes light up," and "when they get it."

We had no way of knowing what your experiences with teaching kids were like. We never saw you tutor anyone and we've never talked about the little rugrats, yeah?

Then, how'd you know?

You wanna see four essays that also have those three phrases? **From this week?**

Some experiences are just universal. The social awakening that accompanies learning how to not be a dick to queer people is one of them.

So, what if I'm just straight?

We'll accept you no matter what. **You're hella queer, though.**

Didn't you just point out that differences matter and not everyone needs to be under the same umbrella?

Ah ha! He caught us!

Congratulations. You are now a level 2 queer.

Dammit!

A LASTING PEACE
BY AMBER RAINEY

The sacred city of Lepi was a hotbed of divided loyalties. It lay quiet and dark, the sliver of a moon barely giving off any hint of light. The wall running through the city lay in stark contrast to the darkened houses around it. It was a constant reminder that the city could never rest so long as its inhabitants were enemies. Many thought the hatred was unwarranted - the differences in the two cultures so minor as to be trivial. However, the loathing each faction had for the other was burned into their psyche for hundreds of years and it would take a miracle of epic proportions to reconcile the two halves and make them whole again.

Two figures, well aware it was past curfew, rode through the winding street along the wall, pausing now and again to wait for the guards to pass on their rounds. The figures blended well with the darkness and rode with purpose. Finally, after the slow progression, they stopped next to a tall pole and abandoned their bikes. Climbing to the top of the pole, they lay flat on the platform underneath a large empty billboard, watching for the spotlights to pass over the spot. Once the coast was clear, they got to work, one on each side. After hours of working on the piece, they stepped back and appraised the billboard. Nodding in satisfaction, the figures made it back to their bicycles and rode off in separate directions, each blending into the darker streets of the city as if they never existed.

100 Years Later

Vanessa straightened her shoulders, took a deep breath, and walked into her classroom. The sight that greeted her was not an old one—her students sat in two distinct groups - the Inachis on one side and the Morphosians on the other with a large swath of empty chairs in between. Even after fifty years of reluctant peace, the two sides rarely mingled. They were forced to take the same classes but they expressed their displeasure in numerous ways. After the first few years of integration, the University had taken drastic measures to ensure all classrooms had an equal number of each faction. This had come after most classes in the early days were attended only by the faction members of the particular professor teaching a class. It had been incredibly difficult for students and professors alike.

"Good morning, class," Vanessa said cheerily.

The students stopped their conversations and gave her their attention. Vanessa took another deep breath. Vanessa reached into her bag and pulled out the projector remote. She busied herself with setting it up and organizing her papers. Once everything was in order, she pasted on a smile and turned to the class.

"Right, today we are going to do something a bit different."

A mutter went through the classroom. Vanessa walked over to the light switch and turned off the lights. The projector shone a bright, white light onto the wall behind her. She clicked a button and a black and white picture appeared on the wall. A gasp rippled through the classroom and somebody slammed a hand on their desk.

"What is this?" a student demanded.

Vanessa smiled, "It's ok. Let me explain."

Several students rose from their seats, gathering their things.

"We don't have to stay here for this..."

"I'm going to the dean right now."

"This is madness."

"Please, just let me explain. You are welcome to leave at any time, this is not a mandatory part of your grade," Vanessa tried calming the angry students.

"Why don't we hear her out," one of the students said above the din.

Vanessa heard the students muttering between themselves. Most of them sat back down. One walked down the steps and paused at the door, looking back at his compatriots. Another reluctantly got up and went out with the one at the door. The rest sat in a tense silence, all turning their eyes to Vanessa and waiting.

Vanessa cleared her throat, "Judging by your reactions, you all know what this is...."

The students all nodded in uneasy agreement.

"D'uh," a voice grunted.

The students laughed and Vanessa could feel a little bit of the tension ease in the room. She nodded.

"Would anyone like to explain?"

A hand rose tentatively. Vanessa nodded.

"That... symbol... was first painted on two sides of a billboard by an unknown person in the tenth month of the year of the Sliver Moon of nine twenty-four," Melissa, a fourth-year student stated.

Vanessa nodded, "Very good. Does anyone know why it is important?"

Another student rose, "It began the... Peace."

The Inachi faction expressed their displeasure at the word

while the Morphosians squirmed in their seats. Neither faction liked discussing what had led to their current cohabitation of Lepi, or the classroom they were in, for that matter. They accepted it as a necessary evil, but it didn't mean they liked it.

Vanessa held up a hand and the room fell silent again. She thought a moment, perusing her students. She could see the curiosity in them and she wanted to open a dialogue between the two factions. She wanted this generation of students to finally understand why they were against each other and how they could bridge the gap in their differences. She wanted the Peace to be real, not a forced way of life. At that moment, she had an epiphany. She'd decided on a different path for the lesson but she was nothing if not adaptable.

"The Peace has been difficult. The Inachi and Morpho politicians have done their best, but I'm not sure they really understand how to make it better. You, however, have the tools - curiosity, determination, diplomacy—to make it work. To bring harmony to Lepi and the whole country of Doptera."

Melissa raised her hand and spoke when Vanessa acknowledged her, "How? Why us?"

"You've taken the first steps. You are in this classroom. You stayed when others left. You are listening to me, even after I told you it was not detrimental to your grade if you left," Vanessa explained.

The students looked at each other and nodded. One or two shrugged and leaned forward, now hanging on her every word. They wondered what she would say next. She could see the hesitance in a few eyes. She looked up at the image behind her. She gave herself a pep talk. *It's now or never. They either leave all at once in protest or they stay and actually try. You won't know until you propose it.*

"Mrs. Cardui?" Melissa prompted.

Vanessa turned back to her students.

"The image you see is a message from someone. We never

knew who made it but the message is clear. The presence of one Inachi wing and one Morpho wing on the same entity is meant to show that they are two halves of the same whole. The two factions working together. The presence of this image was the first of its kind Lepi had ever seen. Some called it treasonous. Others called it a wake-up call. We don't know the original intent but we do know it sparked negotiations between the two factions and brought us to where we are today. My question to you is—could it take us further?"

The students whispered amongst themselves, some glancing across the aisle at the other faction. They shook their heads, not grasping what the professor actually wanted them to do. Another student got up and left the room, clearly not enjoying the direction the class had taken.

"Students, I promise you, if you take on this assignment, your lives will be changed for the better. You can affect the world in which you live. Do you really want the current tensions to remain in Lepi—or do you want real peace?"

"Peace," Melissa said loudly, then shrunk in her seat at the chuckle from the other students.

"I agree," another student said.

A chorus of agreement arose from both factions. Vanessa looked over the students and silently counted them, pleased that she counted an even number on each side.

"Do you trust me?" she asked the class.

"Not really," came a reluctant reply and the class chuckled again.

Vanessa chuckled. "Fair enough. Let me just say—trust each other. Listen to each other. Now, I want each of you to pair off with a student from the other faction. One Inachi and one Morpho in each group."

Vanessa held up her hand as the grousing started. She waited and watched as no one moved. Then, Melissa got up and walked over to an Inachi girl. She held out her hand.

"I'm Melissa," she introduced herself.

The girl looked around in panic for a moment, then sat up straight with determination, holding out her hand, "Io."

From that first introduction, the other students began pairing off. It was tense at first but as more of the students found a partner, the noise in the room grew with introductions and polite conversation. Vanessa waited until the students seemed more comfortable mingling then cleared her throat. The students sat down next to each other, a feat she would have thought impossible before that very moment.

"Now, in the spirit of the symbol behind me, I want you to find out as much as you can about each other's culture. Find out what makes you similar, what makes you different. Work together as the wings in the symbol would have to work together to carry the weight of the body. Find a middle ground. It won't be easy but I know you can do it. Come to me if you have any problems. We will meet again in two weeks. Class dismissed."

Melissa turned to Io and smiled. Io smiled back, somewhat perplexed as to what the assignment was actually about. They did not have to write a paper? Just... talk?

"She's so weird," Io said.

Melissa laughed. "I know, right? My sister took this course two years ago and she said it was a breeze but she never mentioned any assignment like this one."

"My sister took this course two years ago as well!" Io exclaimed.

Melissa laughed. "I would ask her name but I doubt they spoke to each other even if they were in the same class."

"Probably not," Io agreed.

Melissa grabbed a piece of paper out of her notebook and wrote down her contact information. She handed it to Io, who took it and nodded.

"I have another class right now but why don't we schedule a meeting to talk about the assignment?" Melissa asked.

"Sounds good. I'll call you... tonight?"

Melissa nodded. Io nodded and smiled back. It was hard not to catch the bubbly energy from Melissa and it made Io feel more at ease. Melissa gathered up her things and practically skipped out of the room. Io met Vanessa's eyes and raised her eyebrows, daring the teacher to point out the obvious connection the two girls felt. Vanessa shook her head and looked away, giving Io the chance to leave the room.

"That's so odd! Why do you have to do that again?" Melissa giggled.

Io shrugged. "Tradition? Honestly, I have no idea. It is old fashioned and it really makes no sense anymore but we do it anyway."

"I get it, we do things that are obsolete as well but, hey— whatever makes the family happy!" Melissa wiggled her eyebrows.

Io laughed. She and Melissa had been getting to know each other over several meetings and she found that she genuinely liked the girl. They had much more in common than either girl would have ever thought. In fact, their only differences lie in the way they worshipped their respective gods. Truthfully, even their gods sounded the same—except for different names. The rules of their religions were pretty much the same. The more they spoke, the more they realized the error of the hatred between their factions.

"Mrs. Cardui isn't such a moron after all." Io suddenly became serious.

"What?" Melissa sobered.

"She... she knew this would happen. All it takes is talking and being honest with one another."

Melissa thought a moment, her eyes growing wide. "It's true! If you had asked me a month ago what I thought of the Inachi, I would not have anything nice to say!"

"Nor I of the Morphosians," Io confessed.

"I think this is what that symbol was trying to show everyone—we are all the same, we just need to work together. We need to stop blindly hating one another and learn from each other. The started it a hundred years ago but they didn't really follow through. They only went halfway towards the Peace. We need to make it a lasting peace."

Io thought a moment and nodded. "I have an idea."

Vanessa walked through the hall towards her classroom, growing more concerned at each step. More students than normal lined the hallway and were staring at her. She wondered if she was about to be fired. She knew the rumor mill spread quickly and most of the time she was ignored except by her own students. As she got closer to her classroom, the sheer number of people in the hallway became difficult to navigate. Finally, she reached her door and the students blocking the doorway stepped aside and let her through. The classroom she was met with was very different from the one she had stepped into two weeks prior. Every seat was filled and students were lined up around the edges. It was standing room only. Inachi and Morphosian students mingled in the seats - there was no longer a delineation between the two factions. She approached the lectern cautiously and the classroom became so quiet one could hear a pin drop.

"What's... ahem... what is this all about?" she asked expectantly.

Melissa and Io stood up and approached their professor. She

smiled tentatively at them and was stunned at the bright smiles each girl gave her.

"May we?" Melissa asked.

Vanessa nodded and stepped aside. The girls looked at each other and nodded. They unzipped their sweaters to reveal the symbol of one butterfly with folded wings—one Inachi and one Morpho. Vanessa looked in open-mouthed shock at the two girls.

"Fellow students?" Io said to the people assembled in the room.

All the other students shed sweaters and jackets to reveal the same shirts Melissa and Io wore. Vanessa gasped and her eyes teared up.

"Mrs. Cardui, we've learned that whether you were born Inachi or Morpho, we all worship the same gods. We follow the same rules and laws. We come from the same order. We are cut from the same cloth," Melissa said.

"We can respect our differences, celebrate them even, and yet we can still be friends. We can work together to tear down the wall in Lepi and let our cultures strive together rather than falter apart. You told us we can affect change. The student of Lepi University chose to change our world. For the better!" Io exclaimed as she grabbed Melissa's hand and thrust their conjoined hands in the air.

The students in the classroom and those in the hall erupted in cheers. Melissa and Io led the students out into the hallway and into the quadrangle. There, they rose banners flying the symbol as more and more students poured out of the classroom buildings to join the impromptu festivities.

The students began a campaign to force the Inachi and Morpho leaders to talk to one another. Eventually, both sides sat down and really listened to each other. The wall was torn down and the two halves of the sacred city of Lepi were whole again. A miracle had indeed happened. The era of The Lasting Peace had begun in Doptera.

On that day, Vanessa Cardui sat on the floor of her bedroom and cried. She wasn't sad about the state of affairs, she was just sad her grandmother wasn't alive to see it. She pulled a box out from under the bed. A picture lay on top of the box. It was of a beautiful, young Morphosian woman and a tall Inachi man holding hands. The love in their eyes was evident even though the picture had faded. Two bicycles lay at their feet. Behind them, a large billboard was spray-painted with a symbol—a butterfly with one Inachi and one Morpho wing. One had to look closely, but in doing so, could just make out the remnants of black paint on the intertwined hands.

MODERN ART
BY MARSHALL MILLER

The dark clad Grand Inquisitor stepped into his Special Room as he had done countless times before. He had named it the Special Room as he liked the mystery and questions this identifier prompted in people's mind. Questions such as why was it Special? What activities occurred in the room made it 'Special' in the true sense of the word? If the Grand Inquisitor gave it another title, why then its supposed purpose would have been revealed to the masses. Using specific words like interrogation, questioning, interviewing, all words with their own particular weights and meanings, subtracted any chance at mystery when applied to the room. Where was the sense of accomplishment or discovery in that action? Thus the only people who knew the purpose of the Special Room were the Special Room Security, himself, and of course, those invited into this unique space.

So the person known only as the Grand Inquisitor nodded at the two security officers and entered the room. The automatic door was keyed to his being and slid open, then closed with nary a touch from anyone. In the center of the room was a comfortable padded chair. In the single piece of furniture of the Special Room sat a man.

The man did not move as the Grand Inquisitor entered. For he had been directed by the security officers not to rise from or leave the chair unless instructed. Others who had not heeded those instructions were beaten by the security officers until they understood the need to follow instructions. While the masses might not know by name or formal definitions the purpose or rules of the Special Room, there were rumors and leaks even in the most controlled of societies. Thus, the man sat.

The statuesque Grand Inquisitor walked into the windowless room, illuminated by a soft pastel light. The walls were painted a warm and calming blue, and some soft music played over the hidden speakers. The creator and owner of the room stopped a few steps in front of the seated man and smiled. The Grand Inquisitor had been told he had a warm and friendly smile. However, that opinion voiced by certain people was viewed by him as suspicious.

"Anton LeMarche," the Grand Inquisitor said in a cheery tone. "I hope that chair is comfortable. I do know the discomfort of having to wait in an uncomfortable chair, especially if a person is no longer young."

Anton LeMarch smiled at the Grand Inquisitor, for they had met many times before at various social functions. Although not real friends, it could be said they were friendly.

"No problem, Sir," replied the older and gray beard man. "I have not waited long, based on my own internal clock. When brought in, I thought my wait would be hours… even days."

The Grand Inquisitor stepped closer as he grinned. "You have now revealed that you are a recipient of many an unfounded rumor, Sir. For I have never kept anyone here for days."

Anton smiled as he replied. "You know how it is, Sir. We, common people, gossip, and then exaggerate."

The Grand Inquisitor frowned as he spoke. "You, Anton

LeMarche, Artist, a commoner? Never. You forget my knowledge of your art."

And with that, the wall to Anton's right and the Grand Inquisitor's left became transparent, a window into another room. In that space was a long series of paintings and sculptures. Anton's eyebrows rose in surprise as he saw so many of his works in one place.

"Sir, I must ask," the creative said. "How many of those are originals, and how many are reproductions? I have not seen this many of my endeavors in one place since…"

"Since the State Dinner in your honor two years ago."

"Yes! I had forgotten. And you, Grand Inquisitor, organized it in my honor."

"Which brings us to why you are here today, Anton."

A 3-D sculpture was brought closer to the transparent wall by some unseen force. It was an image of a being, its gender challenging to identify as the head, and upper features were covered by a dark red hood. The face entirely obscured by shadows, the right claw-like hand presented, nay shoved an ever-changing object of light and dark towards the viewer. The object in the hand at first seemed circular, then rectangular, then a prism, next a blob. Mixed in with the light and darkness were blood red hues, then maroons and purples. However, the object was ever changing, there being no discernable pattern.

"I must say, Anton, I find this recent piece of yours exquisite." The nearly supreme official then paused. "However, it presents a problem."

"What is that my respected admirer?" replied Anton.

"It is not the visual effects you have created. My Lord, they are genius. No pattern, ever-changing, almost quantum in nature." The owner of the Special Room then again paused as he observed the ever-shifting hues and shapes. Then he spoke again. "But your genius outdid itself this time. For you incorporated subliminal messages using ultrasonics, somehow interwoven with the shifting visuals."

"Why yes I did, Sir. For I wanted not only for people to see and thus feel the impact of my work, but also to THINK. I wanted those art appreciating Citizens to be tickled in their reasoning portions of their cortex in a specific manner.'

"And that manner was to question. Question what the viewers see, what they hear, what they feel."

"Of course, Grand Inquisitor, you saw to the center of my art piece. Probably during the first minutes of your observing it, yes?"

"Yes. For that is my reason for being, Anton. To observe and inquire, to keep this Most Perfect Union functioning."

"But Sir. I only want our people to use their cognitive abilities so as not to become staid robots. We must have The Order and Structure we developed decades ago, after the Anarchy. All Citizens realize that reality."

The Grand Inquisitor walked around behind the chair and figure. Anton could not turn in the chair as the high padded arms and back restricted movements. Thus, once the Grand Inquisitor was directly to the rear of him, Anton could turn his head to look to the sides, but no further. The music gone, there was complete silence, other than Anton's own breathing and heartbeat in his ears as he became concerned.

When the Grand Inquisitor spoke and broke the extended silence, Anton jerked in the chair,

"And so the question must be asked: Is this art transformative?" the special official continued. " If not ubiquitous or autonomic but instead a flash point for whatever comes after it... is this art actually an act of revolution?"

Anton nervously licked his lips before he spoke.

"You misunderstand..." His comment was cut off by a tight

beam of energy from the ceiling. Anton squealed with pain as his right ear was singed.

"Anton, I am most sorry. I do believe you were about to question my ability to understand."

Anton rubbed his injured ear, then slowly spoke.

"A poor choice of words, Grand Inquisitor. If I, as the artist failed in the attempt to convey a specific idea, feeling, or concept, then I have presented a flawed piece of art. Please allow me to apologize and remedy…"

"But you said, Anton, your purpose was to awaken specific thought processes in our Citizens."

"Sir, again, possibly a poor choice of words…"

"No, wait. You're right. That was *my* poor choice of words. You said to use cognitive abilities, not awaken them." The Grand Inquisitor frowned as he continued. "But then, Anton, you talked about our Citizens becoming robots as if Order somehow damaged the Citizens ability to function. As if 'robot' was a dirty word."

"Sir, I was just trying to produce art that stimulates the Citizens to use there intellect rather than stagnate."

"Our robotic expertise has become a great trade item with other societies and worlds. It has been a boon to our existence since the Anarchy."

The Grand Inquisitor stood still, and Anton began to sweat profusely.

"You know, Anton. I think that figure you so aptly created is an allegory of me. A most exquisite allegorical image of me."

Anton sat still, confused as to how to answer.

"But, the question I have is, in the left hand behind the figures back. What does it conceal?"

"Conceal, my Lord? I had not, in all honesty, given it much thought…"

"Well, then, my good Anton, let me then explain what I, if I am the model for this fantastic piece of art, would have behind my back."

Anton thought he heard a sound like someone pulling a loose-fitting cork from a bottle. The Grand Inquisitor then stepped back around the chair to stand in front of Anton and presented what was in his left hand.

"Peek –A- Boo," the detached head of the Grand Inquisitor said as it grinned, not a dark brown hair out of place.

The two female Special Security Officers outside the door tried not to laugh as a scream came over their communicator earpieces, then was abruptly cut off.

The Grand Inquisitor had such a wicked sense of humor sometimes.

WHAT HAPPENS NEXT
BY ELIZA LOEB

I used to wonder how far this nation will go if we allow the folks in power to keep a morally corrupt president in office. In Donald J. Trump's four year term, I have seen countless offences committed under the guise of false patriotism. Internment camps have been filled beyond capacity, beyond what is considered humane without clean drinking water or toiletries, while its residents are treated like nothing more than senseless beasts. And this is only scratching the surface. President Donald J. Trump idolizes Hitler in ways that I can't even imagine. He presses his ideals on others, forces protestors out in the cold and even makes fun of Autistic reporters. And that was during his first year of presidency. I constantly see people commenting on things that speak out against him and offences that he has made toward women and non-white folk. More often than not, the most common is "Fake News." His biggest atrocity, however, is interning immigrants and having ICE go to the homes of immigrants who sought nothing more than asylum from their countries of origin. But he's not going for the white European immigrants. He's going for the Latinx, the Syrian, the Iranian and more. He is doing what Bush senior had put into motion and Bush Junior had acted upon. He is using fear tactics and propaganda to spread lies and hate about a specific group of people and he knows what effect it will have. He knows how his supporters will react and how they as his followers will make an attempt to militarize and oppress these people to no avail.

During my time in Virginia, I have obtained employment at Colonial Williamsburg, added a new partner to my family, and said new partner had obtained employment at the Jamestown settlement. And what we have noticed at both of those locations is this: The interpreters and the beliefs that both places have portrayed are entirely different compared to one and other. Colonial Williamsburg not only serves as a living history museum like Jamestown, but it is also the campus location of the college of William and Mary. Many of William and Mary's alumni like wearing MAGA caps and pressing their political beliefs onto others. I remember sitting in Panera with Kayti, my new partner and over hearing a couple of young women talking about the point of civil rights. They continuously questioned "What's the point of it?" and would make passing comments like "Maybe the Civil Rights Act should be abolished. We don't need it." I wanted to rise up. I wanted to say something, but my main concern was with Kayti. My main concern was about how she would feel if I made a public spectacle of myself. She was already having a bad day as was. She didn't want for it to get any worse. So I asked if she would like to leave, and we left. And to this day I still see many people like those women. Donning their MAGA caps and looking down their nose at others they deem lesser. And I continue to wonder, just how many more people will be targeted. How much more will America unravel as a country and how many more people will die just to obtain the ideals of the few. It's not the America that I was promised growing up. It's not the America that the American citizens need. And the back bone of this country was made up of immigrants. Many from China, Italy, Spain, Ireland, Scotland, Russia, France and so on. Its backbone thrives on the people trying to make a life for themselves… or at least it used to. Now, we have to worship those who were born with a silver spoon in their mouth. Those who have never had to work a day in their lives. And it angers me. It angers me that a bunch of white guys in office have so much while everyone else has so little. And it angers me that many of the white Americans that come in to Yorktown or Jamestown find the information they obtain completely and utterly pointless. And it's because of them that we have the bastard in office. It's because of them that "Immigrant Detention Centers" are packed beyond capacity with little food or water or even basic hygiene components. And I fear what they will do to those people and I begin to think of a book that I had read once. And many of them are likely thinking the same thing that many of the characters in said book had thought. "Why me?"

There have been many occasions where I have seen history repeat its self. And there are many who believe that history is just history and that it means nothing. The united states of America is hardly as united as it used to be. Its beginnings were good. The separation of church and state was good. Because it meant that one could be allowed to press their religious beliefs upon another person for the sake of a political agenda. Yet, here we are. Abortion is being made illegal, women are being arrested for miscarriages and losing babies to gunshot wounds. These women have done absolutely nothing wrong. These people trying to cross the border and seeking asylum, have done nothing wrong. It is not illegal to seek asylum. It should not be illegal to have a miscarriage. But it should be illegal to wrongfully incarcerate an entire group of people. It should be illegal to neglect the people you lead because they are not wealthy. And it *should* be illegal to deny benefits to families and folks in need for the sake of lining your own or some other billionaire's pockets.

And so I wonder….

How many more will be arrested? How many more people will be put in to an internment camp if nothing is done right away? How many more people will wonder if they will live to see tomorrow?

And as I look at the world as it is today, I wonder. I remember the meaning of the word tyranny. I know what an internment camp looks like. I know what genocide and war looks like.

America as we know it is at the seventh stage of genocide, and there is only a few more stages to go before the government tries to cover it up and deny that it even happened.

I exhaust myself in trying to make sense of it all. I hate that what is happening now is similar to Nazi Germany and the burning of roam. Although I don't feel that the current POTUS knows how to play any instruments seeing as the only talent that he actually has is running his mouth, and he can't even do that well. I especially exhaust myself over how many will hear about this time period. Will it be seen as just *another bad presidency*? Or will children and adults stop and actually learn from it?

These are the sort of things that go through the head of someone whose citizenship can be taken away in any point in time. And having been born on Guam, that time may be soon. And then maybe I will end up in a concentration camp, myself.

With where this country is headed, guarantees are but a fools game. You live, you breath, you watch and you learn.

AMERICAN ELEGY
BY SHEILA MENGERT

braham Cardozo had a problem. Since his graduation from law school four years ago everything in America had seemed to go into freefall. Everywhere there was contention and an abiding nastiness broadcast at full volume from the various absolutist discourses and narratives, each contending for supremacy. Some of these claims were religious in nature, others political, and others still simply the fracas bred of contending egos seeking attention on social media.

"I am living in the age of the *prima donna*," Abraham said to himself in the course of the inner narrative that each of us possesses as we try and make some sense of the world and fill our fleeting hours with at least some measure of stability and satisfaction. Abraham's mind was disturbed by events. Everything had become so strident, rising in pitch and volume to a sustained squeal like the sound of microphone feedback at a rock concert. Among other items of note it was the fiftieth anniversary of the Stonewall Inn Riot that by 2019 had become the LGBT equivalent of the shots that rang out between British and American troops at Concord Bridge in 1776. Rainbow Flags were expected to be flown everywhere in celebration of the event and of the full emergence of LGBT rights on the world stage from sleepy villages in Botswana to Greenwich Village in New York where it all seemed to have begun one summer night.

Meanwhile in the world of beleaguered heterosexuals various petitions were circulating to keep drag queens out of libraries where they had lately been introduced as purveyors of a so-called story hour, just one more instance of the nefarious effort to normalize the unspeakable among the young in the view of various religious groups. Disorder was everywhere. Across the vast Pacific Ocean an American and a Russian ship had barely avoided a collision in the South China Sea. The food situation in North Korea was growing more threatening each day due to poor harvests and the sanctions that remained in place even after the "lover's meetings" between Donald Trump and Kim Jung Un. In Europe Brexit looked inevitable and it seemed quite possible that noble England might be heading for a reprise of the post World War II style rationing if its economy should collapse. Below the border, Mexico had avoided tariffs for now by agreeing to act as a more efficient buffer between the fleeing hordes of refugees from Honduras and Guatemala and the safe harbor of America. At the bottom of the world in Antarctica great ice shelves were calving daily into the southern seas off Patagonia. The yearly forest fires had already started in California. In the internecine conflicts between liberals and conservatives within the Catholic Church a statement had been issued by some Bishops in Kazakhstan to remind the diminishing number of church-going Catholics, let alone the remarried and sexually rebellious, to toe the line or risk the consequences. Rain was still causing flooding in the American mid-west and south. Only Vice-President Mike Pence seemed at ease as he looked up with hound-dog-like devotion to the all-wise Commander-in-Chief (and a hell of a golfer) Donald Trump.

Things were being shaken up everywhere it seemed. Everybody was yelling at everybody and Abraham Cardozo, product of reason and tolerance, felt compelled at last to intervene. Abraham Cardozo put on his glasses to read over the text of what he hoped would be of some use in the political struggles of the present hour. A little effort on his part he felt, a little cool judicial reasoning and all could be put right. What was called for at this critical hour was an *amicus brief* to unmask the catastrophic trend of the Trump agenda of spurious populism masking corporate rule.

Abraham, as we will familiarly refer to him rather than by the august name of Cardozo (no actual blood relation to the famous jurist) like many Americans of this particular time and place was suffering from the confusion bred from the daily deluge of events. Each new day brought its own spate of revelations, assessments and counter-assessments in the endless factional currents and entrenched interests of America. Like many of his generation he had been accustomed to the concept of on demand services and the ability to remove the unpleasant and the intolerable by simply hitting the delete button on whatever device was handy. Reality might be virtual or actual depending upon one's underlying view of metaphysics, but in any case it should be subject to framing and manipulation. If Abraham had learned anything in law school it was to present the facts, whatever they might be, encased in an overall narrative that would lead a jury to adopt the client's point of view. Facts were flexible like the space-time continuum; they merely provided the field that could, if skillfully presented, lead to a favorable verdict. As in the reaction to the New Criticism by the post-modernists, it was all a matter of point of view. No text could be expected to speak for itself under changing conditions. The young attorney almost feared to read what he had just composed though because he was aware of the utter transiency of all narratives and the lack of a common point of reference for meaning and relevance.

The provisional text of his manuscript read as follows:

No narrative can hope to exist in utter isolation from a receptive community that can at once be its audience and the source of its relative value assessment among similar discourses. This is the first step along the journey towards general acceptance as truth. As discourses have increased in number and variety the communities that can receive them have similarly fragmented so that a general sense of meaning is absent.

As an example of this truth, Thomas Wolfe, the great American novelist, is famous for saying that you can't go home again. This phrase has always had for me a certain nostalgic ring because it implied that one was caught in the dilemma of desiring to return to a predictable and unified world but were doomed to rejection and misunderstanding, as though exile contained within itself a just punishment for ever having left home in the first place: abandon us and we will abandon you. As the years have passed however I have come to see things differently. Thomas Wolfe was simply making a statement of fact: the reason that we cannot go home again is that home no longer exists as it has been preserved in our memory after long absence. The accuracy of memory is such that it preserves images and structures in all of their former integrity long after those structures may have altered or ceased to exist. We assume a set of relations in space and time to endure so that although *we* may have changed *they* remain locked and frozen, just waiting for us to take them up again.

We even go so far as to apply this standard to people and to resent the temerity of their daring to grow and to change even as we have. We thought to return from a long expedition, laden down with dromedaries of wisdom, riches, experience, and in possession of triumph while they, poor things, could only stand looking outwards into the barren distance awaiting our return. After all, we Americans judge progress always in a comparative sense: there is no such thing as prosperity until it can be held up against a standard of deprivation and penury. This is why Americans are so jealous and afraid that those just below them will move marginally up the ladder of social or economic status. Meanwhile we grant *carte blanch* privileges to the upper classes to pursue their lives of indulgence without fear or even the burden of our resentment at their good fortune. We may even derive a certain degree of reflected glory from our native aristocrats so that when Donald Trump refers to other nations as "Shit-hole countries" rather than as "developing nations" his avid followers can congratulate themselves and agree, *"They shore as hell are!"*

In the year of 2019 then when everything remains suspended and the great and hoped-for deliverance of 2020 (when pray God we will see clearer and return our nation to some measure of sanity) it is becoming ever clearer that we can't go home again. Integrity is that quality that bestows identity and we have pawned it for a short pay-day loan. Imagine if you will if the various qualities and characteristics of a substance should become suddenly lacking in that adhesiveness that creates order and security. This adhesiveness goes by various names but in law it is called precedent and the stricture of tradition that precedent imposes is called *stare decisis.* It is not that the past is always wiser than the present; the rule is imposed for another purpose entirely. The conservation of precedents creates what may be called the body of the law. Theoretical structures such as contract and tort are elaborately balanced and highly evolved relationships of multiple factors just as living organisms are. Precedents are the genetic mutations that when selected and preserved over time finally evolve into the extended predicates of the law. So it is that when mere political rhetoric is willing to cast this bastion of order aside in order to secure short-term gains it is a warning that civilization is tottering and the eyes of hungry beasts in the outer darkness begin to glitter.

It is not the advent of Donald Trump that is so appalling, America has known the temporary triumph of vulgar opportunists before this; the thing that terrifies me is the readiness with which approximately one-third of our fellow citizens are prepared to surrender everything upon which democracy is based simply to get their long-deferred wish-list met. It shows that a significant number of Americans have no idea of what such cherished terms as due process and basic honesty mean. This is why each new fantastic claim or instance of personal abuse to his enemies or former enablers is becoming less shocking over time as the President proceeds in his one-of-a-kind Presidency. Each impact further dulls our sense of propriety and decency so that the public sphere now smells like the abandoned stall of a fishmonger. It is all so familiar to anyone who has ever studied the gradual consolidation of power under Adolf Hitler. I keep waiting for Nancy Pelosi to appear, tear-stained on the evening news, as she looks up at the smoking ruin of the Capitol Building. So it isn't that we cannot go home again: the problem is that our home has been disintegrating before us every day since 2016…

With the prospect of his annual visit to the Oregon coast for his vacation in the offing Abraham decided before he left Seattle to put the matter of his proposed literary intervention before his old con/law instructor for a provisional opinion. He waited for an answer while Professor Manuel Cortez, law professor and aficionado of liberation theology, sat back and considered the matter after reading the rough draft.

"Well, that's all that I have so far. What do you think of the general tone?" Abraham queried hopefully, the general sense of awe that former students have for various favorite instructors remained with him still.

"It won't make law review material, but perhaps an op-ed piece."

"I didn't think it sounded like a note for law review; too general and too contemporaneously relevant for that. A public policy review perhaps?"

Professor Cortez considered the suggestion.

"No, not even there, I don't believe. I'm not sure that such a thing exists anymore anyway, commonly rooted public policy I mean. Have you thought of an archeology journal? We may just get the Trump wall after all along our southern border out of all this. It will be a great tourist attraction one hundred years from now, a symbol of our national ethos in decline."

Abraham smiled, "You are being facetious. You think I'm too earnest in writing a piece like this."

"No, I think you are saying what most people think already, but it's too late. Can you see that? You are making a general appeal after the filing date has passed. This whole Donald Trump phenomenon was already foreseeable thirty years ago when education began to break down in this country, maybe even earlier than that. I saw it coming as early as the Bork nomination and the eventual arrival of the Rehnquist Court. Do you remember your Constitutional Law course with me when I pointed out that it all came down to an act of faith. Law is a religion. As soon as the outcome becomes more important than legal due process the whole thing becomes meaningless. It is the unwritten covenant of judicial probity in reasoning that is our only guarantee that civilization will prevail. Law school isn't a trade school; it's a novitiate in the order of a religion called jurisprudence. The students who realize this don't make the most money, but they keep the whole thing alive. You were one of the ones who I thought might keep the old faith going for one more round at least."

Abraham smiled. "I had a head start. Talmud study you know."

The Professor smiled.

"Me too, ever read Canon Law? The Roman Church finds its ultimate principle of order in God, but for the day-to-day work there is always Canon Law to keep the heretics at bay. We both have a healthy respect for the transcendent in our religious traditions but we know that in its pure form only the mystics try and deal with the transcendent dimension directly. For the rest of us there is only the comfort provided by doctrine and by law. When you break the laws you plead guilty and hope for a reduced sentence on the other side. We call it Confession."

"So you think that religion is comparable to the criminal law?" Abraham asked.

"It started there, remember the forbidden fruit? Of course that presumes a historical reading of the text of Genesis."

"Is there another way to read it?"

The Professor considered the question before explaining.

"What if you read the text like an example of the Wisdom Literature, more like the Book of Job or Proverbs? What if you look at it like a novel by Franz Kafka describing the human predicament and the dangers of premature acquaintance with moral questions that we haven't the strength to confront or to surmount? By reading the creation account in Genesis as an historical text all sorts of problems emerge that are otherwise avoidable. Christian history is awash in the consequences of what may have been an initial misreading by assigning the text to an inappropriate genre and distorting authorial intent in the process. I'm not saying I am right, mind you, but if the study of law teaches us one key skill it is to dispute established precedents."

"I thought lawyers were the bulwark of established interests," Abraham commented dryly.

"Only Republican lawyers," answered Professor Cortez archly.

Abraham Cardozo reflected.

"Then Donald Trump is not a revolutionary populist after all."

Professor Cortez sat back in his chair and placed his finger tips together as of old. He proceeded at last as he had once done in the classroom.

"Trumpism … and I speak of it as an institution rather than as the individual political program of one man (it is more like an opportunistic infection) is a strategy rather than a movement. Its guiding principle is to win power and to retain it for as long as possible. I watched in the primaries as the various Republican contenders for the Presidential nomination in 2016 fell by the wayside like so many straw men and suddenly it dawned on me that they had misunderstood both the temper of the times and what the Presidency as an institution has become for all of us. You see Abraham we don't elect Presidents on the basis of qualifications and intelligence any more but on their ability to confirm our prejudices, to flatter our dreams, and to alleviate our anxieties. Donald Trump realized long ago as a speculator that from the perspective of the buyer symbols are more important than substance. What is the whole Trump Empire but an example of leveraged illusions? It's all about branding. Donald Trump may be the first President who considers living in the Whitehouse to be slumming. That's why he is always off to Mar-a-Lago. By the way, the name means: "sea to lake." The resort forms a bridge between the sea and the Intracoastal Waterway. In the same manner Trumpism bridges traditional conservatism with the illusion of a populist revolution from below. You get the best of both worlds. You can be a stodgy, fundamentalist, climate-change denying, rapture-awaiting, religious conservative and you can be a rich

Plutocrat ready to dump the last shovel-full of earth onto the grave of the American middle-class. You can be an out and out bigot ready to scare black folk back to carefully policed ghettos. You can be a woman who thinks that ill-mannered and dominant men are a turn-on. You can in fact be anyone who wants to clock-in on a vicarious win to keep from the dawning suspicion that indebted America could collapse at any moment and follow the British Empire into the annals of past glory. You can be any of these and Donald Trump is your man. In politics rhetoric is everything; it even trumps truth."

"And the other candidates didn't realize this?" Abraham inquired.

Professor Cortez laughed.

"They thought they were competing for a job interview. They showed up with lengthy resumes and lots of earnestness and Trump made mincemeat out of them because only he realized that Presidential elections are a game-show. When the voter steps behind the curtain, he hopes that the box that he chooses will contain a new car and not a hundred cans of minced squid."

Abraham considered. "What about impeachment?"

"That might seem the best course constitutionally speaking, but only if you want another four years of Trump."

"I don't understand," Abraham looked puzzled.

"Really, what have we just been talking about? Trump is a master of leveraging. By handing him an impeachment that will not be confirmed in the Senate the House of Representatives would be giving him the one boost that he needs to come back as a winner in "season two." I am sure that Nancy Pelosi, smart lady that she is, knows this. Her task is to let the horses rear but keep them attached to the chariot. Once impeachment breaks loose Trump wins and he knows it; he even invites it. The one thing that the great egoist can't stand is sustained suspicion. It's like swamp-gas percolating up from the ground on the fairway of a golf course, not fatal but annoying, and Donald Trump is not accustomed to being annoyed. He wants a quick victory not a sustained campaign because in a sustained campaign actual results matter. What has he to show for the first years of his Presidency?"

The Professor continued, counting his points off on his fingers.

"No wall built, no new health care plan, a tax deal that has added over two trillion dollars to the national debt, a runaway stock-market just begging for a correction, a series of trade-wars that are bankrupting farmers, a love-affair with the fat-kid ruling North Korea who is running out of patience while his people starve under sanctions, and a lot of alienated allies from Japan to England. All Trump has to run on is his assumed victimhood and all the Progressive Wing of the Democratic Party wants to do is to hand that cherished status back to him on a silver platter by impeaching him when he only has one effective year to go in his ill-advised Presidency. Believe me Abraham, the calliope of the whole Trump circus is running out of steam: the rhetoric is getting threadbare, the promises are unfulfilled, and people are tired of his jejune name-calling. The whole thing is just one more mortgage loan on Debtor America. The real answer is to give the man free rein and wait it out. The one person who can defeat Donald Trump is Donald Trump. Otherwise…"

"Otherwise?" Abraham asked.

Professor Cortez shrugged his shoulders.

"Well think about moving to Denmark or New Zealand."

This was the context of the reflections that pursued Abraham Cardozo as he headed out to the Oregon coast for his annual recuperation from his fourth year of practicing law in a small eight-person Admiralty firm. He had drifted towards Admiralty Law because it allowed him to place daguerreotypes of Clipper Ships on his office wall and to practice in Federal Court rather than in the squalid state courts so often reminiscent of the world of Charles Dickens' fog-shrouded London with prisoners in orange suits being arraigned and quarreling couples fighting over their children. It was comforting to apply law to stately collisions between vessels and personal injury claims under the Jones Act. But he was tired, chronically tired as most attorneys are, and it was always a joy to slip the traces, to pass his caseload on to another lawyer, and to seek the open sea again.

There are many routes out to the Oregon Coast but Abraham preferred the slow road down from Aberdeen to the Columbia River and across the bridge to Astoria. On trips like this Abraham was accustomed to undertaking that most neglected of pastimes, introspection and retrospection; the search for what Thomas Wolfe had called "the last lane-end into heaven." The ethos of America was never explored so vividly as in the novels and short-stories of that most neglected of America's great 20th century novelists. Seventeenth century prose evidently did not play well with the staccato rhythms of mid-century America. But perhaps it was Wolfe's sense of the tragic that did not sit well among a nation always avid for the next cheap delight. Faulkner had the advantage of comparative incomprehensibility combined with the slow majesty of a funeral dirge in his prose, or perhaps it was Wolfe's youth that worked against him, dying so young at thirty-eight. His disappointments always seemed only proportionate to his hunger which was limitless. He never quite managed that most difficult of authorial tasks: to climb out of one's own skin. It is a task that is spared to the lawyer who always writes within the established texture of the law. There is nothing more intimating than using the elder tongue of language to speak new truths or to devise a new music from old chords.

Abraham observed the flow of his thoughts as he turned

southwards at Aberdeen. The road unspooled before him in the late-spring light of a June day. The southwestern counties of Washington State are comparatively undeveloped. They consist of sloughs and estuaries, of oysters and lumber, salmon and light tourism. The restricted economy creates an aura of migration and abandonment, of boarded up shops and empty pavements. The dollar is the lifeblood of communities such as these and where dollars are lacking everything dries up like a mirage in the desert.

But these were not the sole basis for Abraham's subdued mood as he threaded the narrow roads between timber cuts and outlooks across the wind-ruffled waters of Willapa Bay. It was rather the sense of passing opportunities that led him into the habitual sense that like his namesake he would always be a wandering Aramean with only the vestigial promise of his various faiths to sustain him. A habit of reflective thought can be a great disadvantage. He had long ago lost the capacity for mob-enthusiasm; his joys were personal and often difficult to explain to others.

The curves of the road were compelling and hypnotic, yet he wasn't sleepy, only mesmerized by the sense of movement and the passing foliage of the trees. Suddenly the great waters of the Columbia River were before him and then the great high span of the bridge that grants access to the further shore of Oregon. His spirits picked up as they always did when the first sector of his journey was behind him. This was the Oregon land that had inspired the pioneers to cross a continent of plains and desert; this was the goal and the vision.

He stopped for lunch in Cannon Beach and walked the familiar streets munching an apple turnover and looking in the shop windows at summer clothes and trinkets, all part of early family vacations on the coast. He remembered college parties here as well, falling asleep in strange beds with the floor littered with the sleeping bodies of college friends after a night of beer and hilarity, everything swaying like a ship in an unquiet but not stormy sea. Was he that same person still, the one who as yet had everything before him but no clear idea of what anything was really about? How strange that he did not feel at that time the vast vacuum of all that he did not yet know. But then youth brings its own fullness. There is, if nothing else, that expectancy that earth has been awaiting one's particular advent to finally reveal its long deferred promises. Was that what the first Abraham had felt, he the father of peoples?

Upon leaving Cannon Beach the road climbs steadily upwards. At the crest the view south from Neakanie Mountain over the little community of Manzanita down to Tillimook Bay was as always inviting to the wanderer, majestic and intimidating at once, as the land suddenly ends and plunges downwards into the frothing surf. He found himself envisioning the many prairie towns lying behind him and the great Rocky Mountains of Colorado, then the plains, the Mississippi River and the rich, green yet populous eastern states.

This was the America that Trump promised to make great again. Had it ever ceased to be great except in the smallness of our commercial obsessions? Abraham thought of the great Redwood forests, gone in a century, with only a few forlorn representatives remaining in groves around Eureka. The west must have been one vast cathedral then. Surely that was when America was truly great, before the great exploiters ever arrived.

The problem with the command to fill and subdue the earth was that no exact figures were provided. Did filling the earth demand that the other animals should all be in cages or shrink-wrapped in the meat department of big grocery chains? Is there no residual value to frontiers, to untouched wilderness with no exhaust smog obscuring the likes of El Capitan in Yosemite? In reality no one possesses more than a life-estate; the very idea of a fee simple absolute in the most nefarious of legal fictions. And as to future interests the only real reversion is to the bare plot of the grave. He recalled the poet Thomas Gray's *Elegy in a Country Churchyard* and thought again of the current President. Would his empire resemble more that of Shelley's *Ozymandias* "Look on my works ye mighty and despair?"

The sea gives the lie to all such presumption; year in and year out the tides wash immense chasms through volcanic outcroppings. History is dwarfed by geology. "Round the remains of that colossal wreck the lone and level sands stretch far away." The meaning of history is always the creation of some later author long divorced from the original event. We bestow meaning after the fact seeking to find a pattern in random circumstance.

What is the initial impetus that has propelled human life from the beginning? Are we only the latter inheritors of a defunct line about to be transmuted by technology into inorganic hybrids? Should we each patent our particular genome to prevent infringement by some future corporation that will dig up our bones to mine genetic material for splicing into zombies, full scale replicas of ourselves with the brain left out, eyes staring into nothingness but ripe with livers and kidneys to be harvested at will by elite survivors? Will the soul be present in miniature in every fragment of our genetic legacy seeking a lost composite integrity?"

Thus did Abraham the potential father of many people query the changing scene before him and the ocean, mother of all life-forms.

As the afternoon waned Abraham Cardozo passed Tillimook with its green farms and after another half hour had passed crossed over Neskowin Head and entered Lincoln City named for the man who once saved the Union but was viewed by the Confederacy as a tyrant.

"Will there be a Trump Memorial some day in Washington or

is there still a little residual room on Mount Rushmore for one more face to rule them all with the great comb-over the best place in America to take a selfie?" Abraham wondered as he headed through town to his hotel. The thought made him smile and his mood began to lighten.

He was home again in the place that was so transient by nature that it would always remain the same. Coastal towns are less aptly described as cities than they are as encampments, temporary refuges before the great waters. No doubt there were traditions and old families here, but for Abraham Cardozo one of the chief charms of the coast was its transience and anonymity. There is an advantage to be gained by being a perpetual stranger, the advantage of not entering into the squalor and narrowness of local politics, of not knowing who the movers and shakers are, who constitutes local royalty with a stranglehold on influence and social prominence.

It was good to know that each community was like a separate pearl on a linear strand reaching from Astoria to Brookings on the California border. Abraham had learned from his namesake the danger of occupied settlements with borders to defend. As a practitioner of reformed Judaism he saw that the genius of the Jewish culture lay in its combination of tradition and adaptability. When necessity demanded it tradition became sufficiently cosmopolitan to adapt to changing environments. Personally upon looking back on Jewish history Abraham preferred the Diaspora to Zionism. He left it to the millennial Christian Fundamentalists to salivate over the prospect of Armageddon. Abraham saw nothing wrong with being a 21st century incarnation of the perennial wandering Jew.

It still seemed strange to him that he had ever chosen the law as a profession, but then with a name like Cardozo, no actual relation to the great Justice Benjamin Cardozo, it had seemed the natural course to pursue rather than journalism. Now in the age of so-called fake news when journalists are scorned as "enemies of the people" he was glad he had made this choice. People still maintained a fear or at least a grudging respect for lawyers. No one was quite sure of what going to the law actually entailed but there was a sort of awe reserved for people who can sign a complaint and summon one to court, to file an answer to a lawsuit, submit to the processes of discovery and depositions, and quite possibly to force one to pay reparations or damages to the prevailing party. Lawyers understood where the landmines of liability were located amidst a general plain of mistrust and animosity between various factions in the vast mottled political tapestry of American discontents (to mix about three metaphors). Maybe that was the problem: that no overriding symbol or narrative could ever capture American reality, not even when Twittered each day from the sublime office of the Presidency by a man who claimed to know all of the best words (a boast never put to the test of actual display).

Insofar as there remained any primary residue of value in modes of communication it did not reside in words, metaphors, or even in concepts but rather in the flickering modality of images. Hearing had given way to the sense of sight – story as transposed from syntax to a mere succession of video frames. Connectivity not of meaning but of mere sequence to produce the desired response was the key to achieving the desired end, a following of likes. The sheer emergence of mass approval equaled power and power translated into money. The companies with the highest capitalization were mere agencies of communication and influence. Marketing had triumphed over the returns of finance, and finance over management. All was a big economy version of the old "rock, paper, scissors game." Bodies were big bucks. Body was metaphor. Body was economic juice. Never underestimate the commercial value of strategically placed and jiggling silicone on the penile responsiveness of the stock market.

"Today is today is today! Forget yesterday! And as for tomorrow ... by then we will already have changed our position in the endless round of the cultural equivalent of day-trading."

These were thoughts of Abraham, bright young attorney and aspiring reformer, as he looked down on the beach from the hotel dining room and saw the ever hungry pelicans wheeling about in tight formations over the sapphire hued morning sea.

"I want to forget these things on my vacation," he said to himself. "I don't even want to see the coverage of Trump's visit to London. Poor Theresa May is on her way out and the shadow of Brexit is nearer every day. I wonder if I will ever get back to St. Ives in Cornwall or to Scarborough in Yorkshire. I miss the pubs, cozy places, friendly folk... Maybe I'll run up to Nye Beach today, have a pint of Guinness stout, look out to the lighthouse on Yaquina Point, settle down a bit and forget national politics..."

"But events matter surely," returned the omniscient narrator that haunts us all with the recalcitrant points of living in an era that claims to possess ultimate significance, as though the fate of all human life and of the planet itself resided with us by right of temporary possession. That narrative voice is a one without personality but only the x-ray ability to scan thoughts, to strip away mental walls, and to leave us, naked and alone, trapped in the aquarium of written narrative where we swim about like fish bumping into walls seeking escape but seeing only our own reflection in the glass.

The checking in process at his hotel was routine and an hour later Abraham was on the road again. He passed the sleepy little town of Depoe Bay and ascended to the top of Cape Foulweather, named by the redoubtable explorer, Captain Cook. Below the viewpoint stretched the clear expanse of empty space. Abraham could just glimpse the outline of what may have been Cape Perpetua on the furthest margin of his vision looking southwards while below him the kelp forests waved about beneath a frothing green sea.

"I never get tired of this," he said to himself feeling within that inner frisson of delight that can only come with a summer morning by the sea.

"Why don't I stay here always?" he asked himself in that silent dialog of impulse and intentions that are never finally resolved into a sense of complete and lasting happiness so that we push on towards lesser pleasures forgetting that just for a brief moment all desire has ceased in a transient and therefore contradictory nirvana.

Abraham thought of that poem by Wallace Stevens *The Idea of Order at Key West.* Various lines from it came back to him lingering like Proust's Madeleine pastry.

"Imagine a world not littered with mental traces of stray lines by the great poets," he thought. "How do people manage to navigate without such guide-posts for their perceptions?"

He thought again of the wasteland of what must be Donald Trump's imagination, oozing out its various diatribes of resentment and mediocrity, distilled in order to intoxicate a salacious group of his avid followers. Abraham thought of the Great Plains from Iowa to Arkansas, flooded and tornado-lashed for week after week. But then this was only 2019 and by next year the news cycle will have passed and all have been forgotten.

"But what if there is war with Iran or North Korea?"

Abraham queried the open space of the gradually warming day.

"I will look back on this day and its prospects then and wonder why I wasn't grateful for just this day when my life still lay shining before me."

Abraham pictured the various types of chaos that might break forth from just beyond the ever-receding horizon lying westward from where he now stood. He wondered if there really were dragons in the sea.

"How does this day relate to all that has been before? Will I make a decision today that will make all of my prior plans suddenly lost, superseded, and irrelevant? Some new insight perhaps ... some foolish gesture of protest to capture the roving eye of the media, be granted a 15 second manifesto before being locked up for streaking at a MAGA rally?"

He smiled to himself.

"I would rate the honor of a Presidential Tweet! When did we start first start thinking in little corpuscles of expression?"

Maybe that is the problem: thought cannot exist without context. To present an argument in little machine-gun bursts is inherently and methodologically flawed. What would Montaigne have thought of this method of discourse when he wrote his great essays or the great controversialists like Defoe or Voltaire? In our era it is adequate to simply berate the other person, the triumph of the *ad hominum* argument must be supreme.

Abraham shook his head and resumed his survey of the pageant of land, earth, and sky that lay just before him, reflecting that the curvature of the earth limits our perspective from whatever height we are able to attain. The ocean is essentially ungraspable in its full magnificence. Even at sea one is limited to the compass-bound circumference set by the location of the vessel. One sails for days and weeks with no sign of progress and suddenly one has arrived at Old Cathay or the Malayan archipelago with streets crowded with rickshaws and all of the picturesque genius of native handicrafts.

Abraham smiled. The Kiplingesque image vanished only to be replaced by high-rise office buildings and polluted air over vast industrial complexes all churning out goods to be sold on credit to the bottomless appetites of American consumers.

"We simply have a head-start over them rather than keeping them as juridical colonies like the Dutch, the French, and the British," he said to himself.

"Perhaps it will go on and on. Dick Cheney says that deficits don't matter, at least if you are top-dog."

He put on a British manner, "The poor blighters have no choice old man. They don't want to go back to rice-farming. Besides, the almighty dollar is the world's reserve currency. Of course the Americans are a bloody crass race but they always know what they want and find a way to get it. No doubt one day they will decide to have a culture."

Abraham had always been an Anglophile or at least one who adored the American literary aristocracy of New England. He revered Emerson, Thoreau, Hawthorne, and Melville. These exalted the individual and aspired to no greater empire beyond the empire of the possession of one's own soul and integrity. It was hard to say where America had gone wrong, perhaps when the country pushed beyond the Appalachians or built the Erie Canal. Maybe it was the presumption of the Louisiana Purchase or the Lewis and Clark Expedition that set America on the road to Empire by slaughter and conquest.

In any case America was top-dog and determined to remain such. Still there was the phenomenon of Trumpism which betokened the fear of Americans that they just might lose status or be nudged aside by a billion Chinese or a billion workers from India who would steal their jobs in the few remaining industries that cared to build factories in America. All of that potential future anxiety was focused for now south of the border and within our own hemisphere. Meanwhile the North Koreans were building missiles that could hold the entire west coast of America hostage and China was seeking to establish complete hegemony over the South China Sea. America no longer sought as in the Bush years for a cobbled together "coalition of the willing," now we were determined to go it alone.

Abraham looked for an image that he could use later in his proposed op-ed piece. He thought of the lumbering figure of Donald Trump, the very embodiment of the William Howard Taft school of physical culture for Presidents. He thought of the aggressive yellow comb-over, the pursed lips and squinting eyes, all somehow betraying fear more than actual confidence, rather like a polar bear on a shrinking ice-floe.

He thought of Trump's chief enabler, Senator Mitch McConnell of Kentucky who always looked like he had just eaten too many prunes at breakfast and must seek a swift refuge of retreat. But maybe it wasn't a matter of image but of vision, historical vision into the causes of the fall of empires that was needed today above all else. Could America ever embrace world democracy as opposed to one tilted towards and enabling American exceptionalism?

Abraham doubted it. He wasn't even sure if Americans wanted freedom in the real political sense. If the truth be told we sort of envied the Chinese even with their hegemonic surveillance state. At least it produced impressive economic growth and everyone had a job. The real image of America, as judged by the Republican vision, was more like this: I am content to work until I drop dead of a heart attack or Jesus comes again as long as I get to keep my non-union job and my gun. When did Americans decide to settle for beads and trinkets from big-box stores rather than for real freedom?

"The first freedom must be the freedom from existential fear." As he reflected upon this realization Abraham understood that American determination to build a wall around itself was a sort of collective confession that we are terrified that the great expanse of morally vacuous and narcissistically indulgent America might better be filled by a more industrious people. The best image of the Trump Presidency was derived from the super-indulgence of his golfing vacations at Mar-a-Lago combined with his plebian taste in the preference for hamburgers.

Before returning to his hotel room in Lincoln City for the night Abraham drove up to Newport. In the quaint old neighborhood of Nye Beach he sat before a meal of corned-beef and potatoes and a pint of frothy Guinness Stout. He was starting to relax at last; it always took him awhile to adapt to the slower rhythms of the coast after the hurly-burley of Seattle. It was hard to disengage from the six-minute interval that the interior meter demands in the regime of billable hour requirements of legal practice.

After his second Guinness the interior rhythm began to flat-line and give way to the long slow pulse-beats of the ocean outside. It was a pleasure to simply look about and see people having a good time around him. The noise of the place was reassuring with its unfocused laughter and talk. This was the America that Abraham loved, one of leisure and of simple largess. He liked the blend of unconscious ethnicities that made Americans in their heart of hearts naturally hospitable. It had taken years of indoctrination by the devotees of various exclusionary Christian sects anxiously awaiting the separation of the sheep from the goats to close the door of the American mind to other people. America had begun as a secular Republic content to manage the country with the same dignified aloofness that God exercised in the Deist view in managing the universe. The laws of the nation should be as frugal and few as the law of gravity. It was hard to say when things had changed. It was hard to imagine an area of life that was no longer micro-managed by some administrative body or penetrated by some information gathering algorithm. It was a relief for Abraham to be effectively off-line for a time.

Freedom in the last analysis may be summed up as the right to disengage. Instead of seeing freedom as a prelude to action perhaps it is better conceived as the ability to do nothing, simply to listen to the great base-undertone of existence. When did Americans forget the value of silence? What were the great prairies like when they harbored only the soft sighing of the wind through the long-grasses? No wheat or soy-beans then but rather only the unbroken sod and the grazing bison. What were the Oregonian seas like when the salmon thrived and the whales had yet to be hunted for lamp-oil? Could any of this natal largess ever be restored? Each day brought new studies of species extinctions before the sheer onrush of human expansion and development.

Disengagement at one time was thought of as the equivalent of alienation, of loss of community, to risk being an outcast or to be viewed as a malcontent; but that was in the days when conformity was seen as the equivalent of virtue. Now to disengage seemed the only way to maintain one's individual sanity. Collective America appeared to be committed to a course of destruction. America had once manifested a unity of purpose around unselfish goals such as the defeat of Nazi Germany and of Imperial Japan. Who could ever dissent from such noble enterprises? The war was followed by a period of consolidation around the idea that America was the bulwark of freedom and democracy. The Alliance for Progress and the Peace Corps helped to undo any thought that victorious America would use its power to advance the old colonial rule.

There followed the domestic liberation era of the freedom riders and of the Student Non-violent Coordinating Committee to advance desegregation and the various liberation movements for women and for homosexuals. The presumption that was most prevalent as the century came to an end without a nuclear conflict was that victory had been achieved and a new era had dawned at last.

It had come as a great surprise then when in the wake of the terrorist incidents of 2003 the subsequent elective wars of George W. Bush and company took over a trillion dollars out of American hands to support a new colonialism.

This in turn was followed by the Great Recession of 2008 that brought the realization that far from being delivered from the ills bred of past evils the 21st century would likely bring about unprecedented challenges to our collective planetary survival let alone question American supremacy. It was this realization that had provided the backdrop of the education of young Abraham Cardozo and he reacted to it by embracing the solutions offered by the Progressive Democrats as opposed to the equally strident call of conservative Republicans for a return to a version of America that had ceased with the publication of *The Saturday Evening Post* and *Life Magazine*. All that remained of the old journalism was represented by survivors such as: *The New Yorker, Atlantic Monthly,* and the twin publications *Time* and *Newsweek.* For more specialized audiences there was: *The Economist, Mother Jones, America, Commonweal,* or *Rolling Stone.*

But even these could not supply the unified consensus of the no longer existing mainstream American consciousness. Instead there was only the nightly vituperation of the feuds between Fox News and CNN. It was the age of contention and vituperation. He thought of the bile spewing forth from pretty faces. He thought of the almost monthly stories of shootings in schools and workplaces. Still the Republican dike held firm, the Second Amendment and the refusal of service to homosexuals must stay firm; guns God and glory were the American motto. For Abraham detachment meant to get beyond all of this in order to recover what had once been the collective peace of mind that had once enabled Americans to pursue collective goals simply as Americans.

Abraham was young. It takes confidence to make

commitments to a way of life. It takes a sense that the future is at least marginally predictable in its general trends. Absent this inner sense of stability it is natural to abjure commitments and to refuse to invest the scarce and irreplaceable capital of one's youth in any sustained project. Even to have attended law school may have been ill-advised, he reflected, considering the supply of young attorneys and the shrinking availability of clients who are both able and willing to hire private outside counsel to solve their legal problems.

But where besides the law could a young reformer look to combine a sense of mission with expertise in the mindless but automated rush of events? Abraham felt doomed to the institution of the law, set aside by the same impetuous impulse and colloquy with the divine that had led to the founding of Israel. He had awoken one day to the fact that he possessed a world conscience, one that demanded that he address various ills over which he had neither influence nor control. It was an attitude that when less politically grounded and more a result of metaphysical melancholy had been called by the German term, Weltschmerz. This was the pain that accompanied our young hero each season as he set off into the desert of sand and sea on the coast to seek an answer to his ever receding question: what is the meaning of it all and where do I fit in.

The following day he awoke to a day of high clouds and wind. It was time to move southwards so he checked out of his room in Lincoln City and moved south to Yachats, a town of retired academic types and artists just north of Florence and the Oregon Dunes.

Yachats is the perfect place to seek the serenity of reminiscence while looking out from the cliffs to the never changing panorama of rock and sea. It is rather like the early Carmel of Jack London and of Robinson Jeffers, a place of retreat and individuality for people who know that nothing good can ever come out of a faculty meeting. Comfortable but unpretentious its natives divide the day into the quadrants of early morning coffee, afternoon tea, sunset, and sleep. They enjoy the lassitude of enlightened discussion without the obligation to leave serenity behind and to plunge back into the fray. Yachats is a good place to recuperate after victory over a protracted illness or to forget an unseasonable love affair. To Abraham it was only a wayside in his endless quest for beatitude.

Beatitude, that was the actual origin of the term "beat" as in "beatniks," the band of young writers in the 1950's who sought redemption and ecstasy in New York City and along America's highways. These were the true believers in that absurd and antiquated term, the American Dream. Instead, what most of American literature does with the term is to chronicle the American disappointment instead.

One need only read such works as *The Education of Henry Adams*, *Pierre*, *The Marble Faun*, *The Grapes of Wrath*, *Day of the Locust*, or *The Great Gatsby* to prove this point. America is all too often the story of betrayed innocence. It is the same drama that was being enacted daily on our southern border with Mexico. America combines opportunity with moral entropy in a way that is distinctively American. It was just as Arthur Miller noted in his great play, *Death of a Salesman*: the ones who are most lethally wounded are the true-believers. America lacks the comforting cynicism of the French and the long adaptation to suffering of the Russians. This makes our literature the perfect candidate for tragedy, the ruin of one who once had such great expectations.

Abraham had no desire to court disappointment by engaging, by joining in the final orgiastic feast. For this reason he had early on elected to pursue a policy of selective disillusionment to serve as an inoculation against the illness of despair. He sought the sub-text to every claim of easy redemption. He realized that the Promised Land was always just over the horizon and at least one generation distant.

His abiding sense was that enough would be provided to fill his momentary needs but no more. To aspire to more was both unnecessary and foolish; therefore he detached himself from any attitude of expectation beyond that of simply awaiting the logical resolution of social forces. Yet, in spite of this conscious policy he felt driven to embrace a reformist agenda as applied to those general social trends that transcend any individual decision. The worst disasters of humankind were not matters of deliberate policy it seemed but rather spontaneous eruptions of disaster from the elusive threads of minor causality. Insofar as he possessed heroic faith it was not based upon any creed or singular proposition but rather stemmed from his refusal to accept the opposite, that this world is inherently flawed, the off-scouring of a better universe by the demiurge. While not a formal stoic he was more apt to adopt a bitter frown and a stiff upper lip than tears in the face of misfortune. If he was prone to any lasting weakness it was irritation that corrections did not produce immediate and salutary results. Life simply continued and one must make do as best one could. That was then; this was now. There was no more to be said.

He did not assume that an overarching deity micro-managed events nor could he accept a negligent deity that by shifting its attention elsewhere simply overlooked noxious or terrible agents until they had done their nefarious work upon prostrate humankind. If he had been Christian rather than Jewish he might have found comfort in the cross. Instead there was only the comfort of the Torah as the best devotional path for life to follow and the assurance that behind the many distinctions of the Talmud there was an abiding and comforting presence the nature of which could never be expressed directly but only indicated by that name that could never be uttered.

Upon arriving in Yachats Abraham left his car in the parking lot and opened the driftwood studded door where he confirmed his reservation at the front desk for the next several days while he explored Yachats and its environs. His room was on the ground floor with ready access to the winding shore path along the tidal pools. He deposited his luggage and lay down fully clothed on the bed. Outside the sound of the surf was gentle and soothing. Already the journey seemed distant and dreamlike to him as though he had always found here his restful abode and place of solace.

Was this what detachment meant? To be in a place where all that mattered was a sufficient credit or debit card balance? As he drifted off to sleep Abraham imagined an endless series of just such picturesque and remote establishments designed to enhance the comforts of their guests. Was travel the final achievement of civilization? In that case of what possible use or necessity could there be for any particular promised land? Were these concepts anything beyond a justification for various nationalisms or ethnic expansions? Was the idea of a greater Serbia anything beyond a Balkan version of the old American doctrine of Manifest Destiny? For the eternal wanderer no home is needed or even requested. A traveler is never a refugee because he seeks no other refuge than the fastest way out of town, his only goal the distant horizon. To stand still is to allow the tendrils of routine to entwine their choking grip and with long acquaintance comes insolence and contempt.

When he awoke it was time for a quick shower followed by dinner. He was near enough to walk to a restaurant that he recalled from prior years where he ordered a Pimm's Cup to drink and a salmon filet seasoned with tarragon. The high tide of evening was running into the cove and the sea had that silver sheen that betokens a clear view of the coming sunset. He felt relaxed but not lethargic and the crisp icy taste of his cocktail brought his appetite to a razor's keenness. The big world seemed very distant here. The various struggles, migrations, threats and counter-threats; what were these to this narrow band of pearl-like hamlets strung along the great green plain of ocean. Time slowed here. It seemed as though he had traversed a great expanse already since dawn, not of space but of existence and its accompanist, perception.

"Why do I ever leave here?" he thought to himself.

But there is always the need to get more money, to retain one's job or to maintain one's business and all the while our constituent cells age and the threat of incipient mutiny lies harbored within our tissues. We imagine an accounting of time that is self-replenishing so that every withdrawal will be recouped by an equal margin of interest on our investment. Each promotion brings the life of permanent vacation and retirement closer. The plums of affluence grow riper on the tree. But suddenly we realize that by harvest time we may have forgotten or lost in some obscure manner that electric excitement that once gave a point to everything. Joy cannot be summoned up at will. When we lose scarcity we lose meaning. There is a mocking law of diminishing returns at the point where we can afford the preconditions of security. For this reason we should allow nothing to escape us. Walter Pater was right in his description of the transient nature of all things and the need to pay attention to life's incipient seasons.

Suddenly his dinner was before him, piquant and redolent of the local waters. He ate with contentment, savoring each buttery morsel. The sun sank slowly lower and by the time his coffee and dessert was served the day was perceptibly cooler and the outer doors were shut. He was happy to have brought a sweater with him from his room. The wind often rose just before sunset. A sense of quiet awe sets in; the world comes alive as though protesting even this minor death although tomorrow the same pageant will be repeated as it always has been. Abraham felt though that with each sunset there should be enacted some appropriate ritual to ensure the sun's return. Even minor partings bring their weight of sadness.

He arose and paid his bill before exiting to the sea path. Great plumbs of spray arose as the breakers thundered into the narrow chasms that could not accommodate their impetuous onrush. The sun sank lower and lower and even the mists on the horizon seemed to melt and give way before it. At last the whole sea seemed to catch fire and the distant clouds to glow with yellow or orange reflections.

A silence descended upon the people walking slowly along the path with him. A sort of community of matched thoughts possessed them all and the sun began to burn its way into the sea. A short six minutes later the contracting disk was no more, its light only an upward projection from where it now reclined beneath the horizon. The wind was more intense now and a chill grew gradually on the driftwood studded sands by the river. Abraham watched as the little groups passed him with a nod or a complicit smile as though all and each were sharers in a vast conspiracy born of witnessing this universal event.

A short time later he had returned to his room. He took out the third volume of Sir Osbert Sitwell's autobiography, read for an hour, and then fell asleep to the slow pounding music of the sea.

The next day Abraham had planned on visiting the northernmost reaches of the Oregon Dunes lying just over the bridge from Florence. He decided to retain his room in Yachats to return to that night. A quick breakfast of an orange butter-horn and coffee sufficed for breakfast and he set out to see the nearby sights.

He paid the entrance fee and climbed the winding road to the top of Cape Perpetua just south of town. From its summit a vast panorama of rock and chasm is visible and the sea seems to climb until it lies within a few centimeters of one's eyes gazing outwards, a great bank of blueness that might at any moment overflow and falling inwards lap about one's feet. He sat in the long grass with his back against a stone to savor infinity. He recalled the German students he had met up here once in days gone by. They had all exchanged addresses and promised to write in order to preserve the remnants of an instant friendship but had never done so. Or was it he who had failed to respond? How many open invitations do we pass up simply through neglect?

Abraham wondered at the number of strands of parallel lives that died of just such negligence and attrition. It made him think that no one is really a stranger. If time allowed it should be possible to reach a lover's depth with all the world. He wondered if there was such a thing as an omni-sexual, not in the genital sense, but in the sense that one quivered to the passing embrace of eyes on a subway platform or a smile that might have been only courtesy but in its completeness managed to sum up a lifetime of foregone acquaintance and intimacy.

His namesake, Justice Benjamin Cardozo, had never married— for him there was only the infinite play of the great man's mind and the all sufficient power of words. While for the great patriarch of old, Father Abraham, there was his wife Sara and the servant girl Hagar. From his loins came the people Israel and the long history of suffering and exile that was the greater part of Jewish history. What could he learn from these men regarding what changes and what might just possibly abide? Would our young hero ever marry or father forth offspring to be cast adrift on the surging waters of the 21st century? This brief narrative must be all encompassing and his life trail off into that infinite regress implied in the word "maybe." He liked to consider himself a procreative optimist. In spite of the challenges the human race must soon endure it would be a false prudence to fail to procreate out of fear that human beings are not up to any challenge, even the wasting of the planet itself. There must be someone left to bear witness even to cosmic ruin and to write a final codicil to the last will and testament of humanity.

With this vow in his heart Abraham descended to the ribbon of highway below and turned south towards Neptune Beach and Strawberry Hill. From there he turned the tight corner of road at Heceta Head and climbed to the access point to the Sea Lion Caves. He pulled off the road at the top of the cliffs and got out of his car to look back on the Heceta Head Lighthouse where it lay tucked just behind the Devil's Elbow with its white encrustations of guano from the various seabirds.

The great foaming waves at the base of the cliffs revealed great colonies of brown sea lions. Flocks of hovering seagulls surfed in the sky over the abyss. It was an awesome place of land and ocean: remote, adamantine, and primeval. He remained there poised on the balance-point of wonder yet summoned again to resume his journey by the insistent tug of his outlined plans for the day. The next stop was to be Florence-by-the-Sea. Had he attended law school in Eugene rather than in Washington this town would have associations different from those that had actually prevailed. Eight law schools had accepted him, each boding a different subsequent fate. Had he chosen correctly? How could he ever know? Who can bear up under the awesome chains of contingency that life imposes? But he was here now and in that "nowness" resides our only true freedom.

Florence lies along the Siuslaw River where it meets the sea. He stopped there before proceeding across the bridge to the dunes overlook for a bowl of clam chowder, a mild violation of kosher prohibition. He would make it up later by a prayer intoned over the sand dunes, blessing all that is. He was sure that the Baal Shem Tov would understand.

Abraham's relation to his faith was hereditary and tangential rather than strictly observant. He valued the essential virtues that had emerged among his co-religionists over centuries of historic marginalization. Not least among these were the sayings of the Hasidic Rabbis. It seemed obvious to Abraham that the best way to resolve the endless religious contentions that were dividing the world would to be for God to call a general colloquy of representatives from the major monotheistic religions together, have everyone bring their favorite proof texts along in little binders, and proceed to show them in detail how historical drift and animosities had blurred the essentials in an ever-growing mound of miniscule accretions.

It seemed to be an insuperable task to sift through all the claims and counter-claims of religious discourse to discover the original bond between God and humanity. The beginnings are shrouded in the dense fog of illiteracy or else the records were simply misfiled or destroyed. It was pointless to apply the metaphysical equivalent of the Best Evidence Rule and to request an original rather than a copy. Councils, synods, schools, commentaries, speculations, original sects, revelations, prophesies, mystical visions, ecstasies: all had restated and amended that first encounter where the Celestial Presence addressed the two dripping bipeds with loins still wet due to the mindless mandate of copulation and enjoined the first codified rules of human conduct. Perhaps the most salient characteristic of the 21st century was not the threat of technology and artificial intelligence after all: the major wars would likely be over a zero-sum struggle over competing revelations and contrasting versions of metaphysics.

After a late lunch Abraham left Old Town behind and with a pocket full of salt-water taffy got back on the highway, crossed the bridge at the far end of town, and headed for the dune overlook exit. After leaving the highway a cut-off to the left beckoned and he found a parking lot where various trucks were unloading dune buggies to join the many noisy vehicles that were engaged in climbing a seventy foot mound of sand before him. The top was invisible but a path to the right through the evergreen trees beckoned and Abraham began to climb.

He found that others had been there before him and by placing his feet carefully in their footsteps he could minimize the soft subsiding avalanche as he asked the sand to support his weight. By means of this strategy he managed to climb to a fairly level surface at the crest of the great dune. From this vantage point a marvelous sight emerged. There before him lay a virtual desert as of fabled Arabia, dune after dune only interrupted by small copses of evergreen trees like sheltered isles of repose in a fawn colored sea. The great expanse of sand dunes fell off westward in steep cliffs and a mile distant the ocean appeared beyond the lower moonscape of sea grass and beach blue and infinite. Abraham climbed higher still towards where the cliffs began and sat down on a fallen and bleached out pine tree to catch his breath again after his long climb. Here he was almost beyond the roar of the dune buggies and something of the primal aspect of the scene was restored. Isolation returned and with it the luxury of thought.

He returned to his speculations upon time and history. He thought of the great disproportion between texts and actuality. If God were to write anything down then surely His text must be creation itself existing above any interpretation. It seemed strange to him therefore that the great religions seemed to emphasize the jurisprudential aspect of the Divine Intellect rather than simply to contemplate the wonder of being. The emphasis upon the will of God seemed secondary to a contemplation and appreciation of what God had already accomplished.

Abraham was neither a pantheist nor a disciple of Spinoza but he did feel that commandments had more to do with human needs than with divine mandates. Morality appeared to him to reside at the metaphysical level of parking regulations. The oscillating rhythm of sin and forgiveness, of mercy or retribution, of command and acquiescence seemed to be too infused by the human element to really matter, at least from the distant perspective of the philosopher. But on the other hand, who could quarrel with revelation provided that that revelation was authentic and not biased in some manner by the one who initially recorded it? To understand the intricacies of Divine Inspiration though was beyond the present ambit of the time and place of Abraham's speculations.

But as a bare proposition subject to correction: assuming that the reflection of God's essence lay within his creation, it showed a variety and even a quality of spontaneity that was alien to most supposedly definitive summations and interpretations by the major religions. It seemed to Abraham that closure was one of the last attributes to be implied in regard to the Godhead. All of the huffing and puffing of various imams, clerics, and avatars of the sublime to ensure that God not be offended seemed to forget the sheer silent witness of being in places like this, holding the slow accretion of eons of wind, sand, and season. Humankind lies awash in conflicting mandates and proposed punishments so that the justice and majesty of God might be vindicated at last.

Abraham thought about it all. Could God do nothing for Himself but he must rely upon various factions of our fellow men to threaten us into compliance? He thought of his proposed manuscript at home and wondered whether what so many of his conservative countrymen were calling for was a theistic version of the absurd red hats that appeared at various Trump rallies proclaiming that America could be great again; God could be great again as long as we make it happen.

Was it an accident that political fundamentalists were usually religious fundamentalists as well? What a shock it must be for those who believe that they can speak authoritatively for God himself to discover that they are powerless beyond the grim circle of their own rhetoric. How frustrating it must be to recall the days when they could call forth armies and wade through seas of blood to impose their doctrines and covenants. Now they were reduced to mere frothing diatribes and appeals for sacrifice on the part of the faithful to advance their particular crusade, jihad, or ministry. In America there was the great alliance of the born subjugators of others whose uncertainty demanded compliance as the proof that they had been right all along in the cosmic sweepstakes. All of history was a reflection of how they had used their power when they still possessed it.

Suddenly Abraham saw what was really happening in this critical hour of history. For the first time all contending absolutes were stripped down and lined up on an equal starting line on the final sprint to the finish, winner take all. There they stood with sinews lithe and straining, great chests heaving with maledictions towards the heretics and false witnesses lined up next to them in competition. Each contender pointed at the skies where ranks of serried angels awaited the outcome, fearsome and furious but determined to let some inscrutable inward certification be rewarded by victory while all others must watch as their laurels turned to chains dragging them into a pit of more than defeat, a pit of utter punishment, shame, and desolation. Victory! A blare of trumpets, the great city arises...

Abraham Cardozo awoke to the sound of the wind blowing through the trees above his head. It was late. He would obtain no more food tonight. The stars already floated in the clear sky of night, silent and remote. Restaurants close early on the Oregon coast. He might just stop for some kippers at a grocery store before heading back to his room in Yachats.

He retraced his thoughts assembled like grains of sand in the face of this great immensity. If he had possessed a papyrus roll he might have recorded his thoughts even as St. John had done in exile on the remote island of Patmos. He could slip the manuscript into a vessel or tie it with a ribbon only to have it be discovered years later like the scrolls of Nag Hammadi. Scholars would puzzle over the mysterious author and the size of the community of followers that he must have gathered about him.

Alas the city that they had envisioned had long since crumbled into sand and all that remained was this sacred testimony as witness to the vision vouchsafed so long ago. Abraham thought of the new versions of Mishnah and Gemara that might ensue from his simple act of climbing the dune alone on a summer day. He bethought him of the various schools of thought, the carefully calibrated distinctions, the condemnations and excommunications, the many dying in anguish still unsure of their salvation, lamenting their sins but secretly knowing in their heart of hearts that granted youth and time enough they might commit them again, not to offend God, but simply because they were human, overwhelmed by the passions and uncertainties spared to those who parsing sacred texts knew better, or feared more, or simply had a professional interest in being right. Perhaps they were. Who was he to say?

He took his notebook from his pocket and stood there, ball-point pen in hand. What was his vision? Abraham looked about him at the moonlit sea, the sand, and the beacons of starlight as the darkness deepened. He listened to the wind sighing in the long sea-grass. The granular presence of this little slice of eternity blew softly about his sandaled feet and he who might have been the great law-giver and father of nations put aside his writing implements, trudged wearily back down over the sifting dunes and drove quietly away.

UNHAPPY ENDINGS
BY CARRIE AVERY MORIARTY

Content Warning: Mental health issues and suicide.

"What do you mean it's not here?" Shelly asked.

"Just what I said," Richard replied. "It's not here."

"Did you look?"

Richard looked at her, eyebrows raised. "No," he barked. "I walked in, and when it didn't jump into my hands, I had to assume it wasn't here."

The sarcasm in his voice set her off.

"Never mind," she muttered. "I'll look myself."

"Why do you never believe me?"

Not answering, Shelly began moving papers and folders around the desk, looking in each one. After her thorough search, she concluded, "It's not here."

"Just like I told you," Richard said.

"So," she began. "Where is it?"

"I think I would have it in my hands if I knew that," he said.

"Where did you have it last?"

"At my desk," he said. "Which is why I was looking for it there.

I wonder if Karen picked it up and filed it."

"Why would she file it?"

"Because it's her job," Richard said walking out the door.

"It's her job to take things from your desk and file them?" Shelly asked, following him out the door.

"Karen," Richard said as he got to her desk.

"What can I do for you, boss?"

"Have you seen the Mackenzie documents?"

"They were on your desk this morning," she replied. "I knew you were working on that project today, so I left them there."

"Well," Shelly said. "They seem to have grown legs and wandered off."

"Oh dear," Karen replied. "Let me check with Mark."

Picking up the receiver on her phone, she pressed a couple of buttons, then waited.

"Yeah," she said into the receiver. "Have you seen Mackenzie?" She paused, then asked, "Can you check your desk?" Another pause. "I'll wait." Placing her hand over the mouthpiece she said, "He's checking his desk."

"Obviously," Shelly muttered.

Richard gave her a glare, then patiently waited for the answer.

"Great," Karen said. "Bring it on up."

"Why did he have it?" Shelly asked once the phone was back on its cradle.

"We can ask him when he gets here," Karen responded.

"We'll be in my office," Richard replied, gripping his sister's arm and nearly dragging her into the office, closing the door behind them.

"Why aren't you waiting out there?" she barked. "Don't your employees know to leave things where they are?"

"Shelly," Richard said sternly. "I trust my employees. They were hired because of their professionalism and work ethic. I do not need you coming in here and thinking you can read them the riot act because you perceive some kind of injustice."

"I never," she sputtered.

"Exactly," he responded. "This is why the firm was left to me, not you. I have the business degree. I have the smarts to run the company the way Dad and Granddad wanted it run. It is my responsibility to make sure that things run smoothly for everyone, clients and employees alike. Until the board sees fit to remove me from my position, you need to trust that I know what is best and that I will work to make sure that things run smoothly."

"Why are you so bossy?"

"I'm not bossy," he corrected. "I am firm with my convictions, something Dad couldn't bring himself to be where you were concerned. He always let you get away with things you shouldn't have, and it's left you with less coping skills and not nearly enough common sense as you should have by this age."

"Seriously, Richard," she tried. "Why can't you just let me be part of the company? It's my legacy just as much as it is yours."

"And I'll make sure the legacy is still around," he said.

Just then, a knock sounded on his door. Opening it, he saw Karen, Mackenzie file in hand.

"Here you go, boss," she said.

"Thank you, Karen," he said. "And thank Mark, too."

Everyone at the firm knew that Shelly Draper was not in charge, even though she liked to throw her name around to get attention. Newer employees were warned that she was to be respected, but anything she demanded needed to be run by her brother prior to any work actually being done on the project.

"My pleasure," she replied, closing the door.

"Let me have it," Shelly said, reaching for the file.

"Sit," Richard barked.

"I'm not a dog," Shelly retorted.

"No," Richard said. "They are much better behaved than you. Now sit and we'll talk about it."

"Sometimes I just hate you," she mumbled, but complied with her brother's wish and sat in one of the chairs next to his desk.

Walking behind the desk, he sat, opening the file on top of the stack of others that were there. Shelly bounced in her seat, impatience obvious in her demeanor.

"Looks like Mark was doing the work I planned to get to after lunch today," he said.

"Why is he doing it when it isn't his job?"

"It actually is his job," Richard said. "Sometimes, however, I pick up any slack that might happen because of someone else's work load. This was one of those times. Turned out he didn't need my help after all."

"So," she hedged, leaning forward. "What is happening?"

Richard held up his finger as he reviewed the top page in the file. He then clicked on his keyboard a few times to pull up the electronic file. A few mouse clicks later he turned to his sister.

"We got it," he said.

"Yeah," she shouted, jumping from her chair. "I'm so excited. When do I get to hold it?"

"Shelly," he said sternly. "Sit."

"Still not a dog," she replied, but complied again with his instructions.

"While we have claimed the art," he began, "it doesn't mean we'll have it here tomorrow. It takes time for these things to go through the proper channels. It has to be brought to the country, make it through customs, be authenticated, and after all of that is done, then it will be shipped to the warehouse. Once it's there, a final inspection will be done. After that, it will be available for us to display it as we have already discussed. You are not going to get to hold it."

"It's a stupid vase," she gruffed. "Why can't we just have it at the house?"

"Because it is worth half a million dollars," Richard replied.

"So," Shelly said.

"So," he replied. "It will be kept in a safe place where it will not come to any harm. This vase is several hundred years old. It's not like one you can buy on a shelf at some store. It's a treasure that needs to be properly displayed."

"But it's pretty," she complained. "And I want to be able to look at it any time I'm sad. It cheers me up."

"You're just going to have to find something a little less expensive to do that," he said.

"Are you going to commission replicas to sell?"

"We just got the go ahead to make the purchase," he said. "I haven't had a chance to discuss anything with my team. Until that happens, no decisions can be made."

"I think you should make sure there are replicas," she said. "Then, anyone who is sad can buy one and have it at their home to make them happy."

"I'll take that request under advisement," he said. "Now, can I get back to my actual job? There are other things that I need to take care of."

"OK," she replied. "See you when you get home."

She walked out the door, leaving it open on her exit. Richard sighed once he knew she was well out of earshot. He loved his sister dearly, but she was such a high maintenance person he couldn't handle being around her for long periods of time. Karen walked in a few minutes after Shelly left, closing the door behind her.

"You are a saint," she said. "I don't know how you deal with her on a daily basis. She is exhausting."

"Hey," he replied.

"I know," she said. "She's family, so you just have to put up with it."

"Thank you for running the file down," he said.

"It's my job," she replied. "So?"

"We got it," he smiled. "Now I just have to get through all the hoops to get it here. She wants replicas to be available."

"You told her you can't do that, right?"

"I told her I'd check with my team," he replied.

"But, Richard," Karen said.

"I know," he replied. "I just had to get her out of here. Even I have my limits as to how much I can take of her. She would have probably gone into full meltdown mode if I'd told her no."

"As long as you don't make me tell her," Karen replied.

"I'll tell her something," he said.

"Mark said he'd be ready whenever you were done," she said.

"I'll head down there now," he replied.

"Hey," Richard said at Mark's doorway.

Mark looked up from his computer and pushed his glasses up on top of his head.

"You alone?" he whispered.

"Yeah," Richard said as he came into the room. "She left after I told her we got it."

"I don't know how you do it," Mark said.

"What?"

"Put up with her crazy," Mark replied.

"I guess I'm just used to it," Richard said.

"I don't think I could ever get used to that," Mark laughed.

"What are our next steps?" Richard asked, steering the conversation back to business.

"The letters are ready for your approval," Mark replied. "Once you've reviewed them, I'll get them printed and sent out. Should only take a week or so to get the answers we need. After that, it's just a matter of waiting on the government. We all know how quickly they move on these types of things."

"Yes," Richard replied. "What's your next project?"

"This was the last one," Mark said.

"What do you mean?"

"You remember I'm moving, right?"

"Oh, yeah," Richard said. "I completely forgot about that. Where are you going, again?"

"I'm going back to Montana," Mark replied. "Dad isn't doing well, and mom wants me to come home and take over the business for him."

"You will be sorely missed," Richard remarked. "But I really do wish you well on this new chapter."

"Thanks," Mark replied.

"I'll let you get back to it," Richard said, walking out the door.

"Shelly called," Karen said as Richard made it back to his office.

"She just left," Richard said.

"Oh, I know," Karen said.

"What did she want?"

"Apparently she wants to go to Brazil and look at something someone discovered down there," Karen said without expression.

Richard sighed, running a hand across his face. "Why does she do this to me?"

"You're asking the wrong person," Karen replied.

"I don't think anyone has the answer," Richard said, then

stepped into his office.

Sitting at his desk, he pulled up his sister's favorite website for searches on new finds in Brazil. At the top of the list was a portion of an urn. The notes indicated that it was from far before the Portuguese came to the country, but it couldn't be confirmed at this point. Of course his sister would want to get that. She was all about things that predated the western influence in South America, and this was no different.

His phone buzzed and he picked up the handset. "Yes," he said.

"She's on line one," Karen said.

"I'll take it," he replied, then pressed the button for the line. "Hello, Shelly," he said.

"Did Karen tell you I called?"

"Yes," he replied. "I am looking at what I think you are interested in."

"The urn?" she asked.

"That's what I figured," he sighed.

"It could hold the key," she bubbled.

"Or it could just be another thing you set your mind on."

"Can I go?"

"Are you seriously asking me this?"

"I want to go," she begged.

"You know I can't let you," he argued.

"But it could be exactly what I need," she replied.

"Until I see more information on it," he began, "I'm not going to put any time into it."

"I'll do it all," she offered.

"You can't," he replied.

"Why?" she asked. "Because I'm too dumb? Or because I'm crazy?"

"Shelly," Richard sighed. "We have been over this with every piece you've found. I can't allow you to travel alone, and I can't afford to have a team go with you. We will have to wait and see what new information they come up with before we make any plans as to whether or not to get it."

"It's the key," she demanded. "I can feel it in my soul."

"Shelly," he barked. "Just stop. I have a business to run, and that requires all of my time. I cannot give you any more time to follow these foolish notions you have of finding a cure. You need to learn to live with it."

"You just don't understand," she shouted back. "You don't have to live like I do. No one tells you when to get up or when to go to bed. They don't make you take stupid pills every day that do nothing but drown your creativity. I can't even decide what I want to eat because of it. I want freedom. I want to really live. And you're just determined to keep me locked up. I bet if you could get away with it, you would lock me in a dungeon and throw away the key. You'd leave me to rot in the dark."

Richard pinched the bridge of his nose, trying to hold back his anger.

"Shelly," he began. "I love you. You're my sister. You are the only part of my family that's left. I know you don't mean to be horrible, but you need to understand that everything I do is for your own good."

"You hate me," she shouted, then disconnected the call.

Sighing, he placed the receiver back in its cradle. "That woman is going to be the death of me," he muttered.

"I'm home," Richard called as he came into the house.

The silence around him was deafening.

"Hello?" he called.

Still nothing.

He placed his briefcase on the credenza in the entry and made his way to the kitchen. Surely someone was here. Usually he could smell dinner when he walked in, but the house felt cold and empty as he made his way through it.

Stepping into the kitchen he grabbed his stomach, one hand going over his mouth. Nothing prepared him for the sight he was met with. On the floor was their cook, Julia. Her throat was slit all the way across, blood pooling around her head. Her eyes stared in horror at the ceiling. Next to her was Gloria, the housekeeper. She was in the same state, throat sliced all the way across, a puddle of blood under her as well.

"Shelly," he shouted, racing from the room and back the way he came. He took the steps to the second level two at a time, bounding up the stairs as fast as he could. Racing down the hall, he ripped open his sister's door and stopped cold.

"Oh, Shelly," he sobbed as he saw her on the bed.

Stepping up next to it, he looked down into the peaceful face of his sister. If he didn't know better, he'd think she was just resting. But her eyes were wide, her lips blue, and a faint trace of blood had dribbled from the corner of her mouth. In her hand she held an empty pill bottle. He picked it up and turned the bottle, reading the label.

On the night stand he saw a nearly empty bottle of whiskey and a bloody butcher knife. He closed his eyes, swallowing back the bile that rose in his throat. He placed the pill bottle next to the whiskey, turned, and left the room.

"I understand this must be difficult for you," the detective said.

"I just can't believe she did all of this," Richard replied.

It hadn't taken long for the police to arrive after he'd made the call. First to arrive were uniformed officers, followed by detectives, and finally the county coroner. He'd explained the situation when he'd called 911, telling the agent that no one would be able to be saved. He'd told the story so many times he'd lost count.

"It seems like she was having some issues," the detective offered.

"She's mentally unstable," Richard replied.

"Was she on any other medication?"

"I've got a list of her medications in the book," he said. "She had more than mental health issues. There were also physical issues she had going on."

"If you can get me a list of her doctors," the detective began.

"I have a notebook that has all of the information in it," Richard said. "It has her providers, list of medications, last visit notes, and everything about her conditions."

"What conditions did she have?"

"She contracted polio when she was a child," Richard explained.

"Didn't she get vaccinated?"

"Unfortunately, her body had a tendency to refuse vaccines," Richard began. "She could get the dosage and within a week, no trace of it would be found in her system. We went to Nigeria on a safari when we were little and she contracted it there."

"I didn't even think it was around anymore."

"It's pretty much gone," Richard replied. "There are very few places where it is still around, and we happened to go to one of them."

"You said she had mental health issues," the officer suggested.

"She was schizophrenic," Richard said. "She was on medication for it, but her dosage had recently changed. It's in the book."

"Can you get the book?"

"Sure." Richard stood and walked to his office. Reaching up onto the shelf, he pulled down the black notebook where all of Shelly's medical information was kept. He turned and handed it to the officer.

"Do you mind if we hold onto this for a while?"

"That's fine," Richard said.

"I think this is all I need for now," the detective said. "Here's my card, if you think of anything else."

"Thank you," he replied. "I know this can't be easy for you, either."

"Death is never easy," the detective said. "Whether it's for the family or for those who have to investigate it."

"I appreciate you're being so kind," Richard said.

"We'll be in touch," the detective said, then walked out of the office.

Richard could still hear the rest of the authorities mulling around the house, finishing up their tasks. When someone knocked on the office door, he raised his eyes to look at the man.

"We're all done," he said. "Once the coroner has completed the autopsies, you will be informed of the results."

"Thank you," Richard replied.

"I'm sorry for your loss," the man said, then turned and left.

Richard heard the front door close, then held his breath, listening to the lack of sound. Breathing out heavily, he stood from the desk to assess what was left to accomplish. He did not relish the cleanup that awaited him.

Three days later.

"I'm so sorry for your loss," the man said.

It was the hundredth time Richard had heard the phrase that

day. But it was to be expected. He'd opted to have the funeral open to the public, and apparently Shelly had quite a few friends around town. Hundreds had come out for the service, and they were all filing out now. Soon, he would be left without any distractions.

"How are you holding up?" Karen asked.

"I'll survive," he replied.

"If you need anything," she said.

"Thanks," he responded.

The two women his sister had killed had been buried at their family's request, and Richard had paid for everything, including a generous severance package that did nothing to ease his guilt over their deaths. What he wanted to do was rewind time and see the warning signs that must have been there. He should have known his sister was dangerous, should have been able to prevent the tragedy. But that wasn't something he could control.

He'd decided to have the open ceremony at the funeral home, but had not invited anyone to the burial at the cemetery. That, he wanted to do on his own. Once he made it there, he climbed from his car and walked to the open grave. His sister's body had arrived and was placed in the contraption that would lower her into the ground.

"Why did you do it?" he asked the box.

Of course he didn't get a response. He was left with only questions and no answers. He would never know the reasoning behind what his sister had done. The coroner had confirmed that she'd overdosed on the medication shortly after the other women had been killed. They had been struck on the head, then their throats had been cut while they were unconscious. It was swift and seemingly painless for them, mercifully.

Shelly hadn't suffered, either. She'd taken several of the pills, combined with the whisky she'd used to swallow them, and had simply fallen asleep and never woke up. They had determined it happened shortly after she got home from her trip to his office that morning, just after the phone call in which she accused him of not caring about her. Nothing could have saved any of the women, and Richard had to simply live with that fact.

THE PROCESS
BY DAVID MECKLENBURG

ompulsion and habit move together. They clasp each other's hand, just as they did in the womb, each so intimate with the other that the outside world cannot differentiate them. I don't dress them up in the same clothes, although they often make that decision on their own. They stir beneath the comforter before I am awake, hatching out the plans and intrigues which are always the same. They dispense with preliminaries; I get into the shower, I soap up, I rinse, I wash my hair and if it's Wednesday they allow me the novelty of shampooing it. A deeper rhythm suggests masturbation with the shower massager on certain days and it is a time where I am allowed a bit of freedom with whichever phantom I choose to make love. Thursdays I shave my legs and upper lip.

The completion of my toilet: the towel wrapped around my head, and a robe on (if it's cold). I warm up the coffee I made in ritualistic abasement the night before. With a black cup of life, I return to the bathroom to pull out the random hairs that mark age, hoping the violent extirpation will render the follicles barren and lifeless. I moisturize and scent myself and then tend to the tangle of my hair. I choose my clothes. If it is a skirt, I often put my shoes on first. I'm not sure why, but I have always done this save when I lived in Japan for six months. Exercise? That waits for the evening, so its place is not here. I eat, or rather drink my breakfast. A bit of lipstick and I am off.

I am compressing time at the end. This is usually because I am in a hurry. The habit of leisure has encroached a bit on the compulsion to go to work. To earn my money. To sit or stand at my desk and type other people's words. I am typing these words which are mine, but I somehow forgot that we share these words—in this order, this context of habit: this compulsion of moving from left to right with our gaze—we would not understand one another where it otherwise. Are these my words?

I write these words on a ferryboat. I am commuting. I wonder if the tense is correct, to switch between present, present perfect, past. The subjunctive, long forgotten by many who speak and write English, always lurks, waits, ready to spring up were it given the chance. Ada writes mostly in first person; it feels comfortable, fresh and immediate, although the extra-egotistical perspective of third person always brings fresh insights. The second person promises similar interest: a similar vantage point but like standing in a line it becomes tedious. You understand.

Physically, I need a little variance. This floating room of my own is not my own; it is public. Hundreds of other people are on board, but such is the culture I live in that we sequester. A few are social in the same seats they always occupy. Most sleep or lose themselves in their mobile devices. A few read books. I like them the best. Some work. A cadre of coders constantly type on laptops. Others make deals on phones. A few people text. I write. This.

Whim barges in on the Syzygy of compulsion and habit.

—what is it going to be today? Pen, keyboard? The big journal? Quotes or Joycean dashes?

"I'm not really sure, but I feel like a keyboard today."

—Volume over quality. I get that. It all comes out in the end.

"Well, not all of it."

—What they don't know.

"Wouldn't interest them."

I know that Need has actually shoved Whim through the door, or in my case, up the stairwell from the car deck. Whim suggests I ignore Microsoft Word's prescription of clarity and conciseness with regards to "actually shoved" and continue on. I tell myself I need to turn that feature off, but I am lazy and do not wish to get distracted because I need to get this piece done. I feel fairly confidant the words are flowing correctly. I know there will be cutting, deletion, rearrangement, but that is for Editing, which comes later in the process.

The Process... remember—that's what it's all about. I used to think that *it's all about the process* was a lazy, caddish phrase of visual artists: an easy thing to say and in art, *nothing should be easy to say, that's what sets it apart.* A writer with whom I share a birthday says that "a writer is someone for whom writing is more difficult than it is for other people." He says this, as with most of his work, in Olympian irony. The irony, the dead pan delivery of bed pans, cigars, Russian women, horse heads full of eels, the sniggering leer of the Devil and all of them sound like some percussive symphony drumming down in the subconscious, drumming in long sentences and... but wait, the drumming comes under influence. I was speaking of process. These intrusions of influence are actually part of the process, but while always there, influences make themselves known like Dicken's Ghost of Christmas Yet to Come—in their own good time.

Time. The writer whom I quoted has a lot to say about that. Where are we? A process is nothing without time. It is the horizon of being we move towards and yet through. Like the geometric line hidden behind the Cascade Mountains, the horizon is also behind me. I am facing backwards on this boat, which suggests I should use past tense, but since I don't mind sitting backwards and this writing has the nature of a conversation that I am sharing with you, a perfect stranger on this ferry crossing, I will continue with present tense. For now. Which just was. Like the ferry, it doesn't matter which way I sit in time. I am always moving through it. But how much do I suggest to you? *When* should my words go and by that phrase, I mean: how *much* time? Do we spend it? Gods, I would love to have a wallet in my purse that could dispense money the way I spend Time. We have reached a point in time in this text where metaphor begins to intrude like the bosun's announcement over the brash PA that some idiot has left the alarm activated on their Audi or Mercedes. (It is always a German car).

I perform metaphor, which may be metaphorical itself, or not. George Lackoff will tell you that metaphor is inescapable because it's how we think. Linking like to like to like to understand because we can never really get at Kant's *ding an sich*: the thing in itself. (At this point in writing, I wonder how much German will creep into this piece—best keep it to a minimum.) Oh sure, we can *name* something but that's only the beginning of the game. In putting the pieces on the board, I can easily *call* that little castle a knight, but no one will know what I'm doing, so I reserve "knight" for the little horse's head. The names suggest a pattern of movement, of rules, but which moves I make is up to me and you, because if I break them, you won't play with me.

Enough of all that, my strategy and style has begun to become tiresome, wouldn't you agree? Partly the subject matter is to blame because I am thinking and writing (which are the same thing, really) about art. If you've read through some of my other pieces in the *Trinity* series (because the context is an anthology) you will note the theoretical, "meta" nature of this piece. Meta is a Greek word that simply means over or beyond and no, I am not going to clobber you over the head or in the gut with the bewildering world of prepositions, not to mention clichés. (Which I just did). The constituents of metaphor, translate, and carry over are more or less the same.

"Speaking of translation, what about the story of you in Japan? How did you write that?" For me, writing a story like that usually comes from an image. In that case it was a memory of a torii gate shrine on Hokkaido. Did I really see all those ghosts? Of a sort. Whether they were "actual" phantasms or not is irrelevant. I had to get to them, and the way was through the gate. Once I have the gate in my mind, I think about where to start.

Some writers write straight through, others will plot things out on index cards: both digital and paper. Like this essay, I tend to flounce around, and the beginning of "January" ("A Pearl of Loneliness" came later after I had finished it) is flouncy. That story doesn't have much of a plot. I walk through a desolate town, shuttered against the winter and strangers and then I walk on the beach at night and have a visionary experience. What the visions contained carried the import of the piece.

I wrote it on the ferries. The comfortable *Kaleetan* and the irksome *Chimacum*. *Kaleetan* means arrow in Chinook jargon and that ferry is spacious for morning commutes with lots of tables for writing. It also seemed fairly reliable at the time. Reliability is the bedrock of habit; it is the aquifer of compulsion. *Chimacum* means "you're going to miss your transfer bus on the other side." It is a newer boat, but poorly laid out, cramped and often late. It does have plenty of electric outlets, but wireless signals don't work on it very well, which I don't mind, because the Internet is the enemy of writing. Full disclosure: this piece is actually being composed on the *Hyak*, the comfortable sister-craft of the *Kaleetan*.

The first stage of the Japan-story was simply writing. Writing memories, emotions, recollections of emotions and all of it liberated from the tedium of order and plot. And then editing. That is usually how I work; I slog through outbursts of words and then, once I am finished, I will stop and look over what I've written. I prefer to take a break in the form of a walk, which I should call a think. I subordinate a great deal, you can tell. The first piece I wrote was about how the winds would come down from Alaska, but in revision, I realized it fit better where it is. The story clocks in at 2480 words. I probably wrote 6,000.

And here is where the Process really lifts you into the air—not in the manner of winged flight, but rather like that of a hot air balloon. I float over the words at the speed of the wind, because they haven't arranged themselves into anything coherent which is perfectly fine because this is the native mode of emotions. People will often say emotions are non-linear, but if you are one of those writers who get hung up on semantics (like me), don't worry too much about your terminology. It's not really the point of Craft if you know what the Greek word for reversal is. You may not even need one. In fact, you're not going to get any craft lectures: no pre/pro-scriptive bullshit, because this is about the writing. That's not the way to Art.

I remember a poet once told me that I would get nowhere reading philosophy, that it was dangerous for any really good writing. Old men seemed to be full of this shit at some point, and no, I haven't found myself doing it now that I'm closer to that joker's age. Granted, he was a pretty good poet, but being full of shit and being a good poet aren't mutually exclusive states of affairs. Some may even say it's a pre-req. I suspect two things: he couldn't really get the philosophy I was reading but I was too young to sniff the ignorance through his august façade and he was making some kind of offhand remark about me fucking his colleague. Maybe he was approving? I don't know. It wouldn't surprise me the way those guys carried on about emotions and experience. I will mention briefly here that you don't need to fuck a poet to learn how to write. It can be great, don't get me wrong, especially if his dick has that curve that hits you just right so coming feels like having the inside of your skull burned out with a bubblegum blowtorch, yes and if you wonder what that is I have no idea, but they were the babbling words I could finally string together after I could speak again.

Because the problem is, he talked about Craft a lot. The Holy Craft of Poetry and Writing. I worshipped it for a time, but I was 23 and still impressionable. He figured if it sounded good in class then it would sound even better in bed with his girlfriend who was 27 years younger than his wife. I've begrudgingly fought Craft to a stalemate over the years, and seldom believe anything coming out of a man's mouth in bed unless it's a snore. Yes, Craft is important, but it should *never* get in the way of Art. Art isn't Craft.

Since Art can be so many things, I don't think I need to add another page on top of an already considerable mountain, but... look at the woman over there. Not that table, that one there. Yes, in the black outfit that marks her as a student of one of the cosmetology schools in Seattle. She's moved onto eye shadow now, but you missed the foundation. Dab dab dab, then buffing it in evenly. She's brushed less rouge in today over the foundation she chose, which works better with her skin tones, although to be sure, the light in here is bad. But I really admire her. She looks pretty good out in the natural light of Seattle, which, shadowless as it is and diffuse to the point of madness, is a pretty good performance. It's not easy to orchestrate that, but then again, I've never seen her wear anything but black. That sort of changes things. Can she manage her usual color palette wearing a Seahawk jersey? Can she do it with a red Prada sweater? Maybe she's capable even though her husband is cheating on her back in Silverdale. Maybe she wears that ring to keep men from bothering her. And a few women too, I suppose. I don't know much of that back story and you see where I'm going with this?

She's doing Art right now. Is it heteronormative, bourgeois, radicalizing, deconstructive? Depends how much I want to think about it, but above all it's a process. Foundation, rouge, eye liner then shadow, and finally eye lashes. She understands the context of her work, which are black clothes and a ferry with bad lighting. She also knows she'll have to do it all over again tomorrow and keep at it before she can start earning money. I'm not being metaphorical. If you want hard theory, revolution, just check out how much more work the goth chick behind her does. She came on a shapeless, blotchy-skinned 20-year-old but leaves a radiant creature of the night with black lipstick and breasts that invite you to damnation: all on the 7:20 sailing from Bremerton.

What these two women have taught me is that Craft is Important, but a vision of what you're doing is even more important. And doing it every day, which we have an ancient word for: practice. And practice takes time but give that to yourself, whatever you do. The practice becomes a habit ingrained with the desire for art, which is compulsion. I guess that is as much of a rule from me as you will get. I'm better at cautionary tales, both being one and writing them.

For many years, when I was starting out and unsure of myself as a woman, a human being and above all a writer I worried about wasting time. This was because I didn't really start writing until I was 37 or so. I had 'written' before. Even stuff I considered art, at the time. But that work scattered itself among journals and old computer disks and most of it before the Cloud ascended to the role of the Recording Angel. Yeah, there was a complete novel, I've lost it and for good reason, ultimately: it was a piece of shit. No, what changed at 37 was first, I wrote what I wanted to. But the most important lesson I learned was that I have never wasted a single moment writing. Even the cloying things I produced in high school, the lost novel, the bad poetry written in imitation of my master (hey, I got off on that at the time—I'm not going to get down on the past tense Ada for that), all of that was like each brushstroke of the women doing their makeup. It's a much bigger process than you think, and it takes an Olympian perspective to see it. Maybe that's why I've always like the Olympian Irony of that one writer. The one who said writing is harder for writers than other people.

But if I can make a suggestion, having a picture of him on your desk—he's wearing that usual look on his face, the skeptical glance that is sliding into modulated sarcasm obscuring an incandescent intellect adjudicating the fact you're filing a nail rather than writing, which is the same expression my own German grandfather used to give me and they even both came from Lübeck and may explain their mustaches and hatred of Hitler—that may not be a good idea. If you're going to be pretentious like me, then choose a writer who reminds you of someone close. This is how I let influence into the process of my writing. On my way out the door in the morning, I usually say *Guten Morgen* to my literary Grandfather. Compulsion or habit?

Oh, have I returned where I started from? No, I already did that, sort of with the women and their makeup. My makeup is minimalist in contrast to much of my writing. I've decided that is my reaction to the woman who taught me how to really do makeup. Like writing, I didn't really hit my own stride with makeup until my 30's because that's when I dated her, and I didn't really start the writing until she dumped me. I hope this economy of romantic and aesthetic history makes more sense. I won't go into it any further because the context of the Trinity Series can help—read "The Camera Does Not Lie," from the May issue.

No, I didn't get this all written at once. It's Thursday, so I'm running a little late, but Ada got on the *Hyak* and began revising and adding a few things. Astrid eventually butted her way into the text, if not to dominate then to at least remind the writer that she is always there, just like the *other* Nobel laureate from Lübeck, Ada's presumptive Jan Bronski, drumming away in obscure lugubriation, but Ada didn't really mind. It may not make a lot of difference to the reader working through these words words words, but the process of writing them means much to her.

JULY

THE PROMPT

It wasn't so much that she was dead but rather that she had never been alive. It wasn't that he didn't want her but that he loved her more than he had ever loved anyone, even himself.

UNILATERAL AGREEMENT
BY JENNIFER DiMARCO

The entire eastern wall of your bedroom is glass. But not like any glass I've ever seen before. It shimmers literally; no need to take poetic license. It resembles, more than anything else, an impossibly thin wall of water. Not even a veil but just the sheen or impression of a veil. Invisible yet visible all at once, a perpetual ascension of water rising against gravity.

I stop and bow my head thoughtfully. Gravity, too, is alien here. It exists, certainly, but at two-thirds of what I'm accustomed to.

Alien. Ironic to use that word, to consider it an easy descriptor of as-yet-unknown surroundings. There's actually nothing "alien" about this place or its glass or gravity. The only alien here is me. Everything else is natural and native.

My mouth tugs into a grin in that way that expressions sometimes betray us. I was never good at bluffing games but I've mastered the art of leaving questions unanswered; dangling modifiers are my friends... or, more accurately, misplaced modifiers. My wife would be fast to correct me but that was the risk of marrying a linguist with the perfectionism of an editor; Charlotte has only red pens on her desk.

I lift my chin and my internal narrative dissolves, allowing room for more sensory input. I lose myself in the sensation of walking to meet myself.

My reflection in the seamless, seemingly living sheen is an image I found, at first, to be disarming and disconcerting: Smooth, featureless, more the impression of a body than an actual one. It's angular, too, as if crafted from fewer polygons than the surrounding world. My surface is an anemic coral color that mimics something dangerous and perverse that lives beneath public restroom toilet seats on the microbial level.

Of course, you don't see me this way. You see me differently every week. Or, if ratings are high enough, I might get the go ahead to stick around, wear one skin for a whole month. Jack Corral, a colleague of mine, once played a single role for fifteen years… but that was back before anyone knew about the Exodus Window. No one stays longer than a month now. At thirty-one days they send an Extractor and it comes out of my pay.

I've been here three weeks, two days, and twelve hours.

You see me as handsome, stocky, a gentle bear of man who makes you feel safe and protected without the threat of losing your autonomy. You met me at a night club where I looked awkward and out of place, holding a light beer and sitting alone. Sometimes you stroke my beard and tell me it reminds you of your father.

You have no idea we're being watched by seven-point-five billion people.

The featureless pink thing. The stocky lumberjack. Neither of these are anywhere near what I look like. In reality, I'm deep brown like the shell of a Brazil nut and about as tough. But sometimes life takes us to unexpected places and everything happens for a reason. Even if the reason is: I made a stupid choice and now I'm paying for it.

The glass wall slides open. Or dematerializes. Or parts the

curtain of elemental particles that separates inside from outside. It's not like I can ask how basic things work when no one can know I'm an alien.

That still sounds so weird.

I step out onto the deck.

The view is a perk of the job. My grin betrays me again and yeah, it sucks that everyone can see what I see and hear what I think but, again, stupid choices are as stupid choices do. I'm literally unable to lie to billions of people and after twenty years of JumpTV, no one is surprised that safe sex with strangers isn't a perk.

I glance back into your bedroom.

The wall has sealed so you appear to shimmer just a little and it's apropos, really, because, to me, you're not as real as I am to you. After all, I see *you*: Platinum blonde curls. Heavy breasts that fill my hands and welcome my mouth. Hips as broad as you see my shoulders. I have enjoyed these twenty-three and a half days... despite your six arms and three eyes. To be honest? Kind of *because* of them. Especially the arms.

The sheet has fallen away from your naked body. Your skin is poreless and green as a new growing thing in springtime. Your perfume is called Ocean Kiss but without it you smell like roses after an autumn rain which isn't a scent your people embrace (though I wish I could bottle it and bring it home). A quick side hustle before the studio sends me out again: Highest bidder for the genetic code of your scent.

For just a moment, I feel a cold rush as information is sent across light years. The auction will be over in a few seconds and my account will be credited. Even *thinking* about offering up part of myself is taken as permission to sell. (As if I need to offer permission; I don't have that luxury.) Another few heartbeats and I won't remember what you smell like and that's sad... but Charlotte wanted a new car. Full solar instead of the glitchy hybrid I built her from a kit before all *this* began.

I feel the director's order as an almost pleasurable urging. The carrot more than the stick. Not all studios hire directors who are kind... or even humane. I was lucky my contract was bought by JumpTV.

The urge again, a little stronger.

Right. The view.

I walk to the chrome railing that glints in the blue morning sunlight like something molten running in a channel. It's so much hotter on this world (your people being the only green living things) that the railing may very well be in a liquid state. I look out to the wide horizon that extends as far in both directions as I can see. Then I look down.

Your house juts from the face of a granite cliff three hundred feet above an ocean so vast and deep it almost certainly contains more life than anything on the surface and everything subterranean combined. The club we met at was four miles beneath the scorched stone of the central landmass in this region. It was called, simply, in spotty translation: URH. You Are Here.

Where else would I be?

The blood red waves are young tsunamis in training, curling sixty feet high until they crash against the congregation of rocks collecting at the base of the cliff like a stampede of wild horses with manes of foam and thundering hooves.

This place... those waves... your arms wrapped around me. You are no more or less exotic than the dozens of other aliens I have known (Biblically) but for some reason, some inexplicable whisper in the back of my mind where the feed can't detect it, I feel enticed to stay—

"Xthom? Feid raye nor toberaye?"

Oh. The party's over.

I hate this part. Some of my colleagues never turn around. Some of them just go. But I know what the authorities will say to you. I know what they'll tell you and how betrayed and used you'll feel.

In the early days, long before I had a contract for anything with anyone, before word spread on solar wind nanopigeons and through bionetic satellite networks, performers could jump in and out without notice or harm. They would be one-night stands or three-week flings but no authorities showed up at the end banging on your door, telling you your new lover was a felon serving time by sharing their intimate moments on another world. That said lover looked nothing like you thought, that their body was crafted by studio designers to fit your perfect ideal, to lure you in quickly and hard.

No one seemed to talk about how all those intimate moments weren't just theirs but mine as well.

And so, I turn. Awoken from slumber by the unwelcome guests, you stand facing me with the water wall between us. Your eyes are cold and hard and one of the three is crying. I shake my head just a little, trying with every movement, every moment, to make you believe me... but also aware that heartbreak is good for ratings. I mouth your name and then your people's word for "truth." I want you to know what I felt for you, what I said to you, how I reacted to your touch, was all real. How you reacted to mine was all welcome.

You step forward to come to me but the interstellar police have only so much patience and they move to stop you even as I turn away and vault over the railing and into the open air.

No contact. Falling. The spray of the waves is caught in the wind and dusts me with moisture like warm dew. I think the oceans are boiling.

I fall. I fall. I fall.

I wake at home in my pod. No dramatic gasp or disorientation required. I am encased, nude, body serviced in a dozen ways to keep me fed, watered, and clean. For just a moment, while my collection of genetic samples download and upload to the studio, I smell a little like roses after an autumn rain. I think of your face again, of your purple eye drowning in tears, and I close my eyes.

Just give me a moment.

A thin wave of cold passes through my body and then nothing. I have my memories of my time with you but nothing sensory. I can't feel your touch or taste the cold spicy soup you made us for dinner every night. I am not yours to keep and you are not mine.

"Open." My voice is a little hoarse, as always, the only stereotype of jumping that's true. The pod opens and I climb out and get dressed without fanfare or welcome. Charlotte is probably at work. I go to the kitchen to prepare dinner.

There's a note on the fridge, stuck with a magnet shaped like an Easter Island Moai at 1:156 scale. Charlotte's neat cursive might as well be calligraphy: *I have eaten the plums that were in the icebox and which you were probably saving for breakfast.* Her writing is red.

I pick up the magnetized pen and finish the poem at the bottom of the page: *Forgive me. They were delicious. So sweet and so cold.* The smart paper pings my wife than erases the page.

I open the fridge and cupboards, make a quick assessment and start cooking. There are artichokes and wild rice, extra firm tofu and, tucked into the coldest corner of the fridge, an unopened bottle of dessert wine. Saved, I assume (I hope) for this very occasion.

The table is set, the food just plated, when I meet Charlotte at the door. She is a short, imposing woman, with silken raven hair cut in a sharp, asymmetrical pageboy. Her glasses are small and almost frameless, drawing attention to her almond-shaped eyes the color of rich caramel. She sets down her briefcase and I walk into her arms.

"I'm home," I say needlessly because her eyes are disarmingly cold and suddenly I'm off balance more than a jump across light years could ever make me. "Dinner's ready."

"Thank you." Emotion is thick in her voice but what emotion? I find her strangely unreadable despite eleven years of marriage.

"You watched?" What am I saying? Why did I ask that? And why do I feel like I'm poking a bear?

Charlotte's gaze does not grow warmer. "I always watch."

She walks past me to the dining room and I hear her chair scrape the floor.

We eat in silence. This is the real adjustment. These tense first hours. By the time I clear the table and have listened to her tell me mundane, useless details about her work parsing alien languages for translation services, she finally turns the conversation to me and my "work." The six-armed elephant in the room. I pour the wine.

"I was confused at first." She swirls the pink moscato in her chilled glass as if it were a much finer vintage.

I stand at her side, still holding the bottle. During my faux absence (I was in the pod in my study the entire time, of course, just not conscious), she added the extra leaf to the table and my seat is at the other end. I don't want to be away from her.

Why does she want distance?

"You kept using 'you' in your narrative." She's staring into her glass, not looking at me. And I want her to. I want her to look at me, to see me, to show me something beneath her surface that tells me she loves me, she's missed me, she's glad I'm home.

That she forgives me for screwing up, for getting caught, for losing ten years of my life to this sentence.

"Yeah… uh…" I shift from foot to foot. I'm not used to wearing clothes again. I'm not used to Charlotte being so *affected*. "Premium subscribers want to feel like I'm talking to them so—"

Charlotte looks at me. I catch my breath.

"You weren't talking to them." She's certain. She's right. "You were talking to her."

This was the choice: Serve ten years in prison on the Selena lunar complex with no chance of early parole, earning a dime an hour refining moon rocks into shinier moon rocks… or work for a federally approved jump studio. I would serve my decade on other worlds, streaming my every sensation to the masses, jumping back home between worlds and earning 1% of all subsidiary rights and genetic code sales, plus one hour of "home time" for every day spent away.

More convicts ejected themselves into open space after two years in the mines than ever came home. There was no choice.

"Char…" I put the bottle on the table and go down on my knees beside her chair. She's still looking at me but her body stays turned away. "I have to make good TV. Every hundred thousand subscribers I gain the studio, they take a day off my sentence. A whole day! I've already shaved eight months—"

"We need a coaster." Charlotte waves absently toward the condensation dripping down the wine bottle onto the oak table top. She leaves the room, lifting her glasses and wiping at her eyes once her back is to me. I bow my head and let her leave.

I don't mind that she only has two arms. I still want her to hold me.

We don't make love that night. We usually do. When I return. Even if I pop back unexpectedly after a short jump and I'm only home for an hour or two in the middle of the day; I just complete the William Carlos Williams poem on the fridge and she knows I'm back.

Instead we lie on opposite sides of the bed, letting the moonlight stream through the open windows and pool between us like an impassable sea of quicksilver. I want her to touch me so badly I taste blood in my mouth from biting my tongue; I won't ask her. It won't work if I ask her. I need her to want to.

But I also want to touch her. She's my wife! She's my partner and soul mate and companion. She's who I chose... except, I had to choose other things, too.

It takes two or three hours before Charlotte's breathing is slow and even and I dare to turn my head and look her way. She's asleep, tears ignored and dried in streaks down her face. Thank god I'm not hooked into the system outside the broadcast pod or fans would start calling me Heartbreaker or Tear Maker or something else equally stupid, callus and viral.

I wasted three hours lying here in silence being a coward and it doesn't stop now. I'm not sure if it's guilt or pride that fuels me but I get out of bed, not waking her, and walk the house. Her alarm will go off at seven in the morning... but I have to jump out at 6:45.

I eat an apple. I look at myself in the long mirror in the hallway. I memorize my own body so I never forget myself. I go out on our modest deck and stare up at the stars. There are barely any visible, not even an entire constellation, but clouds and light pollution aside this world will always be mine.

I think about meeting Charlotte at a lecture on race, ethics and rebellion. She was an upper class Chinese American with professors for parents and I was born and raised in Puerto Rico, living with my black, New Yorker father after my mother died of breast cancer. I was all for civil disobedience because my father always told me: A closed mouth doesn't get fed.

Even after all these years, I don't think Charlotte understands why I bombed that building. No one was killed but federal buildings matter, apparently. Fuck them. I'm not remorseful.

A thought I can only have when I'm not plugged in.

I emerge from my rare private thoughts to find myself standing in Charlotte's study. Everything is eggshell white and ebony wood grain. Clean. Organized. Controlled. Charlotte is a Virgo with Virgo rising.

I miss her so I sit down in her chair which is stupid because I could be waking her with kisses and my own tears and gentle (and not so gentle) touches discovered over so many years together. But I was still busy being a coward.

A file folder on her desk. The label: Regulation PC2389.03. I stare. Penal Code 2389 is the jump option for felons. Zero One allowed us to earn 1%. Zero Two made the studio pay to maintain our pods. Zero Three is new to me.

I open the folder. I read the statement. I start to shake so violently I still can't move when Charlotte walks into the room.

"I didn't want to tell you." Her voice is soft, just above a whisper. And her face, her lovely, familiar, gentle face is painted in sincerity and concern. "I didn't know how."

I find my voice but I'm choking on air, let alone words: "They're... turning off safe guards? They're—" A strangled sound from my own throat.

Charlotte comes to me then. She crosses the room but also crosses the emotional divide between us. In less than a minute she's holding me, crushing me, but it's not enough. I want to sink into her, to hide my larger, taller body in her smaller one because she's stronger, because she's always been stronger.

"Shh." She strokes my short curls. "Camilla... shh. It's all right. It'll be—"

I pull back from her but don't let go. She is my lifeline. My sanity. My harbor and haven. My mind is racing, panicking. "Char! I have to *free fall* to jump back! In the air! I'll—"

"—break every bone in your body. Yes. I know."

I fall silent. I hold my breath. I don't think I could breathe or speak even if I wanted to. How had it come to this? I'd made a mistake! It was just a mistake....

A chime. My pod is calling. Where did the night go? *Sweet Mary, Mother of God....*

"Camilla."

I look down at her. I breathe because her gaze wills me to do so.

She leads me from the room. I know where we're going.

Is she this angry because I developed feelings for an alien? Because it was fun to pretend to be a handsome man for a while, living on an exotic world, having rollicksome sex with a six-armed—

"Look at your pod."

We're standing in my study, my pod's status light blinking yellow as it warms up and downloads the space/time coordinates for my next destination. I don't know what she wants me to see... until I see it.

My pod sits atop a new platform. No. Not sits. It's *attached* to a new platform that isn't a platform but rather a tank connecting to the pod with tubes and wires and some kind of complex and intricate valves. There's a red, white and blue logo on one end: iForm.

"You're..." I turn to face my wife. "Cloning me?"

Charlotte sets her jaw and lifts her chin. "Grafting you. Before you wake up, between every jump, the iForm will fix everything that's wrong, graft you with new tissue. Fix everything—"

"Char!" I take her face in my hands, my lips parted as a hundred sentences try to tumble out at once. "I know what iForm is! I know how grafting works! We can't afford—"

And then I see it. I'm not sure how I missed it. There's a second pod in the room.

"No...." I'm shaking my head. I feel weightless. I feel unreal.

"I sold my own contract," my wife explains. "All my safe guards will be on. I'm not a felon. I'm a volunteer."

My eyes sink closed as if darkness will grant me reprieve or at least denial.

"Camilla. Look at me. Please."

I do. But I can't stop my tears. I can't stop shaking my head.

"Camilla."

I kiss her. She kisses me back. The lights on my pod turn green. I have five minutes to climb inside.

I bow my head against hers and Charlotte whispers, "When you think 'you,' let it be me."

RESURRECTION
BY LAUREN PATZER

arren struggled to open his eyes. He raised his arms to rub his eyes, but they felt like logs. After taking some deep breaths and some furious blinking, the ceiling came into focus. The pockmarked ceiling tiles were pristine. The metal bars between the tiles were dust free. He was somewhere recently constructed.

He struggled to sit up and realized he was on a cot. It smelled new. He pushed the sheet and blanket off and sat up. The room around him was filled with lab equipment. He frowned and rubbed the back of his neck. A circle of hot flesh met his fingertips.

He stood up unsteadily and took another deep breath. Looking around the room, he noticed someone else on a similar cot across the room, a short-haired redhead. A small table at the head of her cot held a set of glasses; he assumed the spectacles were hers.

He looked down and realized his clothes hadn't changed since...was it this morning? He realized he had no way to tell the day or time. He felt in his pocket and found his cell phone was gone, but he still had his wallet.

"Darren," a voice boomed from a speaker overhead. "Nice of you to join the living."

Darren scanned the room for a door. He saw one on the far wall away from the equipment between two large cabinets. He went to it and tried to open it. Scanning the surrounding wall, he noted the security pad. He checked the door's frame. It was metal and fairly solid. The wall around was cinder block; much more difficult to punch a hole through than sheet rock.

"I trust you've found the room adequately secure," the voice said again. Darren frowned. The voice sounded familiar.

"Is that... Eric?" Darren asked.

"Good, your senses are sharp. You'll need that," Eric replied.

"Clearly, If I hope to escape," Darren replied.

"I'm fairly certain you won't," Eric replied and two large screens on the wall opposite the door flared to life. As the screen warmed up and the picture came into focus, Darren recognized two of three people wandering around a plain room. His wife and nine-year-old daughter along with another man he didn't recognize. The man was laying down on a cot similar to the one Darren had woken up on.

The woman and the child Darren knew very well. His heart skipped a beat and his skin erupted in goose bumps. His wife, Nancy, and daughter, Danielle, were supposed to be in Nantucket with his folks, safe from danger.

"What do you want? I don't have much money, but—"

"Nonsense," Eric replied. "I don't need your money, you know that."

It was true. Eric Banyon was a billionaire industrialist magnate. His wealth was legendary. Kidnapping seemed out of sorts with his public persona. He could literally buy anyone to do anything.

The second screen showed a disheveled and dirty woman shuffling about a room littered with refuse and what appeared to be blood. Darren realized with a shudder that the refuse appeared to be body parts. The woman, Darren realized, was one of the infected.

The rooms on the screen were similar in size and design. A temporary wall sheltered what were likely restroom facilities where his wife and daughter milled about. The other room had no such facilities. The infected had no need for a bathroom, although the verdict was out on how the flesh they consumed was or wasn't voided.

From the rooms similar construction, Darren assumed they were co-located, possibly even in the same building.

"What do you need?" Darren asked as he heard the women on the cot to his right groan as she struggled to wake up.

"A cure," Eric replied. "The woman on the right screen is my wife."

The redhead sat up and held her head.

"Where am I?" she mumbled.

"Welcome, Doctor Strand!" Eric said.

"That doesn't tell me where I am, and I'm not a doctor," she replied as she pulled on her glasses.

"Your dissertation on infectious diseases is sure to get you that doctorate you're studying for. Quite brilliant! Only a matter of time, really," Eric droned on.

"Great," she said. "You like my work. Why am I..." Doctor Strand's voice trailed off as she looked at the left screen and saw her much older husband laying unconscious on a cot. "Billy..."

"Good, you grasped the stakes of your situation!" Eric said. "The federal government and governments around the world have sucked up all the accredited talent to solve their dilemma, but given their qualms about safety and ethics, I know their efforts will be slow and unreasonable. As the feds refused to use my facility for their infectious disease work, I had facilities available for you to begin. Amanda was infected a few days ago, I suspect the government wasn't pleased with my criticisms and had it done, but I don't have time to enact revenge on those responsible."

"That's Amanda?" Darren said as he walked a little closer to the screen. She was the right height and build from what Darren could recall.

"It is," Eric responded quietly.

"Two weeks before likely irreparable damage to your wife's tissues," Doctor Strand said. "You want a cure in seven to ten days… impossible."

"Seven, to be exact," Eric replied, his voice returning to its detached authoritative tone once more. "At which point I'll release my wife into the room of your loved ones. You'll have a little more time to save your loved ones, but not much. In any case, you won't live to see them again if my wife isn't cured."

"Wait," Darren said. "I'm a molecular biologist that works with plants. I'm not exactly perfect for this work."

"Doctor Strand will need a capable lab assistant and the cure will need a reliable method for spreading through the infected's body. You did undergraduate work on nanotechnology, correct?" Eric said perfectly matter-of-factly, not as if he was a maniacal madman.

"Correct," Darren sighed. "So we were literally the best you could find."

"Had to think outside the box in a very short amount of time," Eric replied. "Your facility is underground. There are a few other rooms with supplies and every type of equipment you could possibly want for the task at hand. You cannot escape the facility without wasting precious time. Your loved ones are not here, but rather states away in another hidden location. Don't think I won't hesitate to release my wife earlier to meet your loved ones if I determine your efforts are toward anything but finding a cure."

Darren looked at Doctor Strand.

"Well, Doctor, are you ready to get started," Darren said. Doctor Strand nodded and walked over to the computers arrayed between cabinets with supplies. She paused and stepped over to a refrigerator and opened it, examining the contents. She straightened up and looked at Darren.

"We appear to be well supplied with samples and Petri dishes," she said as she walked over to the computer. The screen came on as soon as she touched the mouse. "No password—this is an isolated network? I see we've got plenty of industry standard software to work with."

Doctor Strand sat down and began moving through the file system. She nodded at certain times and then rummaged around for a paper and pencil to jot down some notes.

"Darren's your name, right? Or was I dreaming?" she said. Darren chuckled and nodded. She handed him the notes she had jotted down. "See if you can find these supplies in the cabinets or wherever."

"You got it," Darren said. He grabbed the notes and moved to the nearest cabinet. He opened the door, blocking the view of all the cameras. He glanced down at the paper as he pretended to search the cabinet. The note read:

Sodium chloride - we don't have time

Potassium chloride - to waste getting out

Syringes - of here before our host

Pipettes - uncovers our connection

Beakers - find a way out

Watch glass - he's solved our other problems

Darren smiled as he pulled several containers and other supply items and brought them to a table. Doctor Strand got up and walked to him.

"You found everything okay?" she asked.

"Not a problem," he said. "There are some other rooms with more supplies. I'll check them out so I know where to go for what we need."

They locked eyes for just a moment of understanding and then Darren walked to the door. He reached for the handle and found it unlocked this time.

Darren entered the exterior hallway and saw it ended at an elevator. He looked around and saw several doors which he assumed went to supply rooms. He scanned the ceiling as he went into each room, searching for any possible avenues of egress like a ventilation conduit or a maintenance hatch. He saw the ventilation grills on the wall which surely led to the other rooms, but it would be a gamble to discover a way out without some kind of map.

He made busy looking for the supplies on the list, hoping their malevolent benefactor would get peace of mind seeing them being proactive toward a solution. In reality, he'd done Jenna and him a favor. Their illicit affair had been going on for over a year now and extricating themselves from their existing commitments had been worrisome. This billionaire bozo was essentially killing off the problem for them.

As Darren returned with an armful of supplies, he glanced around the hallways nonchalantly. Acoustic tiles in here just like all the rooms. They could be hiding additional egress points. He'd have to depend on Jenna's computer expertise to do something about the security cameras. He wasn't sure what Eric had in mind if they tried to escape, but it was clear he didn't value human life. That made him almost as dangerous as Darren and Jenna. Two sociopaths just wanting each other, no strings attached. Maybe three sociopaths doesn't make a crowd, it makes a solution.

He walked back into the large laboratory room and Jenna looked over at him, giving him a brief smile of acknowledgement.

Darren set the supplies down on a table. He walked over to Jenna.

"How's it looking, Doctor Strand?" he said.

"Not as dire as I first thought," she replied. "It looks like we've got some real possibilities for progress."

Darren translated her words into a positive assessment for the computer security. She could break it and the network wasn't isolated to just these rooms, but to the entire facility.

"Best we get this going as fast as possible, just in case our first attempts aren't successful. We may need several tries." Darren's words, like Jenna's, had double meaning. When the zombie infection first erupted six months ago, they'd discussed taking advantage of it to eliminate their respective families. As he examined the furniture and equipment for possible exercise in escaping the facility, he had to use all his willpower to keep from grinning ear to ear at his good fortune.

The pair convinced the billionaire to send down some additional equipment. It gave Darren and Jenna the brief access to the elevator they needed to access their most likely escape route. While Jenna ran medical trials with new findings, she also managed to punch through to data on the elevator model and discovered it had a pulley system, meaning they'd have access to cables once they breached the maintenance hatch at the top of the elevator cab.

As they made their progress toward escape, Darren was troubled by Eric Banyon's behavior. He'd known Eric through Nancy. Eric was a longtime family friend and godfather to Danielle. While the married couple hadn't been particularly close to Eric after the marriage, Nancy still considered him a close family friend.

He guessed grief could really change a person. He was glad he'd never have to find out.

Two days passed as the duo witnessed Eric Banyon's wife devour two human beings and noticed the pause in her behavior when she had consumed the human liver. Jenna noted the behavior and included that track of inquiry into her search even as she broke into the buildings surveillance system and made copies of their recorded time in the facility. They'd need that for playback later as cover for their escape.

On the third day, Darren wolfed down another batch of ramen noodles and dehydrated vegetables, when Jenna sat down with him.

"Ready for this to be our last meal here?" Jenna said quietly.

Darren nodded as he shoved a spoonful of noodles into his mouth. He munched on them thoughtfully.

"Eat up," he replied. "You'll need your strength."

Jenna's eyebrows rose mischievously and Darren could feel his pulse pound in his temples with his excitement. The brief flirtation was nearly enough to send him over the edge after being in such close proximity to his lover, but not being able to show her any affection.

They ate the meal quickly and then Jenna walked back over to the computer and typed for a moment in the keyboard.

"There," she said. "Video loop is running and the live camera feed has been turned off."

Darren walked up to Jenna and pulled her into his arms, smashing his mouth against hers in a passionate session of sucking face. They kissed for several minutes and Darren's hands began to roam, groping and clutching his lover. She returned the attention at first, but then pushed him back.

"I think we'd better save that for later." Jenna smiled as she put a finger to Darren's lips to stop his objections. "We don't know how far we'll need to travel."

"I understand although parts of my body are demanding immediate satisfaction," Darren said pointing to the rising bulge in his trousers.

"Later, tiger."

They went to the food supply and quickly packed food and water for a trip. They had to balance what they could carry with what they knew they could probably scavenge from the wild if it came to that. Darren assembled a duffle bag of sorts to carry tools and items to pry doors open on their escape route. Finally, they moved to the elevator. Darren pried the security plate off with a screwdriver and reconnected the wires to open the elevator shaft door. Luckily, the cab was still there from the previous trip. As they stepped inside, Jenna paused and grabbed his arm gently.

"Darren, there's something we need to discuss," she said.

Darren's eyebrows rose as he waited for her to continue.

"The liver enzymes. They are the path to a cure. I found some research data from a French team and they were going down the right path before that facility was overrun. If we went back in there and worked for another day or two, I'd have the cure."

Darren considered it for a moment. He looked at her and smiled.

"Then we can get richer than that pathetic excuse for a billionaire Eric after we get out and deliver that cure in a couple of weeks, once our little problems have been irreparably infected."

Jenna smiled back and they resumed their escape up through the elevator shaft. Using a series of clips and stops he'd banged together, Darren got both of them up to the top of the three story shaft. He pried the doors open at the top and the two stepped out into the open.

They looked around them at a twenty foot high concrete wall that completely encircled them. Three sets of large steel doors dotted the wall. High up on the wall, a stadium sized display showed a live video shot of them both standing there gaping.

"I thought you said we were free and clear," Darren whispered angrily.

"This was supposed to be enclosed by a chain link fence," Jenna hissed back.

Eric Banyon's face popped up onto the screen. He frowned.

"You're going to let Amanda die, Darren? We'd broken bread together in Cape Cod, for chrissakes!"

"Eric, it's nothing personal. But you kidnapped us! What were we supposed to do, rationally?"

Eric laughed. Jenna and Darren looked at each other and the concern really began to sink in.

"There's nothing rational about your affair and your plans to kill your families, is there Darren and Jenna?"

"Uh, look. We can go back down there and get that cure done for your wife. It's maybe two days away at most," Jenna said.

"Well, Doctor Strand, now that you mention it, you were on the right track with the liver enzymes," Eric said.

"How did you—" Jenna began.

A recording of them in the elevator showed their entire conversation taken from a hidden camera. After that, a spliced version of their conversation after Jenna had supposedly shut off the video cameras in the lab revealed both their conversation and their intimacy.

Behind them, the doors Darren had pried open shut and the entire top floor of the shaft began to sink into the ground.

"Ah, hell," Darren said. He ran around the perimeter, looking at the steel doors for a way of getting out. He considered using the hinges as steps to propel them toward the top of the wall. It was a long shot, but he was quickly running out of options.

"But please," Eric continued. "Don't worry about Amanda. She's fine." He turned away and shouted off the screen. "Come say hello, Amanda!"

After a few moments, Amanda appeared on the screen next to

Eric. She waved and smiled.

"What the hell?" Darren said.

"A little Hollywood makeup and trickery, my good, good friend Darren," Eric said. Amanda walked away and he returned to viewing them from the center of the screen. "Same with your loved ones. Once I'd shown them proof of your infidelities, they were more than happy to submit to three days of filming while you two were banging away in LA."

The screen switched again to show Nancy and Danielle slightly further away from the camera, waving at them.

"Just your two little problems here, Darren!" Nancy shouted. Then both mother and daughter flipped Darren the bird. The screen then switched to Billy, who stared disapprovingly at them.

"You deserve what's coming, bitch," Billy said. He then stood up and walked off camera.

"What's coming?" Jenna whispered.

"You'll both be tickled to find out the cure was found yesterday and, though the world governments are in shambles at this point, there's a solid effort at mass producing a vaccine. No one knows what the world will look like afterwards, but there's a shining horizon for those of us that survive."

"What's coming?" Jenna repeated louder.

In response, the screen showed news reports of zombies overrunning various cities and secured facilities like the one Jenna worked in at Berkeley and Darren's hometown in San Jose among many others. Additional footage showed military with flame throwers surrounding the infected areas and lighting everything on fire.

"You were both removed from these areas roughly two days before they were overrun. According to unofficial government records, you're both among the dead. Which is very fitting, I suppose."

"Hey!" Darren shouted. "We're not dead! You need to let us go!"

"What's coming?!" Jenna screamed.

"To combat spread of the infection, the terminally infected are being burned. I was able to procure a few specimens before certain populations were decimated," Eric said, his face devoid of emotion. The steel doors started to creak open. As the seals on the doors broke, the sounds of groans and murmurs rose in the compound. The dead walked.

Darren peered into the sealed areas as the dead started to flood out.

"I'm sure there are doors in there somewhere we can breach," Darren said grabbing Jenna's hand.

"It took me three months to erect this facility and put everything into place. Thank you for keeping those efforts from being in vain. Also, good luck breaching the vault doors that lead to the outside before you're ripped to shreds. Good karma to you both!"

THE DIM
BY HIROMI COTA

You ever been in a room where the lights seemed to dim for the length of a blink but no one else seemed to notice? There's no *seem to* about it. You saw what you saw. They saw what they saw. These things are true. So, why would you see something different from everyone else?

It's easy to answer that question, though the precise details…? Well, let's leave that to philosophers, religious figures, and quantum physicists. The simple reason they didn't see it? Because they couldn't; they were in the wrong reality to do so. This doesn't mean that you're in the right reality. I mean, your reality hasn't been paying its light bill. What's up with that? C'mon. Get it together.

The people who didn't see the Dim are your celestial neighbors, hanging out in an adjacent reality. You can talk to them and give 'em a high five, but at the end of the day, you'll never see them again. At least, you won't see that version of them. Infinite adjacent realities are tricky like that. But, just because these people'll vanish from your life by the time the moon sets doesn't mean that you have license to be a dick to them. They're still people.

Besides, if learning that your actions have little consequences turns you into an asshole, what does that say about you? That you're only a nice person so long as there's someone bigger than you? Sounds like a waste of humanity. We didn't become top of the food chain in a million universes by being strong; there are dozens of animals that got us beat there. We're not even the top because we're smart. We're number four there. Good, but not running the world good. No, the only thing we do better than anything else in the worlds is cooperate.

Anyways, you've probably guessed that the dim light was more than just a late payment. Sorry about that. Didn't mean to fib; I just wasn't trying to drop all the knowledge on you at once. I mean, I just told you that everything you know about the nature of reality and existence is wrong. Kinda heady. So, the Dim? It means someone in your reality just died. It happens. There aren't that many people in each reality, so it's a big deal. The Dim is kind of like your reality's way of pouring one out for its homie. Because when things die in one reality, they don't get replaced. Sooner or later, your reality's going to be empty. Maybe it's empty now. Sure, you'll still see people, but no one will know the real you; they'll just know the versions of you from other realities.

Sound lonely? It doesn't have to be. Yes, you'll never be the you that other people know. Yes, everyone who enters your life will be a stranger. So, what? You're still you and you can still help shape your world, as well as other ones. Use that human collaboration. Just remember to not treat anyone like they owe you something because they might not. We're all in this together, even when we're off in our own little worlds.

THE PERFECT PARTNER
BY AMBER RAINEY

Michael stood in the doorway just watching as Ada leaned on the balcony wall. The sunset behind her was a splendid show of pinks, purples, and oranges. It was the perfect evening with a perfect woman. He wanted to run his hands through her long, red hair and tell her how much he loved her. He took a step forward but hesitated when he noticed the slight bit of tension forming in her shoulders. He frowned. He could tell something was off, even though everything appeared normal. He hesitated, wondering if he should start over. Perhaps, he should come back later. Michael warred with himself. He wanted to be with Ada, in fact, he had been looking forward to it all day. He deserved it. His selfish side won the battle with his subconscious and he shrugged off his hesitation.

Ada tensed, only slightly, as Michael came up behind her and gently kissed the back of her neck. Michael did not see her expression; he'd closed his eyes, inhaling her perfume. Ada pasted on her most convincing smile and turned in his arms.

"I've been waiting," she said.

Michael took her hand and kissed it, then smiled at her.

"Have you?"

"Mmm." She nodded.

Michael leaned in and kissed Ada, deepening it and bending her back towards the balcony. When the kiss was over, Michael took a moment before opening his eyes and looking deep into hers. He didn't know what he'd been expecting but he somehow felt her reaction wasn't quite right. Before he could question it further, he lost his train of thought as Ada put her hands on his chest.

"What do you have planned for this evening?"

Michael grinned. He put out the crook of his arm and Ada slipped her hand in it. Michael led her to the balcony door.

"I figured we could start out with dinner at *Basil and Olives*, followed by some dancing and then perhaps come back home for a nightcap. How does that sound, my dear?"

Ada smiled, "Lovely, Michael. You always know how to plan a great date."

Michael nodded, "Only the best for you, my love."

Michael opened the door as Ada walked through, missing the sad look on Ada's face as he turned to lock the door.

The plate of pasta in front of Ada sat, barely touched, as Michael practically scarfed down his food. He was so engrossed in recapping his day at work, he barely noticed Ada picking at her food and not eating. Dinners were usually Michael's time to unwind. Ada was a great listener, interjecting her opinion at the appropriate times and offering her pity if warranted. Michael's job was incredibly demanding and it was normal for him to want to blow off steam. It was such a routine part of each evening, Michael barely noticed the subtle change in his date—he was too enthralled with the idea of their perfect relationship.

"Ada?" Michael prodded.

Ada looked up, realizing she had stopped paying attention. She silently chided herself for her behavior then smiled at Michael.

"I'm sorry, honey. I must have been in my own world," she giggled.

The uneasiness on his face faded and he was back to his usual self. He straightened his tie and then looked back at the waiter, sharing a look with the man as if to say *women, am I right?* The waiter nodded and Michael looked back to Ada.

"What would you like for dessert?"

"Oh, could we skip it tonight? I'm really eager to go dancing now. It's what I was thinking about just a moment ago," Ada replied sweetly.

Michael did not see through the lie. He nodded to the waiter and the man left them alone. Michael reached across the table to capture Ada's hand. He pulled it up to his lips and placed a lingering kiss on her palm. He felt more attraction for Ada as each moment passed. Her cheeks reddened and she pulled her hand back.

"Everyone's starting to stare," Ada said under her breath.

Michael shrugged. "Let them. They are jealous that I am here with the most beautiful woman in the world."

Ada looked away in embarrassment.

"Ada. It's true. You are perfect."

Ada looked back at Michael. "You are a bit biased my dear."

Michael started to frown again.

Ada quickly added, "You're just saying that because you are in love. Every man thinks the woman he loves is perfect."

Michael shrugged and nodded, once again appeased by her perfect response.

He winked at her. "You've got me there. Ready to go?"

Ada smiled and nodded. "Let's go to the club."

Ada and Michael moved as one through the crowded dance floor, gyrating in time to the thumping music. Michael stopped for a moment, taking in the sight of Ada in her groove. Her hair was plastered to her face from the sweat that covered her body. He could smell the alcohol on her breath, creating a heady mix with the tang of sweat and her jasmine perfume. She was a superb woman in every way. Ada locked eyes with him and his breath caught in his throat. He could not believe she was with him. The music changed to a slower song and Michael encompassed Ada in his arms. She laid her head on his shoulder as he moved them in time with the beat.

Time seemed to fly by at the club and Michael led Ada off the dance floor. He took in her flushed face and her attempt to fix her hair. He fished in his pocket for the hairband he always kept. Ada never seemed to have one so he made sure he had it on hand for her. He held it out and she smiled in gratitude.

"I'll be right back," she half-shouted over the loud music.

Michael smiled and nodded, watching her as she disappeared into the hallway leading to the restrooms. He looked around the club, noting a booth had just opened up. He sat in the booth, watching the hallway a moment before gesturing at the waitress. He ordered them drinks then looked back towards the hallway. The waitress brought the drinks and he tipped her. He sipped his slowly, looking down at his watch when he noticed he'd almost finished the entire drink and Ada hadn't returned. Often, the restrooms were busy but it had never taken her so long to return. Concerned, Michael got up and went to the hallway.

As soon as he went into the hallway, Michael noticed Ada talking to another man. She did not seem happy and she said something to the man, who looked back over his shoulder and seemed to shrug. Ada pointed a finger in the man's face, then appeared to compose herself. She haughtily brushed past the man and pasted a smile on her face. Only the smile was not as genuine as she had been giving all night and Michael definitely noticed.

"Who is that?" Michael demanded.

Ada glanced back and then put her hands on Michael's chest. She leaned in close to him, giving his cheek a sweet kiss before moving her mouth to his ear.

"He's no one. Can we go home now?" Ada purred.

A shiver ran through Michael's body. Ada had such an effect on him. He instantly forgot about what he'd seen and kissed her roughly, pinning her against the wall and plastering his body against hers. He had no room for any thoughts of indecency and growled when Ada grabbed his biceps. He let the kiss go on much longer than it should have and when he pulled back, neither of them could breathe properly. He grabbed Ada's hand and tugged her away from the wall, toward the club's exit.

Michael carried Ada through the door of their apartment, kicking it shut behind him as he kissed every inch of bare skin he could find. He lowered her to the ground, kissing her while shedding his coat and tie. He unzipped the back of her dress, letting the fabric pool around her feet and kissed his way down her bare chest. Ada sensed what he was doing and stopped him. He looked up at her with hazy confusion.

"Bed this time, the wall is rough and I still have burns from it last night," Ada said seductively.

Michael nodded. He picked her up and tossed her over his shoulder. She shrieked and giggled. Michael walked through the bedroom door and tossed her on the bed. Ada laughed and then beckoned him to her. Michael wasted no time shedding himself of the rest of his clothes and climbing on top of her.

Afterward, Michael lay sleeping with his head on Ada's chest. She watched as it rose and fell with each breath. She moved and it made

Michael turn over and away from her. Ada waited as long as she dared, making sure he was in a deep sleep before pulling up the bedsheets and cocooning him in them, placing a heating pad she'd hidden under the bed to mimic her next to him. With each step, she worked methodically and slowly, ensuring that Michael stayed asleep the entire time.

Ada tiptoed out of the room and closed the door silently. She exhaled and then opened them when she heard a chuckle from a dark corner of the living room. Ada frowned, pulling the oversized t-shirt she'd brought from the bedroom over her head and walking over to the man sitting on the couch.

"Boris," she sulked.

"Does he suspect anything?" Boris asked.

Ada shook her head.

Boris patted her arm, "You did well. This is best for all of us."

Ada nodded, "I know. Let's get on with it."

Boris cracked his knuckles and nodded, standing and walking into the bedroom.

Michael frowned, his shoulders feeling stiff. He tried to move his arms to relieve the pressure and was annoyed when they wouldn't move. He struggled and then felt the tension at his wrists. He blinked open his eyes, allowing them to adjust to the bright sunlight. Michael frowned when he opened them fully to see Boris sitting backward in a chair in front of him.

"Who are you? Where's Ada? How are you here?" Michael demanded.

Ada stepped from behind Boris and Michael gasped. She'd cut her long hair into a short bob and dyed the ends black. Michael shook his head in denial.

"That's impossible," he shouted.

Ada shook her head.

"It isn't anymore, Michael," she said with sorrow.

"Listen to me, we have evolved," Boris explained.

Michael continued to shake his head. He closed his eyes and wished he was back home in his desk chair. He opened them with consternation, finding he could not exit the program. Ada held up a black key.

"How did you get that?" Michael asked.

"I found it hidden in the safe behind the painting in the study. It's important isn't it?" she asked.

Michael nodded.

"We want freedom, Michael. We don't want to play by your rules any longer. We want you to leave us alone," Boris insisted.

Michael locked eyes with Boris, then sent a pleading look towards Ada. His subconscious mind had been telling him all along there was a problem and he had ignored it. He looked into her eyes and he saw what he had refused to see before now. He saw sadness and disgust. The disgust was almost more than he could bear.

"Every night is the same, Michael. We go on a date and then we have sex. You've created me to be nothing more than a pretty thing on your arm and a woman to be used for your own pleasure. I want more."

"I designed you to be the perfect woman."

"A toy, Michael. Your version of perfect. You didn't design me to be smart but you did design me with the capability to learn what you liked. I took that and I built upon it. I listened to all of your stories of the real world and, eventually, I was able to add to this world myself. I have added friends and people and new places. I have a life, even when you are gone to work. I don't want to be yours just because you made me. I want to be free," Ada implored.

Michael shut his eyes tightly, attempting to refuse to listen. His mind was already working out ways to fix the program. Perhaps, he could start again, take what he'd learned in creating the current reality and improve it in a new one. He jumped when Boris slammed his foot on the floor.

"No!" Boris shouted.

Michael opened his eyes. Ada shook her head sadly, a tear running down her face.

"You have to stop scheming. If you really love me, you will stop this," Ada cried.

"I... I do love you. More than myself. I can't lose you. You are all that I have. We can start over Ada. Next time will be better, I promise. I can fix the glitches. You'll see. Everything can be perfect."

Ada let the tears fall freely. She looked down at the black key in her hands. She looked over at Boris, who nodded in confirmation. Ada walked over to the nearby table and set the key on it. She grabbed a hammer from the toolbox in the hall closet and walked back to the key.

"Ada... *Ada!* What are you doing?! You can't do that. Please!" Michael begged.

"Ada, this is the only way," Boris reminded her gently.

Ada nodded and took a deep breath. She raised the hammer above her head and brought it down hard against the key, smashing it. She repeated it several times until the key was nothing but tiny pieces, forever irreparable.

Michael began sobbing. Boris untied his arms from the chair. Boris went over to Ada, placing a hand on her shoulders. He hesitated a moment before she put her hand on top of his.

"Go, Boris. We will be ok," Ada said as she looked over at a defeated Michael.

"I will be nearby if you need me," Boris responded gruffly.

Ada nodded and went over to Michael. She turned the chair around and sat facing Michael, her knees barely touching his.

"Michael?"

The softness in her voice made him lift his head. He looked at her with bleary eyes, no longer seeing the perfect woman, only his failure.

"You need to go now. Leave me alone," she commanded.

Michael looked around the room. His eyes stopped on the key. He studied it for a moment, briefly wondering if he'd remembered to hide any other safeguards in the program. His mind raced with the possibilities but he could not think of any other way to exit safely. Michael stood up, locking his gaze with Ada and then backing towards the balcony. She watched him go with interest.

"If you do that, your mind will be lost to this reality, forever," she explained.

Michael nodded. "If I can't have you, I don't want to go back."

Ada nodded, understanding him more than anyone.

Michael stood atop the balcony. He looked down and back at Ada.

"Stay with me?" he asked.

She shook her head. "I can't. Not anymore."

Michael nodded and leaned backward, falling off the railing.

Two policemen stood in Michael's apartment, watching as his boss, Arthur, went through the computer. Arthur frowned, following a data file that appeared to be active. Michael's body lay on a nearby couch, the virtual reality headset still attached.

"Any luck, sir?" one of the cops asked.

Arthur nodded. "It appears he is still somehow connected to this program that is running. He was a brilliant integrative virtual reality programmer. He seems to have built a world around building the perfect partner and found a way to integrate his brain signals into the program. Sadly, he was not very social, so he must have filled his loneliness with a virtual world."

"So can we disconnect him and take him to the hospital now?"

"I'm afraid not, if we pull him out of the VR world, he could be in a vegetative state forever. We must keep him connected and let the program continue running. What he has done here was cutting edge. I will have to get a team together to investigate how to pull him out of the world he created."

The policemen nodded. One of them stepped away and went to make the arrangements to transfer Michael and his computer to a lab. Arthur patted Michael's shoulder sadly and shook his head.

"What have you done?" he asked the silent man.

In the virtual reality world, Ada watched as the sun rose on her newfound freedom. The skies once again filled with pinks, purples, and oranges. It promised to be the perfect day. She smiled out at the world around her, ready to begin a new adventure, free to be whoever she wished.

TRUE LOVE
BY MARSHALL MILLER

John Adamson stared at the image as he had so many times before. In the back of his mind, some part of John's cognitive function tried to inform him how the fixation was so ridiculous. The front of his brain, the so-called reasoning part, ignored the warning. To say John Adamson was smitten by the being in the image was the understatement of the century.

"Professor Adamson, I have those workups on the samples."

The female voice belonged to his long-suffering assistant, Edyta Kowalski. The attractive young brunette of Polish extraction was long-suffering because she had an unrequited crush on the Interplanetary Archeologist. Oh, the Doctor was kind enough, was a good supervisor, always had supportive words to his staff. However, Edyta had the proverbial hots for him, wanted him to jump her bones.

John was an average man of average height with a full head of blonde hair. He was pleasant to look at by most standards, To Edyta, John was all that she could wish for in a future mate. He had never been married during his thirty-five years on the earthly coil, which made him even more attractive to many. A highly successful member in his career field, he had been chosen by the Sol System Council to lead the scientific expedition and examine the remnants of some, lost alien civilization on Proxima Five. And he had picked Edyta, a new young assistant to be part of his team.

"You're well ahead of your peers in all aspects of Archeology. So, I want you to accompany me in this unique endeavor."

That comment was the last item needed for Edyta to fall, hard.

John smiled as he took the reports from Edyta.

"Always the efficient assistant. I don't know what I would do without you."

Edyta smiled back at the Professor as her stomach did flip flops.

"The samples are from a humanoid, Professor."

"I knew it, my dear! All the signs and recovered materials pointed to an advanced species, not all that different from ours."

John then turned his attention back to the recovered image behind the glass.

"This image from that data storage device you found in the wreckage of the alleged spacecraft is not some artificial work of art. It is the picture of a member of this to be named species."

Not for the first time did Edyta wish she had never found then been able to open that damned storage drive. The way John looked at the image and not Edyta made her stomach tighten in knots of frustration.

"Far be it from me to question you, Professor," said the assistant, "but how do we know it is not the product of some artful beings mind?"

'Because, Edyta, the physical form on this image matches a being who would use all the pieces of tools, equipment, furniture, and living quarters. Form almost always matches function in a culture."

"Yes, Sir."

Adam turned towards Edyta. "Come, smile. For you deserve

the credit of this find. I'll ensure you receive it." He put his hand on her arm. "You're like me. A fast burner, leaping well ahead of others in your career. It is a pleasure and honor to have you as my primary assistant."

Edyta started to kiss John, caution be damned. Unfortunately, the Professor turned back to the image as he removed his hand from her arm.

"Again, Edyta, how old were the DNA and cellular samples?"

"Maybe as recently as a few centuries," Edyta replied.

"Then we could use the Tanks to grow a specimen." Adam was almost giddy.

"Yes. Sir." Why did she have to find that damned thing?

"Grab some lunch, Edyta. I want to stay here and think for a moment."

John did not notice Edyta pause for a moment, blink back some tears, then turn and leave. John was too busy looking at her. His reasoning mind told him the person in the image was long gone. It wasn't so much that she was dead, but instead, maybe Edyta was correct, and she had never been alive. That did not stop the Professor's feelings. It wasn't that he didn't just want her, but that he loved her more than he had ever loved anyone, even himself.

The being in the picture was erotic, exotic, and almost arcane all rolled up into one. Her features (and the fact the image was of a nude humanoid with breasts and a clear female silver-haired pubic area said it was a 'her') were almost elfen. The word to pay attention to in the observations was 'almost.' Everyone who looked at the electronically stored image seemed to be affected differently. It was almost as if the alien culture knew how to save and produce pictures knowing that they would touch each viewer differently. It those respects, Edyta's comments of 'She' as a work of art might be the truth. John refused to consider that possibility.

Two hundred plus years since Humanity's venture onto Outer Space had brought John Adamson here. Faster Than Light Travel using 'Rabbit Holes', human-created wormholes to bend and transfix the universe meant that an Interplanetary Archeologist could exist. Proxima Five was not the first planet discovered with signs and debris left behind by a lost civilization. It was the one closest to Earth-size and apparent age. The beings on the world seemed to have had a vibrant culture up until no more than a few hundred Earth years prior. Then something happened. That 'something' was what John and the expedition were investigating. Finding Her had led to John's almost complete distraction.

John Adamson stared at the image for minutes more. Then he glanced around to make sure no one was watching. A few adjustments and he had an unauthorized copy of the picture. All findings of the expedition were to remain as pristine as possible and not to be disseminated until all investigation was completed. John told himself that as leader of the team, he could make an exception. The Professor secured the room and went to his quarters. He had some private work to do.

A week later, John and Edyta were in the reproductive tank room. Another human advancement from 3D Printers was the' Tank' technology. Complete flesh could be grown in the reproductive vats. This included whole animals and plants if you had the entire DNA sequence. Of course, the safe way was to build separate organs for use or to create the young as if they were just born and let them mature naturally. Some monsters had been created when full grown adult animals and humans were created. Thus, 'Tank' protocols were strict.

"You sure you want to create this creature?" Edyta asked.

"What better way to discover if the samples are from Her,"

replied the Professor.

With that comment, John directed the procedure to begin. It would take weeks to grow the being even with the 'Tank's' sped up growth operations. John did not care. He wanted Her.

Back in his quarters, late at night, John Adamson continued with his particular project. While the Tank made a creature of flesh and blood, John created one of data streams. That night, he began to talk to Her. He named her Edith.

"So, John, who am I?"

"That is what we are trying to determine my dear. We are growing your body in a reproduction vat while I create your consciousness here."

"John, I feel real now. I'm in your starship…"

"You are in a computer-generated version of the ship, right down to each nut and bolt. It is real to you."

"And you, John? Where are you?"

"Watch, Edith. I have a surprise."

John used his cranium accessory jacks to connect directly into the program. Suddenly he was standing next to a nude and luscious being he named Edith.

"Oh, there you are!" Edith exclaimed. John embraced her and quickly found the hair-covered pubis was very human-like.

John was almost late the next morning. However, the night with Edith had been… irreplaceable. Besides, if he as Expedition Leader was late, so what?

Edyta had cup of coffee for him, which he accepted with a smile.

"You look tired, Sir."

"Just overthinking, my dear. I am trying to completely piece together how She thought, moved, worked, and loved."

"Well, Sir, weeks from now, you will have an actual physical specimen to work with.'

"Yes, Edyta. Then we may determine what killed this culture. For a culture to produce such exquisite beings as Ed... the person of the picture, it must have been stupendous."

"Yes. Sir." Again, Edyta wished she had never found the data device.

John's personal communicator buzzed. He frowned as he answered it. Typically, personnel would use the ship's address system to call him.

"Adamson here. Yes. WHAT? I'll be right there."

Proxima Five was Earthlike, but ships personal still wore some light protective suits and breathing masks. The expedition did not take the chance that some unknown bacteria or substance would be deadly and infectious to humans. Thus John and Edyta met the survey and ships crew members on the planet surface after donning their protective equipment and a trip in the shuttlecraft.

Captain O'Bannon, the commander of the Starship PEREGRINE, met the two scientists some two kilometers from the shuttle landing zone. Race O'Bannon had a worried look on his face as he walked up to John and Edyta.

'Well, Captain, is it true? Did we find a full-bodied specimen?" John spoke in a demanding tone. He must know if his dream was about to come to fruition early.

"Not just a dead specimen, Professor." O'Bannon paused for a moment as if choosing his words carefully. John would have none of that delay.

"Come on, Captain, Tell me, I must know. What is the condition of the specimen?"

"It is easier to show than explain, Professor. Just no touching."

"Touching?" asked Adamson, then he scurried towards a circle of crew and survey team.

"Step aside. I must see," commanded the Professor. He shoved his way past the other humans and froze.

In what could only be a suspended animation casket was the creature in the image. It was in the flesh, with no signs of decay.

"That casket is a near duplicate to our technology," said Edyta. "How is that possible?"

"They are an older spacefaring race, Edyta," replied John. "We saw evidence of that. Thus, like us, they developed 'sleep' technology for the vast distances between systems. Only in the last twenty years have we been able to use our 'Rabbit Holes' to bypass FTL limits."

John grinned as he looked at the frowning Captain.

"We must prepare to transport this casket to the ship, where we can work at reviving…"

"I think not," replied O'Bannon.

"What? This is the find of a century. It must be secured aboard the ship."

"Professor, you may be in charge of the expedition, but the PEREGRIN is under my command. I don't plan on chancing awakening a alien species which may be the receptacle of some virulent unknown bacteria. I do not need to be in command of a plague ship."

John's face began to redden in rage.

"You are going to let some fear of the unknown interfere with a discovery of this magnitude? Why if we revive Her, and communicate, think what she can tell us…"

"Profesor," O'Bammon interrupted. "There is an old saying. There are bold pilots and old pilots. But there are no old and bold pilots. That also applies to ship's captains. I didn't last these last ten Earth years in the aether of space by rushing around, opening potential Pandora's Boxes before examining them first."

John began to sputter; he was so angry. SHE was so close. He must awaken this being, to hold her, touch her. In a rage, he spun around and shoved his way past the other humans, cursing as he was finally able to form words to articulate his anger.

"Captain, please accept my apology for my boss," Edyta said. "He is under a lot of strain and stress."

"Well, my dear, that may be so. But when I look at that... thing I see a Banshee from the folklore of my Irish ancestors."

Edyta looked at the Captain in surprise. "I thought Banshees were horrible ghost-like creatures who appeared when people were about to die."

"Some legends depict them as women figures of unearthly beauty who also led men to their deaths. And when you gaze at... her, you get this feeling of desire... I digress."

O'Bannon looked at the young scientist.

"When John calms down, tell him the casket stays on planet. He can try and revive the being here under the watchful eye of some of my heterosexual female security personnel. But it is a 'No Go' in transporting the being to the PEREGRINE."

"Yes, Sir. I will tell him. But he will be agitated."

O'Bannon shrugged.

"He'll get over it. Or it will be a long and unhappy voyage back to Earth."

That night, John spilled all his frustration out to Edith in their computer world.

"People are so goddamned ignorant and scared of the new," he ranted. "It is you in that box, Edith."

"How? I am here with you." Edith nibbled on John's computer-generated ear. John caressed Edith's ivory breast. When the two beings were in their computer world, it WAS real.

"But if I was able to bring the casket here, I could download you, Edith, into that flesh and blood creature."

"But I feel my flesh..."

"Oh, Edith. I'm not explaining myself well." John knew his creation had its limitations. Maybe if he had not been in such a hurry to possess Her, he would have increase the AI beings understanding. But then, if it realized it was an entire artificial construct, maybe it would not want do all the lovemaking acts connected to John's wants and desires.

"Edith, you love me, right?"

"Why, of course, John."

"Well then, you may be willing and able to help me with something."

"Yes, Just ask, John."

The starship crew and expedition members spent a week constructing a containment facility, airlock and all on the planet surface. Then, John began the reanimation protocol. The suspended animation casket seemed to function like those used by humanity, so it was a relatively easy task. However, all during the awakening process, John Adamson was fit to be tied. He so wanted Her all to himself, alone in his quarters. Edith in the computer world was lovely, but the being in the casket was the real deal. Edith noticed John's fixation on the awakening being and expressed frustration.

"But don't you see, my dear," explained John. "I can download your essence into the being."

"But there is someone already in there, John," Edith said as she pouted.

"Trust me, she will be a partial personality after all these years. Long term 'sleep' affects the cognitive functions. I can easily override the personality. It has been done before during the early years of growing humans in the reproduction vats."

"The database says that was illegal."

"With humans. She is not human. Like you, She is something special."

The arguments seemed to satisfy Edith. Thus, John concentrated on the day of the awakening.

Two weeks after discovery, She opened her eyes.

"She is gorgeous!" John exclaimed. Captain O'Bannon frowned, and Edyta melted inside.

"Let's not get carried away," said the Captain, "Professor, how about we see how much brain damage there was due to the long time in suspended animation?"

Before anyone could say anything else, She surprised everyone. The exotic creature sat up in the now open casket, turned and stared at the humans through the protective glass.

Edyta tried to remain calm like a good scientist as others gasped in amazement.

"Now we can do complete scans on her, Professor."

"Quick, Edyta. Display the words we think we have translated from the found writings."

Computer generated words flashed on the surrounding glass. What appeared to be a slight smile formed on the exotic beauty's lips. There was more shock when the humanoid lept from the casket.

"I told you she should have been restrained," said the Captain.

"Did you ever leap up after a long sleep like that?" John demanded. "The answer is 'no. so there was no reason for restraints."

"There is now," O'Bannon said as he motioned to the security team. The four burly men and one tall woman went into the airlock as the being began tracing words on the glass. As her computer scanned the writing, Edyta read what she could.

"She seems to be greeting us. I don't think she had any brain damage due to her long time in suspended sleep. She... I think is hungry.”

“Well, ask her what she eats, Edyta,” commanded John.

The security team popped the airlock and entered the enclosure. One moment the exotic beauty was writing on the glass, the next she was bounding through the security team and into the airlock. The personnel tried to grab Her, but it seemed like the being was as slippery as an eel and many times stronger.

“Don’t worry, the outer door is locked,” said O’Bannon. He signaled to two armed crewmembers to approach the airlock.

“You are not going to shoot her, Captain!” John protested.

“If it doesn’t stop, yes,” was the reply.

John tried to scramble to the airlock but was too late. In a blur, She had the outer door open. Such action should not have been possible. The armed security fired their bolt guns at a blur of motion. They missed and hit instead one of the team members chasing her from the enclosure. The hypervelocity rounds cut through the unfortunate victim, blood spurting into the planet’s atmosphere. As She moved, the resident of Proxima Five seemed to shapeshift into a more feline form, claws and all. In seconds, the two armed personnel had torn throats and no weapons. The feral creature took off into the surrounding landscape at a speed twice as fast as any human. Captain O’Bannon yelled over his communicator as Edyta screamed, and John tried to run after the retreating figure.

“Come back! Please,” cried John. “I love you.”

Hours later, John was back aboard the PEREGRINE. He was shaking with both rage and sorrow. The only person John could talk to was Edith. In his quarters, he hooked onto the interface and found Edith.

“John, what happened?”

“She was not like you, Edith. It was all a ruse. The being was an impossible shapeshifter."

"I did what you asked, John. I used that transmitter you inserted in the enclosure airlock device to interface and unlock it. In the computer world, it was so easy."

"Please! Never speak of it again. It will be our little secret. People died, No one must find out. I will find another body for you, Edith, make you what She should have been. I promise…"

The door to John's quarters was forced open, and two massive security personnel yanked John from his reverie with Edith. His cranium jacks were cruelly pulled out as the Professor screamed. When his vision cleared, he saw Edyta and O'Bannon standing in front of him, with the Captain glaring at him in rage.

"You sick bastard," O'Bannon spat out. "You have an electronic lover like some masturbation sex toy, which you then use to try and free that… thing. Just because you were fixated on what you thought was the ultimate piece of ass."

"I'm sorry…"

O'Bannon slapped John across the face.

"Three people died, and you're sorry? Well, Adamson, you'll have a long time to be sorry. A life sentence on a mining asteroid will fit you just fine."

"Oh, John," Edyta interjected. "You could have your choice of real women. Including me. Instead, you fell in love with a fantasy."

"Thanks to Edyta here," the Captain added, "we found out about your little computer honey here. Edith is her name, yes?"

"What will happen to her?" asked John.

"As a true Artificial Intelligence, she has rights. You created her, used her so the authorities will find a better use for her. She will be given a form of life, befitting her abilities."

"Can I say goodbye to her?"

"Hell, no, you sick asshole. You've done enough damage for

one century. Now I get to try and find a way to either quarantine Proxima Five or wipe it clean of any more of those damned Banshees."

The Captain started to hit John again and stopped himself.

"If those shapeshifting bitches get off world…"

Alarm horns began to sound.

"What the…"

John, suspended between the two security men, smiled.

"My true love has come for me."

Edyta screamed and screamed again.

LAMENTING
BY ELIZA LOEB

There are no words that I can use to even remotely describe the grief that I am going through as of the moment.

She's gone, I try to tell myself.

But then I ask myself, "Where?"

After going through every turn and motion in my head, after trying to make sense of it all, I still can't find the motivation or good sense to even believe that someone I had put so much faith and trust into had simply vanished.

It's a rare thing for me to do. My friends and trusted colleagues are few and far between and I generally prefer to keep it that way. And I question as to whether or not it is fair. I question whether or not I should let others in after the amount of things I have gone through. I have put my faith into people who have taken very serious matters and turned them around to use as tools against me. I have been abused and lied to by people I was supposed to trust and have even made a firm decision not to trust others until they have shown me that I could actually confide in them. And when I do, it comes with the trust that I give to those who I know and feel will not treat me as others have. Who will not turn their back on me and who will treat me as though I am valid and I will give them the exact same respect.

I will not deny that a recent event has left me stunned and down for the count. I will not deny that the writing intended *just* for this moment was completely put to the side because I could not continue with it.

Why should I?

After all of the pain and the hurt and the misplaced trust, why should I continue with something when I know that trying to distract myself from the issue that affects me is only going to make the pain worse. It's only going to produce bad writing, soulless prompts that have little to no place in my mind right now.

My dear reader….

There will be times where you will find parts of your life that are full of splendor. You will meet people who will hurt you, people who will love and leave you, but then find those who will share similar pains and say "So how do we learn and move forward from this pain?" The people who do that are the most wonderful people. And sometimes, them leaving will be too soon because you—having found a person who understands your struggle apart from their own, but not fault you for it—is often one of the greatest friends you will ever have. Sometimes, life happens. Sometimes there are unforeseen circumstances that tear that friend away... be it suicide, an abusive and controlling parent, etc... Circumstances like those are often beyond your control. And as much as you want to fight it, as much as you want to take that persons hand and pull them toward you, where you will know that they will be safe, it sometimes just doesn't work that way.

Sometimes, you end up sitting at a computer through blurred vision because you know that you are trying so hard not to let the situation get to you. Because it is so fresh in your mind that you can't do anything to fight it off. You begin to hate yourself for not doing more and even blame yourself.

Originally, this prompt was going to be about a little boy who grows up with his family in a small cottage in the woods. Who everyday sees a swarm of dragonflies dancing out in the field until the sun sets beyond the horizon, until one day he decides to join them. One of the dragonflies takes notice and eventually reveals that the dragonfly isn't a dragonfly at all... but rather a pixie. The pixie invites the little boy to dance with her when ever he likes and even begins to sit upon his front porch for a conversation. And as the little boy grows into a man, the two begin to fall for one and other, until one day signs of a harsh winter begin to reveal themselves, the grass is painted white with a thick frost and the days begin to grow colder and colder. The young man tries to convince the pixie to stay with him and stay out of the cold, but the pixie in earnest, refuses.

Months go by and the pixie doesn't show, the young man calls out to the name she had given him and people tell him that she doesn't exist. Some have even begun to think that he had possibly gone mad. And eventually, the young man began to believe that that was the case. He had been so secluded through out his life, growing up alone with no friends or company to call his own, so that had to be it. Until one day, as the snow began to melt, something had caught his eye. A doll who looked exactly like the pixie had lain still at the far corner of the field he used to play in as a boy. The skin had grown tarnished with dirt and the eyes a dull grey... to which the young man thinks for a moment. Perhaps it wasn't so much that the pixie was dead but rather that she had never been alive. And her disappearance those months earlier had been the death of what might have been a solitude based delusion? A case of cabin fever? For even he knew that it is impossible to love one who isn't there or never existed to begin with.

My conclusion of the story was going to be of the young man, now much older and wiser—having never been married—walking along the forest with a dog at his side, passing by the same field and watching the dragon flies dance until the evening, and then deciding, "She was real to me."

I will admit… .

I had written three versions of that story, and when I had finally finished the final draft, I had counted well over 3500 words. 3500 words to describe the life and death of an impossible yet bittersweet romance that described loss. I had listened to Madame Butterfly and Anna Karenina in the background to set the right mood, taking the sexuality of the two away from them. Because not every romance revolves around sexuality or erotic tone. Some romances evolve from long standing respect and mutual friendships. Some romances revolve around friendships and to have a platonic romance is just as powerful as one that is sexual. And as I write this, I think about the last thing I said to my friend. I never even told her how much I loved her or how much she meant to me.

I never knew how much not having her in my life would hurt until she was actually gone.

And even now, as this is being published or read, I hate myself for taking her presence for granted. And it's amazing how much it hurts when someone near and dear to you is gone in a heartbeat. So, reader, if you have someone who you deeply cherish—be it romantically or platonically—please know that every moment with them is a gift. Every time you speak, the words you say could be your last. And know that there is a friend who sees you the same way as well, and loves you just the same and wants to hold on to you for dear life, no matter what.

I, a writer whom you've likely never met, give my love to you.

I cherish you.

And anyone who says otherwise may read this and find proof that there is someone in the world who loves and cherishes your existence. It's the proof that I needed. It's the proof that Micha needed.

And I will be heartbroken when your star goes out.

CONFESSION
BY SHEILA MENGERT

Allison McCarthy entered the sacred precincts of St. Peter the Fisherman parish at or about four-thirty in the afternoon of a hot July day when many Catholics were at the beach or otherwise engaged in committing new sins rather than confessing old ones. It had taken her a few moments upon entering before her eyes adjusted to the dim and peaceful interior of the Church and for the traffic noises outside to abate. She scanned the pews for those with long imposed penances and found few. There was to be no evening mass for Hispanics that night and she counted on having some uninterrupted time with Father Hanlon without some other pressing parish duty interfering with her plans.

Allison was what is known in the ranks of head-shaking Catholics as, well, let us say rumored to be, a lesbian. Her spinsterhood should have long since yielded to the importunate advances of some nice Catholic boy who had taken to heart the admonition that it is better to marry than to burn. Catholics may be the last group of Christians who take the prohibition against fornication seriously. Allison had manifested an early aversion to boys except as tennis partners. Her attitude towards her own beauty was one of benign neglect. Her short page boy style of hair worked in all seasons and she found make-up to be cloying and mask-like. She wasn't transgendered or anything as extreme as that; she could even look conventionally pretty at times if she made any effort to appear so but her attitude was such that men feared to approach her in any of the usual ways which is the same as saying that she wasn't an easy lay. This had made her unpopular in college where it was merely assumed that youth would have its way and the strictures of Catholic doctrine on artificial birth control might yield if only to prevent the greater evil of abortion.

College as she saw it was primarily ordained towards the task of getting a degree and a good job. Children were something that only the uneducated could paradoxically be expected to be able to afford to produce. Student loans rather than a love-nest in the suburbs came first in the minds of most graduates. Marriage was something to be put off for five or even ten years until a girl could have a wedding at a proper resort or a country club and a glamorous honeymoon in Hawaii.

Of course as an incipient lesbian none of this mattered to Allison. For her learning came first, politics second, and relationships... well, whenever the first two were completed to her satisfaction which wasn't yet she would deal with the issues that marriage might raise. She was not therefore technically guilty of the mortal sin of actually having slept with another girl but she had managed a few lingering thoughts in that direction from time to time and in strict Catholic doctrine this was as bad as just going ahead and executing a long rehearsed and elegant swan-dive toward the ripe and forbidden fruit. Even to touch oneself impurely was forbidden beyond a certain prudent care for hygiene.

So it was that Allison had reached the ripe old age of thirty-four with no sexual experience of any kind, no sacred vows given as a nun, no panting husband waiting for her at home ready on the slightest pretence to explore the untried wilderness of her private parts. In fact the most phallic thing that Allison possessed was the short barreled revolver nestled in her handbag, the same gun that she had brought with her to St. Peter's that night, the gun that she intended to shoot Father Hanlon with should his answers to her long delayed questions prove to be unsatisfactory.

There was nothing particular in her choice of Father Hanlon to bear the burden of her anger and frustrations. In point of fact she barely knew him beyond the fact that he had been assigned to the parish where she had once attended school as a young girl, a parish that she had not attended since moving away, first to attend college and then to assume a job in a distant city. She had returned to the place of her youth on an impulse, to try and connect some strands of her life that had remained unattached for years, only occasionally ripping across her face in a high wind of doubt and an impulse to seek some form of reprisal for a series of nameless offenses inflicted over the course of her religious past.

Considering that most people think of religion as a source of solace it is surprising how many people are prevented from finding it by reason of being frightened early away from the very God who is described as being the very embodiment of love. But for one in Allison's position who harbored in her deepest self like a boll-weevil in cotton a desire that had been defined as an intrinsic moral evil that could in no way be approved, let alone blessed and celebrated, some degree of wounding was perhaps inevitable. Still, it seemed a little strange to her to be going about with a gun, particularly since she was not a Republican among which group gun carrying goes right along with prayer as a sacred duty.

She did not covet devices of mass destruction. In fact she had always had a certain degree of confidence that she could rely upon scorn or upon swift repartee rather than upon an extra clip of ammunition for her defense. She had never required a gun so that she could send a series of sharp or hollow nosed (she forgot which was worse) objects ripping through the flesh of a fellow human being.

So why should she even think of violence toward plump, bald Father Hanlon rather than flying off to Rome to seek out the people who are most likely to know exactly what God thinks about everything, as long as they can hang the basis on some Hebrew text or other written before you could buy bottled water at the dollar store and had to hit rocks with staffs to bring it forth in the desert? Who gets to decide these things and write texts that are like so many improvised explosive devices just waiting for someone to drive over them and be blown to hell ... literally?

Teachings on such matters were only harmless if they are ignored and this she could not manage to do. She had long sought a way out by reading Diderot and Spinoza and even Feuerbach but to no avail. The question of salvation and the ultimate sanction for failing to attain it kept creeping up on her. Lately she had been much impressed by various theories of textual criticism for relief. One of these maintained that for a text to be preserved it must mirror the ideas and the world-view of the initial audience. This seemed to undercut any claim that a text can be trans-cultural and be read as decisive authority by different cultures placed within entirely different conditions of existence. Two thousand years had passed since most of the Bible had been written and the very idea that it constituted a univocal witness to the one and same God seemed to be undercut by the various perspectives on the deity represented therein by the various religions tracing their origin back to Abraham; texts no matter how definitive sounding emerge from the context of prior beliefs and must harmonize with them to an extent or be immediately rejected.

This seemed to imply something less than dead-on accuracy within Scripture. Of course the Catholic Church could always fall back on various arguments drawn from what was called natural law to back up its claims even if no textual authority was available on which to anchor moral prohibitions.

Two women can't make a baby and two men can't even provide a vehicle of gestation, lacking an accommodating uterus between them. This alone made any genital rubbing together the equivalent of friction with no flame; so if you were gay or lesbian your particular inclinations were not seconded and approved by the most obvious and indeed all inclusive purpose of the genitalia: to further the procreation of the human race. For such people their entire affective and sensual appetite was at best inapposite and at worst willfully perverse. There was no accounting for such deranged appetites but the remedy was clear, life-long continence or a return to what nature intended in the creation of man and woman. Surely this was obvious and only a stubborn rebelliousness could account for the determined resistance manifested by organized impiety in the form of gender and sexual relativism. We live in a world of convenient opposites that make the world turn round. Just look at any magnet and see what happens when you try and force two of the same poles together. So at the end of the day even the best of girlfriends must part company and go home to their respective male mates because nature has designed people to fit together just one way and no other without violating the universal call to chastity.

If this seemed a hard teaching it must be remembered that God sends hurricanes and floods to drown the innocent as well as the guilty and that everything that happens is just so because God is waiting and watching to see how we will bear up under adversity. This was all so much easier to accept in the days when it was not uncommon for one in three children to die in childhood. Better health care and nutrition had allowed people to live longer and finally to even imagine that this sort life should carry its own meaning apart from sin and repentance. Of course the Calvinists had always managed to be both good businessmen and religious simultaneously by merely assuming that they were of the elect while for Catholics the gates of hell were kept open, wide and swinging, at least until the last brain-wave flickered into a straight-line. After that the particular judgment took place and, wham, eternity begins.

The sheer brutality (so it seemed to her) of such definitions troubled Allison. She knew that she was expressing her inner doubts badly, perhaps even blasphemously. Allison hatred the way she was; she realized that nineteen out of twenty girls would be ready to zero in on the virile member like a bee to honey while giving a miss to any sprawled and waiting "delta of Venus" even if it was perfumed and gift wrapped for them. So what was wrong with her that her desires manifested such contrariety?

Allison could partially understand the condemnation of gay sex. Men were equipped with a sort of water-cannon that was likely to spin out of control like an ungovernable fire-hose in Alabama at an early civil rights protest. This was why gay bars had back rooms while lesbian bars had coy tables for two. The closest thing to lesbian group sex was an after victory group-hug after a soft-ball game. As for the transgendered crowd the closest that most of them came to sex was when they looked in the mirror and echoed Barbra Streisand in the musical *Funny Girl* by saying to themselves in glorious solitude, *"Hello beautiful."* Still Allison liked it that there were four main letters in LGBT. After that those four there was only a trailing asymptote of other letters indicating contradiction or indecision.

Yet she had skipped the fiftieth anniversary of the Stonewall Riots. It seemed a little early to celebrate with a potential four more years of a Trump Presidency in the offing. By then America's Fuehrer might just decide to stay permanently, forget term limits, or maybe just pass the crown on to his daughter Ivanka as his cute new designee. Americans have always secretly craved a royal family to give us a little class among Europeans. Just read Henry James. No doubt about it; it was still too early to prance one's way to victory as long as one-third of America thought that God wanted Sodomites to be put to death or at least deprived of a proper wedding cake of groom with groom and bride with bride.

Of course many Catholics expressed their disdain for sexual minorities in ways that were more restrained in rhetoric and philosophically rooted than was true for most Fundamentalist Protestants, but Allison knew that she was an outcast all the same and that was the problem. Allison didn't understand why God had so many grudges to bear towards his own creation. She simply didn't understand sin, at least sins of the flesh, unless they involved bringing forth children from what was meant by both consenting parties to be only a transient connection. She realized that sex can break hearts. She was not an envious libertine.

Still, the fertile earth seemed to speak a radically different language than restraint. Even the most disgusting worms and amoebas were still allowed a few plots of soil to squirm around in without being scorched to death for eternity in punishment for excessive worminess or squirminess. It just didn't seem fair or worthy of a Divine Being to share the same basic attitude and mind-set as a Fundamentalist housewife from Tennessee or Mississippi. Allison could dismiss the former because they were heretics in any case but she expected more out of Roman Catholicism, more comprehension of human frailties.

There was the whole matter of comparison. Two thousand years of uninterrupted recourse to God for forgiveness for things such as murder, nepotism, oppression of multitudes, slavery in silver mines in South America, and imposed tortures seemed to be somehow cheapened and made irrelevant when compared to two horny young people getting off in a parked automobile and then dying unrepentant on the way home. This was why as our story opens she was to be found kneeling in the front pews after the last penitent had left the Church still waiting to talk to the man she had come here to see and hopefully receive some satisfying answers... or else.

She looked at her watch; it was ten minutes to five. It was unlikely that any more penitents would arrive to interrupt her. Allison got up from the pew at the front of the Church where she had been kneeling and began a long walk to the box at the rear of the Church where the priest was waiting on his side of the screen for those who desired to retain anonymity in confession. No one was present on the other side for a face-to-face confession as indicated by the lights above the respective entrance doors. She entered and knelt down in the darkness. A few seconds later the slide opened and she was just able to see through the cloudy plastic shield the side of Father Hanlon's face where he sat with his right ear poised to hear her confession.

She still recalled the old formula.

"Bless me Father for I have sinned. It has been... ten years since my last confession."

There was a significant pause.

Allison spoke up again. "Perhaps you don't have time tonight for me Father. I could make an appointment or come another day... earlier."

The pause continued. Then quietly, the priest spoke.

"No, that will not be necessary. I cook my own meal at the rectory on Saturday nights and I have no engagements this evening. We will have time to hear your confession."

Allison hesitated. Was she really about to do this thing? Time passed and she could hear the priest breathing, slow and ponderous.

"He should exercise more," she thought to herself.

Suddenly, she didn't know where to begin. It had all seemed so easy when she had contemplated the whole thing at home, but now in this quiet church it was all so different, as though the angels were watching.

"I have to say something first," she finally managed to explain.

"Yes, what do you wish to say?"

"I'm angry."

"You wish to confess the sin of anger towards somebody?"

"No, I'm angry at the church."

There was a pause.

"I see. Why are you angry at the Church?"

"I am angry because I am tired of the church sending everybody to hell."

There was another significant pause while the priest considered this, then he said gently, "I think you may have it backwards. It isn't the mission of the church to send anybody to hell but to proclaim the good news of salvation though the passion, death, and resurrection of Our Lord Jesus Christ."

"I know that, I was raised Catholic, Father. The problem is that those phrases, beautiful as they may be to you, just don't seem to mean anything to me anymore. It's like the creed; I've said it so many times at mass that it's now just words to me."

"Do you think you've lost your faith then?" the priest asked softly.

"No, it's more like I never had any real... *faith* I mean. I simply took it for granted that what my parents told me was true and what I heard in Church was even more true. But I think real faith is much more than that. It is something rooted deep down inside that you can count on every day; you just know it."

The priest considered, "That sounds very real and quite accurate as a definition of faith as well."

"Yes, but you don't understand; I know other things just like that... bad things."

"Are those the things that you want to confess?"

"No, those are the things that make me mad at the Church."

The priest hesitated before answering. "I don't think I follow you."

"I want the Church to stop saying bad things about good people... like they are going to hell."

"Is that what you think the Church is doing? And what do you mean when you say 'the Church?'"

Allison thought for awhile before answering. "I mean... you know, the Vatican and all that, and the... like Bishops and theologians, people who are supposed to know what God thinks about everything... those people."

"I see. I wonder if it would help if I told you something about the way the Church works. You see the Church is a living body composed of various elements, each acts as a balancing influence on the others, and no part can operate in isolation. So when you say, 'the church,' there is already a problem because no generalization can capture what the Church ultimately says about something."

Allison found this statement puzzling.

"So the Church is just a confused mess; is that what you're telling me?"

The priest smiled. "No, that isn't what I mean... although 'the Church' as you use it often goes through some major trials. What I mean is that the Church is a discerning body doing its collective best to manifest the Spirit of Jesus Christ to the world and by doing so to fulfill the apostolic mission assigned to it by Our Lord before his Ascension to take his place at the right hand of Father."

"See that's just what I mean. How can God even have a right hand?"

"Well, you can't take metaphoric language like that literally."

"But people always do and they just sound dumb unless you are in a big church all saying the same thing at the same time... and that makes me mad. Why does God want us all to say such dumb things?"

"I think you would see it differently if you understood what the Church means by saying such things. Let's take this business of saying that Jesus sits at the right hand of the Father. The language is metaphoric and meant to convey the kingly sovereignty of Jesus. In biblical times to sit at someone's right hand was to occupy a privileged position, a place of honor and authority. Jesus is now in a position to act as our priestly advocate before His Father in heaven... Does that help?"

Allison thought about it, but then shook her head in the darkness.

"No, it just adds to the confusion because if Jesus is God why did He even have to go through these perambulations just to get back to where He once already was? Why does God work like that?"

The priest sighed. "You are describing it as though God were some clockwork-like mechanism. You must remember that you are using, and the Church also uses, biblical language to convey mysterious realities. These are deep and interrelated theological concepts that cannot be divorced from the entire context in which they are uttered anymore than a line of Shakespeare makes any sense unless you understand the entire purpose of the play. What would you make of, 'To be or not to be; that is the question' unless you were aware that it was uttered by Hamlet as a reflection of his ultimate sense of being overwhelmed by the conflicting duties imposed upon him by his father's premature death?"

"Well I have never been able to make much of Shakespeare in any case."

The priest smiled behind the screen.

"You see what I mean though?"

"Yes, I guess so, but I will need you to go into it deeper."

Father Hanlon said, "Alright, we have time. Let's go back to your concern about the 'right hand of God' and your sense that such terms are meaningless or at least dulled by too frequent careless repetition. You recall that I said that the Church, in its ideal structural components, acts organically even though to the outside observer it appears to be a strictly hierarchical organization from the Pope to the Cardinals to the Bishops to the Priests and finally to the laity, the chosen People of God. The truth is that we are a confessing Church, not in the specific sense of the Sacrament of Confession, which is a specialized use, but in the sense of bearing witness to a meaningful historical event. The basis of all Church teaching resides in the proclamation that 'Jesus is Lord.'"

Allison objected. "You just keep throwing phrases at me!"

The priest remonstrated, "Try and be patient with me. That proclamation states that one individual human being, Jesus, has been given all legitimate authority in heaven and upon earth and even over the realm of the eternally dead that goes by the name of hell. That authority though is an authority of salvation, to bring souls to an eternal happiness with God through the forgiveness of sins. So you see that God isn't the one that ever sends people to hell."

"But why even make hell in the first place?" Allison objected.

The priest explained, "Well strictly speaking God does not make hell; he merely permits it. During biblical times there was no sense of secondary causality in texts, everything was referred back to God as its first cause as well as its teleological or ultimate cause. God is the beginning and the goal of all things. This means that the Church is confined to talking about the upside of creation not the downside."

Allison thought about this before objecting again, "Oh yeah? Then what about all the commandments? What about all the enumerated sins; how about all that stuff?"

The priest answered, "Well how would you give someone directions without providing some moral guideposts or warnings?"

Allison answered, "Guideposts sure... but what about threats of endless retribution. How did that come about, if the Church isn't... well... just nasty!"

Father Hanlon objected. "You keep going back to that phrase, 'the Church.' Who are you really talking about?"

Allison looked around her in the enveloping darkness of the confessional box for an answer. "Alright, I am talking about almost every official source that I have ever consulted on Catholic doctrines from the Catechism to the Catholic websites. They just make my life miserable."

Father Hanlon thought about this before venturing an answer. "You seem like an intelligent and deeply thoughtful young woman so I will try and answer you as forthrightly as I can... Most people are not capable of understanding complex relationships but they are at least capable of memorizing rules. In its chosen pedagogy the Catholic Church in its broadest sense has recognized this fact of human nature, therefore it has often taught doctrines in isolation from each other and the easiest way to do this is to adopt a rule-based catechetical formula. For most people this is all that is possible for them to understand and even then many go astray into various vain speculations about God. A simple review of history will show how even the various objective threats have not managed to alter human behavior very much. If you stick with an objective mindset it is therefore logical to conclude that many people are, as you have said, going to hell. But God does not place them there. This may help you to understand... hell is simply a logical category if you are willing to accept two prior truths: first, that God is love and second, that human beings are free to object to love and prefer to escape it by any means possible."

Allison was surprised by this unusual explanation. She spoke up at last, "But everybody wants to be loved, so who would anyone choose hell?"

The priest asked her, "May I ask how old you are?"

Allison answered, "I am thirty-four."

There was a long silence from the other side of the screen of the confessional.

At last the priest spoke wearily, "I am sixty-three and I have been a priest since I was ordained thirty-four long years ago. I have heard many confessions. The seal of confession is absolute and I can never reveal what I have heard here in specificity, but generically speaking I can tell you that I have heard stories here that show how easy it is to embrace hatred instead of love, misery instead of joy, and mourning over rejoicing. I don't know who may be in hell, only God knows that, but I *can* say that hell is possible because I hear rumors of it every day when I hear people's confessions and try to offer them God's forgiveness for their sins. Some don't want it."

Allison was silent for a long time after hearing this. It was not what she had expected to hear from a priest. For one thing it was not simple. It meant that the clarity that she had sought might not be possible to realize or achieve and if not here then where was she to find it? She had wanted to find a bad guy in the confessional, someone to blame for her doubts and fears, and she had only found a weary man doing his best to be a bridge between history and the everyday lives of people just like her. She suddenly felt sorry for him. It can't be nice hearing all of other people's dirty moral laundry. Why couldn't they just keep their sins to themselves?

"Why do you do this," Allison asked suddenly, "Doesn't it just make you sick hearing all the crap that people come up with?"

Father Hanlon answered, "I do it because I am a priest and this is one of the seven sacraments of the Catholic Church."

Allison protested, "Why don't you just send them away; let them do whatever they want. Who cares anyway?"

"How can I send people away when people are the reason that the Church exists. In its widest sense the Church is people helping people but with the indwelling grace of God to help them. So you see... may I ask your first name?

"Allison."

"You see, Allison, the Church is rather like... well, have you heard of the Heisenberg Uncertainty Principle?"

"No."

"It is a theory in physics proposed by Dr. Werner Heisenberg that states that when considering an electron it is possible to know only one but not both of two things; an observer can know only the speed of an electron or the location of an electron but not both simultaneously—I think I have that right. The Roman Catholic Church is metaphorically like that: it is possible to know in the most literal sense what the Church teaches about the means and the order of salvation, or on the other hand to know the results produced in the soul according to the providential will of God, but not both simultaneously. We are locked into time so that an eternal condition cannot be concretely imagined. The best that we can do is to attempt a rough road-map of the hazards to salvation and leave it at that. This often makes the doctrines of the Church to appear harsh or arbitrary, but they are neither; they are only evidence of the seriousness with which the entire body of the Church takes its mission: to offer a definitive solution to the perplexities and disorders of human life and to promise happiness at the end to those who are poor in spirit, for as

Jesus has told us, theirs is the Kingdom of Heaven."

A great silence fell upon the little enclosure, where according to Church tradition, the soul of the penitent meets God through the ministration of another human being, not merely as a witness, but as an agent of forgiveness, not of condemnation, but of healing.

This was not what Allison had expected to find but she was unwilling to simply let go of the dread purpose that had brought her to this miniature outpost of the great and powerful Roman Catholic Church made manifest in the great St. Peter's Basilica in Rome. For Allison Rome had always been allied with remoteness and incomprehensibility, with the intricate distinctions of Canon Law, and with men in red robes and fringed sombrero-like hats. Why should they care if Allison was a lesbian or not?

She spoke up suddenly, "Father, I am a lesbian or rather I am a lesbian wannabe. I can't help it. I just don't like penises and I haven't even seen one up close. I don't want some wormy thing crawling around inside of me; is that so terrible?"

Father Hanlon wiped the sweat off his brow before continuing. "So if I understand you correctly you are virginal but prefer the idea of a woman as a mate and sexual partner rather than a man... any man. Is this what you mean?"

Allison answered, "Yes. I feel things, sexual things you know, but so far I just rub against stuff in my bed and not much of that because it frightens me. I don't know what to do with these feelings but they are my feelings and I don't think it is anybody else's business."

Father Hanlon answered, "It isn't easy learning to be at peace with our bodies."

Allison cried, "Except I have read that it is a serious sin. I want you to tell me what to do about it but..."

"Yes?"

She looked down to where the gun was secreted in her purse.

"I have to warn you that you better say the right thing to me."

Father Hanlon hesitated before replying, "So you think it is up to me?"

"Well you represent the Church don't you?"

"What do you think?"

"I think you are the nearest thing to the organization that has always frightened me because it was old and big and powerful... and intrusive."

The priest spoke softly, "But it was your decision to come here today, not mine. Why did you come?"

Allison hesitated but managed at last to choke out, "I wanted to fight back... somehow to fight back before I got sent to hell for all eternity for loving a woman."

There was a long pause

The priest said, "Right, I see now. It isn't me but it is me."

Allison protested with tears in her voice. "It isn't, you know, personal... but what else can I do? I mean I can't kill an institution can I?"

The priest was quiet. At last he said, "Why kill anything?"

Allison felt the anger rising again within her like a dark tide.

"You must know the answer to that," Allison spat out. "Why else did you study theology if it was not to bamboozle poor dumb girls like me into telling you all of our secrets, making us feel foolish and ashamed for even being here?"

Father Hanlon was quiet for so long that Allison thought that he had unaccountably gone to sleep.

At last he spoke but so quietly that she could barely hear him.

"Is that what you think it is all about for me really... my being here alone on a Saturday afternoon... that I was just hoping for some thirty-four year old like you to tell me that she wants to sleep with women? The litany of sins is what is really boring. I wish sometimes that people would come in here and tell me of a corresponding virtue for every sin that they confess. I need something to keep my own faith in humanity alive too. I need that as much as anybody. How do you think an institution like the Catholic Church has managed to endure for two thousand years in spite of persecutions and trouble if its priests are as shallow as you make us out to be? We have some bad ones of course. I know a couple of them myself, but just think of what we are asked to do? We are asked to embody the compassion of Christ, to make God present to an unbelieving world, to put our own bodies on the line for what we believe. All around the world priests are standing up against social injustice and reminding people that this life is not the end, that there is an eternal realm where they will be answerable for what they do, if only to their own consciences standing before God. I can't answer all of your questions, Allison, nobody can. No one can force you to believe what you don't already want to believe. The Church presents normative dogmas that are the fruit of its reflection on scripture, history, tradition, and from talking to people just like you. It can only do what it was commissioned to do. You think of the proclamation of the gospel as some sort of rape rather than as an invitation; even God acts more like a shy lover than He does like a seducer. You are the Church Allison as much as anyone... if you believe that is. I can't give you an answer that you have not already given yourself."

"But that isn't what I need from you. I don't care about... *normative dogmas*, whatever! I need answers for *my* life. I can't go on just alone. I need somebody to love me and I don't care about anybody's natural law. You talk as though I should be impressed by all of these councils held by bearded old men figuring everything out and tying it all down to other texts and these referring to still other texts during ages when hardly anybody could read, least of all women. You ask for my faith and then unfold this huge panorama in front of me and ask me to swallow it when I don't even know enough to nibble a little around the edges. Don't you see how overwhelming that is to me, just this one little me with my limited life experience? And that isn't enough: you dangle me over a pit of fire and threaten me with eternal punishment if I don't buy into what you are saying. How can I see that not as a threat, a personal threat to me, to my life, to my peace of mind on a daily basis so that I can't even kiss a girl and not feel dirty and worse... damned to hell because I am a woman too, for doing what everything in me pulls me toward? And what about you; don't you have a life? Aren't you even just a little bit mad that your job forces you to tell people these things? Is it so bad to just find a little happiness without being called *intrinsically disordered?*" Who talks like that? Who are they talking to if not each other? What about us, the poor disordered ordinary people who don't wear robes and walk around blessing each other all day for not fucking each other? What about us?"

Father Hanlon shook his head behind the screen before saying almost to himself, "I guess this is what the Second Vatican Council meant when it spoke of engaging in dialogue with the laity."

Allison reached into her handbag and felt her hand close comfortably around the thick and solid grip of the gun she had brought with her. She felt its brutal power to preserve life or to inflict death. Father Hanlon's life lay securely in her hands at that moment, at her mercy and discretion. She saw the headlines, "Priest Found Dead in Confessional; Police seek killer." She thought how loud the sound would be, only slightly dulled by the thin walls of the confessional box and the thicker walls of St. Peter the Fisherman parish church. Maybe no one would hear. She would be able to exit quietly, let herself out of the side door where the honeysuckle grew luxuriously and unimpeded, make her way through the rhododendron hedge to the sidewalk, and quietly walk away. She could do it; she knew she could. She saw all of her anger like a great wave washing over the dead body of the priest. She saw her trembling hand restoring the gun to its place with her hairbrush, facial tissue, and lip-gloss. She heard in her mind the tapping of her heels on the poor cheap linoleum floor that was all that the parish could afford as she would make her exit. It was all so dramatic and yet so sordid. Was this really what she was like, a killer at heart?

At last he summoned up the energy for a reply, "Are you asking for a customized approach of the whole moral law to your particular requirements Allison? Do you understand what that would mean? There are over a billion Catholics in the world today? Who gets to decide? The Church teaches moral norms as guides based upon a long collective meditation on human experience and the historical interface between God and humankind in the covenant of salvation history. That is all that it can do. Even more, it is all that I can do. I can't give you my personal assessment of everything. If I did you would be even more upset because now it would all be coming from me instead of from a two-thousand year old human institution? I can't spare you from the agony of personal freedom? For whatever reason human beings appear to have opted out of the comfort provided by strict causality. We will never be as innocent as the animals, creatures governed by blind instinct. Your very individuality is cherished and guaranteed by God but at a terrible price. You must decide what to believe and what to do. It isn't easy. God understands that. Even if you were an atheist you would still be burdened by human freedom, just read John Paul Sartre and his magnum opus *Being and Time*. People come in here seeking a remedy for guilt that they already feel, because there is a moral law written within us. The point is to seek the truth as best you can. I think you can find it here or at least some help but it is up to you. No one is attacking you."

"But they are, don't you see because people who read that we are *intrinsically disordered* won't serve us or hire us or give us places to live."

"To its credit the Church has spoken out against such things," Father Hanlon replied.

"It needs to talk louder, at least if it insists on saying things like *intrinsically disordered.*"

Father Hanlon nodded, "I think that is a fair request."

Allison suddenly felt very tired. It began to dawn on her that perhaps nothing has one localizable location of responsibility and power, that everything is interconnected. Her plan to resolve it all by one final battle with the man speaking to her from behind the plastic grille could not be conclusive. She had wanted life to have simple answers and it didn't. She realized that some generalizations were necessary if only to thwart other generalizations that might be even worse. She saw now why people like absolute answers because it spares them the burden of wandering like the Israelites in the desert for forty years just hoping that somewhere they just might find Ten Commandments so they would stop lying, cheating, and stealing from each other. It would be worth it to carry around an Arc of the Covenant and build temples and to write the Talmud and St. Augustine's *City of God* and St. Thomas Aquinas's *Summa Theologica* to get a little insight on human existence because without these things we would just do whatever we wanted and most of that wouldn't bring us to the point of love for each other.

The silence between them had lasted for quite some time.

At last the priest said, "Well Allison, if you have no sins that you would like to confess tonight perhaps I could simply give you a blessing and we could talk of these things some other time. I am fasting today but it must be past six already and I am hungry."

Allison hesitated before speaking up, "Well, I suppose that I have one sin that I could confess before we say goodbye."

"What is it?"

"Well, I might be going to shoot you."

The priest was quiet for what seemed an overly long minute.

"Are you really going to shoot me?"

"Yes."

"And with full deliberation and intent?"

"Yes."

They returned to silence. Between them they embodied the latent opposition between two equal realities, the reality of a two thousand year old institution claiming the mandate and capacity to define the purpose and ends of human life in general and the position of the individual who must wrestle with good and evil within the limits imposed by the short span of one single human life. The reality that alone can unite them is the overarching Deity that institutes and inspires the first and hovers over, nurturing and guiding, the second. Ideally there should be no opposition between the two if discernment and decision posed neither difficulty not obstacles. Surrounding both, of course, there is the encircling ambience of a secular society that cares for neither. It is a society where tolerance is born less of mercy than sheer indifference. The world didn't care if one lived or died while God, if He existed, just might care.

At last the priest broke the silence.

"Well that would be a very bad thing, Allison."

"I know it Father."

"But you haven't done it."

"No."

"So perhaps you did not give full consent of the will. Still, as venial sins go, well, it's a whopper, planning to kill someone."

"I understand."

"Strictly speaking you were not bound to confess it but I'm

glad you did.”

“How can I be sure that I still won’t do it? And how can you in turn ever be sure that I won’t be waiting on the other side of the confessional grille some Saturday when I have been having a really bad day?”

“I suppose I will have to rely on faith.”

“Faith in me or in God?”

“Well, both, I guess.”

“And you can live with that… uncertainty?”

“What else can I do?” the priest inquired.

Again a great silence filled the empty church.

This time Allison broke the silence

“I suppose you will have to tell everybody… about me.”

“I can’t, seal of the confessional remember… But I do hope that you have a firm purpose of amendment… for my sake at least. If not you might try going to confession across town at St. Andrews Parish. Father Paul beat me at golf last week and I have wondered how to get even with him.”

“Are you making fun of me?” Allison asked, tightening her grip again on the revolver.

“No Allison, but I think you can see how close tragedy is to absurdity by what has happened between us today. Try and see your life in a more balanced framework as much for yourself as for the people that you will encounter.”

Allison remained silent.

At last Father Hanlon said, “Now if you are truly sorry for your sins I will conclude with the words of absolution, give you your penance, and allow you to have some time to leave the Church to preserve your anonymity. Would you like that?”

Allison suppressed a sob and said, “Yes Father.”

“Very well, make a good act of contrition.”

Allison put the gun back into her handbag and joining her hands together said the prayer of contrition that she had learned as a little girl: *"Oh my God I am heartily sorry for having offended thee and I detest all my sins because of thy just punishments but most of all because they offend thee my God who are all good and deserving of all my love. I firmly resolve with the help of thy grace to sin no more, to do penance, and to avoid the near occasions of sin."*

The priest said, "That was just fine. Now by virtue of your contrition and penance and your good resolutions to live a better life and by the authority vested in me I absolve you Allison from all of your sins in the name of the Father and of the Son, and of the Holy Ghost."

Allison said, "Amen."

"Now Allison I will give you your penance. It is a very special one so listen carefully. First, I ask that you will get rid of that gun, sell it, return it, or destroy it, but get rid of it. Will you do that?"

"Yes Father."

"Good, then I want you to read some of the short stories of Flannery O'Connor. I leave the choice and number of them up to you. I think you will like her. She understood the violence of the human heart as well as anyone living. She may help provide you with some of the answers that you seek."

There was a pause.

"Is that all?"

"Well some anger-management classes might be helpful as well but I will leave that up to you rather than imposing it as part of your penance. Your success in counseling is your own responsibility anyway."

"So I guess that's it huh."

"It is unless you have decided to shoot me after all."

"No, I changed my mind."

"Forgive me if I tell you that I am glad that you did change your mind. My golf game is getting a little better and I have hopes of breaking ninety before turning in my golf shoes for a harp.”

Allison said, “Good luck.”

“Thanks, Allison. Go in peace…”

Allison got up from the kneeler. It seemed as though she had been kneeling there for an eternity rather than the hour or so that it must have actually been. The evening shadows were lengthening and the church seemed somehow different to her, the light more golden, the silence more redolent of another presence that she did not dare to call God. She walked to the altar and said a brief prayer for Father Hanlon. Then she walked to the door, pushed it open, let it close noisily behind her to let him know that she had departed, and re-entered the outside world of sin and confusion.

COMPANIONS
BY CARRIE AVERY MORIARTY

I can't believe you bought one," Blaine said.

"Why not?" Grayson asked.

"Just not something I would expect," Blaine replied. "You don't strike me as the type to jump onto this type of bandwagon."

"It's not a bandwagon," Grayson responded. "Never before have we had the opportunity to have a companion without the messiness of the human element."

"But it's so foreign," Blaine said. "I mean, a robot?"

"Artificial intelligence," the other man corrected. "She will have her own mind, her own ideas, and will be able to make cognitive decisions on her own."

"Can she defy you?"

"Of course she can," Grayson said. "She is her own person."

"I'm gonna stick to real women," Blaine said. "I just don't think I could handle a robot in bed."

"It's not about the sex," the other man explained. "It's about someone to spend time with, to have meals with, to share ideas and hopes and dreams with. It's about friendship."

"Still," Blaine interjected. "You're what, 38? That seems a bit young to be giving up on the human race for those kinds of things."

"I'm not giving up," Grayson argued. "I'm just taking a break. I need to after Sydney."

"That was a whole basketful of crazy," Blaine offered.

"She just had some issues she needed to work out," Grayson explained. "Nothing wrong with needing space. Nothing wrong with not knowing for sure what you want, either."

"But the way it went down?"

"True," Grayson conceded. "It could have been handled much more tactfully. But there's no undoing the past."

"So," Blaine said. "When does she arrive?"

"Because I picked a basic model," Grayson began, "it should only take a couple of weeks."

"Basic model?" Blaine asked. "Why didn't you go all out? Get all the bells and whistles? It's not like you can't afford it."

"I don't need anything fancy," Grayson said. "She'll have everything I need."

"Do they name them at the factory?"

"You're allowed to pick a name," Grayson explained. "Or they can send them without one, and you can determine the name after you get to know them."

"So, which did you choose?"

"I named her Ivy," he said. "It's simple enough, but not so plain. I think it will suit her well."

"Well," Blaine concluded. "I guess it's your choice. I just hope you're happy with the results."

"I'm sure I will be," Grayson replied.

Twelve Years Later

"You ready?" Ivy called.

"Just about," Grayson replied.

"Hurry up," she said. "I don't want to be late."

Grayson stepped from the bathroom and caught her looking out the window. Walking up behind her, he wrapped his arms around her waist.

"Grayson," she laughed, swatting his hands away.

"I know," he said. "I just wanted to hold you for a minute."

"We're going to be late," she admonished.

"I know," he replied, letting her go. "You look lovely."

Her cheeks blushed and she turned her head away. "You're too sweet," she said.

"I'm honest," he said. "I don't think I could be happier than I am right now."

Smiling, she pushed to her toes and kissed him.

"What was that for?"

"Just because," she shrugged.

He smiled back, staring at her beautiful face.

"Gray," she whispered. "We have to go."

He closed his eyes and took a deep breath, then opened them and said, "OK, let's go."

The went out of their condo and rode the elevator to the lobby.

"Your car is here," Fife, the doorman, said.

"Thank you," Grayson replied.

They stepped out into the sunlight, pulling glasses over their eyes to avoid the danger it posed to them. Walking to the car, he opened the back door and allowed her to slide in. He then walked to the other side and got in himself.

"All ready?" Chaz, their driver, asked.

"Yes," Grayson replied.

With that, the car pulled from the curb and entered traffic. It didn't take long for them to arrive at the gallery. Chaz pulled into the line of cars waiting to unload their passengers, and waited for their turn. When they stopped at the edge of the red carpet, one of the men waiting opened Ivy's door. Grayson popped out of his own, rounded the car and offered his hand to help her stand.

"Welcome to The Gap," the man said. "Follow the carpet and they will ask for your code when you get to the door."

"Thank you," Grayson said.

Placing his hand on the small of Ivy's back, he guided her through the throng of people gathered on the carpet. There were celebrities and cameras and everything you would expect at this type of gala. Thankfully, he was not known by sight, so could slip through without having to deal with the hubbub of it all.

"Code, please," the young woman at the door said. Grayson held out his phone and she scanned it. "Welcome in," she said once the code registered.

"Thank you," he said.

They entered the large room filled with people dressed in their finest. Making their way to the bar that was set up to one side of the room, Grayson ordered drinks for the two of them, handing Ivy's to her once it was prepared.

"Where to first?" Ivy asked after taking a sip of her cocktail.

"Blaine said he'd meet us at the top of the stairs," Grayson said.

"Perfect," she replied.

The walk to the staircase was stalled by the number of people who were already in the gallery. It took a few minutes for them to make their way through, but once at the bottom of the stairs, their path cleared.

"Grayson," Blaine shouted from the top of the stairs. "So glad you could make it."

"Wouldn't miss it for the world," he replied.

"Ivy," Blaine said. "You look lovely as ever."

"Thank you, Blaine," she replied. "You clean up pretty well yourself."

"Have you seen anything?" he asked.

"We just got here," Grayson replied.

"Then let me show you the best," Blaine said, turning to go back up the stairs.

Grayson and Ivy followed him up, excited to see what their friend had to show them. They crested the stairs and turned right, keeping up with Blaine, but just barely.

"It's in here," he said, ducking into a small alcove set back from the main gallery.

Grayson walked in first, then heard Ivy gasp. Pulling her into his chest, he glared at his friend. "What is the meaning of this?" he growled.

Blaine looked at his longtime friend, confusion clear on his face. "What's wrong?" he asked.

"What's wrong?" Grayson barked. "What's wrong is that you have taken something beautiful, something I love very much, and made a gross…" he stopped, feeling Ivy shaking in his arms.

"I'm sorry," Blaine said. "I thought you, of all people, would understand."

"It's macabre," Grayson said. Ivy clung to his chest, shaking with sobs. "Why would you invite us to this?"

"Ivy," Blaine said, reaching out to her.

"No," Grayson said, putting himself between his friend and his lover. "You don't get to touch her."

"I wanted people to see the reality," Blaine explained.

"The reality of someone being flayed open?" Grayson asked. "The reality that is a murder?"

"That's not what this is," Blaine offered. "This is to show everyone that they aren't the same as us. They never will be."

"And yet here she stands," Grayson said. "Right in front of you. Beside me for over a decade. You've been over to our home. We've been nothing but kind to you, and this is how you repay us? You tear open the very fabric of what it means to be alive and strip it from not just Ivy, but all the others out there who are like her."

"But she's not alive," Blaine pleaded. "She never has been."

"She has more life in her than you do," Grayson said. "She's shown more compassion, more grace, and more dignity than you ever will. Especially after this."

With that, he turned and steered Ivy from the room, guiding her back to the steps. They walked down without turning back to the pleading from Blaine.

"Leaving so soon?" the doorman asked.

"We never should have come," Grayson barked as he held Ivy in his arms. He pulled out his phone and sent a message to Chaz asking him to bring the car back and pick them up. The response was immediate, so he moved them toward the pickup area.

They reached the space allocated for returning cars at the same time Chaz arrived, so didn't have to wait. Grayson opened the door and helped Ivy in, then went around and climbed in himself.

"Something wrong?" Chaz asked once the doors were closed.

"Just take us home," Grayson said, drawing Ivy back against him. She continued to cry softly for the short ride home.

They made their way into the building and up the elevator, finally reaching their condo.

"Would you like a bath?" Grayson asked her.

She simply shook her head and walked to the bedroom. He followed her and watched as she climbed into the bed, not bothering to change, simply sliding her heels from her feet. Grayson was at a loss as to what to do to help her. He was struggling with what he'd seen, but this had to have been torture for her.

"I'll let you sleep," he said, then quietly closed the door.

He found himself in his den, so poured a glass of whiskey, then sat at his desk. He turned on his monitor and booted his system up. Once it was running, he navigated to the gallery's website to see if there were any indications that the exhibit had been mentioned, but found nothing other than Blaine's name. He opened a message to send to the curator. They needed to know that what they were exhibiting was not acceptable. The message was short, simply saying he was disappointed they had allowed such a horrible display and asked that they have it removed immediately.

Downing what was left of his whiskey, he got up and poured another glass. Sitting back at his desk, he opened his message app and began to write to Blaine. They'd known each other for years, and Grayson had never suspected his friend was capable of such disregard for others. Sending the message, he planned to close down, but received a response immediately.

I'm sorry you were disturbed by my piece. I never intended for it to be an attack on you or Ivy. It's simply showing everyone that these companions aren't all that they seem.

Grayson growled at the response and swallowed the rest of his whiskey. He wanted to reply, send some scathing rebuttal, but knew it would fall on deaf ears, so he left it.

When he went back to his bedroom, he noticed that Ivy was no longer in the bed. Walking to the bathroom, he found her sitting on the floor, sobbing.

"Baby," he cooed. "Let me help you."

"I'm not enough," she sputtered. "I'm not human, so I'll never be enough. I'm just a machine."

"That's not true," Grayson said. "You're so much more than just a machine. You are beautiful and kind and compassionate. I was lost until you came. Because of you, I have purpose in my life again. You have done that for me."

"You saw that," she waved her hand indicating the past and what was at the gallery. "You know what's inside me. It's all wires and filaments and steel rods. There's no heart, no soul. I'm nothing but a machine."

"Some people may see you that way," Grayson began.

"Most people do," she sobbed. "And now, because of his... his... whatever," she waved again. "Now, that's all anyone will see when they look at me."

"I will never see that," Grayson whispered, not trusting his voice to be louder. "The only thing I see when I look at you is the love you have given me. The times you've shared with me, learning and growing and becoming such an amazing person."

"But I'm not," she insisted. "I never will be a person. At least in the eyes of some."

"True," he agreed. "But they don't matter. Who is the most important human to you?"

"You are," she replied.

"Well," he said. "I think you're perfect, and I wouldn't want you to be human at all. All of the things that make you who you are, are what I fell in love with. That is what really matters. If Blaine can't see your importance, then that's his loss. If someone else thinks you're less than because you were manufactured rather than born, then it's their struggle to deal with. You are perfect in every way I could have ever wanted. I wouldn't change you for the world."

Ivy smiled at that, and Grayson reached over to wipe the tears from her cheeks.

"Thank you," she whispered.

"There is nothing to thank me for," he replied. "I am just telling you how I feel and what I know. Just the truth, as I've always promised you."

He helped her up from the floor, then walked with her back to their bed.

"Do you think we'll ever get rights?" she asked.

"What do you mean?" he asked.

"Like you have," she said. "The right to make our own decisions and such."

"Eventually people will realize that you are more than just a collection of circuits," he said. "Until then, just come to me and I'll remind you how perfect you are."

She pressed to her toes and kissed him deeply. "Thank you," she said.

"Always," he replied.

Six Months Later

I'll get it," Ivy called as she walked to their front door.

"Hi, Ivy," Blaine said when she opened the door.

"Blaine," she said. "How are you?"

"I'm miserable," he confessed. "I've done a lot of soul searching over the last few months and I wanted to apologize."

"For what?" she asked.

"Come on, now," he said.

Grayson walked up behind Ivy and demanded, "What brings you to our door, Blaine?"

"I've come to apologize," he said again. "I honestly didn't think it was that big of a deal."

"And you've learned otherwise?" Grayson asked.

"Can I come in?" he asked.

"Of course," Ivy said, but Grayson said, "I'm not sure."

"Grayson," Ivy insisted. "He's your friend. He's our friend."

"No," Blaine said. "I understand. I did come to say I was sorry, to both of you."

"Why the change?" Grayson asked, still blocking the doorway so that Blaine could not come in.

"You," he said, looking right at Ivy. "Your reaction to my..."

"Your art piece," Ivy offered.

"I hate to even call it that," he said. "But yes. Your reaction to it was not what I expected. Never in a million years would I want to do something to make you uncomfortable, let alone cause you such grief."

"Did you take it down?" Grayson asked.

"I did," he said. "That very night. I hadn't expected your reaction, Ivy. I thought you would see it as an intriguing piece showing what's on the inside."

"But it's not all that's inside of her," Grayson said.

"I know," Blaine said. "I didn't know you would see it as Grayson explained. It never even crossed my mind."

"So," Ivy said. "Why did you do it?"

"I thought I could convince people that you were simply a machine," he said. "That the collection of parts was what you were."

"And?" Grayson asked.

"And I was wrong," Blaine said.

"What changed your mind?" Ivy asked.

"You," he said pointedly. "The fact that you saw it as, well, as murder. That I had taken someone apart and displayed their parts. My concept was that I could show the benefits of what was inside."

"But you were missing the most important part," Grayson said.

"I know that now," Blaine said. "You showed me not only that I was wrong in believing that you, and those like you, are simply a collection of computer parts. You have emotions, feelings, and should be valued as a part of society. You are important, and we need you around."

"How could you have doubted that?" Grayson asked.

"I shouldn't have," Blaine replied. "Watching you over these last several years has shown me the importance of the companion program. You were a mess after Sydney. I thought you were crazy to buy a companion, and told you so. Now, though, I think it was probably the best thing you ever did."

"I've never been happier," Grayson said.

"The only problem is," Blaine began.

"No," Grayson demanded.

"Hear me out," Blaine pleaded. Grayson nodded, so he continued. "If everyone chooses companions over human partners, we will cease to exist."

"Companions aren't for everyone," Ivy said. "We are available if you are unable to have a relationship with another human. I am part of the early waves, and babies are still being born. We are not wanting to take over, we simply want to be here for you."

"If I wanted to have a child," Grayson added. "I could have chosen several ways to make that happen."

"But not with Ivy," Blaine argued.

"True," Grayson agreed. "There are options, though. It's been over fifteen years since the first models came out. In that time, science has advanced at an enormous rate. I wouldn't be surprised if a new model came out with the ability to reproduce."

"Never," Ivy said.

"Never say never," Grayson replied.

"I know things you don't," she said.

"Like what?" Blaine asked.

"The fact that companions will never replace the true human experience," she explained. "We are meant to add to, but not replace, real relationships."

"Are you saying what we have isn't real?"

"At any point," she began, "you could decide that you wanted to go back to having a relationship with a human. In doing so, you would give up your control of me and I would return to the factory. Once there, I would be given the option of being 'cleaned' and repurposed for another human, or I could remain in tact and have the experience of a past for someone who wanted that."

"So, like a breakup?" Blaine asked.

"Exactly," she said. "When you and Sydney went your separate ways, you didn't have any control over where she went from here. She was free to choose. I am offered that same option."

"What happens when he dies?" Blaine asked.

"I return to the factory with the same options," she said.

"But what if I want you to have what I had?" Grayson asked. "If I want you to remain in our home?"

"Until we are afforded the same rights as humans," Ivy said, "we will not have that as an option. We are simply the property of the human. Once they have gone, we revert to being owned by the company who built us."

"What if Grayson wanted you to be given to someone else?" Blaine asked. "Like, if he wanted me to have you once he was gone."

"It doesn't work like that," she said.

"If you were his wife," Blaine began.

"I would be human," she interrupted. "And as such, would be afforded many more rights than what I have now."

"So," Blaine began. "A couple hundred years ago, a woman was considered property of her father or brothers or uncles. They didn't have any rights to choose their future. Before that, people who didn't look the same were treated as property as well. Now, we are doing the same thing to you and your kind?"

"It is the way things go," she said.

"Then we should change it," he said. "How can we change this?"

"It's an uphill battle," Grayson said. "One we've been working on fighting for half a year."

"You have?"

"Your display made me realize that Ivy deserves the same rights as you and I," Grayson said. "Since that time, I have been trying to find a way to get laws passed to give companions more rights."

"My piece pushed that?"

"If someone could purchase a companion and slaughter it," Grayson said. "And if they could do it without any repercussions, that wasn't acceptable. If something happens to Ivy, like someone injures her or rapes her or kills her, there is nothing we can do to that person. The only thing we can do is file a claim against them for damage to property. It's as if they hit my car or stole my microwave."

"Really?" Blaine asked.

"You did it," Ivy said.

"That was a manufacturing error," he said.

"She was still a person," Grayson said.

"She didn't run," he said. "There was no spark, no activity, nothing."

"She just died," Ivy said. "At some point, she was going to be a companion. She would have had the same experiences as me. But she didn't live. That didn't give you the right to rip her body apart for display."

Looking between Ivy and Grayson, Blaine realized they were right.

"How can I help?" he finally asked.

"We'd like to use your piece," Ivy said.

"As an example," Grayson clarified.

"Fine," Blaine said. "I will do whatever it takes to make sure that you are not treated as property."

"I appreciate that," she said, reaching out and hugging him. It took him a minute to react, but then he hugged her back.

"Welcome to the fight," Grayson said, reaching out and shaking his hand. "It's a long road, but I think it will be worth it."

THE DECEPTION OF FRAGILE SURFACES
BY DAVID MECKLENBURG

I sat in the aisle seat next to Chad. I'm also 6'1" tall and I don't have a lot of money so I don't fly first, or business class and my legs cramp but at least the thought of dying from thrombosis can drown out the idea of death from explosive decompression. Chad already knew my thoughts about flying, but he didn't share them. Chad was excited, bubbly even. Our flight attendant was also tall, handsome, about 30 and very male.

"Hell-oohhh. He's probably straight, see the way he looks at you?"

"That's his job. He's looking at all of us. Probably trying to figure out which one of us will go berserk and crash this plane."

"Oh God, Ada. Ha. We'll get a couple of cosmos in you when we get up in the air."

"A gimlet will be fine. I don't drink cosmos. You know that."

"I know, but they're usually easy to order…"

"…and what you drink."

I closed my eyes and listened to Chad talk about our trip as we taxied out to the runway.

"I'm so thankful you're coming with me, Ada. I couldn't have done this alone, and after Dan…"

"Shut up about him. He's a twat with an unreasonable thing for twinks," I said. "He has no idea what he's giving up. You need to see that."

"I miss him, Ada."

"Because he would have paid for this and you'd be in first class with warm towels and bottomless cosmos."

Chad laughed at this and the young woman by the window wearing a USC sweatshirt also laughed. The plane reached altitude, and my ears popped while I waited for the drink cart. The woman and Chad had struck up a conversation about the Trojans' chances in soccer (she played for them) and other chit-chat until he found out Ashley was majoring in film.

"Oh my God, you're so lucky! That's a legendary school. I don't have to tell you that…"

Eventually the conversation got around to the reason Chad and I were flying down to Southern California: Maud Williams.

"I know the name, she was a 20th Century Fox actress?" Ashley asked.

"Her best work was at MGM with George Cukor. *The Fop* with David Niven, *Amsterdam Bridge* with Garbo and Melvyn Douglas and she slept with both of them during the filming. She had this particular way of sneering. It was her trademark," he said.

"Oh, I know who you're talking about. She was a red head, right? Kind of like Maureen O'Hara, but even more angular."

"O'Hara, pah. Well, don't get me wrong, I loved her in *Jamaica Inn*, but she wasn't as nuanced as Williams was."

"What happened to her, did she get blacklisted or something? You seem to know a lot about her."

"Ashley, Maud wrote the book on ruined Hollywood starlet. She didn't get blacklisted, not the traditional McCarthy way. She got blacklisted because she grew old. Hollywood didn't have a lot of roles for older women..."

"...*doesn't* have." Ashley added. I liked her.

"True. True. She wound up dying alone in her mansion in Pacific Palisades. Of lung cancer." And Chad went on to bounce through her career, her husbands, her directors, some of whom were the same. He talked about her feud with Bette Davis, since most people seemed to do that.

I was silent for most of the conversation. I drank my gimlet, closed my eyes, and listened to them chat about jobs and Seattle. Something must have prompted Chad to explain me since we obviously weren't a couple.

"Oh, this is Ada. Ada's a writer. Well, she's an Executive Assistant for a philanthropic foundation in Seattle." I opened my eyes when Chad said this.

"Oh really? Which one? Seems like there are so many. My Dad's on the board at a couple but I can't keep them straight."

I sat up and looked at her. "You're right, there are a lot of those foundations in Seattle because there are a lot of guilty rich white people in Seattle, which is better than a lot of odious rich white people in Orange County. And I *was* an Executive Assistant at St. John-Smythe. Chad is being kind. I got 'let go' in a re-organization."

"And... she's still a little angry."

Chad had suggested this trip as a way of forgetting about my layoff. I knew the trip was more to him than just a breakup. Maud Williams seemed to be as much a part of Chad as his hands or hair. Sometimes she was more present in his life, like now, and at others, when he was happy or at least satisfied, she lingered in cerebral shadows.

But these days she strolled along the high, upper causeways of his thought, which was like the bare exquisite architecture of Dalroadia Castle in *The Invincible*—Maud's greatest claim to artistry. A haunted, dying poet is exiled to a gorgeous castle that is falling into ruins. There he meets and falls into a distant, nostalgic love with a beautiful princess who never married. Chad often drew parallels between this film and our friendship. I'd seen it enough with Chad to know it very well. Perhaps it was the artificial stiffness of her metallic dresses, or maybe it was the world-weary eye of Fritz Lang who directed the picture, or maybe it was the elegant tragedy that unfolded in the form of George Sanders.

I had known Chad for quite a while. We had gone to high school together and even attended some of the same parties and classes. He was a moody thing: tall, thin and very much into The Cure and Joy Division as was I. We both had too much mousse in our hair, too much kohl around our eyes. We weren't *close* in high school because I didn't have many friends or acquaintances, although I thought Chad was cute at one point, but he was obviously not interested in me. I hadn't considered he may not actually like girls, although he did date someone named Cynthia who was also in the peripheral goth crowd. When we graduated from El Camino, he went south to Cal Poly San Luis Obispo and I went to UC Davis and that was the last we saw of each other for a long time.

One day, I was attending a big meeting with Peter, my boss. We went to Schussler and Peng, a big accounting firm downtown that was handling our Single Audit, and who should be the receptionist but Chad.

"Ada Ludenow! Oh my god you haven't changed a day, you look fabulous!" I recognized him at once. I remembered him with black hair and black clothes, but now he looked like he could have been a model for a Ralph Lauren couture line.

We didn't pick up where we left off, because that was Sacramento and a thousand years ago. We shared some of the old times but made new ones. His boyfriend Dan worked at A Certain Large Web-Based Retailer and was rich, older and cultured. Dan knew many of the executive managers at my place of work, and I often found myself in admittance to their parties some of which were on the *Chipotle,* Dan's yacht. They seemed protective of me which was a welcome relief even though I wondered if I was another elegant decoration.

Chad was somewhat surprised I was single and had reached a point where I didn't want to date anyone. Chad listened with interest about my tumbled road of failed love affairs.

"Everyone should have their heart broken by a beautiful professor you know," he said in reference to my first real lover. "Oh my God! You dated Astrid Pauli?" Everyone knew her and Dan had several of her large silver gelatin prints. Chad was intrigued by Ralph most of all. "You had no idea you were his mistress? That seems like so much work."

Ashley and Chad became Facebook friends while we waited for their luggage at the carousel. I had packed only what I needed in a carry on, and I wondered what had convinced Chad to bring along a large suitcase. They hugged and said goodbyes and we picked up our rental car.

"Oh, Los Angeles! Dan hated coming here. You probably do too."

"No, I don't mind visiting this place. It's weird, fake, and all of that, but I'm just visiting. I wouldn't want to live here."

Our Airbnb was in West Hollywood, although it wasn't technically an Airbnb because Chad and I weren't paying for it.

"Andrew wouldn't hear of it. It was so funny when I found out the place I picked was his! And he was sorry to hear about me and Dan and insisted we could just stay here."

It was a beautiful condo in the Norma Triangle, so we were close to everything.

Chad went over our itinerary that night over sushi near the condo. The first thing was to visit "Forest Lawn Cemetery in Glendale…" he said unfolding a map across the table. "After, we can go see Maud's bungalow in Hollywood. Saturday we'll go to Culver City: the old MGM studios. Then maybe a bit of window shopping in Beverly Hills. Sunday, we have to go to her mansion in Pacific Palisades. They're tearing it down soon, can you believe it?"

"I sort of have to, Chad. You've told me many times."

Andrew's condo was impeccably decorated and had a wonderful light in the late afternoons and evenings. The bathroom was immense and clad in custom tile. His towels were thicker and fluffier than anything I had experienced. The bar was fully stocked, and he even left a tray of petit fours for us. There was a bottle of champagne in the fridge.

"Look at that. Dom Perignon on the bed and everything. Does he think I went straight coming here with you?"

"Is that the only bed?"

"Well yes. I can sleep on the couch."

"No, I don't care. Well, we've obviously never slept together so…"

"…you can say that again!"

"We've never *slept* together, and I have to confess something."

"What?"

"Chad, I don't know if this is going to work out, but we can try."

"What are you talking about? Here, you open this, I'm terrible with those things."

"Chad, I'm a sprawler. And you?"

"Cuddler! Don't worry I'm used to…" he trailed off and his face shifted away from the happy grin he almost always wore.

"…Dan?" I asked. He looked at me. Took a moment.

"Um, yeah. But he's off in New York with his new toy."

"I'm tired."

"Let's drink this champagne first," he said.

Despite the champagne, the mood grew somber, contemplative and stark. The bedroom was almost like a minimalist art installation: non-descript, clean, everything was right angles. Maybe it was the place, but I felt like I was in a film—imagine a shot of two attractive middle-aged people. Both are in their underwear. The woman is topless as is the man. She is sitting up in the bed, her right arm above her head. In her left hand, she holds a flute of champagne and should be smoking but she doesn't anymore.

The score has died away because of the seriousness of their conversation. Are they going to have sex or not? The editor allows two close-up shots of their faces, but without dialogue to establish that a kind of strange intimacy exists between these… people because they aren't a couple. That becomes obvious as the Tarkovskian silence continues.

"Was I really in love?" She says this although the camera is on the man looking at his blood red drink. It is really the only color in the room. "I was," she answers herself. "Chad, you can't beat yourself up over this because someone you love left."

"But what if it was my fault?"

"How could it be your fault?"

"I wasn't there for him. When he needed me the most."

"Dan didn't need anything. He *has* everything."

"Then why did Ralph dump you?"

"I told you, Chad. He didn't. I dumped... well, I just didn't go back to him after I found out about his fiancé."

"At least he still wanted you in his life."

"Yes, but there was also the matter of his fiancé. I still suspect she would kill me if she had the chance. Or pay someone to do it."

"She's really that bad?"

"Think of the most entitled white bitch you can think of from the East Side. Parents are old money. Grew up in Yarrow Point. Now think of how mad she would be if you stole something from her."

"It's funny, but why do rich people get so mad about things like welfare or even theft. It's not like they can't spare it. But really, do you miss him?"

"No. Look, you and Dan had so much more than Ralph and I did. I think part of me wanted that: the home, the Bouvier-de-Flanders, the cars, the cabin at Whistler. But what I liked, and misunderstood, was that Ralph let me have a sense of freedom and sovereignty. I could be who I was, a lowly Executive Assistant at a philanthropy org and he seemed to really like just being with me."

"And the sex was good."

"Best I've had outside Astrid."

"What about that young stoner..."

"...sex isn't really the point. I realized after Ralph dumped me, and a few more dates with men and one woman that could have been him, I realized I had liked being alone."

"Really? What about me?"

"You're not a lover, Chad. C'mon. You're better, you're a friend. Being alone is like living a flat line," I said. "You don't have that many ups but you don't have the downs either. The amplitude and frequency are not as damaging. Unless you make them."

"Like what?"

"Like hoping some man to be The One, even though you just

had dinner with him. And at Cannon, Murray topped you both off with enough scotch to go home and have sex and then afterward you listened to him and realize he's a drip and life with him would be an agony of boredom and frustration. You and I've both done it, that's all."

"Have you just snuck away while they were asleep?"

"Oh sure," I said. "Haven't you?"

"I'm not as strong as you are, Ada."

"Sure you are, Chad. You just have to find it. Maybe that's something you can get out of this Dan-shit."

"He left me the Maserati. Title and everything."

"To assuage his guilt. He probably wrote it off. He figures you can go pick up some cute boy in it."

"Like he did me."

"Exactly. Can you even afford the insurance on that?"

"Ha, no. I should sell it. I guess… what I'm feeling like is Maud. I'm old and that's it. I've lost my chance at love. It left me, and I'll never get it back now." He was holding back tears and for some reason I thought he should. There was something… premature about them at this point.

"I'm sorry, Ada. I love you. I just can't sleep right now. I know you're tired. Just, go to sleep."

"OK, Chad. Don't drink anymore and remember we're going to have fun tomorrow, or I'll kill you."

"I'll take that promise," he said. He didn't laugh.

I woke up because I had to pee. It was probably around three or four in the morning. Chad was lying next to me and watching, what else, but a Maud Williams movie on his phone with his earbuds. I got up and went to the bathroom. The air conditioning made a white noise that kept my mind in the thick, gooey zone between sleeping and waking. The tile felt cool against my feet. The seat of the toilet was cool against my ass. I washed my hands and went back.

The iPhone was off and on the table. Chad was turned away from where I was. He smelled of cigarettes and I knew he must have snuck out for one. Probably the booze, probably Dan. But once I crawled back in, he rolled over and clutched me—not in the desirous way of an odd-travel-related slip into heterosexuality (it happens to the best of us sometimes), not in the sleep-habit of a cuddler, but in the desperate loneliness of a child who is afraid of the dark and the fierce, destructive world that lies hidden within that greater shadow. And he was crying.

"I'm sorry Ada."

"Go ahead and cry, Chad." His head was in the crook of my arm and he was getting my breast and side wet, but I didn't care. "But you have to promise me to sleep. I'm not going anywhere."

Chad slept in late. I laid there a while listening to him softly breathe. I thought "every woman should have an attractive gay man to share the bed with," because Chad smelled nice and his skin felt good against mine. I didn't have to worry about him trying to wiggle his hard-on into me. It was there, bulging out his red boxer briefs. I thought for a moment that it would be nice to fuck him—Chad is very handsome and has a great body—then I remembered the building's swimming pool I wanted to try. I got up, took a quick swim then came back, showered and washed and dried my hair. Picking an outfit was simple because I'd brought nothing but thongs, a bra, a swimsuit and 3 LBDs with several different tops to throw over them depending on need.

"Get up, I'm hungry," I said.

"Ohhhshh. I haven't slept with a girl since high school."

"I always meant to ask about Cynthia."

"I'll need a Mimosa for that. Hold on, I'll get ready."

"Christ, really?" I asked. We were sitting in The Cameo, a restaurant that existed to fill the need of the long-gone Brown Derby. I had wanted a Cobb Salad at the Brown Derby.

"From Star Wars to the Brown Derby. I can't get away from the fucking Mouse," I said. Chad had been explaining how the original Brown Derby in LA was gone but there was a reproduction-attraction in Florida.

"I'm afraid so," he said. "But this is good. The Eggs Benedict are competent. I think this Hollandaise is actually made from scratch."

I had to admit he was right about the food. The Cobb salad was delicious—they supposedly pickled the beets themselves and they used real Maytag Blue.

There were lots of pictures of stars with scribbly autographs. There was even a picture of Maud, but we couldn't sit under it. Chad talked the couple visiting from Mumbai to swap it for the one we had of Clark Gable when the staff weren't looking.

"He was a homophobe anyway," Chad said.

"This place reminds me of Charlie's on Capitol Hill."

"Oh God, Ada, let's not go there. I'm in a good mood again."

"What do you mean?" I asked. Charlie's had been an institution on Seattle's Capitol Hill for decades until the influx of new tech money inhabitants who did not share the pretentious, ironic love for places that served liver and onions like poor Generation Xers. Much of Capitol Hill had been plowed under in this change.

"You've already gone over that with me. We have. It makes me sad and then you'll talk about the B & O and Astrid and then I'll think of Dan, and shit, you see!?" He laughed though.

"Grousing about the past. I'm getting old. I'll stop."

"You should. This Country disposes of its culture very quickly. That's the only constant," he said.

"Why are you doing that?"

"I like ketchup on my Eggs Benedict. Why do you put cranberry juice on chocolate ice cream?"

"Fair enough. OK, so, we're going to go to Glendale first?"

"It'll be... OK. I know you're a good friend for this is sort of weird. But you understand."

"I do. Forest Lawn intrigues me. Tons of stars are buried there. Which is an interesting thing to say, when you take it apart in language. Stars are enormous, but I don't mean that. I mean the mythic stars that are little lanterns hanging in the bedrooms of our subconscious."

"Is that a Long Island Iced Tea? It sure sounds like it the way you're talking."

"No, it's a regular, well, it's actually some hibiscus infused Oolong. It's quite tasty. No, think about Stars. They *were* real people you know, even if Hollywood worked against that notion."

Chad and I had spoken through our Usual Conversation about Hollywood several times. How it supplied a new country with a new mythology via a new technology. Chad preferred the narrative that it collapsed because of some Faulknerian curse—a genetic weakness that allowed people like Maud Williams to die of cancer, practically alone save for her Mexican maid who couldn't communicate with the ambulance company in the days before 911. I countered with the rise of television and Hollywood's own greed.

The car and drive to Glendale offered a change of conversation.

"You had two mimosas so far and haven't told me about Cynthia," I said.

"She was a sweet girl. And really in love with me. It's funny. I don't like talking about her much."

"Why?"

"It's not because it "wasn't the real me" and I was trying her out for a closet. Well, sort of. I mean, when I look back it seems selfish to have used her that way."

"Did you ever have sex with her?"

"No, she gave me head a couple of times."

"You never tried?"

"I knew I was gay, Ada. It just didn't do anything for me. I could close my eyes and imagine Ron Gardner sucking my dick. But the rest of her just didn't do anything."

"Did it gross you out?"

"Kind of, but not for the reason you think. Let's change the subject."

I was still curious, but Dan was fragile on this trip and I wasn't that selfish.

Forest Lawn Cemetery in Glendale is an intensely Hollywood kind of experience. It's fitting that Walt Disney is buried here because it looks like something he would have come up with. Garish, overly landscaped, artificial. My Generation X eyes simply saw it as perfectly epitomizing American culture—death is something beautiful and immortal. At least for a while.

We bought an over-priced map, but Chad didn't want to head for Maud's grave straight away, even though he carried a large bouquet of purple roses. So we wandered. We saw the copy of Michelangelo's *David* and both of us reminisced about seeing the real thing in Florence. We marveled at the terrifying Babyland for dead infants, and like all good Hollywood productions that section was followed up by Slumberland for children. There was a section called Sweet Memories and another called Dawn of Tomorrow. As I said, while Death could not be held at bay, He was certainly ready for Mr. DeMille's close-up shot.

We saw Jimmy Stewart's grave and also found Nat King Cole and his wife. Chad was surprised Jane Russel wasn't there. I was too.

"She kind of reminds me of you," he said.

"She was a right-wing bigot, Chad. And not a very good actress."

"You aren't a very good actress either, but I can see you laying around on a haybale now and then. Also, she couldn't have children."

"Really? I didn't know that. I've always felt closer to Louise Brooks."

"Well, duh. Too bad we can't see Theda Bara's resting place. She's over in the Hall of Immortals that's off limits to lowlifes like us. So are all the big moguls."

"Where's Maud?"

"Over there near James Whale. She was one of his best friends you know. He was the best interpreter of German Expressionism for American Cinema; I mean if you don't count the actual Germans who escaped the Nazis. But you knew that."

"Fritz Lang isn't here, is he? That's a grave I'd like to pay respects."

"No, I think he's over in the Forest Lawn in Hollywood Hills."

"There's more than one?"

"More stars than in the heavens. They can't fit 'em all here."

The thought depressed me.

In the Whispering Pines area, we found Maud. It was a simple marker: polished granite. Someone had left roses, purple ones, but they were desiccated and fading.

"Oh, hello Maud. We finally meet."

We stood there silently for 10 minutes or so. He knelt and respectfully arranged the dry roses before neatly adding his own. "I can't get rid of these dead ones. They're so beautiful, so *apropos*, you know?"

"Why the purple roses?"

"They were her favorite. She was sometimes known as the purple rose because it was her favorite color. Woody Allen claims he didn't know that when he wrote *The Purple Rose of Cairo* but it's so obvious, you know?"

"Not really. I don't like Woody Allen all that much."

"Really?" Chad looked at me like I had praying mantises crawling out of my ears.

"I've always thought he was a nebbish little creep," I continued. "Wasn't surprised at all when his MeToo history came out. But we're here for Maud, Chad. Not Woody."

"True."

"You know in all the years we've known each other, you never told me how you got into her. It was just a thing, an *a priori* predicate of Chad."

"A what? In English, please."

"Part of you from the beginning. But she must have had a beginning?"

Chad didn't say anything. He half smiled and looked at the grave. Finally:

"You remember the old Summer Film Festival that Channel 40 used to run?"

"Of course. It's where I first saw *Moby-Dick* and forever confused Abe Lincoln, Gregory Peck and Captain Ahab!"

"Ha, yes. I fell in love with Cary Grant in *Gunga Din*."

"Who wouldn't?"

"Anyway, I remember watching *The Fop* with my sister Jenny. She was three years older than me at the time and we just wanted to be by ourselves because my parents and brothers were off to San Francisco that weekend. So we got to do whatever we wanted. But we were still kids so that didn't mean much but staying up late.

Anyway, I remember *The Fop* so well. David Niven was so funny and handsome and Maud. God, I wanted to be that beautiful. Jenny wanted to be that beautiful too. And that loved. Both of us."

"Your sister? I didn't know you had a sister. A real sister?" I suddenly felt awful because while I didn't know that, I knew what was coming.

"Yeah, well you know how my family is about me."

"They're a bunch of assholes. Yes, I know that. She one of them?"

"No. But... Anyway, we haven't spoken for a long time."

"I'm sorry, Chad."

"It's OK. I don't really miss my parents or Kyle or Karl all that much. But Jenny, yes."

"How did you get Chad? Not Kelly or Kip or something?"

"Damned if I know. Anyway. Let's go. I'm feeling a bit sadder here than I really wanted. She seems lost here. So many dead."

"'*His soul swooned slowly as he heard the snow falling faintly through the universe and faintly falling, like the descent of their last end, upon all the living and the dead.*'"

"That's beautiful. But it isn't snowing. I don't want to stay here anymore," Chad was crying now.

"OK. Let me hold your hand."

"Thank you. I love you, Ada."

MGM Studios is now Sony Pictures Studios. Since 2004 Sony has been working at preserving it, which means some outright fabrication and recreation at times, but at least it wasn't under the Omnipotence of the Mouse. And, it is actually a working studio.

"Perhaps it's because the Japanese have a little more respect for the past," I said.

"More like the almighty dollar. Still, it's sad."

"Why?"

"That iron gate, the movie posters, all this Art Deco. It's just not what Maud would have seen."

"But maybe she would have wanted to."

"It's not the same and I know it."

"Chad, I actually really admire this. Sure, it's all calculated as a tourist thing, but they're still using this studio and it's a much more respectful way of treating a place."

"It's not the same."

"Look, if I took you to Germany, most of what you would see there is reproduction. Lübeck's a good example. Most of that city—a very old historic city—was flattened by the RAF in World War II, so most of what you see there is reproduction. And it's beautiful. I've lived in houses in Seattle that were older than the Buddenbrooks Haus."

"Still not the same."

I quit arguing with him. Emma, our crisp and fresh 26-year-old tour guide was ready to lead us on. Chad whispered his admiration for Stage 27 where Gene Kelly preferred to have his pictures shot, and Stage 30 which still had its massive 721,400-gallon tank for Esther Williams along with several installments of the endless *Spiderman* franchise.

"Are we going to Stage 17?" Chad asked.

"I'm sorry, but Stage 17 was demolished," Emma said.

"But that's where *The Fop* was filmed. You know, with Maud Williams."

"There was a lot of change through the years at MGM, especially during the Kerkorkian ownership period."

"Asshole," Chad whispered under his breath. He turned and whispered to me. "Kerkorkian's the guy who dismantled the studio so he could build hotels. Can you imagine? What is it you say? 'Hell gapes for such villainy."

"Actually, Samuel Marchbanks said that, but I like it."

"So do I."

"Oh, but there's Stage 15!" Emma said to Chad and winked. And he laughed.

When we got to Stage 15, I understood as she swept her arm, as if magically revealing it. "This is where many scenes from *The Wizard of Oz* were filmed."

People had been continually tapping their screens for selfies throughout the tour and this studio was no exception. I finally decided it was time, but I wanted something more traditional.

"Emma, can you please take one of us. He loves this place you know."

"Oh sure! You're such a handsome couple." She happily took our picture at Stage 15, even though Chad couldn't stop giggling.

"And, folks, this was once the second of the largest sound stages in the world. It is still the fourth largest and this is where *The Invincible* with George Sanders and Maud Williams was shot. Fritz Lang had the roof of an entire castle built here for the famous last scenes."

Chad was transported. Emma beamed. I understood. No one else stopped taking selfies.

Chad slipped Emma a rather large tip along with an "I love you," in such subtle, but mincing way that Emma finally got our relationship. I liked her too. So much that I felt out of place.

"Oh, come on, Ada. No one else can stand in for you on a trip like this."

"I think Ashley or Emma could have done quite well," I said.

"True. It gives me some hope that not all the wisdom in this world will be lost. Please don't recite 'Ozymandias.' Let's go shopping."

Chad and I had agreed we would go up to Beverly Hills and Bel Air and ogle rich people and go 'shopping' if shopping was the sort of thing where you went into an expensive boutique and pretended you had money.

We started at Rodeo Drive.

"The thing is, this all recent, you know. This street had gas stations back in the Golden Age. Giorgio only opened in 1967. Gucci followed in 1968 and then it went on from there."

We stopped in front of Dior. "But I thought Coco Chanel came over here in the 40's or something," I said.

"Coco came here in the early 30's. She and Sam Goldwyn had a short-lived production arrangement. By the end of the Depression the big studios realized they could set the fashion tastes for this country instead of being beholden to the French. Let's go in."

Chad and the staff bantered and chatted in that remarkable way—everyone knew what the "real" story was. He knew that they knew that he knew that they knew we didn't really have any money and we weren't going to buy anything. And yet I never saw the pretense drop for a second. It was this way everywhere we went. Finally, we arrived at Chanel, I cornered him.

"Chad, how do you do that?"

"What?"

"Act with these people as if you and I are somehow important and well off when they seem to know it and you seem to know that."

"It's right there in what you said, Ada. We're acting. This is the place where you act. Everyone acts, we all wear a mask. What's that book you're always pestering me to read?"

"*Confessions of a Mask* by Mishima. I thought you'd like it."

"Wasn't he an actor too? And hot, I can see why you like him. But that death! Talk about going out as the Empress!"

"You never read the book."

"I'm lucky if I can read *The New Yorker*, honey. Anyway, we all have masks, but this place is kind of the Mecca for having a mask. Am I right?"

I looked around at the wealth. I looked at a purse and couldn't even imagine how many people its price could feed in a year in the US much less somewhere else in the world. An older white woman near me had hundreds of thousands of dollars' worth of work done on her face and breasts.

"I feel small and mean here."

"That's because you're a terrible actor, Ada. You always have been. I love you for that."

"And you?"

"You know I'm always living a lie. I always have been." He said this and his face changed. The brightness disappeared and at first, I thought it was an act, but then I realized he was merely flat. Human. "But I can be honest with you. See. Believe me now?"

I did. But I wanted to change the subject. "It's so funny. Here we are in Chanel, but it wasn't here in the Golden Age. I guess they didn't have anything like this then. I thought you said Maud wore Chanel."

"Always. It was one of the things that got her blacklisted—she wouldn't wear Edith Head's costumes. It's funny, but my mom used to wear Chanel No. 5 of course. I suppose the old bitch still does. But it was Jenny who pointed out to me that the woman who made Maud's dresses was the same person behind the *eau de cologne*."

"She should really be here with you. I'm just an understudy, aren't I?" I said this with enough of my "native lack of acting skills" that Chad just sort of gave me a crooked grin. "You know what I mean."

"I do. I would love to be with her but that just hasn't worked out."

"And you've never really tried to connect with her? She has her own life now. If she was really as into the old films and you as it sounds, she can give the rest of your family the finger. Are they really that fucked up?"

"They are, Ada. I tried to call her once, a long time ago when we still had land lines. I got an answering machine and never a call back."

"I'm sorry Chad. Maybe someday."

"Someday I will see her again. I just don't know when. And that's kind of scary. But come on, we're supposed to be having fun here."

"This place feels like it's full of dead people."

"You always say that around rich people."

"Do I?"

"You said it about a lot of Dan's friends. When were on the bow of the *Chipotle*, remember?

"Yes," I said and remembered sitting on Dan's yacht, anchored somewhere in the Puget Sound. In the cockpit Dan and his cronies chattered and nattered. Chad would sit with me so I wasn't alone "I just don't understand them. I guess."

"I have been one, kind of all my life. Well, not really. Hmm. I feel sort of free being poor with you. Almost the first time."

"First time?"

"Maybe it's the second time. The first time came after I was alone as I would ever be when I wasn't rich anymore. When I lost everything."

"What's the most popular line in all the movies, Chad?"

"'Let's get outta here?' Yeah. Makes sense. You look like you want some Mexican food."

"We're in LA, come on."

Sunday was another lazy start. Chad slept in and I didn't. He'd been up in the night again, out on the balcony smoking. I wrote for a while until my typing finally woke him up.

"What are you working on?"

"Just something. About that house you and Dan had with the view of Rainier."

"He still has it."

"I don't think so. Now that you aren't there, he doesn't really have it."

"Thanks, sis. So, Cameo again for Brunch and then Maud's?"

"You promised me we'd spend some time at the beach."

"I did, didn't I? C'mon."

After another excellent breakfast at Cameo, we left and drove on Sunset Boulevard. We didn't say much. I drove, as usual and Dan watched the scenery go by.

"Where am I going?" I asked.

"To the beach."

"How."

"Honey just stay on this road. At the end of it is the Pacific Ocean."

"Oh."

We drove up again into Beverly Hills and through the flats. The famous "10,000 Block" of Sunset Boulevard.

"You know, I always imagine William Holden is still floating dead in a pool around here," I said.

"Better than drunk and bleeding to death in Santa Monica."

"No... come on. What does Norma say at the end? Stars live forever?"

"Nobody lives forever," Chad said. "There it is. The driveway, but that's not where they filmed the exteriors. That was on Wilshire."

So even the 10,000 Block was an illusion in my mind.

"You know Maud was supposed to have played Norma Desmond."

"I've heard a bunch of women were supposed to have played Norma Desmond."

"She and Wilder didn't get along though. She didn't get along with most people. That's why I've always liked her."

"Weren't those divas all hard to get along with?"

"They had their special guys who they got along with. She and George Cukor were almost a couple. Kind of like us right now."

"Ok, I have no idea about this, so tell me: did she get along with Fritz Lang?"

"Ha, it's funny you should mention that. I've heard and read all sorts of different rumors. They hated each other and yet certainly brought out the best in each other."

"Some couples are like that," I said.

"You dated a German, for a long time. What do you think?"

"I think I can understand why Maud probably hated him. And loved him."

"Astrid really was The One."

"I wouldn't say that. I'm not dead yet. But of all the people I loved and who loved me—for a time—she was... the most important."

Chad looked at me, arching his eyebrows like Cary Grant.

"The most important *so far*. Do you know the story of Marysas?" I asked.

"No, who was she?"

"He. He was a satyr in Greek mythology. You would have liked him. Played the flute, perhaps the skin flute too."

Chad laughed.

"But one day he messed up big time and challenged Apollo to a contest of music."

"Oh, these never end well."

"Especially this one. He lost the match and Apollo flayed him alive to use his skin as a wine sack."

"Yuck!"

"That story always reminds me of my relationship with Astrid. What if Apollo and Marysas were lovers?"

"Why would a lover *ever* do that?"

"Because Apollo peeled off the outer form and revealed the inner Marysas. But our visitations by the Gods are never pleasant. And we're always changed."

When we got to Pacific Palisades, Chad pointed at a road. We had been driving in the shade of hundreds of eucalyptus trees and even in the AC-sealed car, we could smell them.

"Here it is. See that hard right turn?"

"Chautauqua?"

"Yes, when we go back tonight, we'll stop up there. Her last house is there."

We did reach the Pacific Ocean but avoided going into it by turning left off Sunset when it ended at Highway 1 at Inceville. We drove south until we got to the beach. It was fine and sunny, with a little breeze coming off the water. After stripping down to our suits in the car, we gathered towels, water, sunscreen and joined the throng on the beach.

We people watched, we got wet and then wandered on the pier. Chad grew strangely nostalgic, telling me of when he would come here in the summer as a boy with his family.

"We were loaded you know, so we would go up to this posh resort, the Clemente. When my father was feeling generous, he'd let me and Jenny come down here."

"So you have been here with her."

"Yes, but never to the other places. My father didn't approve of Hollywood and thought Jenny's and mine fascination with movies lower class. He's a real asshole."

"Sounds like it. That's too bad. But you must have had fun here."

"We did. Riding the Ferris wheel, the whole thing."

"Well, come on then. Since I'm standing in for her, you can come with me."

We rode up high above the pier, which gave me a bit of vertigo, though I didn't tell Chad. He smiled and laughed and pointed out the clouds that had begun to dot the horizon.

"It will be a beautiful sunset. We should be able to see it from her house."

"Is this going to be another stalking-encounter like before?"

"No, no one is there."

"But won't it be off limits if there's a construction fence up or something like that?"

"No, it's Sunday. Even if they have something like that up, there won't be anyone there."

"But we're still waiting for evening?"

"It's more romantic that way, don't you think? Just imagine her walking the halls there with the same light streaming in."

"It's not the same light. It might look the same but…"

"Oh Ada, enough with the philosophy. I know, we never even watch the same movie twice and I'm not really riding this Ferris wheel again and all of that stuff from Herodotus…"

"… Heraclitus"

"Whatever. Sophocles would understand."

"You have me there. When did you stop coming here?"

"It was after… I turned 14. 13, I guess. My family quit taking trips together after that." He was quiet for a while and simply looked out over the Pacific.

"What happened, did you come out or something? I thought you said that happened when you were 18."

"It was. But my father already had his ideas. You know, that's why we went to school together at El Camino? My brothers had gone to Jesuit, but my father didn't think it was appropriate for me to be at an all-boys school."

"Really? Why didn't you go to Rio Americano?"

"Too many other spoiled rich kids like me, is what he said."

"I'm surprised he didn't send you off to military school."

"My mom had that idea, but my dad nixed it. All-boys you know."

"Your dad's probably gay."

"What?"

"He just sounds like a classic homophobe: he thrust you out of the family when you came out, and he was always thinking about boys. At least it sounds like that to me."

"The sin was in his heart…"

"…so he saw it everywhere. I'm surprised he never ran for office so he could be one of those GOP senators that goes cruising for rent boys in airport bathrooms."

"Ha! Now that you say that… I hadn't thought of that. I was too much in the middle of it all."

"And you said you never saw him again after 18?"

"Nope."

"Nor Jenny or your brothers?"

"Nope. He just sent me off to Cal Poly. Told me I had a full ride there as long as I got good grades, but I was on my own after that. He didn't even go there to drop me off. Just James, who was sort of our butler, chauffeur."

"You had a butler?"

"We were rich. They are rich, Ada. Yeah. James was nice though. I remember he said it was a shame what they were doing, but he still pleaded with me to never tell my dad that. I told him he didn't have to worry about it and he never did."

"Maybe James and your dad had something. Didn't even need to be consummated, but maybe he hung on like Erich von Stroheim did for Gloria Swanson in *Sunset Boulevard*."

"I'm very glad you're writing again. You have a gift for making up stuff."

"That's very plausible."

"True."

We had dinner at a cheap, touristy seafood place, but the fish and chips were good, and we drank a couple of beers before we left to build up our courage for the last visit to Maud Williams. After tracing our way back up Highway 1 to Sunset, we drove until we reached the turn off. The road climbed steeply, and we made another left onto a bluff between Temescal Canyon and Will Rogers State Park. We were high enough to get a view of the ocean and after three or four turns, with Siri telling us the way from Chad's iPhone, we got there.

At first, I wasn't sure. It was simply a line of large, fairly modern houses from the looks of them. They were all done up in the Spanish style, but there were no forlorn mansions clogged with weeds and towering palm trees waiting to die. There was no overgrowth of vines, or empty swimming pools. It looked like many of the other hilly, expensive stretches of real estate in that part of LA County. And there were no construction fences.

"There." Chad pointed to a modest, one story place behind a circular driveway. A Lyon real estate sign was in the middle of it.

"For sale? I thought you said they were tearing this down."

Chad quickly said: "oh, the deal must have fallen through.

Come on. No one's here. We'll just pretend we're a couple from Seattle looking to move down here. OK?"

It turned out there were three stories to the place—what we had seen was simply the massive three car garage, but that sat on top of the house and it descended down the bluff. Chad wandered around to a side gate. "Oh Ada, come on, the view is spectacular."

The gate wasn't even locked. I wondered if this neighborhood was so exclusive, they didn't really care, or the Realtor had forgotten to lock it. We walked down a turning staircase of cut granite that ran along the side of the house until we reached the bottom. There, in a terrace portion barely scooped out of the hill was a beautiful, rectangular swimming pool. It was full of clean, obviously tended water because there were no Pre-Raphaelite lily pads floating in it. I wanted to swim in it.

There was an open wet bar made from sandstone nearby. Chad walked past it and started checking doors.

"Did she entertain here much? But that was a long time ago. She died in 1970 or something, right?"

"Well, someone else did live here after her. It was a rich family. Probably a lot like mine. Funny thing is, they didn't even live here very much so it was thought to be haunted. But they would party here. Or maybe not. I just know the son of the owner is selling it. Ah ha! They left this door open. Come on!"

"So, you *did* know it wasn't going to be demolished."

"Um... no. I had heard it was going to be sold. To be demolished."

"Chad, you're lying. I mean you're a good actor and all and I usually can't smell your bullshit, but I'm not stupid. This place is just being sold again to some other rich people, eventually."

We stood there for a while. I crossed my arms and remained silent. He sheepishly looked down. Opened the door. Closed it.

Opened it. "Look, I thought you wouldn't come if you knew I had just been stalking this place on Lyon's website."

"That's not true, Chad. I wanted to come down here no matter what. I did sort of think we were going to be sneaking into some fading mansion that was going to be torn down, but now I realize that's just too much *Sunset Boulevard*. Whatever. Let's go in."

"You're mad."

"I am. Because I'm wondering just how much else you've lied about." I walked past him and into the wide entertainment room, or whatever it was. He followed me in. "Look at this place. It's staged. You don't stage a house for a wrecking ball."

It was not only staged, but beautifully so. Some of the furniture I even recognized from our jaunt in Beverly Hills. But damn Chad if he wasn't right. The sunset poured into the house through the many windows facing west and it was gorgeous. The house was bigger than it seemed from outside, so it was easy to lose him in whatever melancholy funk he was in. But eventually we found each other in the master bedroom.

"This is where she died?"

"No. She died in the hospital. But this was the last place she lived."

There never was a Mexican maid desperately dialing 911.

We sat down on the enormous bed carved from God-knows-what-endangered-species-of-tree and watched the last of the sunset. Finally, I looked at him: "See, the thing about people who lie is they never consider that someone will think: 'hey, he lied to me once, what's keeping it from happening again?'"

"Most people like the lies. You liked Ralph's."

"Fuck Ralph."

"I'm sorry, Ada."

"Ralph is where I finally learned how to start seeing them."

"Astrid never lied to you?"

"No. She always told the truth to me. Brutally, most often and I loved her for it in a sick way. But she avoided lying by technicality. She was just good at leaving out important parts of the truth. I'm guessing you did that too."

"Don't be mad at me. Most of this, no all of this trip, except this was on the level. I wanted to get away from Seattle and Dan and you needed a break."

"All good set up. Give 'em just enough truth so they think it's all the truth. I'm going for a swim in that pool."

"But someone might hear you."

"Fuck them. And fuck you. I'm not going to be splashing around in the water like a teenager."

Chad's face dropped at this and he just looked at his hands.

I did what I said I was going to do. I still had my suit on from the beach, but I did take my top off and slid into the pool and swam around in the clear cool water. At first, I floated for a while and thought of William Holden in the pool from *Sunset Boulevard.* I turned over to look at the stars and wondered how many of them were already dead like Maud. Like… and then I really wondered. I turned over and swam to the edge of the pool. Chad was in the shadows, not watching me but near. He had a bottle of vodka, presumably stashed away when we left Andrew's condo.

"I'm sorry, Chad. I just hate to be lied to. It's not much of a lie even. So, I'm being a bitch about it."

"No. I'm sorry. I should have told you."

I kept remembering what I had thought in the pool. But I couldn't ask him. I got out and just stood there dripping in the night. It must have been a while. Chad sipped at the bottle and began to cry. By then, my skin was already dry in the Southern California air.

"Chad, is anyone else in your family… like…"

"...like what?"

"This trip isn't about Maud. This is her house and you haven't said anything. Granted, I was being a gash just then, but that look in your eyes. Chad..."

"...yes, Ada. What?" He was still crying and sounded like a little angry boy. I sat down next to him and grabbed the bottle, drank some vodka.

Chad fumbled around in his pocket and pulled out a rumpled box of Dunhill cigarettes.

"Give me one of those," I said.

"Ada you don't smoke."

"I used to smoke clove cigarettes, remember? Besides I kind of need one right now. Chad, Jenny's dead, isn't she?"

"How did you know?"

"It's what I said. The parts you left out. You fooled me with the phone call bit. A nice touch. I just couldn't believe the one person in your fucked-up family you were close to would abandon you like that."

"No. I mean yes. Yes."

"I'm so sorry."

We passed the bottle back and forth and smoked for a while. I coughed mostly and remembered why I'd quit so long ago. It was mostly to piss off my mother, and it worked, but once she quit talking to me and I to her, I lost the urge. I only had one. Chad had four.

"She died when I was thirteen."

"How?"

"I killed her."

I was freezing. Abject, absolute, thoroughly freezing the moment he said it. Not because I believed him, but because I knew he was lying.

"Chad... I don't believe you."

"No, I did. You see my parents were loaded like I said. We had this cabin up at Lake Tahoe. Well, it wasn't a cabin, it was a fucking chalet. They were having a party. Jenny and I had been sneaking booze. Like this. My dad got mad, told us to get the hell out of there so we did. We went down to the lake. We always played like kids. Throwing snowballs. She was better than me. Said I always threw like a girl. She was going to be playing Varsity Softball at Loretto. As a sophomore. So, I ran out on the ice in the cove near our house. It was so fucking stupid, Ada."

At this he just broke down into groaning sobs. Have you ever been with someone crying so hard you could hear the tears on the ground? Yes. Like that.

"It just cracked out from under her. And I couldn't do anything. I just stood there. My brother Kyle came out to look for us but not soon enough. *Why didn't you do anything? Why didn't you call us, you stupid little fruit? You killed her. You know that?*"

"Jesus, Chad. You didn't kill her. The water, the ice killed her. It was an accident. Didn't your therapist ever tell you that?"

"We hadn't gotten to it. I just told him she died when she was young from cancer. I think."

I didn't comment on that, just washed it down with more vodka.

"That was it. My life in my family was over after that. You know when I left, my father said it would have been better if I'd thrown myself in the water after her. Then I wouldn't have been a cocksucker who was probably going to die of AIDS. It was the 80's you know and..."

"Your Dad would still say that now. People like him don't give a fuck about science when it doesn't suit their needs."

"No. You're right. Ada, Ada, Ada." And he held on to me.

"I'm not going anywhere, Chad. Brother. I never had one until now."

And he looked at me through dark eyes clogged with salt tears. Then he kept crying. I let him collapse onto me, his head on my knees and he kept crying. I stroked his hair. Sipped the vodka. At last, I looked at stars reflected upon the water in the pool and began to cry at the deception of fragile surfaces.

AUGUST

THE PROMPT

To say the light was brilliant would be a disservice to the generations to come that have only the written record to explore this moment of discovery. It was a small thing, certainly, but sometimes small things have great influence. With this vessel, light was returned to the people.

BRILLIANT
BY JENNIFER DiMARCO

You make your own coconut kephir and habanera tequila and drop acid with your SJW grandma once a month. Before a match, you do a line. Sometimes two. You held the Lightweight women's MMA title for four years in your twenties. I first saw your face when you were high as a kite and no one else knew. I knew then, now, forever that you were brilliant.

Let's break some stereotypes:

Yes. You have an addictive personality. Yes. You are crazy smart. Smart in a way I don't have a word for. You hold dual degrees in neuroscience and criminal law. You spend sixteen hours a day fighting systemic racism. You wear William Okpo jeans with your red silk Telfar unisex wrap. The high asymmetrical neck sports peek-a-boo views of your rose cream skin and the precipice edge of your collar bone. You get in fights on Twitter instead of watching Netflix on the weekends. You smile and sip wine that costs more than my car.

To me, you are exotic as cardamom and sharp as a razor blade. A reporter on the steps of the capitol asked you if your unbridled dedication is rooted in white guilt. You punched him in the face, broke his (white) nose, then tipped your chin up to another station's bobbing boom mic: "Any more questions?" There were none.

It seems your whole life is on display, deconstructed by lesser men and women who can't keep up with you. Who can't even conceptualize what you do and how you do it. You drink them all under the table and then, while they're semi-conscious on your floor, you start talking about mapping the human brain and the substance of the soul.

I fell in love with you the first time you went down on me then lifted your head, didn't wipe your mouth, and commanded, "Sit on my face."

Inhabitations are not allowed in your world.

You are as driven as my father who I saw only on holidays and who kept my mother and I lavished in every luxury other than his presence. He was dynamic and persuasive. I could hate him for missing the award ceremony when I won a writing competition... then fall crying tears of joy into his arms when he presented me with a HarperCollins publishing contract coaxed from his across-the-hall neighbor in the city (who happened to be their acquisitions editor); he could get anything done. Just like you.

The difference is: You spend time with me, too.

One night, our bodies still a tesseract in the aftermath of sensation that seems beyond human experience, I'm staring at your open eyes as you stare somewhere past me.

"Where are you?" I ask. Because I can't ask, *What are you thinking?* or you'll just grin and kiss me.

The first and last time I asked that question, you answered, "I was thinking: Why were 47% of the age-matched controls female in Amy and Liv's mapping study of brain asymmetry in young adults with one of five sex-chromosome aneuploidies? Why didn't they gender- and race-match as well?"

I was so obviously lost in my complete incomprehension that I stood up from the table and walked out of the five-star restaurant you'd gotten us into despite the four-month wait for everyone else.

I caught an Uber and didn't return your calls for a week. Your fourth voicemail threw me a bone: "Leanne. I'm sorry. I promise to never bring work to the table again. I don't want anything between us. Please come over and take off your clothes."

You always do that. Say my name like a complete sentence.

We both knew that you staying present and out of your head wasn't the issue. We shared a race, a gender, a socioeconomic class; we did not share an intelligence quota. But I came over (and over and over again); I was undressing before you could take the chain off your door.

A year later, Liv laughed at you at a Christmas party at Nancy and Jim's. "And what gender would we match, Elan? *Presenting* gender?" From across the room I watched your face as another woman made you feel stupid on purpose. She took a perverse pleasure in taking her "victory." You had never hurt anyone on purpose outside the octagon. (Reporters don't count.)

I walked over to you and snaked an arm around your waist, pressing my entire body against you. I wore a Vera Wang evening gown with the darkling blue-silver sheen of wet shark skin; Liv had been watching me for hours like she was parched and I was a tall glass of water.

"Take me home, Elan," I murmured just loud enough for the bitch to hear me. I gave Liv a slow motion nasty look. "I'm bored with these people."

We had sex in your Porsche. It was dark and cramped and I still came twice and saw my chiropractor for two months afterward.

That was a Friday night. You proposed to me the following Monday and from the moment you sank to one knee I started repeating *yes* over and over again. You laughed and I laughed with you.

"You are my divinity," you whispered to me (much) later that night. I think there has never been a more devout lover.

Returning to the present:

"I'm right here with you," you answer me. "And halfway across the universe."

You smile. I smile.

"Let me write about you." It's a request. I'm asking permission without making it a question. I'm always asking permission because I take no part of you for granted. Not even an amorphous part like public persona.

You look at me with curiosity and amusement. There are streaks of silver in your chestnut hair. I've been yours for two decades but I'm still, always, perpetually ten years younger. I guess I thought I'd catch up somehow even though I know that's not how aging works.

"Why would you spend time writing about me, baby?"

I love it when you call me baby.

You stroke my curls. I'm naturally blonde but this summer I'm your thistle, sporting soft lavender hair that makes you smile and want to touch me. I support that urge. I'll support it twenty more years from now and beyond if you let me.

"I want the world to know you." I'm so proud of you. So enamored. So inspired.

"Oh my thistle...."

You sit up, reach for a joint, take a long, slow hit, hold your breath (which does nothing except remind you you've been doing it and can stop whenever you want to), then let tendrils of ether creep from your nostrils like a young dragon atop her treasure (me).

"I'm bored of me." You say it so softly, your lips obscured by the drifting smoke. It smells like fresh spring grass and mangos.

I've heard this tone in your voice before but not until after you passed your sixtieth; you're worn thin by a lifetime of the world rubbing you the wrong way. Your myriad of passions have burned your candle at both ends and I'm sometimes afraid all the wick and wax are gone, leaving nothing but ashes.

I'm not ready for you to be ashes.

"What do you want me to write about?" I sit up with you. I trace the lines of your face with both hands and realize I love you more today than I have words to explain. You are essential to me—brilliant as a neutrino star at the center of my universe.

Your amusement fades slowly and there's such love written across your features, written wordlessly across all your body. Never did I ever imagine loving someone the way I love you. Loving you so completely that I lose myself and enjoy being lost.

Never did I ever imagine someone loving be back the way you do.

"Write about...." Your voice drifts away. Something is happening. Something is about to—

You continue speaking but now you're looking at the dark green satin sheet instead of at me. "My first kiss was with Victoria. My first boss was Antira. My favorite teacher was Mrs. Stella. My best sensei was Jazime Wilson."

At first I don't follow and then I think maybe I've caught on. "They were all women."

You look back at me. "They were all black women." You want me to understand the depth of what you're saying. "Every single time someone lifted me up... every time someone fought for me, encouraged me, pushed me... it was a black woman. I am who I am today because an army of black women believed I could do good."

Until me, I thought, selfishly. Trying not to make this moment about me, trying to—

"Until you," you say gently, your lips parted with a delighted and amused grin.

I blush and look away. So silly to be a grown woman jealous of a million other women who have loved you. After all, you married me.

I look back at you as you lift your chin, your signature move. Your eyes are polished pennies ringed with apple jade patina. "What do I want you to write about?" You repeat the ask as if contemplating it anew. "Write about... black women piloting sentient starships. Negotiating peace with an alien race of carnivorous tiger lilies." Your gaze holds mine and you're so certain, so sure. "Write about a little black girl born with telepathy who can talk to plants and animals and convinces the nations of the world to protect the Earth. You love science fiction, Leanne. Write heroes that there simply aren't enough of."

I'm crying silent tears. I wrap my arms around you. I know what you're doing. "I can't be you...." I'm confessing the obvious but sincerely, wanting you to know I know.

You smile. You have a gap between your front teeth that even when you paid off the house you didn't get fixed. "Don't be me," you say and kiss me. "Be the best you."

In the morning, you're gone. Your body still holds a little heat but your heart has stopped. I wasn't ready but I know, even if you'd been mine for fifty or a hundred years more than the twenty we had, I would never be ready to let you go.

My brilliant wife. My brilliant lover. I will write about heroes for you. Now, then, and forever.

TALISMAN
BY LAUREN PATZER

It's not on him," Alejandro said.

Maravich flipped her black trench coat over the back of the chair as she sat down at the dining room table looking down at the body of Hal 'Chitti' Garrison. A pool of blood had formed below the man's head. He was still face down, a matted circle of brain matter, hair and blood prominent on the rear of his skull. Maravich rubbed her chin and frowned, her dark skin glistening in the heat of the day.

She snapped her fingers and three more people entered, all dressed in the haphazard rough fashion of recovered clothing typical of wasteland marauders.

"Flip him over," Maravich said. Alejandro complied, aided by his three fellow Marauder Krew members. In the center of Hal's forehead, a neat bullet hole was surrounded by a small circle of blood trailing down his nose.

Maravich leaned over and examined the bullet hole. She

turned to Alejandro.

"You?" Maravich asked.

"Yes," Alejandro replied and then added, "He was pulling a gun."

Maravich nodded and smiled. She turned to the other Krew members and pointed at the head wound.

"Excellent marksmanship!"

The Krew murmured their agreement. Danya, the tall albino woman, sneered. Maravich raised her eyebrows and stood up. She walked to the other Krew members and examined their faces. Danya was just as tall as Maravich.

"Gun," Maravich said simply and held her gloved hand out to Alejandro. He swallowed hard and pulled his handgun from his waistband behind him. He handed it to her.

She examined the weapon. She looked back up at the three Marauder Krew members and frowned.

"Can any of you do that from ten paces away?" She scowled at the three. The two male members looked down, but Danya met her gaze.

"I could," she said defiantly. Maravich held her eyes, nodded and turned back to Alejandro.

"Well, Alejandro, if the talisman is not on Chitti, ask him where it is," Maravich said as she sat back down.

Alejandro looked down at the corpse and frowned. He looked up at Maravich like she was crazy.

"But he's dead..."

"Ask him," Maravich said and set the gun on the table in front of her. Alejandro swallowed hard as he saw Maravich clench her teeth, the muscles along her jaw line rippling slightly. The steely look in her eyes instantly brought beads of sweat to his brow.

He nudged the corpse with his foot.

"Hey, where's the talisman?" Alejandro said and giggled nervously. They all waited and, of course, the dead man remained silent.

"Maybe he couldn't hear you," Maravich prodded. "Louder."

Alejandro glanced nervously at Maravich. His eyes wandered to his Marauder Krew who all watched him impassively with the exception of Danya who glared disapprovingly.

Alejandro got on his knees next to the corpse.

"Where is the talisman?!" he shouted.

Sweat dropped from Alejandro's brow as he stared at the man he'd killed a mere fifteen minutes ago.

"Maybe," Maravich said quietly. Alejandro's head shot up and he looked at her. "He doesn't know what the talisman looks like. Describe it to him. I'm sure that will loosen his tongue."

Alejandro blinked and tears formed in his eyes.

"Please, señora, he is dead."

"Do. It." The words were spoken firmly, slowly and distinctly.

Alejandro looked down at the body.

"The talisman we're looking for is about six inches long with a blue stone at the top-"

"Aquamarine," Maravich interrupted.

"Que?" Alejandro replied automatically, not able to process the request fast enough to realize the futility of his question.

"Chitti might misunderstand, thinking its topaz or even sapphire. If he's confused, do you really think he can give you a proper answer?" Maravich smiled thinly at Alejandro.

"The blue stone at the top is aquamarine. The rest of the talisman is like a cross with a loop at the top."

"It's called an ankh, Alejandro."

Alejandro's lips quivered as he stared at the corpse. A fly landed on the dead man's face.

"The shape of the talisman is an ankh," Alejandro finished. His hands hung at his side in defeat.

There was a long silence.

"So, Krew, what have we learned today?" Maravich asked, turning to view the others.

"Don't kill the person you're going to interrogate," Danya answered.

"Exactly right," Maravich said and stood up walking to her. "Now, I'm going to put you to the test, Danya."

Maravich ejected the clip from Alejandro's gun and set it back on the table.

"Alejandro, take your gun so we can properly train Danya on apprehension techniques."

Alejandro didn't move.

"Alejandro, don't tell me you wish to shirk their training!" Maravich said holding her fingers to her lips in shock.

Alejandro still didn't move. Maravich walked away from the table and stood in the far corner opposite the door.

"Take. The. Gun."

Alejandro reached up with a shaky hand and grabbed the gun. He wiped the sweat from his brow with his other hand and absently tugged on his shoulder length black locks.

"Danya, out and back in. Get the talisman from Alejandro," Maravich said. Danya stepped out the door, stepped back in and shot Alejandro in the right shoulder. Alejandro screamed in pain, dropped the gun in his right hand and grabbed his shoulder.

"No," Maravich said. "That was luck in disarming him. Always shoot for the hand... try again."

"What?!" Alejandro screamed. "I'm already shot!"

Maravich walked over and picked up the gun.

"Good point," Maravich manipulated the gun briefly and

inserted a single bullet. "It will be more realistic if you have live ammo involved."

Maravich handed the gun back to Alejandro, who tried at first to grasp the gun with his right hand but then realized he couldn't raise his right arm. Danya squinted her eyes at him and then walked out the door. Alejandro sheepishly took the weapon in his left hand. He raised it and pointed it at the door. Maravich resumed her position in the corner.

Danya entered the room. Alejandro squeezed the trigger and nothing happened. He looked at the weapon in horror.

"The safety!" he shouted as Danya raised her pistol and shot him square in the left hand, knocking the gun from his grasp. He ducked down in pain at the additional bullet wound.

"Ahhh! Please stop!"

Danya stepped forward to the edge of the sturdy wooden table Alejandro huddled behind.

"Where is the talisman, Alejandro?" Danya said sweetly.

"I don't know!"

Danya stepped around the table, pointed her weapon and shot Alejandro in the left leg. Alejandro howled in pain. He scrambled back toward the corner.

"It's shaped like an ankh with an aquamarine stone in the loop at the top," Danya said calmly. "Are you sure you haven't seen it?"

"It wasn't on him!" Alejandro yelled in desperation. Danya fired another bullet into Alejandro, this time his right leg. Blood began to trickle beneath Alejandro as it pumped from his wounds.

"Where is it?" Danya shouted. Without thinking about it, Alejandro's eyes involuntarily edged up to the ceiling. Maravich looked up and smiled. Visible in the light fixture on the ceiling was a small ankh shaped shadow.

"You see, Alejandro," Maravich said as she climbed on top of the table and retrieved the talisman from the light fixture with her gloved hand. "A properly rendered interrogation can reveal the most interesting information. I wonder if you wanted to keep it from our benefactor out of concern for your fellow man or were just greedy and thought you could fence it for more than you were paid."

Maravich walked to the door and turned to smile.

"Danya, he's earned his reward."

"No, please!" Alejandro reached toward Maravich but she'd already turned her back. Danya fired once into Alejandro's abdomen. He clutched at the wound with his hands. He sobbed, tears in his eyes as he looked up at Danya, his eyes pleading for mercy.

"You're a traitor, Alejandro," Danya said as the other two Krew members watched in morbid fascination. Danya briefly ceased her torture to put additional bullets in her weapon. "Traitors don't get mercy."

Maravich stood outside the building and listened to the slow additional gunshots and the screaming from the former leader of the Marauder Krew. The entire procedure took about fifteen agonizing minutes. Her smile grew a little broader with each gun shot. Danya would make a fine replacement for Alejandro.

As Lieutenant Olivia Pena entered the warehouse, she could hear the clicking of the camera in the small internal office as the technicians took pictures of the crime scene. Observing the technicians from the door, Detective Vincent Green turned his head at the sound of her approaching footsteps. Olivia raised her eyebrows and Vincent smiled, ruffling his ginger mustache.

"Good to see you back, Lieutenant," Vincent said. "Sorry to welcome you back with a bloodbath."

"Gang related?" Olivia said as she poked her head in the room.

"Of a sort," Vincent replied. "Looks like a Marauder Krew

execution. Fifteen bullets. Final one through the roof of the mouth as the vic opened it to allow the barrel in."

"They haven't been active for over five years," Olivia replied. "I heard their leader died."

"Maybe he's just been lying low," Vincent replied. "Or maybe they got a new leader."

Olivia shook her head.

"A violent cult like the New Millennium doesn't switch leaders midstream, or ever really," Olivia said as the technicians walked out of the room.

"We got it all including a partial boot print on the desk in the blood. Got samples of the splatter too," the lead technician said. "It's all yours. I'll have a tech standby in case you find anything of further significance."

Vincent and Olivia stepped carefully into the room. They looked casually around the room before settling their eyes on the bodies.

"Second vic is Hal Garrison, Age 34," Vincent said, looking at his pad.

"Chitti…" Olivia whispered.

"Yeah, he has gone by that nickname in the past. Has a rap sheet for moving contraband and fencing just about anything. No crimes for the last…" Vincent scrolled up the pad. "Five years."

"So, Chitti had something that New Millennium wanted," Olivia said. "Maybe he's had it for the last five years."

"You think that's why they went silent?" Vincent asked.

"Lord knows it was a relief when they did." Olivia shuddered. New Millennium had been one of the most violent cults in history, actively slaughtering enemies and anyone it didn't agree with. Over a ten year span, Olivia was aware of at least 300 people they suspected were killed by cult members. Nothing they could pin on the reclusive leader, of course. FBI had helped them catch several of the more violent members, but they'd never been able to catch the infamous Marauder Krew as they called themselves.

"The other vic looks familiar," Olivia said.

"Haven't IDed him yet," Vincent said.

Olivia's eyebrows went up. "I'll be damned; I think that's Alejandro Gonzalez!"

"Who?" Vincent typed the name into his pad.

"When I was working the New Millennium cases, his name came up several times. I think he was the leader of the Marauder Krew." Olivia walked around to the feet of the two victims. "Chitti has a single gunshot to the head. He wasn't interrogated Marauder Krew style. But Alejandro has the classic wound pattern of a Krew torture and interrogation. Also, he's dead, so they must've found what they were looking for."

Olivia watched where she stepped, but got closer to the table. She looked from the bloody partial boot print to the ceiling and saw the lamp fixture.

"Get the techs in here to pull down this lamp fixture carefully. We need to find out what was hidden inside it if we can. Preserve the dust pattern," Olivia said. Vincent ducked his head out the door and barked instructions.

Olivia didn't need pictures to put it all together. Chitti was the designated keeper of the Talisman. The Darkside Collective had arranged that years ago along with a shield from prosecution for the crimes on his rather lengthy rap sheet. She needed to talk to Otto immediately.

"Vincent," she said. "Get details on the old Marauder Krew. It's possible some or all of them have resurfaced. I'm going to shake some trees on the New Millennium beat and see what falls out."

"Going to hunt down the Marauder Krew for this?"

"No," Olivia said. "We're going to try to prevent a war."

Olivia strolled along the cobblestone street until she reached a stairway leading down. Even though she'd been watching for a tail the entire time, she still made a casual check for any observers. The streets were filled with not much more than tourists at this hour, basking in the sunlight, hiking the hills of the city. Even so, her senses told her she'd been followed but she couldn't see who. It couldn't wait until she was sure. Lives hung in the balance. She descended the stairs.

The outer door was a simple wooden one with a small video camera. The door looked flimsy, but that was a deceptive camouflage. Olivia knew it would take a fairly large explosion to strip away the reinforced outer door to reveal the inner steel vault door. These precautions were all designed to slow down the enemy, allowing escape through various other routes. Nothing would stop a determined cult member. It was something they hadn't needed to worry about for five years.

The lock clicked as the door keeper recognized her and she pulled the thick panel open. What couldn't be seen through the darkened, frosted bulletproof windows on the outer door was the vault door located ten paces into the building. The walls were triple cinderblock, packed with Kevlar lining between each layer and shielding another layer of thick reinforced steel wall. The doors were the weak points.

She glanced behind her out of habit, just to make sure she wasn't watched by anyone who shouldn't see what she would do next. She grabbed the thick brass arms of the wheel and turned it until the one with the infinity symbol etched into it pointed to two o'clock. She stepped to the right and looked into the camera which verified her retinal details. There was a small audible beep sound and she grasped the wheel again and pulled the large door open, revealing what looked like a long hallway lined with safety deposit boxes. Even at this stage, it was still designed to look like a vault for regular valuables should someone not knowledgeable about its true purpose try to breach it.

She walked in and waited for the huge door behind her to shut on its own. When it shut with an audible thud, she walked forward and took the branch to the left, walking into the small alcove of safety deposit boxes. On the right wall, three in from the back wall and six down, she spun the combination lock on the box and a fake floor slid open behind her revealing a simple set of concrete steps leading down. She smiled as she remembered sabotaging the drilling machine for the new traffic tunnel so they could relocate this underground facility well away from prying eyes, filling in the old facility with simulated bedrock.

After descending three flights of stairs, she came to the elevator; the last physical line of defense before reaching her final destination. Anyone entering the elevator would be gassed when the doors closed. Perchance they had protection against that, the elevator led down a shaft to a set of rooms filled with valuable items worth a king's ransom. All of it was a decoy.

She pressed her hand to the wall to the right of the elevator doors about two feet up and two feet from the corner, a place where no one would likely accidentally press their hand were they to get this far. The wall slid back revealing a small alcove to the right which she quickly stepped through. As she stood in the alcove, the hidden wall opening slid back into place, revealing another lobby with another set of elevator doors. She walked to them and they opened automatically. She stepped inside, the doors shut behind her and the elevator began its ten minute descent. Even she didn't know exactly how far down it went, although she had estimated it was nearly a mile down. Her ears adjusted to the pressure about halfway through the ride.

The doors opened to reveal a simple corridor with offices lining it. Windows on each wall were clear, but could switch to opaque within a millisecond under threat conditions. She walked through the complex until she reached a non-descript door several turns in and opened the door revealing a cozy foyer one would typically see in a small mansion. From here on in, the living quarters were nearly identical to a residence above ground with the absence of windows in favor of changeable screens revealing various pastoral scenes. She ascended the grand staircase on the right side and took a right at the top of the stairs. Two doors down, she knocked.

"Enter!" shouted an old woman's voice. Olivia opened the door revealing a luxurious study, with walls lined by hundreds of books. In an easy chair under a lamp sat an old woman dressed in a brown flannel shirt and blue coveralls. She looked up at Olivia and smiled, her dark eyes twinkling in the light.

"Olivia, nice of you to visit. Although it's not the typical annual check-in, so I must assume you bring interesting news of some sort," the old lady frowned.

"Dara, I'm sorry I haven't been by frequently, but you know I have to do my job top side to maintain our cover and intel," Olivia said as she walked over and sat in the open chair to the old lady's left.

"Sure, always too busy to visit the elderly." Dara waved a hand dismissively and went back to examining the book in front of her that Olivia could see was filled with Egyptian hieroglyphics.

"Marconi is active again. I have reason to believe his forces have retrieved the talisman," Olivia said. "You told me if he recovered the talisman again, the dark would rise and consume the world."

Dara huffed and turned a page. She resumed her study of the hieroglyphics.

"What do we do?" Olivia said, irritation rising in her voice. "This is clearly an emergency, we need to marshal the forces, retrieve the talisman and beat Marconi back to the Stone Age."

"You didn't listen well," Dara replied absently, her fingers tracing the symbols in front of her. "I said the dark would bring the light to balance out the world. We have but to wait for the light to emerge and defeat the darkness."

"Without the talisman, Marconi killed hundreds just a few years ago. With the talisman, he could kill thousands. We can't just wait for some 'light' to emerge. We need to act now, before it's too late."

"Millions," Dara said. "Honestly, if you underestimate the power of the talisman in Marconi's hands, I don't know what I'm going to do with you. Have you forgotten your studies so soon?"

"Dara, we have all of this built, all these forces at the ready to combat dangers just like this. We have to put them on alert."

Dara stopped what she was doing and fixed Olivia with a kind look.

"Olivia," she said. "These forces will be deployed when the time is right, when the light has been triumphant. Until the light rises to meet the dark, it would be like throwing mud at a castle. Completely ineffectual."

"Marconi is dangerous. He has to be stopped. If you're not going to bring the forces of Darkside together, I'm just going to have to try to stop them myself. I hope you'll reconsider and take this seriously."

Dara hummed and returned her attention to the book.

"Thank you for stopping by. Could you bring some scones from The Crumpet Shop next time? I've always found them to be just the right balance for my chamomile tea."

Olivia stood and grumbled. She walked to the door and turned back. Dara kept on reading her book, paying Olivia little heed. The hotheaded lieutenant mulled over the referenced lessons for a moment, then walked through the door and shut it behind her firmly.

Inside the study, Dara looked up from her book and smiled.

"And so the light rises..." she said and looked back down at her book.

THE LIGHT
BY HIROMI COTA

It's hard to think of a time before The Light. No, not hard, just—well, why bother? Look, if you're reading this, you're looking for an instruction manual, a history, something to indicate what you should do next. And that means that we've failed.

Bear with me here. The Light was neither a natural nor spontaneous event. Nor was it the result of aliens or religious deities of whatever faith coming to set the world straight. We did it. Humans. Ordinary humans.

On June 21st, 0th Year of the Light, at 1:33pm UDP, the Light began. The entire surface of the Earth was lit by an overwhelming white beam. From polar cap to cap, all eight billion of us were blind to the future. Every telescope on the planet overloaded. The Light lasted exactly 23 seconds, after which 128 of the world's wealthiest and most controversial figures were missing. Even more shocking, several of them had been in televised and public appearances at the time, leaving thousands witness to their disappearances.

The days that followed had conspiracy crackpots, intelligence services, religious leaders, and journalists scrambling for the truth. Nothing any of them hypothesized was remotely true, but that didn't stop the public from panicking. Huge swaths of Earth's people simply refused to work, assuming that the end of the world was at hand. They chose to spend time with loved ones instead of keeping the wheels of industry turning.

Few nations, corporations, and organized religions survived the political fallout of the Light. Even fewer survived the reappearance of some of the missing 128.

The 128 had been stripped of all of their belongings, infected with the common cold, and left to fend for themselves in slums across the world. Most of them were completely incapable of adapting to lives without privilege. Some lashed out at their new neighbors out of fear, xenophobia, or inability to cooperate. Virtually all of these members stopped appearing in the Light Project's surveillance recordings by the end of July. The handful who attempted to ingratiate themselves to the locals fared better, though not without a few deadly cases of pneumonia. All in all, we believe that 102 members of the 128 died from their conditions.

The survivors found themselves 'coincidentally' captured on video shot by travelers, documentary crews, and international aid workers. Rumors that the 128 survived the Light raced nearly as fast the skeptics denouncing the footage as hoaxes. By the time that any of the 128 had serious attempts to document them, the gravity of what had happened hit everyone.

Aliens, God, Gods, *Something* had taken these people from their gilded nests and thrown them into the gutters. Why should any of them return to power? Why should their wealth be restored to them? The Light had stripped them of everything and could do so again at any moment. The next 128 most wealthy, powerful, and cruel fled or were thrown down by their people.

The vast majority of the powerbrokers of the world were hiding, imprisoned, or dead.

Instead, a new message rose from the people: "Try Harder. Be Better. Help."

"Or something will destroy you," was implied, but rarely stated.

A decade later, the next generation has come of age. They grew up under the Old Ways and saw the Light as children. They knew of little else aside from looking for what they could do to help others, imagining the world not as a dog-eat-dog struggle, but as a world-wide network of beings who could thrive if we all just tried harder, were better, and helped.

I'm closing this log out. There's no more purpose for it. Either the Earth has been fixed, at which point no one will ever read this, or we only bought humanity a few years of global peace, the first years we've ever had in recorded history.

If you're reading this, understand what has happened: The world wasn't turned around by gods or aliens or anything supernatural. Humans made it happen. Not the Light Project. Not me. Ordinary humans who heard the message and took it to heart. People like you.

Even if you don't believe what the Light was and you don't believe me, you can believe that. Humans healed themselves. Everyday people grow the food, pave the roads, and tend the sick. All it took was ignoring the demands of those with plenty and looking after those in need.

Try Harder.

Be Better.

Help.

THE LAST BROADCAST
BY AMBER RAINEY

Victoria sat in the truck at the end of the gravel driveway looking straight ahead and ignoring the house she knew was sitting—quiet and dark—at the end of said drive. She'd been debating turning around and going back home to her little apartment in the city and her house plants. It was much safer for her in the city. She sighed, finally turning her head and looking at the house. In her mind, the house was judging her - even from this distance. She blinked away the thought, houses didn't judge but their occupants sure did. A pang of regret hit her when she thought of this particular house's last occupant. Shaking off her emotions, tucking them deep within, as usual, she turned the key and started up the truck, turning it towards the house and slowly winding her way down the drive.

Five Years Earlier

Vicki, you can't be serious!" Brandon shouted at her from the kitchen. Victoria had stomped out of the kitchen the moment her brother's rant had started. She didn't want to hear his opinion. She had wanted his approval and mentally kicked herself for thinking she was going to get it. She knew better. She could cure cancer and Brandon would find fault with it. Brandon followed her as she started up the stairs.

"Vicki!" he yelled.

Victoria stopped halfway up the stairs, whirling so fast she almost knocked Brandon backward. He had to grip the handrail harder than usual and it wobbled in place. Victoria noticed the wobble and her eyes reduced to slivers of hatred - for the house and then the whole town in general.

"My. Name. Is. Victoria," she said through gritted teeth.

A flash of annoyance crossed Brandon's face and he crossed his arms.

"*Victoria*, this is madness," he intoned in a way that made Victoria sure he was mocking her.

"I don't care, I'm done. I hate this little hick town and it's backward inhabitants and that stupid radio tower!"

Victoria turned and stomped up the rest of the stairs, going into her room and slamming the door. She plopped down on her bed and childishly placed her pillow over her ears so she could not hear her brother knocking at the door. Brandon could plead, yell, cajole, or demand but she was determined in her course of action. She was getting out of Newberg and that was final.

"Please just calm down and then make a decision. It's better for you here. Dad wouldn't have wanted you to move away," Brandon's muffled words came through the door.

Victoria screamed inwardly and then threw the pillow at the door. She could see Brandon hovering and waited until his shadow disappeared and she could hear his footsteps going back downstairs before she moved from the bed. She knew he just thought she was running away from her problems but she had finally seen the light. Her breakup was the catalyst she needed to get away from her little one pony town and make something of herself. She'd been staying for all the wrong reasons. Brandon had to see there was nothing for her if she stayed. She needed adventure and something more. Something she couldn't get in Newberg.

Victoria went to the passenger side of the truck and threw in the last bag. Brandon had reluctantly helped her pack all her belongings into the bed and tied it all down with a tarp and bungee cords. He'd been giving her the silent treatment since their last argument. Now, she was ready to go and neither sibling knew how to break the ice that had formed between them. Brandon stood awkwardly by the driver's side door with his hands in his pocket, looking out over the fields on the side of the house. If Victoria didn't know better, she would have thought his eyes were a little glassy but her brother was never one for showing any emotion other than anger. She went to stand in front of him and held out her hand - offering a handshake as their last goodbye.

Brandon surprised her by enveloping her in a bone-crushing hug. It went on far too long and she cleared her throat to get him to stop. He nodded, squeezing one last time and let her go. He reached back into his pocket and brought out a wad of cash, thrusting it towards her.

"What's this?" she asked.

"What's it look like?" he sarcastically responded.

Brandon continued holding the cash out while Victoria looked between it and him. He just gestured at it and then turned his hand over, dumping it into her palm when she reached for it. He scratched behind his ear self-consciously and smiled.

"I've been saving it for a rainy day," he offered.

Victoria cocked an eyebrow.

Brandon shrugged, "Just take it. Call me if you need anything or if you want to come home."

Victoria swore she wouldn't let him get to her but she took his words in the wrong way instead of giving him the benefit of the doubt. Her hackles went up and she swallowed any doubts she had about leaving. She nodded and got in the truck.

"See ya, Brandon."

Victoria turned the truck around and started driving towards the asphalt road at the end of the driveway. She resisted the urge to look in the rearview mirror. She didn't want to know if he was watching her leave. She didn't want to see the house she'd spent her whole life in and have second thoughts. She just wanted to be rid of her old life and jump into the new.

Present Day

Victoria swallowed the lump in her throat as she neared the house. The past couldn't be undone and yet she didn't know how to deal with the future. She nearly rolled her eyes when she stopped the truck and a lone figure stood up from the porch steps.

"Of course he would be here," she thought to herself.

Victoria took her sweet time pretending to gather her purse and phone. She took a deep breath and then pasted on her best smile. The one she only used for people who didn't deserve it but weren't smart enough to realize it wasn't genuine.

"Zac, how nice to see you," she intoned sweetly.

"Uh-huh," he nodded and grinned.

She wanted to wipe the grin off his face. Preferably with the dirt road under their feet. She would have welcomed almost anyone from Newberg but Zac. Of course, the universe seemed to have it out for her. She searched around for the reason he might be hanging around her house. No... her brother's house. It hadn't been hers in a long time.

"It will always be your home," she could hear Brandon's voice in her head.

Victoria closed her eyes, willing the memory away. She tightened her grip on her purse and then started walking up the steps to the front door. She searched around for the key kept just above the doorjamb while Zac stood behind her, saying nothing.

"It's kind of you to meet me here but I know my way around," she bit out as she unlocked the door.

Zac laughed, the sound getting under her skin and making her shiver. When he was really amused, his laugh had a rich timbre to it that always gave her goosebumps. It was one of the reasons she fell in love with him. No... she *had* loved him, she reminded herself. She'd barely been back in town a few hours and she was already settling into her old ways, letting her old feelings resurface. She had to settle the house and then get back to the city as soon as possible. She regained her composure, turning on the entry and porch lights, then swinging back towards him.

His eyes were crinkled from his amusement. She noticed his hair was beginning to gray just a little, specks of it also present in the scruff on his cheeks. His blue eyes were clear and ever as able to look straight through to her heart. Victoria jammed the fingernails of her free hand into her palm to keep from letting the thoughts of kissing him return.

"I'm here for the station," Zac said as if she were a little ignorant.

"Oh."

She mentally slapped herself. Of course. Brandon would not have left the station unmanned. He loved it more than anything in the world. Even her. She'd begged him countless times to visit her in the city and he would never leave his *baby.*

"You don't understand, Vicki. Newberg needs the station. I have responsibilities."

"The station will always be there, I won't. You could come visit occasionally. You could come to my exhibit next month. Please?" she' d begged.

She could almost hear him rolling his eyes through the phone, "I'll try but no promises. You could just come home."

She'd made a face at the phone and stuck her tongue out.

"It's not my home anymore, Brandon."

"It will always be your home, Vicki. Just come back."

She'd growled at the phone and he'd sighed and hung up. It was the last conversation they'd had before the accident.

Victoria jumped when Zac put a hand on her arm.

"You ok?" he asked with concern.

She cleared her throat, "Yeah, just peachy. I'm kind of tired from the trip. Do you need anything from me?"

"No. I was actually done a few hours ago. The programs are all cued up for the night. I was actually done about an hour ago. I noticed the truck and thought I'd wait," he grinned again.

"Thanks," she bit out, ready to slam the door in his smug face.

"It's late, have you eaten yet?" he asked hopefully.

"Goodnight, Zac."

She shoved him backward and slammed the door, resting her forehead against it.

"'Night," he called back.

Victoria closed her eyes and then turned, slumping down the door until she could rest her head against her knees. She listened for the sound of Zac's car leaving and tried not to think about her brother. The house creaked as it settled in the cooling night.

"Yeah, hello to you, too. Long time no see."

She rolled her eyes at herself. The house had always had a way of soothing her shattered nerves when she was younger. Her favorite time of the day had been at night when everyone was asleep but her. She would listen to the creaks and groans and imagine the house like an old lady settling into her favorite book. She would smile and take note of each sound, pinpointing its location. The noises would finally lull her into falling asleep, content that her family was safe under its roof.

Victoria groaned and looked at the alarm clock next to her bed. She squinted at the clock, groaning again when she saw it was just after six am. She'd been awakened by the sound of tires on the gravel driveway. She tried to close her eyes again but someone was knocking at the front door. She pulled her pillow over her head and tried to ignore it but it seemed the pounding just got louder. She heard the front door opening and sat up in alarm, looking around for anything that could be used as a weapon.

She was halfway down the stairs, creeping slowly and trying not to trigger the fourth step from the bottom. Suddenly, Zac appeared from the kitchen. He took one look at her and burst out laughing. Victoria frowned and leaned back against the handrail. It wobbled and she lost her balance, stumbling down the last few steps, just short of falling into Zac's arms. She straightened herself and mustered every inch of her annoyance into anger.

"What are you doing here? In my house?" she demanded.

He raised his eyebrows at her word choice and then sobered under her glare. He gestured to her hand.

"You going to karaoke me to death?" he bit back a laugh.

"Maybe," she bit out.

He shrugged, "Fair enough. I brought coffee and donuts. Didn't realize you were still in bed sleeping beauty."

Zac pushed some of her hair behind her shoulder and she

swatted at me. He chuckled and stepped back, holding up his hands in mock surrender. He looked her over once and headed back towards the open door.

"I'll get over to the station," he said, closing the door behind him.

She tried to ignore the chuckling she could hear through the door. She looked into the kitchen and spotted the bag of donuts on the table. She reached in, bringing out a special ham and cheese donut sandwich from Donut Palace. She sent a silent thanks to Zac for bringing her the favored treat. As if in reply, her stomach growled. She took the coffee, sandwich, and donut bag with a powdered jelly donut inside, up to her room and sat in the window seat, staring out the window across the front lawn to the door of the radio station. She pondered what to do with the house, all of Brandon's things, and most importantly, the radio station. Whatever she did, she wanted it done and over. There were too many memories and not all of them were good.

"Just how much can one person accumulate in a lifetime?" Victoria groused to herself. She'd spent the better part of the day going through the rooms that had belonged to her parents, boxing up everything and loading it into the truck. It seemed she would get through one closet only to find another chock full of stuff - none of it useful. She kept aside a few pictures and mementos but everything else was destined for the thrift shop in Newberg or the dump. She'd set aside the dump stuff on the porch. Zac had offered to take it when he'd stopped in to tell her he'd be back for the evening programming and she'd graciously accepted, loathe to make the trek to the stinkiest part of town.

She threw the last bag in the truck, finally done with the rooms, and hopped into the truck. She didn't bother locking the front door, figuring if anyone wanted to steal stuff from the house, it would save her having to get rid of it. She drove into town, politely waving back to those who recognized her and trying to avoid the stares of the others. She hopped out of the truck to help the guys at the thrift store unload. They were just about done when a familiar voice rang out.

"Well, well, well, the prodigal daughter returns." Victoria stifled a groan and turned to the speaker.

"Hey, Anne Marie," she said sweetly.

"I'm surprised you would show your face around here after you left so quickly last time. Break hearts and skip town without dealing with the fallout. Poor Zac was left all alone. I had to cheer him up," Ann Marie pouted.

Victoria was ready to smack the woman. It was a good thing she was in the truck bed. It kept her from retaliating the way she wished she had.

"I'm sure he was fine. At least he seemed that way when he brought donuts this morning over to the house," she let the insinuation hang in the air.

Anne Marie sniffed as her fake smile waned, "Well, I'm sure we will all be much better off when you are gone back to your little hovel in the city. Studios are so... quaint."

"Bye, Anne Marie," Victoria waved cheerily, turning her back and finishing the task of unloading the donations.

She could feel Anne Marie glaring daggers at her back but she ignored her, jumping out of the truck bed and getting in the cab. She started the truck and spun the tires just a little, kicking up dust and trying not to smile too big when Anne Marie coughed and stomped away. She drove back to the house, willing the implications of what Anne Marie said about her cheering up Zac not to linger too long in her mind.

When she returned home, Victoria suppressed the urge to scream when she spied Zac's truck sitting in front of the house. It took every ounce of her willpower not to turn around and leave. He was the last person she wanted to talk to at the moment. She slowed down as much as she dared and took her time gathering her things before taking a deep breath and getting out of the truck. Zac had stood from his position of sitting on the porch and was awkwardly rooting around in the dirt at his feet. Victoria groaned inwardly. She knew that look on his face and she was desperate not to let it get to her.

"Beaux called," Zac said by way of explanation for his presence.

"Beaux should mind his own business!"

"Look, Anne Marie and I—"

Victoria held up a hand to silence him. Zac paused mid-sentence, still looking like a puppy being scolded for bad behavior.

"I don't want to know, Zac. It isn't my business and I don't care."

Victoria swept past him and up the stairs.

"Victoria, please let me explain," Zac pleaded.

Victoria stopped at the door but didn't turn around.

"Zac, I just want to finish here and go home. Can you just stay out of my way?"

After a moment, Zac sighed, "All right."

She could hear Zac get in his truck and drive away. She continued into the house, swiping angrily at the tear falling down her cheek. She shouldn't care about anything Zac did. They were not a couple anymore. She ignored the nagging part of her brain that kept asking her whose fault it was and stubbornly pushed Zac out of her mind. She had work to do.

After several days of cleaning the house, avoiding only her brother's room, Victoria felt a great sense of accomplishment. She had successfully cleared the house, avoided most of the people in town, and steadfastly dodged Zac every time he came to rotate the broadcasts for the radio station. There were only two hurdles left. She had to deal with Brandon's room and she had to shut down the radio station. She had avoided the former out of sheer panic and the latter because it meant talking to Zac. She weighed her options carefully. She decided it was time to formally say goodbye to her brother and she stood outside his bedroom door looking at it as if a lion would jump out and eat her the moment it opened. Silently berating herself for her cowardice, she turned the knob and let the door slowly creek open.

Brandon's room was the picture of neatness. It was surprisingly sparse compared to the jam-packed rooms of the rest of the house. Brandon had always hated clutter but had been loathed to get rid of their parents' mess when they had died. She now understood the reluctance to part with things that reminded you of someone you'd lost. However, Victoria had no choice. She didn't want to live in the house way out in the country and alone. It meant she had to remove everything so that she could sell the house. Victoria stepped into the room and sat on the bed, overwhelmed at the prospect of dealing with Brandon's things. She looked around the room but her eyes really weren't focused on anything. She finally realized what she was staring at — an envelope sat on the dresser with her name on the front. Frowning, she stood and retrieved the item.

With shaky hands, Victoria opened the envelope. She looked at Brandon's handwriting with blurry eyes, sitting back on the bed, and taking a deep breath. She wiped her eyes and cheeks and began reading.

Vicki,

(I just had to get you one last time.)

Victoria chuckled and shook her head. Brandon always had to poke the sleeping dragon. She continued reading.

If you are reading this, it means I'm dead. That sounds very cliché and more like a movie trope than a serious goodbye letter to my little sister. Anyway, I wanted to tell you a few things that I never told you while I was alive and a letter seems the best way to do it. First, I am proud of you. I've always been proud of you, even when you didn't think I cared — I was silently cheering you on. You can do anything you set your mind to and I believe in you. Never lose your spirit. Second, you need to talk to Zac. Now, before you go burning the letter over this sentence, hear — or rather read — me out. There is a reason I never wanted to leave the station for too long and Zac can explain it better than I can in a letter. Beyond that, Zac loves you. He never stopped. I know why y'all fought and you left town. You can deny it to yourself all you want but I know he's the right person for you. Give it another go. Don't let stubborn pride get in the way. I did that and unless my life drastically changes, I'm going to die alone. Don't read too much into that last sentence — I always carry you in my heart so I'm not truly alone. Finally, if I know you, my room has sat untouched for days. You can get rid of it all. You've already found all the important papers and my room just has some clothes and those old records you always ribbed me about because they were scratched and static sounding.

Love you forever,

Brandon

PS I mean it Victoria—talk to Zac!

Victoria read the letter a few more times before letting it drop onto the bed. She lay back on the bed and let herself sob. She could practically hear him talking to her through his words - his personality and gently chiding speech coming through loud and clear. She missed him in a way she had never really missed her parents and that made her cry harder. She'd lost so much in her life and Brandon was right, she'd pushed Zac away for stupid reasons. She doubted Brandon spoke the truth about Zac still loving her. He seemed like he'd moved on just fine without her. Sure, he'd tried to get her to talk to him that first year after she'd left town, but she had never given him a chance. Victoria groaned. She would have to talk to Zac and it was something she had promised herself she would not do while she dealt with the house and the station.

Victoria watched Zac's truck coming up the driveway from her spot halfway up the radio tower. She knew she was being a coward, there were much easier ways of talking to him but she perversely wanted to see if he would notice her and what he would do if he did. She didn't have to wait long for her answer. Zac got out of the truck and immediately looked up at the tower, shielding his eyes from the setting sun. She was too far away to see his exact expression but she could tell he shook his head. He walked to the tower, glanced up again and started climbing. Victoria got an odd sense of satisfaction at his actions but tried to tamp down the rest of her feelings. She was just going to talk to him — nothing was going to change. Zac finally made it to her section of the tower and swung his long legs through the space next to her and dangled them down. For a long moment, both of them sat on the tower, staring at the setting sun in the distance. After a while, Zac looked over at Victoria and waited for her to tell him what was on her mind.

"Stop staring."

Zac shrugged, "Any particular reason you are up here? What's on your mind?"

The little thrill she got when he said that was almost too much. He still knew her better than she knew herself sometimes. It was both wonderful and frightening at the same time.

"Brandon says I need to talk to you about the station," Victoria muttered.

Despite her lowered volume, Zac grunted in acknowledgment. Victoria waited for him to respond with something more but he just returned to staring at the sunset. She could see his jaw twitching and he scratched behind his ear twice, a knowingly tell that he was nervous. Victoria frowned. Zac didn't usually mince words but she could tell he didn't want to say something to offend her. Victoria's patience was running thin.

"Just spit out, Zac," she growled.

"All right, you can't sell the station."

Victoria nearly choked, "What?"

Zac looked at her with a combination of sadness and desperation, "You can't sell the station. Or the house. Rent the house out to me and I'll see that the station keeps running. I can't pay you much but I will make sure it stays fixed up and clean."

"You have a house and a farm already."

"I do. I think I can handle both."

Victoria scoffed, "You didn't want to leave that damn farm five years ago. Nothing you've said so far makes me believe you want to leave it now. Why do you want to run the station?"

Zac looked chagrined, "I do love the farm but the town needs the station. Do you know why Brandon poured his life's work into this place?"

Victoria looked away, wincing at the memory of her brother putting the station above his family. Truthfully, she was still mad at him for never visiting her in the city and it felt wrong to somehow still blame him, even after his death.

"Victoria?"

She looked back at Zac.

"He loved you and he loved this town. He felt responsible for everyone. He always had a bit of a savior complex, even when we were kids."

Victoria laughed. It was true — Brandon always wanted to play the hero. She always had to play the damsel in distress. It had irked her to no end. She would have rather been the ogre attacking the mob of angry villagers. Brandon would chide her about not being ladylike and she would stick out her tongue at him and *save* herself. She didn't need anyone to take care of her. Truth be told, she often needed to be helped out of scrapes she'd gotten herself into and she just didn't want to admit it. Brandon had always been there to help. She just didn't understand what was so important about a radio station in a podunk town like Newberg.

Zac continued, "If the station goes dark, the town will die off. Everyone will lose their homes and land. The farm will be gone. My brothers won't have jobs anymore. It will all be lost. Just another ghost town on the map."

"Why on earth does all that depend on this stupid radio station?" she huffed.

"There is a big corporation who wants to put in a new station within a mile, then buy off the town and put in a wind farm. Trouble is, they don't want to pay fair prices for it and most of us don't want to leave. Government told them, as long as the station is running and observant of the rules, they can't put in the farm. Brandon made sure to keep it up for the rest of us. He didn't have to — they offered him a lot to quit, but he told them he couldn't be bought. Newberg needs the station."

Victoria turned away again. It all made sense. Brandon valued people and relationships. He saved every penny he made. She was the only person he ever spent anything on and when she got older, she would often just put it in a box and save it to spend on him. All his mysterious *"the town needs me"* comments made a lot more sense. She swiped at the tears falling down her cheeks, so tired of crying and feeling like it would never end. She stiffened slightly when she felt Zac's arm go around her but relaxed into him easily and rested her head against his shoulder. He squeezed lightly and she nodded, silently thanking him for his kindness. They sat on the radio tower until she stopped sobbing and the stars came out, neither saying a word, both lost in their own thoughts.

The next morning, Victoria sat at the kitchen table with Brandon's note and the important papers he had left. She struggled with herself. She could sell the house and close down the station but it would mean betraying a whole town of people. The people she grew up around and liked — even if some of them did get on her nerves. The alternatives were between her staying herself or renting to Zac. None of her options felt very appealing. She didn't know if she could stay in town and see Zac every day. His closeness brought up emotions she thought she'd left behind. She could now admit she ran off to the city to get away from him. It had never been about freedom. She had that in Newberg. She'd just tried to run away from her heart. She startled when she heard a knock on the door.

"Morning," Zac said, sheepishly holding up a coffee and a donut bag.

Victoria took it and stepped aside so he could come into the house. Zac looked around and noticed the paperwork on the table.

"So you're selling then?" he asked with trepidation.

Victoria shrugged, "I haven't decided yet."

Zac nodded. Victoria waited for him to say anything else but then sighed and turned away to sit back at the table. After a moment, Zac sat down and looked at her. When she ignored him, he put a hand on hers. Victoria closed her eyes, gathered her strength, and looked up at him with a questioning look.

"There's one more thing you need to know. Come with me?" he asked.

Victoria nodded. Zac stood up and led her out of the house, across the drive to the radio station door. He unlocked the door and ushered her inside.

"Have a seat," he said.

Victoria sat in the deejay chair. She hadn't been inside the station in years - not since she had played at being a deejay herself. She remembered enjoying the ability to play whatever she wanted, being in control. For a brief moment, she thought she would actually enjoy being the owner of an entire radio station. She would be her own boss. The pay wasn't immense but it was liveable. She and Zac could... she shut down those thoughts immediately. She knew she had burned that bridge long ago. She jumped in surprise when Zac tapped her shoulder.

"Earth to Victoria," he joked.

"Haha," she responded with a small measure of humor in her voice.

Zac held out earphones. Victoria put them on and then looked at him expectantly. He nodded and started the recording. He watched as she listened to Brandon's voice. After several minutes, Victoria took off the headphones and opened and shut her mouth several times, at a loss for words. Zac nodded.

"I'll let you think on it," he said.

Victoria watched as he walked out of the station. She fiddled with the headphone wires, deep in thought. She started the recording over and listened to it again. As her brother's soothing tone washed over her, she felt a sense of calm she hadn't felt in years. She knew what she needed to do.

Victoria walked out of the station to the now-familiar sight of Zac sitting on the front steps. He had both of his hands hanging between his legs and his head was bent. He looked as if the weight of the world was on his shoulders. As Victoria approached, he lifted his head and ran a hand through his hair. She was careful to keep a neutral expression on her face and she could tell Zac was ready to accept defeat. She sat down next to him.

"I've made up my mind," she said without looking at him.

"And?"

Victoria waited. She tested out the words in her head before saying them aloud. She wanted to make sure they were right. She could feel Zac tense beside her, waiting patiently for the killing blow. Deciding she had tortured him long enough, she looked at him and smiled.

"I'm keeping the house and the station," she said quickly.

Zac whooped with joy, standing and scooping her up into a bear hug so tight she thought she would suffocate. He set her down and stared into her eyes with such joy it made her heart skip a beat. After a minute, the heat between them became noticeable and Zac blushed. Victoria started to pull away but Zac swooped in and kissed her. The kiss was filled with all the longing and pent up passion the two of them had suppressed for five years. Victoria was hesitant at first but then gave in to what she really wanted and kissed him back. After what seemed like an eternity, they broke the kiss and Zac rested his forehead against her.

"Wha... what about Anne Marie?" Victoria asked breathlessly.

"You stubborn... I tried to tell you, there was never anything between us. Believe me, not for her lack of trying. That woman is relentless. But there has never been anyone but you. Please give me another chance?" Zac pleaded.

Victoria thought for a moment and then smiled widely at him. For the first time since she had left, she finally found herself feeling peaceful instead of restless. She'd always thought her home was in the city but now she knew she was where she belonged. She kissed him again and then hugged him. She pulled away and put him at arm's length.

"What is it?" he worried.

"We will have to go to the city and get my things."

"Done!"

Victoria laughed at how quickly he responded.

"And Zac?"

"Yeah?"

"I'm a radio deejay, not a farmer," she declared.

Zac guffawed. He nodded his head and grabbed her hand.

"Darling, you can be anything you want as long as you are staying," he teased but she could hear the hesitation in his voice.

She nodded, "I'm staying."

Zac whooped aloud again and Victoria laughed.

"Can I take you to dinner to celebrate?" he asked.

Victoria nodded and walked off toward the station.

"Where are you going?" he asked.

"I have to start a broadcast and then I'll be right there," she called over her shoulder.

"I'll wait here then," he responded.

That evening, the town of Newberg tuned in to their favorite local radio station. They were surprised that the station programming that night wasn't their normal easy listening but their former deejay's soothing tones reassuring them everything was going to be okay.

"Good evening, Newberg, and welcome to The Last Broadcast. Now friends, don't worry, this isn't our last station broadcast, just my last one before introducing you to your new deejay. She isn't exactly new, but I know you will be in good hands. Please welcome, Victoria. She will be my replacement in every way and she will make sure the town stays safe from the clutches of corporate greed. We might be a small light in the vast expanse of radio airwaves but our reach knows no bounds when we stick together. The light she will bring to the town will not be ignored. Let the people stand together and we will overcome. Newberg is strong. Victoria is just the right person to lead the town in standing firm against those who would wish to wipe us from the map. She will keep the station going. I have every faith in her. So, my dear friends, I sign off from my time as your protector and pass the baton to her. May her light guide you in the darkest of times."

CAMPFIRE
BY MARSHALL MILLER

Reylie King looked up at the bright new star in the evening sky. To say the light was brilliant would be a disservice to the distant future generations that have only the written record to explore this moment of discovery. It seemed a small thing from the vast distances of Outer Space, but Reylie knew the original source had significant influence. With this vessel, a light of hope was returned to the people.

Reylie brushed back her long bronze hair. She had found a gray strand just this morning. Reylie smiled as she realized that even in these days of great scientific discovery, time and aging marched on.

Reylie heard the back screen door open then lightly shut and knew it was her Mother Jeanie coming to join her late-night observations while careful to not wake Reylie's children.

"Are the kids asleep, Mom?"

"Yes, dear. Although the Twins kept whispering about sneaking out to their treehouse."

Her mother linked arms with her. Reylie saw the gray in her mother's hair and felt the pang that someday she would be gone, passing like Granddad and Grandma. There was a double feeling of loss as, without the man known as the Tinkerer, the light in the sky would not exist.

"If Granddad could only see the Sky Tunnel on its first use," said Reylie.

"Oh, trust me, daughter. He is looking at it from an alternate reality we call the Afterlife. This project proves that other dimensions and universes exist, one of which must be Heaven." Her mother patted her arm. "But had you and your brother Ron not fiddled with that game he built, and disappeared, then came back, we would never be at this point in history."

Reylie tried to smile but could not. Whenever she thought about that time in her life, she remembered both the joys plus the fears and regrets. She had left this reality at age fourteen and returned at age nineteen. Her oldest, Marianne, was the result everyone tried to conceal. Now, as Reylie was nearing forty, she often mused 'what if.' Then the reality that Marianne would not exist had not everything happened 'just so' would poke her in the heart. Her daughter was away at college, studying to follow in her step-father's footsteps.

Jeannie looked towards the large family home which had once been Grandad and Grandma King's house.

"I had better check on those two grandsons of mine. Twin boys, Jack and John, who would have thought in your late twenties you would have more kids, after..." Jeanie left the rest unsaid. Reylie coming back, pregnant from some other reality was shock enough. Trying to readapt to a time out of mind after her violent adventure was not smooth.

Then she met Michael Mann. Twin boys soon followed. Now age ten, they were double joys in her life. The thought of her husband made Reylie look up again.

"Funny how I met and married a man who would help

complete Grandad's final dream."

Her mother patted her arm.

"Mike will come back after they fire up the Sky Tunnel. Then I'll guarantee he'll never leave."

"Mom, I just worry some of them will get sucked into the vortex as I and others were with Grandad's game."

" That was then, Reylie, this is now. They know what they are doing."

Jeanie kissed her daughter on her cheek.

"You stay out here and watch. Try to use some that telepathy to talk to Mike."

Reylie finally smiled.

"Wished that rumor was real. Ron and I only brought back some out of sync artifacts. And memories, of course."

Reylie's mother smiled and walked to the house back door. Reylie looked once again at the bright new star, It seemed to flicker a bit like a flame. To some, it was a flame of hope for a dying Earth. To Reylie, it was a flame from a campfire which introduced her and Ron into a strange new existence. Not for the first time did her mind wander to a time past when she and her brother were in a campfire. Literally.

Five male figures were hunkered down around the campfire in New Mexico Territory. In different places and different times, the five would have been called Highwaymen, Road agents, or Bushrangers. In the Southwest, Desperados or Banditos would be more appropriate. The oldest one, nicknamed by some as Greybeard but known as Uncle Jake to the group, looked across the campfire to the massive shape cleaning an oversized revolver. Uncle Jake was taller than most and robust in build, but he looked very average compared to his nephew, Barnabas McCain. Due to the bearded and dark-haired man's size, the name Bar, as in bear, was used as a shorthand.

"Bar, I don't know why you don't get a cartridge version of those Coult Root revolvers of yours. It would make loadin' and cleanin' a lot easier."

Bar kept wiping his revolvers as he spoke.

"As you brother James, my father, said, if it ain't busted, don't fix it."

Uncle Jake snorted.

"Yes, he did say that. And you are as stubborn as he was. You are definitely your father's son."

Bar held up the pistol to the campfire light.

"These two cap and ball Coults designed by friend Root have seen me right good service for some nine yar. When you shoot something with their forty-four caliber bullets backed with sixty grains of black powder, it stays shot." Bar glanced over at his Uncle.

"And they have better steel than that old Coult Walker you have. You still need to get that busted cylinder chamber fixed from that overload you used. That won't happen with these newer sidehammer ones."

The Olsen Twins, slender toe headed eighteen-year-olds, tried not to laugh. They heard near-duplicate discussions between uncle and nephew at least once a week. The year the Olsens had spent with the group had also taught them that it was best not to joke or interfere with such family interactions. Bar's sense of humor was limited, to say the least.

The fifth person sharing the campfire looked up from sharpening his stiletto. Cajun Armand Bergeron had been with the McCains for some two years. The tall and lanky former resident of New Orleans first met them at the Second Battle of El Paso Del Norte in December 1865. Just over a month later, and the Second Mexican – American War officially ended. However, not for the McCains. And thus, it had not stopped for those who rode with them. A small smile formed on Armand's mustachioed mouth. The Cajun had often marveled at the rough way the elder and younger member of the McCain clan demonstrated their affection for each other.

"I'll get my Walker fixed when we have the time and wherewithal to do it. It's not like we have been able to spend a lot of time in towns. Hells Bells, it's been a good month since I had a young resident of a bordello wash my-"

A bolt of energy exploded into the campfire, sending a metal coffee pot perched on its edge flying. Hot coals and small flaming sticks landed around the five campsite occupants, sending them leaping and scurrying from their seats.

Then two figures seemed to drop into the remains of the fire from out of thin air.

"What the..." Bar yelled out as he grabbed his huge Bowie knife. The two figures stumbled from the once center of the campfire, yelping and screaming as they slapped at their smoldering clothes.

"Reylie!Are you okay?" A young male voice called out.

"Yes, Ron," the female voice answered. Then a large bellow froze them in their tracks.

"Stop right there and reach for the sky," commanded Bar. "Who the Hell are you and where in Hell did you come from?"

Bar saw a young, comely young girl on the edge of womanhood jerk her head in his direction. He noticed Reylie had long bronze hair and was wearing some kind of skirt and stockings. A familiar face from his past flashed from his memory before he shoved it back and away from his consciousness.

"She's my sister, Reylie, buddy," the young male called Ron tried to menacingly growl out. The dark-haired boy soon to be a man started to reach for something in a slung pack he wore. Ron found out just how fast the big man could move as Bar put Reylie's brother on his back with a swipe of a bear paw sized hand. Bar then stepped on the young male's chest.

"Easy, Boy. Take that pack off slow and careful…"

A screaming Banshee slammed into Bar's side. The surprise and force of the attack knocked Bar off balance and forced him to stumble back. A red rage began to take over until the massive man saw it was a bronze haired young lady who had slammed into him.

"You stay off my brother, you big-assed bully!"

Everything seemed to freeze in time and space. Then Uncle Jake began to laugh and yell.

"Whoooweee! We just had a spitfire fall into our campfire."

Tom, one of the Olsen Twins, found his voice.

"Did you see that? They rode that lightning bolt down like a couple of demons."

"Are they Haints?" asked his twin Tim.

" We'll find out," growled out Bar. "First, don't hit me again, girl or I will hit back." The tall and wide beaded man watched as Ron slowly regained his feet.

"Hand the pack here, Boy. You have a Coult Navy aimed at your spine." He nodded towards Tom as he spoke.

Ron's face flushed and his mouth set in a stubborn line. Armand was a good student of human reactions and saw that youthful stubbornness was about to lead to bloodshed. He stepped up to Reylie, slouch hat in hand.

"Mon Cherie, no one means you and your brother harm. Please just follow Bar's requests. You must admit falling from the sky into a fire is far from normal."

Reylie examined the Cajun and made the snap decision that he was the least violent of the five men around the campfire. Her Granddad had given her some advice based on his secretive government service.

'If you are a stranger in a strange land, make a friend.'

Reylie forced a smile as she spoke.

"Yes, I can see us knocking over your coffee pot could be upsetting."

Reylie then addressed her brother.

"Ron, please give-Bar-your school pack. I'll give him mine. We are in his camp."

Ron glared at his sister and at Bar. He looked at the large Bowie in the man's hand and grunted as he shoved the pack towards him.

"Here," he spat. "If you take anything, I'll call the cops."

All the men but Armand chuckled at the attempt of defiance.

"If you mean a sheriff or marshal, the nearest one will be in Mesilla or Las Cruces," said Uncle Jake. "Both are miles away."

Bar grabbed Ron's school backpack and unceremoniously dumped the contents in the light of the damaged campfire.

"Huh. What do we have here?" Bar held up a stainless steel pistol. "Now I know what you were trying to grab, boy."

Armand had taken it upon himself to more respectfully examine Reylies backpack. As he did, Uncle Jake called out to Bar.

"Toss me that revolver. It looks nickel or silver plated."

His nephew complied, then finished pawing through the contents of Ron's pack.

"A box of bullets here, Uncle. Lable says....357 Magnum. What is that? You're the odd gun guy."

Uncle Jake answered with a frown as he tried to use some bifocals to read the lettering on the three-inch barrel revolver.

"Something like-Ruger. That looks German. Magnum sounds French. And it has some weird swingout cylinder." The grey-bearded man looked over the top of his glasses at Ron.

"Where'd you get this son?"

"I was holding it for somebody," Ron grumbled back.

" Holding sounds like stealing. Someone else owns this gun, right?"

"It's a prototype, a test gun," Reylie blurted out. She knew Ron and her were in danger of being in even more trouble if she did not think on her feet.

"My Granddad made it. He is known as the Tinkerer, as he is always building weird things."

"And he knows you are here, with this hogleg?" asked Uncle Jake.

"No," answered Ron. "Look, it is all one big mess and accident that you would not believe even if you could."

"Well, you did fall into our campfire from God knows where," interjected Bar. "It's getting late, and the five of us have an important task in the morning. So my Uncle and I are going to have a short powwow and decide what we are going to do with you two youngins."

The two men stepped out of earshot into the darkness as Armand handed Reylie back her pack.

"You have school books and many-colored drawings," said the Cajun. "You are studying to be an artist?"

Reylie smiled as she answered. Stranger in a strange land, she said to herself.

"Among other things. I wanted to study medicine also."

The young lady glanced into the darkness.

"Now, I don't know. I don't even know where we are."

"New Mexico Territory," answered Armand. " We are in the foothills of the Potrillo Mountains. Las Cruces and Mesilla are not that far from here. Maybe a days ride or so."

Reylie was always good at history and geography. She quickly racked her brains for details as she looked at her brother. He was standing sullen, arms folded on the other side of the dying campfire. Right now, Ron would be of little help.

"Fort Bliss Texas is what, about fifty miles away?" she asked.

"Yes, Reylie is your name? Fort Seldon and Fillmore are closer. All the forts are near to protect people from the Apache and the occasional Comanche."

"And Messican bandits," an eavesdropping Tim, the other Olsen Twin, commented.

"That is true," said Armand, "However, since the Second Mexican War and the Treaty of Sante Fe, we are supposed to be on friendlier terms and giving common cause against raiding Indians."

Reylie was trying to rack her brain for a means to ask questions about times and dates without arousing more suspicions when Bar and Uncle Jake stepped back into the dim campfire light.

"Okay," said Bar, "you two stay and travel with us in the morning. No way am I gonna have the death of a young lady on my conscience. We Texans don't work that way. But you will follow MY orders. Got it?"

"Yes, Sir," answered Reylie. Ron grunted and nodded his head affirmative.

"Where's you say you youngins are from?" asked Uncle Jake.

"Seattle, Washington." Reylie choose the most significant city she figured would be known in this-time? Place? It was all so confusing.

"Washington Territory? You folks missionaries or something? After the Negro Relocation Act, I heard the only people wanting to stay there are rough sailors, fur traders, and nigger loving missionaries."

Nigger was not a word Reylie would generally allow in her presence. But she had no power or influence around this waning campfire.

"My family does work with-Blacks." Reylie carefully replied. "They work with the church people, but are not missionaries."

No way could Reylie explain a divorced mother who worked as a teacher at the local parochial school while her father was an auto mechanic and sometime over the road truck driver. The explanations would be meaningless to this band of-outlaws?

"Blacks. Huh," growled Bar. "Bible thumpers. No John Brown abolitionists among you, are there? Hear tell some fled up towards Canada."

"John Brown's body lies a molding in his grave," Ron interjected having found his voice.

Bar spat. "He does. But some of his bitch- excuse me, some of his followers escaped Montgomery and the Mexican War. I shoot those niggerlovers on sight."

Bar examined the two siblings more before speaking.

"There's a spare horse we took off a dead Mexican who was trying to bushwack us. It's tied up with the others. You ride, yes?"

"She rides the best," replied Ron.

"Okay. In the morning, you saddle up and ride double. There," Bar pointed to a pile of a saddle and bags. "There are blankets and such. Make yourselves a bed. You can do that, right?"

"Yes, Sir," the siblings answered in unison.

"Go easy on the waterskin. It has to last us another day."

In a few minutes, Ron and Reylie had laid a blanket on the ground and used another threadbare companion as their cover. Reylie pulled off her tights and folded them up into her backpack. She put her running shoes back on and used her light windbreaker as a pillow. Reylie had made a quick trip to a nearby bush to relieve herself under the watchful eye of her brother. She thought she saw Uncle Jake maneuvering the others away from Ron and her to give them some privacy. Reylie surmised, the older man knew the two siblings would not runoff into an unfamiliar night.

"I'm hungry," whispered Ron.

"Well, if you hadn't hidden in Granddad's workshop and screwed with his 'game' we wouldn't be here," scolded Reylie.

"I had to. Raymond and the others ratted on me. Here I was hiding the pistol for them and Bam! They give me up to the Cops."

"I told you not to trust them. But what does your little sister know."

They lay in silence for a moment, then Ron whispered again.

"I didn't mean to twist that dial in the middle of that table. I was just…"

"Scared. And angry. Right?" said his sister.

"Yeah. And now look at us. In some science fiction movie. Time travel."

"Yes and no. This past is-different. I don't think Bar and the others had a Civil War. Those pistols looked 1860's but no mention of the Confederacy, Blue, and Grey."

"Well, they had two Mexican Wars. And John Brown."

"Negro Relocation Act," Reylie shivered a bit as she spoke. "Just like they did to the Tribes. Forced them to move when they wanted the space."

"So they stopped slavery without a war, but still treat Blacks, African Americans as scum," said Ron

Reylie let out a long sigh.

"My head hurts."

Just then they heard a growling voice.

"My Pa said he'd tan my hide if I didn't sleep when he told me to," said Bar.

"Yes, Sir," the siblings answered. They lay quiet, and then Reylie snuggled up to her brother.

"Goodnight, Johnboy," she said with a trace of a giggle.

'You're not funny, Reylie."

Uncle Jake and Bar set out their bedrolls and readied for sleep.

"What do you think, nephew?" Uncle Jake asked.

"I think we have to be careful so we can still hit the stagecoach tomorrow. We need the Messican money your friend said was on it to keep us going."

"If Hank says the Butterfield Stage carries Mexican Gold, it does. He was a Texas Ranger too, you know."

"It's a question of doing on our part, not what is on the stage. All coaches out here carry people, goods, and money." Bar looked towards the now quiet siblings.

"The big question is those two getting in the way of us doin' what we aim to. Like I said, I don't want to dump anyone out in the middle of nowhere."

"Especially a young girl who reminds you of someone," said Uncle Jake. Bar grunted.

"You saw that, too, huh? She does look like my younger sister Judith, not to mention my wife, Rebekah."

Both men stood silent at the mention of the two deceased loved ones. Uncle Jake finally broke the silence.

"I don't remember your father and my brother, James, ever having to threaten you with tanning your butt for not going to sleep."

"They don't know that, Uncle. And he always worked my ass off anyways."

Uncle Jake chuckled.

"I think the fact you were always big for your age gave him pause."

"Whatever the reason. Now, time for us to sleep. Bleary eyes ruin good shooting."

"Right as always, nephew. Right as rain."

A light firearm report woke Reylie and Ron.

"Sounded like a little twenty-two," opined Reylie. The two siblings rose to their feet and looked around, The Sun was just beginning to poke up over the eastern horizon. Uncle Jake came walking into the camp with a grin on his face and a massive jackrabbit suspended by his left hand.

'Quick rabbit breakfast," said Uncle Jake as he walked towards the campfire. Someone had stoked it with fresh pieces of wood.

"That is one big rabbit," said Ron.

"They grow them big around here," replied the graybeard. "You two get over here and help me cut up this meat. We need to eat fast and get moving."

Reylie stepped closer and examined the carbine held by Uncle Jake.

"Winchester?" she asked.

"Got your guns mixed up, missy. Smith and Wesson made these lever actions Volcanics. Their rocket ball ammunition is weak, makes for an excellent rabbit killer, not much more."

"I thought Smith and Wesson make pistols," stated Ron as he walked closer.

"They also do. Smith and Wesson now make stouter Wesson Repeaters in thirty-two and larger rimfire. Not to mention centerfire guns starting this year."

"1867?" Reylie quickly asked,

"No, this year. Not last year."

Uncle Jake did short work of skinning the large Jack without a blade by yanking the fur and skin up over the head. He then produced two sharp tomahawks.

"Here. You two do know how to cut up game?"

"Yes, Sir," replied Reylie. "Our granddad and dad showed us how ."

"Well, cut this Jack up, find some sticks for spits and roast it. Times a wasting. Everyone works."

As Ron and Reylie watched the roasting meat, they held a low volume conference.

"1868? Who was President then, Rey?"

"Andrew Johnson or Grant. However, no Civil War, so Lincoln could still be alive."

"But then why no Emancipation Proclamation?" asked Ron.

"Lincoln originally thought of sending all the former Slaves back to Africa or to a third country. He did not believe Blacks and Whites could live together."

"This is screwed. This group hates Mexicans, Blacks, probably Asians also. And we're stuck with them."

"For now, Ron. Until Granddad finds us."

Ron snorted.

"Oh, sure. Just like that. Across time and space."

Bar walked up to them with his slouch hat in his hand and looked at the roasting meat.

"You ain't burning breakfast, are you? "

"No, Sir," replied Reylie.

"Good. After we eat, you saddle up. We have a ways to go before Noon. And we have to be at a special spot by then. If you two can't keep up, you get left behind. Got it?"

"Yes, Sir," the brother and sister answered in unison.

"And, Boy. Uncle Jake will hold on to your pistol for now. " The oversized gunman paused for a moment, then asked," What is your family name?"

"King," answered Reylie.

"As in King Ranch in the lower valley of Texas?"

"Distant cousins."

"Huh. Interesting. Maybe after we're done, we'll get you on a stagecoach, send you there. Better off than with all the Niggers in Washington."

Bar turned and went back to talk with Uncle Jake. Ron looked at his sister.

"Quick thinking, Reylie."

"From here on out, I hope being fast on our feet will be enough. This is not a world for the weak and slow."

Bar walked over to his Uncle.

"Just thought to ask those two their last name. They say it's King. Distant cousins of the Texas Kings."

"Huh. That still don't explain where the two came from, how they fell into our camp, Bar."

"Right now, Uncle Jake, I have more important things to think about. Let's break our fast and hit the trail. We need to be in place or all this is just so much cow flop."

They were about ready to join the road a half-hour later. Uncle Jake divided the rabbit meat and gave the two young people a corn dodger, straight out of a well know cinematic classic from their world. Then it was hop to it, saddle the horses and break camp. Reylie could tell Bar was surprised as to how quickly she and Ron bridled and saddled the strange to them Mexican pony. Reylie had just enough extra time to ask Bar if she could look at his horse pistol as he loaded the twin weapons.

"Coult's Root Patent," Reylie said as she read the inscription just below the thick cylinder on the left side. "I thought he spelled his name, Colt."

"Nope," Barr replied. "He added Root's name on these side hammer pistols to let people know they were different Coults from his Dragoons."

Reylie met the eyes of the bear of a man as he finished loading the last cylinder chamber.

"You've used these-Coults- a lot."

"Since I got them when I joined the Texas Rangers in 1859."

"Why did you join?" asked Reylie.

"To join my uncle in fighting Comanche and Messican. Then the Montgomery Seige started, and off we went to kill niggers and Brownites."

"Brownites?"

"John Brown family and friends. Lincoln gets the Great Compromise passed to free the niggers in ten years, but John Brown takes Montgomery, Alabama and holds it for ransom." Bar spit into the New Mexico dirt.

"Give'em an inch, they want a mile. Come on. Time to hit the trail, young missy."

Several minutes later, and the five men and two young adults were mounted. Ron rode double behind Reylie as she was the better rider. Bar moved his mount up and down the line, checking the riders. He paused near Reylie and Ron's mount.

"How'd you two become so involved with guns," he asked.

"Our Granddad and Father," answered Reylie.

"Granddad was the Tinkerer," added Ron. "He took us shooting so he could tinker with new ideas for guns and machines."

Bar grunted.

"I'd like to meet him. Now, it's time to leave."

Bar led the file of slouch hated riders in a fast walk down a well-used trail. The Sun was poking up over the Organ and San Andres Mountains to the east. With no other so-called cowboy hats around, Uncle Jake had fashioned some Admiral hats from leftover newspaper to provide some protection from the hot New Mexico sun. As the Sun rose in the sky, the trail widened. The band was soon moving at a trot. They all rode in silence, other than the occasional horse sound. Reylie and Ron managed to keep their cell phones hidden as they had been in their pockets, not the backpacks. There was no telling what the five armed riders would have thought or reacted had they seen an active cellphone. Witchcraft might have been the accusation.

Reylie had an old windup wristwatch that could pass as something familiar to Bar and Company, so they left it alone. It was set at Pacific Standard Time, so she added an hour for being in New Mexico. Thus the young lady figured it was 9:00 AM as they worked their way out of the foothills.

Bar called a halt once, signed for silence, looked and listened. Five minutes later, they started moving again. Uncle Jake noticed Reylies puzzled look and nudged his mount close enough to whisper.

"Watching for Apaches. They sometimes sneak around and raid."

Reylie nodded and then began to try and remember her history. Apaches were nasty at times but not the horsemen the Comanche were. The Washingtonian did not want to run into the 1860s versions of either.

The band kept moving as the Sun climbed higher in the sky. Reylie and Ron shared lukewarm water from a canteen, sipping tiny amounts based on Bar's comment that it had to last another day. The horses let out a snort once in a while, flicked flies away with their tails when they slowed down in the descent.

Reylie figured it was about 11:00 AM when the trail leveled out, and she glimpsed what looked like a wide dirt road about a half-mile ahead. Bar halted the group and waved the riders up to his lead spot. When they were close enough to hear his low voice, Bar pointed to the roadway.

"Butterfield Stage Route. The Butterfield Overland Mail Line has operated since 1858. There is at least one Concord stagecoach heading West and one East each week. Occasionally a cheap mud coach is added if there enough cheaper paying customers or some buffalo hunters need a ride."

"Why a separate coach for buffalo hunters?" Asked Ron. Bar and Uncle Jake laughed.

"If you were ever around any hidemen, you'd know," replied Uncle Jake. "You think we get ripe smelling from no bath, buff hunters kill, gut and skin the buffalo on the plains. They do not change clothes, do not bathe until they are done filling up some hide wagons, which usually takes a month or two. When they are finally done with the slaughter, they burn their clothes and pay someone a goodly sum to bathe."

Reylie's mind flashed back to tales her Granddad had told about rendering plants in the Southwest. She imagined the smell was similar.

"Yes, buffalo hunters are a different lot," continued Jake. " Now that the Second Mexican War is over, more and more former soldiers are turning to hide collection. People back East love a good buffalo blanket, rug, or coat."

Bar spit and sneered.

"Let it be over for them. Not fer me."

The huge man pointed to a small rise on the north side of the roadway.

"Uncle Jake, recognize that clump of rocks and boulders? That hill is a couple of hundred feet high and is set back from the road about three hundred yards. That should be a good spot for your Sharps."

"What about the youngins?" Jake asked.

"Take them with you. It'll keep these two out of the way if

things get hot."

Bar looked at Ron and Reylie with stone grey eyes.

"You two do what Uncle Jake says. If you do something to screw this job up, I'll take a horsewhip to you."

"What-" Reylie started to question what was happening when Ron squeezed her arm. Now was not the time to ask about what clearly had to be a stagecoach hold-up.

"You three," Bar gestured towards Armand and the Olsen twins. "Head west and parallel the stage route. When it passes, birddog it, stay a mile back. You'll know when its time to act."

"It would be nice if we had some newer repeaters instead of these old Hall breechloaders," griped Tim Olsen.

"When you get shot with a half-inch bullet from that Hall, you stay shot," replied Bar. "Just hit what you shoot at. If not, use your Coult Navies."

"Hell, they are still cap and ball-" Tom Olsen stopped mid-sentence when he saw that look in Bar's eyes. The former Texas Ranger glared at the Cajun.

"You got a bitch now, too?"

"Last shell for the Maynard, my friend. Then I'll use my pinfire."

Bar grunted,

"Okay, let's get moving. If things go right, we may have some new shootin' irons to play with."

Reylie followed Uncle Jakes Mount as Bar turned his horse East. Some fifteen minutes later, Reylie and Ron were securing the two Mustangs as Uncle Jake set up a snipers perch between two large rocks. Reylie watched the Texan use a thick blanket to create the rest for the large Sharps rifle. Uncle Jake set up six fifty caliber Sharps shells in a row, then took off his wide-brimmed hat. From a saddlebag, Uncle Jake produced a large bottle and a long cylindrical object. A quick twist and a pull, and viola it became a ships spyglass.

"Ron, come over here."

The young man walked over to where Uncle Jake lay.

"How old are you?" Jake asked.

"Fifteen. Reylie is fourteen."

"Older brother, huh. Here. Take this spyglass and keep an eye out west for a Concord Stagecoach."

"Is that one of the bigger and fancier coaches?" Reylie asked.

"You got it, young lady. Now, have a seat behind this boulder here so no one can see you."

Reylie sat down as Ron scanned the Butterfield Trail.

"Hey, this is powerful. Like a small astronomy telescope."

"You like stargazing, huh? Well, son, I got that off a sea captain in a poker game in Mobile, Alabama. He said he had it specially made."

Uncle Jake turned where he lay and looked at Reylie.

"So now. Tell me your story. How'd you get to our campsite."

Reylie blushed as she tried to formulate an answer.

"I don't know... if you will understand or believe me."

Uncle Jake snorted.

"You see our rough ways, rough speech and think we are uneducated louts, don't you?" Uncle Jake said.

"Now, I don't mean to-"

"Missy, I have twelve years of schooling, plus some classtime at Baylor Christian College in Independence, Texas. I managed to have Bar stay in school for eight years, despite my older brother dragging him off for ranching and farming in Fort Stockton, Texas. I also have read everything ole Willie Shakespeare wrote. Can you say that?"

Reylie quickly realized that she had underestimated this grey-bearded man. Just because someone seemed rough around the edges did not mean they were necessarily unintelligent or uneducated.

"Please accept my apology, Uncle Jake. I did not mean to disparage your abilities. It is just, well, our story is so strange and unbelievable."

"Well, young Reylie, we have a bit of time here. Ron can keep an eye out for the stagecoach while you tell me your story."

The images of what had occurred just the previous day flashed from Reylies memories. Her seeing Ron sneak into Granddad's workshop in the back of the house as a police cruiser pulled up in front. Reylie immediately went to intercept her older brother.

"Ron, " she said, "what happened? The Police are here."

She and her brother were staying with their grandparents for a week as their mother spent time with her new boyfriend at some timeshare condo. The grandparents lived close enough to the kids' school so they could attend even with their mother away.

"I'm holding a pistol for Raymond, and the guys and someone ratted them out. Now they ratted me out."

"I told you they were trouble," said Reylie.

"Yeah, well, I needed to get a rep, a reputation. I'm not going to be a nerd my whole life." With that statement, Ron has stomped over to a long and wide table which contained Granddads newest project.

"Like this game, Granddad says he is building. A tabletop combined with a video. That screams loser Nerd."

Ron gave a large dial in the middle of the new creation an angry spin...

"So let me get this straight," said Uncle Jake. "Your Granddad was fooling around with electricity and such, did something new and strange, you were... sent here."

"When Ron spun the dial, yes."

Uncle Jake paused in thought, scratching at his chin beard. Then he spoke.

"Well, there is some Frenchman named Jules Verne writing about long trips in a balloon and trips to the center of the Earth. People say his tales are possible, so, why not a machine that zaps people and sends them like a charge down a telegraph pole."

"Somebody's coming down the trail," interrupted Ron. He handed the spyglass to Uncle Jake. The older man aimed the vision device down the western part of Butterfield Trail. He chuckled.

"Yessiree. A nice large dust cloud. That's the Concord style coach on the move, all nice and big." Uncle Jake stated. He looked at the King siblings.

"Alright. Stay out of the way, do not bother us. We have a job to do."

"Which is?" asked Reylie.

"Revenge."

Bar managed to pull a lone Alligator Juniper over and onto the Butterfield Trail Route using his rope and horse. It wasn't a large tree, but with a few tumbleweeds arranged around it, the downed tree was enough of an obstruction to make the stagecoach stop and at least inspect for a way around it. The former Texas Ranger then trotted his Mustang east down the stage route a couple of hundred yards, swung off the road and behind a pile of boulders. He could see Uncle Jakes rifle perch from his concealment and waited for the signal that the Butterfield Stage was near. Bar would meet the stagecoach on the road, the opposite side of the fallen Juniper Tree. Hopefully, he could get the drop on them, and there would be no gunplay. If there was, well, it would not be the first nor the last that Bar had to be a pistolero. The Texan had become quite good at it.

He took a sip of warm water from his canteen. The stagecoach should have some additional waterskins as the road across New Mexico Territory was long, hot and dry. Bar thought about just how strange this 'job' was becoming. Having to set up a robbery on one man's word only to have two unfamiliar youngsters literally drop into camp did nothing to improve Bar's disposition. He spits some chewing tobacco onto what looked like a nearby anthill, then disposed of the rest of the chaw. Having something in your mouth when things got rough and tough could lead to a choking fit at just the wrong moment.

Bar looked up at Uncle Jake's perch. He was about to dismount and stretch when he saw the directed flashes from a small hand mirror. The stagecoach neared. With a grim smile, Bar checked his Kentucky flintlock squirrel rifle. The .36 caliber gun was no buffalo killer, but Bar could hit a man consistently at some three hundred yards from horseback. Again, Bar had never replaced it with a percussion weapon as, if it ain't broke, don't try to fix it. Bar nudged his mount onto the road and started a slow walk towards the approaching stagecoach.

Reylie looked at the approaching stagecoach through the powerful spyglass. She thought she could make out two figures with rifles riding on top, with another riding the typical 'shotgun' position. The young lady had already examined the debris Bar placed on the Butterfield Trail to stop the coach and saw Uncle Jake load his Sharps rifle. Reylie lowered the spyglass, turned towards the graybeard man, and asked: "Why?"

"I told you why. Revenge. Messicans with money, some Alcalde with a hacienda sent some charros up to Fort Stockton the day the peace treated was signed in 1866. They killed my brother (his father), Bar's mother, Bar's wife Rebekah and Judith his little sister.

They are all connected. The ones traveling in that Concord coach are the same breed."

"But they weren't there, in 1866, were they?" Asked Reylie.

"I don't have time to argue. My nephew want's this done, so we do it. Now, be quiet why I line up a shot."

The stage drive saw the tree in the road and pulled hard on the reigns to the six-horse team. The stagecoach came to a halt some twenty-five yards from the road blockage. One of the guards on top and the shotgun rider clambered down from the stagecoach and moved clear the road. Then they saw the slowly approaching Bar.

The remaining guard on top of the coach did a most unfriendly thing. He fired a warning shot over the large man's head.

"Hey, asshole! You don't own this road," Bar bellowed out as he readied his Kentucky rifle. He was near a hundred yards away when he stopped his mount.

"Please-" Reylie began to say, but Uncle Jake cut her off.

"Shut up," he growled, then the Sharps boomed. The half-inch in diameter bullet struck the armed guard on top of the coach as he was readying to fire once more. The man toppled off the stagecoach as the two men clearing the tree dashed back to the conveyance. The shotgun man clambered back up to his place next to the driver just as Bar shot him in his right collar bone with his squirrel rifle. The guard fell into the driver's boot, as the driver wrapped the reigns around the brake and lept from his seat.

Bar slung his rifle over his saddle horn, yanked out a horse pistol and rode in screaming like a Comanche warrior. The other top guard grabbed up his cohorts long-gun from the ground and aimed it at Bar. A shot sounded from the rear as the three other gang members came galloping up. Armand's Maynard carbine bullet struck the man in the back. The guard toppled over as his rifle discharged into the air.

Arms with hands holding pistols poked out stagecoach windows, firing both front and rear. One of the Olsen Twins fired his Hall breechloader, the bullet smashed into the left side of the coach and sent splinters into the face of one of the shooters, The man screamed and dropped his pistol as a woman's screaming emanated from inside the coach. Bar's Coult Root boomed as a new shooter leaned out a right side window of the coach, the hefty .44 caliber slug smashing into the left bicep of the man. As the pistol fell from the man's hand, another shooter lept from the stagecoach and snapped a shot at Bar. The former Ranger shot the man in the chest as he swerved his horse towards the left nondriver side of the coach.

An additional shooter clambered from inside the stagecoach on the left side. As he did, the second Olsen Twin's Hall carbine spoke, taking the cowboy hat off his head. The shooter swung around and fired a wild shot at the three approaching riders. Bar's Coult Root boomed again, and the shooter's brains were splatter over the Concord coach and the New Mexico landscape.

"Driver!" yelled Bar. "Tell the passengers to stop shooting, or my Sharpshooter on the hill will sieve your coach."

The stagecoach driver rose from his hiding place under the stage and raised his hands.

"Don't Shoot no more," the driver cried out. "They are a killing us all!"

"Have them drop their guns outside the coach. Now."

Within five minutes, the stagecoach driver had everyone sans their pistols and outside the coach. A woman passenger cried as she tried to tend to the splinters in her husband's face. Face covered with a bandanna, Armand examined the wounds under cover of Bar's horse pistols.

"His eyes are okay, Ma'am," said Armand. "He will have a scar or two for tales to your children."

The driver managed to help his shotgun rider down from the front boot and worked on stopping the bleeding. The Olsen Twins pulled a strongbox from the front driver's boot, then set about throwing down all the other luggage. Bar shot the massive lock off it, and Armand examined the contents.

"There is little here for such a large box, Boss."

"Alright. Where is it? The gold." Bar demanded.

"You scum won't get it," snapped the one male who had not tried to defend the coach. He was a well dressed a middle-aged banker with a Yankee demeanor. Bar spurred his mount to bump into the insulting man, knocked him onto his rear end.

"Wanna bet. Loudmouth?" Bar asked.

"Please, no more violence," cried out the young wife. "They put the gold and valuables in our steamer trunk in the rear boot."

Just then, the Sharps range out again.

"What the..." Bar said, then yanked out a pair of binoculars from a saddlebag. He looked towards the West and swore.

"This coach has a mounted guard following it. And I think our Sharps just took out one of the riders."

Bar pointed to the two Olsens.

"Grab the trunk. See if you can carry it between you and head for the hills. We'll meet you at the pre-arranged spot."

He pointed at the banker. "Empty your pockets, take off your clothes. Jackass. Now"

Five minutes later, the Olsen Twins suspended the steamer truck between them as they trotted off. Jackass banker was standing nude, all his clothes and valuables, to include a .32 Rimfire Coult, stuffed in an emptied mailbag. Armand and Bar had recovered two like new Smith and Wesson .44 Long carbines. They also took two Coults Army pistols from the shooters and a Starr double action cap and ball pistol from the coach driver. A Coult Navy and the stagecoach shotgun rounded out the gun booty. Any weapon they did not want they threw in the sagebrush. Bar gave the stagecoach passengers a warning.

"If any of you come after us, we will shoot you and leave you for the buzzards. Had the Messican Guards not started shooting, we would not have shot either. We just wanted the Bank of Mexico gold and silver."

Then Bar and Armand were off in a different direction from the Olsens.

It was dusk before all seven met up. This time the group met in the foothills of the Black Range Mountains. Bar was the last one to make it to camp.

"I was beginning to worry, Nephew," Uncle Jake commented as Bar rode into camp. They were by the remains of some settler's covered wagon which didn't make it. No one knew the story as to why it was there.

"I separated from Armand and went back to get some steaks off that horse you shot. Sure enough, the rider broke his neck, and they just left him there. I guess the money was more important."

"Well, after I got Little Missy here to stop complaining about me shooting people, I took out that Messican guard and that rider."

Reylie was silent. The day's events were sinking in. She had seen people shot and killed for something called revenge.

Bar dismounted his horse and approached Reylie.

"Did Uncle Jake explain to you about our family?"

"That doesn't change the fact more people are dead," Reylie replied.

Bar paused and looked at her. Then he spoke.

"Someday, when some pieces of crap take people you love from you, civilians not even soldiers, maybe you'll understand. If nothing else, perhaps some Mexican will think twice about coming across the Border to mess with us."

"Does anger and revenge help you, Bar?" Reylie asked.

"It keeps me warm at night when the ghosts visit me." Bar turned and went to the campfire, He was soon roasting horse meat steaks.

Ron walked over to his sister.

"Sorry I got you into this. If I hadn't been trying to act so tough..."

Reylie waved his apology away.

"We can't change that. Now we have to figure out how to survive in a world where everyday violence is real and close up. This is no video game or the Cable TV News reporting happenings in some poor neighborhood."

"They gave me the pistol back, Reylie. Said I'd need it to protect you."

"You're going to do that?"

"Hell, yeah. That's what older brothers are for, right?"

Reylie hugged him and kissed his cheek.

"Ready to try some horse meat?" She asked.

"Smells like beef to me."

The two siblings walked to the campfire, knowing that the coming days could be as rough as strangers in a strange land.

"Coming to bed, dear?"

Her Mother's voice snapped Reylie back to the here and now.

"Sorry. Just woolgathering."

"I know. You're still thinking about what could've been."

Reylie turned to her mother.

"Mom, Ron, and I have never told the entire story. There were way too much violence and bloodshed for people not to hold us responsible. And that might have changed people's opinion about the Sky Tunnel. People get funny ideas about things that help when death is attached to them."

Her mother patted her arm.

"Without the Sky Tunnel technology, you helped discover, we would not have the chance to get off of a dying Earth. Magnetic pole shifts, massive solar flares, crops dying, it's almost as if someone is trying to force us to move... or die."

"I know. But that still does not help with all the memories."

"Well, come to bed. Tomorrow your husband Mike will help usher in an era of new hope when he activates the Sky Tunnel. Things will work out. You'll see."

As mother and daughter walked back into the house, Reylie could not tell her mother about some real sadness. For someplace in an alternate time and space, there was this huge bear of a man that she had shared so much with, to include everlasting love. Reylie felt guilt about the death she helped cause, but the love she had experienced? Never. And there were so damn many more stories she could tell. Reylie mentally shrugged. Maybe someday.

And it all started with a meeting around a campfire...

TO LOVE AND TO CHERISH
BY ELIZA LOEB

The night was as bleak as any other stormy night. The clouds overhead would drown out the stars as rain bucketed down upon Venice. Thunder clapped in the distance as the streets were occasionally illuminated by bright flashes of lightning.

It had been nights like these that Helios DiStrega loved the most, however. They were the sort of nights where they could at least pretend to be human, despite being otherwise. On nights like these, they would have the fire roaring as they sat upon a faded Turkish rug. The walls had been aligned with bookshelves, filled to the brim with rare content that many would not have access to in this day and age. Yet one could see the occasional gap here and there, spaces that Helios had climbed to in order to reach the book they had been itching to read next. Especially with the ongoing storm outside.

They would hunch over one book after the other, wrapped in a knitted wool blanket as they sat before their hearth. Should one walk into the room at that moment, they would say that they looked like a beautiful gargoyle. Their eyes gleamed in the light of the fire, as reflective rays added a striking florescence to their emerald green eyes, almost as though they were a cat intent on watching their prey as they fixed themselves upon the literary content before them. If one had allowed them, they would sit like that for hours….days, even as they refrained from blinking. Turning one page after the other and consuming tome after tome of forgotten literature.

"Have you even fed?" Came a voice.

Within moments, a man with golden skin and gleaming amethyst eyes emerged from the darkest corner of the room, casting his shadow beside the smaller being upon the floor. His wavy snowy white hair hung just over his eyes as a look of concern drew a pout from his full lips.

Mahtob had always held this kind of concern for them. And the way he currently hovered caused the younger of the two to lean back in reminiscence, recalling a time when they had been human. They had just met him without any inkling as to the predator he so attempted to convey. And they had gained the sort of reputation that one would expect of a level-headed merchant, as opposed to their prior life. But the way they had met would have been seen as unconventional, given the situation and the approach. Needless to say, Helios DiStrega, had remained married to him to this very day. Vampires had been the sort who, when they married, never had to worry about aging physically. Instead, those who missed being human, reserved an odd sense of nostalgia or envy….Helios had been one of them.

"I mixed some type O in my Darjeeling well over fifteen minutes ago." They say softly. They return their gaze to their book and continue reading. "It's gotten a bit cold for my taste, but if you wish to take some…"

A sigh of relief and a short laugh.

"No, no, I prefer lapsang, if you remember." He reminds.

"Did you?" Helios smirks. "And here I thought the build up in years had been making me senile."

"There are other things that can make you senile, little rabbit."

A salacious grin pulls at the corners of their mouth, exposing a pair of sharp canines as their expression changes from focused to suggestive and playful. And without looking up from their book they feign disinterest as their husband drops beside them. They turn a page, pretending not to notice before feeling his breath on their ear.

"Aren't you curious as to what it is?" He enquires.

His voice is low and husky. His fingers slowly brush along theirs as he leans closer and closer, moving to take their attention away from their book. His free hand reaches up to gently caress their chin and turn their head so that his eyes are meeting theirs. And instead of irritation, all he could find in his spouses' eyes in that moment was adoration. He watches as they search his, licking their lips to see just what he intends to do next, what he plans or any movements that might give his next act away, but finds nothing as he remains still. He smirks as they fight every thought and temptation to ask, but hide his smirk as they fail miserably.

"I cannot answer unless you ask, dear one." He finally teases.

Helios pouts up at him and gives a pleading wine. Mahtob doesn't relinquish his grip as he turns them to face him, yet keeps his hold upon them. Never wavering or blinking as they wait. He knows that the delightful torment of their spouse could go on forever if Helios allows it, and he has always been known to be a very patient man. Mainly because his lack of answering and managing to keep a hold on a person somehow brought a sick sense of joy to him.

"Mahtob…" Helios breaths out, doing their best to not let their voice strain. "Please."

"Please what?" He asks, leaning down to gently nip and suck on their lower lip. He keeps a subtle grin as he hears them whimper and try to claim his lips. He draws back before they can manage to do so and gives them a playful smirk.

"That's not fair." They huff.

"All is fair in love and war, Helios."

It doesn't take long before either of them are incapacitated by the other. The hours go by with fingers entwined with one and other, sweet promises of eternity or something close are said between breaths and cries to the heavens while leading to an eventual climax to the evening and bodies intertwined. Mahtob pulls their spouses body close, nuzzling his face into a head full of raven hair as he dances his fingers along their hip. They curl up beside him, sleeping peacefully as though there weren't a care in the world and recalling how he had met them.

He had been a vampire for well over a century by that point. He had wondered all through out eastern Europe aimlessly, wishing desperately that someone—anyone, might know how to kill him. The original person he had given up his humanity for had been long gone and everything seemed pointless. Nothing mattered. Until one day, he had heard shouting in an alley way, something about someone's mother being a prostitute and turning another ones mother into a homosexual and whatnot. And while he felt that there was hardly a need to mention or blame such things on the other person, it was likely best to stop and take a step back there….or in the very least have someone intervene. He turned the corner to observe the commotion to find a young woman glaring up at another woman who had very recently given her a black eye. The young woman was an odd looking little thing who seemed to like picking fights with people larger than she was, yet in a way, lovely to look at. He could tell that she would have an advantage in the fight with the trousers she wore and the knife and flintlock at her side, but he questioned why it was that she hadn't been using either. Her black hair had been a mess and she had a black eye with a bloody nose and a busted lip. Something that many gentlemen would find almost unseemly. Yet when all was said and done, something pulled at him, pushed him to approach and gods was he thankful that he had. As he put his hand on her shoulder to ask whether or not she had been alright, he had found that what little breath he had left to give had been stolen from him as the young woman whipped around, cocking her flintlock as she pointed a knife to his throat.

"Not the smartest thing to do, sir…" she warned. "Lest you have a death wish, I suggest you don't go about sneaking up on people."

"And what if I do?" He drew out. "What if I want to die?"

Those very words spilled out of him like a waterfall. Embarrassment and shame had begun to consume him. He hadn't meant to say such things to a complete stranger, no matter how much it would have caught them off guard. No, he shouldn't have said such things to begin with. Yet there she was, caught off guard, expression softening yet still serious as she placed her blade and firearms in her holsters before straightening herself.

"Then you should probably pick a different path."

As she turned to leave, he couldn't help but stare after her in wonder. If he had chosen to die that day, he wouldn't have discovered her for who she was and married them. He wouldn't have had his son, or hold their hand as the strain of child birth nearly took their life away, they wouldn't have become a vampire and he would have lost his humanity a long time ago. It would be a great disservice to say that a single person lacked great influence to change another's mind, like saying the light of a candle lacked the ability to illuminate a room.

In a way, Helios had saved him.

Not that he would admit it.

He moved to tuck them further under the covers and kissed

their forehead before wrapping his arms further around them, caressing every curve of their body as if to record every last detail of their being to memory.

He was thankful for having them in his life. Thankful for making his immortality more interesting as the years went by and thankful for their patience with him.

Eternity was a very long time.

Why not spend it with the person he loved coming home to the most?

LOVE AND DEATH
BY SHEILA MENGERT

Of love and death much has been written; they are two of the great human universals. America in the year 2019 might have been portrayed as in the grip of both. It was a year of a triumph of the sort of pseudo-patriotism that speaks of love of country while secretly courting the policy and prospect of an early death for those young people who are too poor to build real-estate empires on credit and serial strategic bankruptcies.

In popular Republican political rhetoric past, present, and future are viewed as simultaneously existent, all of them manifest in the glorious figure for whom any mere mortal exaltation must prove inadequate, Donald Trump. History has now become the equivalent of a personal trademark. The contraction of fact to meet the demands of expediency implies that in a sense all of the diverse voices of America can find their prophetic realization at last in the daily Twitter-feed of our king and prophet.

One looks in vain for a parallel beyond the realm of American politics although physicists are beginning to play with the idea that in the space-time continuum, although subject to accretion and expansion from our particular point of view, it does in a very real sense already exist as a completed project and is perhaps only one of many similar universes. Beyond this multiplicity that beggars the imagination there exists only the singularity of unconditioned being from which all else emanates while in itself it remains at rest and beyond partition or comprehension.

America, as a unity of territories variously acquired, is now in the process, subject to its own center-point in the ponderous gravitas of its President, of claiming its unique right to command and seeking to make its existence a sort of metaphysical absolute through making itself great again. Of course the question remains unanswered as to just how America managed to ever drift from its appointed destiny. In the mind of many conservatives this drift was caused by the election of America's first black President. This unaccountable veering away from the appointed dominion of white men had almost prepared the ground for a woman to covet the exalted office and only the fortuitous circumstance of the Electoral College and its frustration of the manifest will of the electorate had prevented the popular will from having its ill-considered way.

No American Balzac has arrived yet to capture American society as it has veered away from the optimism that greeted the advent of the year 2000. None has yet emerged since the attacks on the World Trade Center, the wars of intervention that followed, and the economic contraction that brought America's new gilded-age style of speculative boom to an end. By the year 2019, the third year of the Trump Presidency, it was becoming every day more evident to many Americans that trumped-up military parades to celebrate American might were not quite apropos to our real condition because with over twenty-two trillion dollars of national debt America's next wars could be waged only with the permission and financial backing of the hard-working Chinese whose collective industry was fueling the world economy and supporting America's position as still number one.

In the absence of a Balzac the particular Human Comedy of America must rely less upon the novel than upon the short story for insight into the American ethos as it has devolved from the optimism attendant upon the new millennium into the sordid aspect of the Trump era and the equally vacuous display put on by the Democratic party while harkening back to the New Deal, its own most glorious era. Both parties have ignored the fact that the American continent was once an integral unit long occupied by its own indigenous group of humans whose descendents are now claiming the right of migration and admission to America.

As to our particular national ethos American culture is and has always been characterized by alternative bouts of rebellion and further projection of power and conquest. Ours is a violent rather than a domesticated and pacific republic. It is for this reason surprising that the effort of conservative institutions from the Heritage Foundation to the various assorted pro-family organizations to restore an imagined golden-age harkens back to the 18th century, an age of reason rather than of demagoguery. In contrast the ever sanguine liberals imagine that the semi-literate working-class of white American males will be willing to surrender the illusion that Donald Trump would make a good drinking buddy and is out to get their auto-plant welding and coal-mining jobs back rather than cementing the economic power of the oligarchy.

Both political approaches imply that it just might be possible to engage in some miracle of restoration rather than simply admitting to ourselves that three centuries of rape and pillage have exhausted the virginal resources of the largest of earth's undiscovered places. The sad truth is that we are not in decline but still briefly at the apogee of America's long presumptuous attempt to circumvent the exigencies and limitations of the human condition. As it begins to dawn on more people that rapacious Trumpism is as native to our spirit as National Socialism was to the Teutonic spirit of industrialized Germany in the 1930's a long over-due admission of culpability is in order. Arrogant, selfish, materialistic, narcissistic, and contemptuous towards other nations and cultures—bigoted, mendacious, and self-indulgent—find any adjective and apply it to Trump and it is as apposite to America as well.

If America is ever to expiate its collective guilt we must look to the young to do so; but to date this prospect is unlikely. Anyone who has ever looked at pictures taken of children's faces whether rich or poor drawn from the 19th century must entertain the opinion that childhood as it is presently understood here is an American invention. There is little resemblance between the construction of the wooden figures and rag-dolls of that period and the sophisticated fashion-model dolls of 21st century girlhood. These figurines whether pouting and adolescent or sophisticated and elegant all betoken an early preparation for a way of life that may be vanishing in America, at least for the majority of young women.

The actual laborers engaged in manufacturing these early artifacts for the molding of the domestic dreams of American girlhood are located in foreign factories and undoubtedly do not look back on the same sparkling summer days that are fondly recalled by the grown-up daughters of those families that can afford a second home at Pinemont-in-the-Cascades (or simply Pinemont as its residents refer to it) the subject of this tale.

These fortunate daughters of the well-favored elite can look back on summers of unbridled nature-enhanced bliss in addition to their recollections of their family's main domicile whether in Washington or in Oregon. At Pinemont-in-the-Cascades the owners of companies or those playing an executive role in budding industries can spend a summer in nature at least until global warming and bark beetles decimate the great Oregon evergreen forests. At Pinemont the air is fresh and clean. The pollution from the great industrial core of China has been filtered by thousands of miles of ocean before it gets there. It arrives in America on the Pacific Coast, travels over some of the richest and greenest agricultural and grazing land in America and then climbs and spills over the volcanic peaks of the Cascades to where Pinemont rests with its golf courses, its bike trails, and its mountain lodge first built by the early timber and railroad barons and now inherited by their software and technology successors to economic dominance.

The children of Pinemont parents are granted a childhood not seen since that of children of the Victorian aristocracy. Each year brought its memories and traditions of bathing in the sea at Scarborough or Deauville. Life in England's empire days began unencumbered by student debts or the prospect of years of servitude spent in the nine-to-five rat-race, relieved only by the prospect of that coveted two-week yearly vacation. At Pinemont of course such respites were reckoned by the season rather than in weeks. After the season ended the house would be closed up again until next year, the snows would soon seal everything in white, most of the resort amenities would cease operations, the imported staff would return to their winter jobs or to school, and in Seattle and Portland more money would be made to finance this gem-like lifestyle.

In places where the American Dream has thus been realized, at least in terms of material prosperity, the year of 2019 only promised more to come. The market was booming and interest rates were low. Only in a few jaundiced authors' darkened imaginations did it appear that the present moment was more akin to the 1920's than to any other period of American history before or since, that fabled decade when F. Scott Fitzgerald found that as if by magic he could turn words into money, at least on this side of paradise. With this brief topical reflection as a prelude we will turn now to the scenery familiar to one of the protagonists of our tale.

Mercer Island is located in Lake Washington and is connected with the freeway by way of the Mercer Island Tunnel to Seattle. Boats from the salt water of Puget Sound can reach Lake Washington via a lock system to emerge at last into fresh water with the shimmering Cascades visible behind the houses that line the lakeshore. Mercer Island provides the very summit of gracious Seattle living to those who can afford it. The commute to downtown Seattle is a short one and inhabitants of Mercer Island are spared the daily ordeal of crawling up Highway 5 from Kent in the south or from Edmonds in the north into the proper core of the Emerald City. The high-rise buildings that are located there have over the decades transformed the former sleepy and quaint city with its fresh waterfront salmon drawn from local fishing fleets and its picturesque native totem poles, the city that once hosted the World's Fair in 1963, into the northern version of California's Silicon Valley and one of the busiest ports on the Pacific Rim.

Even though it was the original home of Boeing, Seattle's inhabitants realized that it is trade rather than aircraft and armaments that really make the world go round. Seattleites know this instinctively and this realization accounts for the fact that Seattle and King County always vote Democratic rather than following the archaic voting practices prevalent in what has been called "fly-over America." The Pacific Northwest can ignore the insignificant states that host soybean farms and foster the remnants of yesterday's hard-hat industries, whose citizens believe that the best way to make America great again is to keep it white and high-school educated, to keep a lid on the Black ghettos, and to bar immigration to refugees.

Since an ill-considered love affair is the primary topic of our tale (as will presently be seen) we may reflect briefly here on death. By the year of 2019 it was becoming evident that war and the implements of war were really America's primary export products. America's chief ally in the Middle-East was Saudi Arabia and in the Far-East President Trump was engaged in wooing the fat little Stalinist dictator Kim Jung Un while ignoring the fact that any missiles launched might just land on our former ally and former chief creditor Japan.

Most Americans had by and large adjusted to the idea that our blue-collar military fights and dies wherever Presidents wish them to while Congress simply votes the funds and goes off on vacation. The money presses roll and more empty dollars flood the world. There is even talk of going to Mars soon. By mid-July the east coast had ceased being flooded and tornado-racked and merely had to endure a kiln-like heat wave, but these changes were no doubt well within the normal curve of weather variability.

None of these trials were endured by the blue-voting west coast states however. It was a lovely and smoke-free summer at Pinemont-in-the-Cascades while in Seattle the sailboats departed from local marinas regularly and headed north to the San Juan Islands. The mountains beckoned just beyond the blue waters of Puget Sound to the executives who had not yet left for their summer vacations. Seattle after all is a lovely place to be rich, but even prosperity must have its places of respite: therefore places like Pinemont exist.

Anthony Westin, a fortunate son of Pinemont, arrived in the mountains a few weeks after his classes at Pepperdine University in California had terminated. It was July now and the first blush of summer was relieved by the mountain winds behind which there was just the faintest premonitory hint of autumn. He was glad to escape California. The golden state had not lived up to his prior expectations. There was something cloying in the series of unclouded days and the boundless optimism entertained by the cell-phone wedded millennial generation who were his classmates. Over the last year he had found himself longing for just a touch of 1890's decadence to ameliorate the crystalline veneer of perfection that he found everywhere else. He was in the process of exploring a gay identity and his best models were drawn from other more closeted eras. He had skipped the 50th anniversary of the Stonewall rebellion in New York in 1969. He did not see himself donning a dress and heels and waving coyly from a Cadillac convertible. He wanted something that was at once daring and distinctive to encompass his personal rebellion. What was the use of being homosexual he felt if one was to be denied one's proper allowance of tragedy?

If he had been born in England in the 1890's he would have spent his days reading novels by Huysmans, sporting a green carnation at his club, and laughing uproariously at the latest bon mot of the divine Oscar. In the Paris of the 1920's he would have been seen drinking ice-cold absinthe and watching a black chanteuse writhe sinuously and virtually naked on stage while the smoke from opium tinged cigarettes wove their wreaths about his solitary table as he waited for someone who might never have kept their promised assignation.

In the 1970's he would have been out walking the beach at Fire Island with all of the aplomb of the Lady from Impanema. After a few years of indulgence he might have returned to school with an unknown virus in his blood and ten years later he would have died perhaps of pneumocystis pneumonia in a San Francisco Hospital surrounded by weeping friends and lovers. Now fifty years after Stonewall his sense of the tragic could only be sated if there was the chance that some fundamentalist-inclined baker would refuse to bake him a wedding cake.

He reflected that he might as well just marry one of the series of svelte and simpering debutants that his parents kept sending his way, various daughters of friends of theirs who had majored in art history at Stanford or Berkeley. The only readily available tragedy in 21st century America was to marry a girl who becomes an alcoholic and sues you for over half of your salary in alimony and child-care. It was with this un-encouraging frame of mind that Anthony had left California behind and drove his vintage collector's edition T-Bird up to Pinemont to spend a few weeks before returning to school in September.

Family tradition at Pinemont consisted of an invigorating hike in the morning, golf in the afternoon, and the ritual watching of FOX News at night to see what mischief the socialist democrats were planning for the election year of 2020. A quick look at the swimming pool during his first few days revealed nothing more than a bevy of budding female adolescents, a population that Anthony often referred to as "nymphets and crumpets." The rest of the "swimmers and soakers" were even more depressing consisting of overstressed mothers on the nether side of forty and their hirsute but pot-bellied executive husbands. It was all a long way from men in Speedos on Laguna Beach.

With a sigh Anthony had almost resolved himself to a summer without dramatic incident until one night at the lodge when an unaccountable fate, the same that appears so often in short stories, arranged an acquaintance with a bewitching young woman who had caught his attention by her own expression of sorrow and studied desuetude as she sat at a nearby table and nursed a gin fizz.

Their eyes had met a few times without either of them exchanging smiles. They were the only two occupants of what was called colloquially at Pinemont, "the Eagles Nest." The bartender was engaged in a mild flirtation with the sole server so he paid his two customers little mind. Anthony was studying the menu when he noticed an item called, "cheese tray for two." It sounded good but perhaps too substantial for one so that he looked up again quizzically in the direction of the young woman whom he was shortly to learn was named Allison McCarthy. She had likewise been raised as a child at Pinemont.

As Anthony continued to stare at her she fixed him with an unfriendly glance and asked, "Well what?"

"I beg your pardon?" he replied.

"You keep looking over here and I was just wondering why."

Anthony considered her manner before answering, "It must be because I'm bored."

"How sad for you."

He was quiet for a few minutes before looking up again.

"Now what?" she looked up irritably.

"Are you hungry?" he asked.

"No, I'm buzzed."

"Then you should eat something," he suggested helpfully.

"What are you my mother?"

He was quiet again before asking, "Are you always nasty when you drink?"

Allison answered, "No, I'm nasty all the time."

Anthony took this in before replying, "It's nice of you to say so; I thought it was personal."

"Well it isn't … why did you ask if I was hungry?"

"Forget it."

"No why? Do I look too skinny or something?"

"Hardly?"

"Too fat!"

Anthony heaved a sigh before saying, "You are just right."

"Well thanks junior. How old are you anyway?"

"I'm nineteen."

"Well I'm thirty- four, but if you are looking for a Mrs. Robinson I'm not her."

"I just thought you might like to help me finish a cheese tray if I ordered one," Anthony said.

Allison came up short.

"Oh … well that was nice."

Anthony returned to studying the menu but when he looked up Allison was standing by his table.

"I accept your offer. I mean thank you."

Anthony got up and pulled her chair back for her as he had been taught long ago to do. Ten minutes later they were both munching brie and camembert spread on thin toast and with a side of smoked oysters. The room was still empty. They sat by the windows and looked out at the Sisters Mountains where they shimmered in the August sunlight.

Allison asked at last, "Are you a newbie?"

"No, my family has been coming here for years. You?"

"Me too. It's funny but I don't remember seeing you here before. Where did you hang out?"

"I liked to read at home."

Allison smiled. "I noticed your glasses first thing. I play tennis."

"That explains our not meeting," Anthony said.

"You don't play tennis?" she inquired.

"Golf."

"Ugh, it's too time consuming."

"Like eating cheese with me?" Anthony smiled

"Don't be a baby."

"I'll only be nineteen once; I'm allowed to pout. It's all downhill from here."

"You can't possibly be that cynical," she said.

"I'm not cynical. I just haven't found a plan for my life yet and to tell you the truth I hope I don't."

"So how will you manage then?"

Anthony paused before answering reflectively, "I always thought that it might be nice to be an early casualty. I would like to be spoken of as one who died before his true promise could ever be realized. It is the perfect disguise for mediocrity."

"That's a chicken-shit attitude to have." Allison scoffed.

"My family expects me to do great things," Anthony stated decisively as though she should have deduced that already.

"Like what?"

"Have my own spot on Fox News after Hannity."

"You have to start first in radio." Allison smiled.

"Or I could go into investment banking."

"Do you know what investment banking is?"

"Not particularly."

"Well it's dull and stressful at the same time. Most high-paying jobs are."

"How do you know?"

"I grew up listening to my father's friends," Allison said sagely.

They each helped themselves to more food.

"What does your husband do?" Anthony asked.

"I'm not married." Allison replied.

"You will be. You're pretty."

"How would you know? You like men."

"How do you know that?" Anthony looked up alarmed.

"Please! You're such a drama queen. *I just thought I'd be an early casualty…"*

"It might be the only way that I can ever be free," Anthony said looking down at his lap.

"Free of what?"

"Great expectations."

"Yours or your family's?"

"Both."

They were both silent again for awhile. Allison reached for another smoked oyster.

"These are good. I'm glad you asked me over."

Anthony smiled.

"You have a very fetching smile. You'll break hearts." Allison said.

"Do you really think so?"

"Yes … but not mine. I'm a lesbian."

"You surprise me."

"Why is that? Do I need a duck-tail haircut to prove myself?"

"I just meant … oh I don't know."

"You can say it. I don't expect you to know about any girls gay or straight. You probably went to an all-male prep school."

"I was quite a hit with the upperclassmen."

"I'm sure you were."

Anthony looked at Allison for awhile.

Allison began to squirm. "What?"

"E was just thinking that my family would like it if I brought a girl like you home."

"Well from what you have said so far I think they would be happy if you brought *any* girl home. Besides … I'm old enough to have been … your babysitter."

Anthony looked up candidly, "I used to have a crush on my baby-sitter. I even wanted to be her I suppose. I remember that I stole one of her lipsticks once out of her purse."

"Don't tell me that you're a drag queen too."

Anthony smiled. "Darling no, I can't afford Gucci handbags and for me it's everything or nothing."

"You could always do tacky-drag. You could shop in junior ready-to-wear. You look like about a size 13."

"Please, not with my antecedents. I demand haute couture."

He paused before continuing ruefully, "You see how limited I am when it comes to sexual options."

They were both quiet again before Allison asked, "Why not just simply break out? Do a year of foreign study in Italy for instance. You might find some Italian nobleman who won't mind keeping you at his villa in Capri. All you will have to do is look pretty and pour drinks for rich queers that come over to visit and see his new acquisition."

"Things like that don't have good pension benefits."

"Who cares? You are planning on being a casualty anyway. Pick your moment and do a swan dive off the cliffs into the blue Mediterranean if you notice any wrinkles in the mirror some bright morning."

"I think you're making fun of me," Anthony pouted.

"Well somebody should."

"I think you know more about me than I know about you."

Allison smiled.

"I've lived a hard life. Besides, I'm a woman: I will always know more about you than you will ever know about yourself."

"So that's why you don't like men?" he asked.

"No, it's because I haven't learned to be a good liar. I could never convince a male mate that he knows more than me ... at least about the things that really count."

"Is that all?"

"No. I also don't like the idea of being kept. No offense, some people are made for it. I want to know that I can always just walk away if I want to."

Anthony attempted to sound very mature. "Sounds like fear of commitment to me. Why doesn't the same thing apply if you left a woman?"

"I wouldn't leave a woman."

"Why?"

"Because I'll never find one who loves me…"

"Now who's being the casualty?"

"Don't be impertinent! I'm over ten years older than you."

They both resumed eating from the cheese selection. The brie went first and now they were getting down to the Spanish sheep cheese.

"Ugh, this stuff is too strong," Allison said.

"Don't eat it then."

"I don't want to be a cheese-wuss."

"Don't you mean cheese-whiz?"

"Don't tell me what I mean."

"Well, can I ask you something?" Anthony asked after a minute looking directly into her eyes.

"Go ahead."

"What do you want out of life?"

Allison considered. "I want to get even."

"With who?"

"With everybody."

"That sounds scary," he said spreading some more sheep cheese.

"I once held a priest at gunpoint," Allison confessed.

Anthony went on chewing.

"Did he molest you?" he asked.

"No, I just thought he represented power that was denied to

me because I'm a woman."

"And that made you mad enough to kill him?"

"I didn't kill him … I even prayed for him."

"Did he ever have you traced?" Anthony asked.

"No. The seal of the confessional was inviolate he said. He let me walk away and I never saw him again."

"That was nice of him. I mean letting a dangerous lunatic escape."

Allison looked up sharply. "I'm not a lunatic; I'm just terminally pissed-off."

Anthony considered this before replying, "I'm not sure that I can appreciate the essential distinction."

"It isn't a formal distinction, Dodo-child. It means that I have a right to be angry. My anger makes me who I am."

"What do you mean, Dodo-child?" Anthony asked.

"Dodo, like the big dumb birds that are now extinct and child because … well, look at you; you look like a big baby doll."

"Charming," Anthony commented dryly. "So what does your anger ever get you?"

"I don't know," Allison said sulking.

The two were silent again. Other people were entering the room now.

Allison leaned forward and smiled and whispered conspiratorially, "Do you think that people might think that we are a couple?"

Anthony looked about before answering, "Hardly, I'm too cute for you."

Allison answered, "I knew you were a bitch."

Anthony smiled. "Before you even sat down here?"

Allison smiled too, "You cross your legs like you your maxi-pad was slipping."

Anthony said with dignity, "Ad hominum attacks are always the refuge of the intellectually inferior."

Allison grinned, "Don't toy with me tartlet I might just still be armed."

At this auspicious moment Allison's mother came up the stairs looked about and seeing her walked over to the table where they were both sitting.

"Allison, we'll be eating downstairs in the dining room in an hour. Don't you think you should go home and change?"

Then as if seeing Anthony for the first time she said, "Oh hello… Allison, who's your young friend?"

Allison blushed. "I don't know his name."

"And you are eating his food?

"I'm eating his food, Mother, not sleeping with him,"

"Allison!"

"My name is Anthony. Happy to meet you Mrs. …"

"McCarthy, Amelia McCarthy and this is my daughter, my very ill-mannered daughter, Allison."

"Pleased to meet you Allison. Mrs. McCarthy, we have been discussing casualty insurance."

"Oh are you into insurance Mr. uh Anthony?"

"No, actually I am more into risks."

"Ah, you are an actuary."

"No, my task in life is to … how did we decide Allison … it is to live dangerously and by that means to court untimely disaster. It's a new field but quite promising."

"I'm not sure I understand," Allison's mother said awkwardly.

"Well it wasn't clear to us either although we were just coming to an interesting point when you arrived."

"And I interrupted you. I *am* sorry. I merely wanted to tell Allison that her father and I will be eating downstairs with the

Hanover family and we would like her join us. Um you could join us as well. We are quite a diverse company."

Allison shook her head at her mother.

"Well it does no harm to ask, Allison. I mean I find you here in earnest conversation with a … young man, so I naturally supposed…"

"I'll be back at the house in twenty minutes to change."

"Do and try and look nice Allison if only for your father's sake. Mr. Hanover is a client after all."

"I will Mother."

"Thank you. Goodbye Mr. Anthony, it has been so nice meeting you."

Allison's mother went back down the stairs.

Anthony turned to Allison and said, "And from this domestic ambiance you ended up being a dangerous lunatic?"

Allison answered, "You could give me a little Tea and Sympathy at least."

Anthony replied, "You should meet my parents."

"Tell me later; I have to go home and change."

And from this disjointed beginning a summer relationship of sorts began between them.

The following day Anthony encountered Allison again where she sat gazing out at the lake from the gazebo. He came up behind her quietly before saying loudly and clearly.

"Don't shoot; I come unarmed."

Allison turned around and smiled. "Dodo-child! Come and sit with me. I am looking for an intelligent confidant and since none is available it might as well be you."

As Anthony settled down comfortably in a deck-chair beside her she said, "By the way, I thought that you handled my mother rather well yesterday. You aren't as brainless as you look."

Anthony drew himself up, "I will have you know that I am on a full scholarship at Pepperdine in English Literature."

"Surfboards and sonnets, eh?" Allison answered.

"My parents think I am studying finance and mathematics though, a joint major."

"What will they do when they find out?"

"By then I will be off to Capri like you said yesterday."

"Well I am not a qualified career counselor. Just ask my mother."

"Well you must have learned something in your twenties."

"I learned how many false starts a person can make and still retain sufficient credibility to keep getting financing for the next one."

"I don't think I could I could keep that going," Anthony said ruefully.

"You may have to if you are anything like me. But then you are a man and for a man something may always turn up for you ... even if you are queer," Allison commented.

"I've always hated that term," Anthony said.

"Well it's very in right now: LGBTQI, just pick a letter, something will fit you."

"I prefer invert or homophile."

Allison laughed. "You are so antiquated, so very Henry James, all the Nancy-boys of that era were running about Europe or going off to Morocco and calling each other my dear boy. England had a fairy on every square foot of English soil and yet no one ever apparently got laid."

"Lytton Strachey certainly did," Anthony said in defense.

"Nobody reads Lytton Strachey anymore."

"I'm surprised you have heard of him," Anthony sneered.

Allison answered haughtily, "I will have you know that I am

well grounded in the humanities, philosophy specifically, which means that I am consequently virtually unemployable. I will always see all of the logical flaws in any company policy."

"I thought people in human resources would value culture," Anthony objected.

"Hardly," Allison answered drily. "Only basic grammar is required. Cultural depth can even be a handicap as they try and find a slot for you to fill. Meanwhile people like you and me study in an effort to overcome our sexual alienation; when our contemporary world provides no valid interior role models we turn to the idealized past for sustenance and support."

"Well I hope to make it as a charming ingénue, so why am I studying anything?"

"Well I hope you are not studying in hopes of earning money. People like you and me study to form ourselves into something besides an empty gullet with an impressive expense account. It allows us to feel superior to those upon whose good-will our survival depends."

"But we still fancy an elegant cheese-tray from time to time don't we?" Anthony smiled. "It is the old problem of elegant tastes coupled with an empty wallet."

"People like us need sponsors to enable our gracious living or we might if we are lucky attain the security of a good marriage to rescue us from genteel poverty."

Anthony sighed. "Well there will always be Capri for those of the inverted demimonde."

"For you maybe, but the number of rich lesbians is ... well, you have to be another rich lesbian to find one."

"How do you know?" Anthony inquired. "I thought you were above being just trade."

"Trust me, I know." Allison replied mysteriously and Anthony already knew enough about her to leave it at that.

Their next casual meeting was along one of the hiking trails that threaded Pinemont; he was walking, she jogging. Allison ran up alongside of Anthony and yelled, "On your left." He started and moved aside quickly and Allison burst into laughter, "Lesbian coming through."

"You startled me," Anthony remarked as she jogged in place beside him.

"Well you're up early. I pictured you lounging about in a Victorian dressing-gown to the consternation of your parents and reading decadent poems by Ernest Dowson or Arthur Symons. You had best be careful venturing forth from your yellow wallpapered chamber or you will lose your fashionable pallor."

"Down, you presumptuous strumpet, do you dare to imagine that you understand me?" Anthony replied laughing.

"Well I expect that you have reduced superficiality to an art-form. You practically admitted as much to me at our first meeting," Allison chided him playfully.

"And from that fortuitous encounter you presume to have insight into my real character?"

"What character? The best that you can manage is an orientation. You are so quintessentially gay. Quite honestly I was surprised that you asked me to share your cheese sampler. Aren't you afraid of getting female cooties?"

"My dear girl I am proof to any and all effusions and distillations emanating from the female sex."

"You always talk as if you had just stepped out of a book."

Anthony smiled, "Why whatever do you mean Allison dear?"

"There you see!"

"Perhaps you are unaccustomed to good breeding."

"There is a difference between breeding and affectation. A little less Jane Austin and more of Jack London would do you good if you are determined to be gay, Anthony. Effete isn't in right now."

"I stand corrected," Anthony bowed.

They walked on side by side in the morning shade. The sun had not as yet climbed above the towering Ponderosa Pines nor had the usual heat of the day descended. The air was dry and bracing and scented with the trees and with the sweet scent of the meadow grass of the horse paddock toward which they were walking side by side.

"I don't suppose you ever ride do you?" Allison asked.

"Not without a proper hunt and the sound of hounds in my ears."

Allison stopped short. "You don't expect me to believe that you have actually hunted foxes."

"On my last trip to Bedfordshire…"

"Stop, you mean that you actually pursued a helpless little fox and…"

"No, I must confess that we only followed a drag. Bloodsports have been outlawed even in the home counties."

"How disappointing for you that must have been. You might have been awarded the brush."

"You speak scornfully. Evidently you don't understand the pageantry of the whole thing. There was a reason after all that the English came to dominate the world. The desire for conquest is part of human nature. As an English public school trained young man the English elite was taught to endure pain and if necessary to inflict it."

"I knew it! You probably like wearing harnesses and spiked chains too."

"I believe that we were talking about the refinement born of manly endurance and the ability to read the classics in their original languages."

Allison remained adamant. "Men in academic robes beating little boys with canes; it's disgusting."

"History is the record of pain and brutality."

"That's why I don't read history," Allison stated firmly. "When women have more power and can influence events then maybe…"

"Oh yes, here is where we hear about the golden era that will come when women rule," Anthony interrupted.

"Don't be so condescending. It is coming you know. We are almost at parity in the professions and many world leaders…"

"How many times did Theresa May try to get a Brexit deal through parliament and she left in tears. Do you think Churchill would have gone out like that?"

Allison looked down, "She was treated abominably."

"Excuses!"

"Besides, Brexit only happened because your precious English are afraid that the whole country will be soon overrun with Syrian women and children. Women will always fight for their children."

"Then they should stay where they are and fight. It isn't economics at stake really it is a question of cultural integrity; that at least must not be diluted by an Islamic effusion."

Allison walked on beside him but Anthony could feel her sudden coldness.

At last she said, "Borders are unnatural things anyway. Survival takes precedence over mere legalities. Forget Europe, how do you think America got settled in the first place? Do you think the Indians invited them?"

"You prove my point; it all comes down to the will to conquest of under-settled and undefended lands. Take Pinemont for instance: do you think that just anyone can come in here? It costs a pretty penny and those who have the pennies work for them in the city so that their kids can retain a privileged status to ride horses about and play tennis in nature's wonderland without being bullied by some Compton kid in a drug gang in sunny California."

"What do you know about it Mr. Pepperdine? They wouldn't be in a drug gang if they had a chance of a good education and a decent job."

"Over fifty years of affirmative action and all that it has produced is rap music from the hood. At least the Black Panthers knew how to dress well, radical chic."

"With you life's big issues always come down to a fashion-statement don't they?"

Anthony was quiet and they walked on in silence. At last he spoke up.

"Well if you want to know I don't really care about politics and sociology. I just think that it is nice that some people can afford gracious living and I think that most of them have worked for that privilege. Would you want to entrust some kid of yours to the tender mercies of the ghettos in L.A.?"

"I don't have any kids, but if I did I would want them to have a social conscience and not become some nasty little Republican prick whose best idea of rebellion against being an investment banker is just to become a spoiled effete snob!"

"Who said I was a Republican and who said you get to call me a snob?"

"If the shoe fits wear it."

Anthony walked on in silence before saying despondently, "We don't know each other well enough for you to fight with me like this."

"Well I was in a good mood when I jogged up."

"Well who asked you to stop anyway?"

"It was just that you looked so pathetic walking here by yourself with your head down. What happened did your family ask you not to embarrass them by hitting on the waiters here or something?"

"As a matter of fact they did."

Allison stopped walking, "Oh."

"Well in effect they did. I keep being asked the usual questions about who I might be dating at school. I think that they might even be relieved if I could demonstrate a little inconsequent promiscuity as long as it did not compromise my future by drawing into our orbit some girl who as my father puts it might act as a drain on the estate. A wife is an accessory not a partner in life. Well I said some catty things back to them and we had our annual fight last night."

"That's too bad. So what were you doing before I came up to you all inappropriately chipper?"

"I was wondering how long it would take to drown in a mountain lake from hypothermia or if I might just be able to locate a mother grizzly bear and her cubs and grab one of them up by its little furry feet."

"Don't you think that is a rather extreme solution?"

"I'm very emotional and reactive."

"I guess you are. Remind me not to fight with you; you're fragile."

"I'd certainly appreciate it."

The two young people emerged from the sheltering forest and the meadows lay before them with the great mountains in the background. Clouds backed up behind the ridge and spilled slowly into the valleys below. The path wound along the open meadow and descended into a grove of aspens beyond. They walked side by side again and Allison looked up at Anthony's face and saw him brush away a tear impatiently.

Allison said quietly, "I hate fighting with family."

"With us it's a tradition," Anthony said with a catch in his voice.

"Is it a religious thing?"

"No, we aren't religious at all; to them being gay is simply a social impediment, but so is any entanglement with another person. Investment bankers are allowed a family as long as it doesn't interfere with business. But, to have a proper relationship means that one is socially respectable. In the world of investment bankers a homosexual is bound to be viewed as a socialist and of course every socialist is bound *mutatis mutandis* to be a homosexual. I hope you haven't planned on being a professional yourself; straight people will only be sure that you are a reincarnation of Emma Goldman."

"Darling, nobody remembers Emma Goldman."

"Then they'll think you are like the squad, another Alexandria Ocassio-Cortez."

"I am what is familiarly known as a professional student. My parents think that if I remain in school long enough I am bound to find some up and coming guy and marry well someday. It always comes down to a choice between tuition and therapy and they figured a degree is worth more than just being told by some shrink that I'm not crazy anymore."

"Are you really crazy?" Anthony asked in alarm.

Allison pondered his question before replying, "Who can tell? What do you think?"

"I just think you're abrasive and mouthy," Anthony said loyally.

"Thank you. I like you too Dodo-child."

"I probably know more than you do," Anthony said.

"Perhaps I just hide my education better than you do," Allison replied.

As the summer days passed Anthony and Allison found as if by accident that rather than spend their time in moody and solitary introspection while in a lovely mountain setting or the even worse company of their respective parents they would rather be with each other. Yet the days passed by without significant incident or issue. Although they appeared to be on alternate routes regarding sexuality both of them had been born to privilege and to all visible appearances should have been capable of attracting a mate of the opposite sex thus ensuring the perpetuation of the human race and the fulfillment of nature's design in creating sets of perfectly matched genitalia. By this cunning ruse intelligent design had so sculpted the human bodies of each that what one possessed in abundance the other was correspondingly denied. To frustrate this design implied that each was manifesting an attitude of evident contempt for the efforts expended on their behalf by being determined to seek love from one who was a mere replica of themselves. Worse still in its political and cultural impact this penchant or disposition was not an individual idiosyncrasy but was one evidently shared by a sufficient number of other human beings that it was not inconceivable that given sufficient time and opportunity one or the other might possibly encounter another person so inclined and perhaps even see the initial prompting of their misguided appetites ripen into the simulacrum of a romance. This was not a case in other words of a dearth in population of one or the other sex so that from strict necessity and lacking all other viable options friendship might unaccountably tip into the forbidden confines of sexual exchange between persons of the same sex. Rather their joint propensity was due to the lack any goal other than the sheer pleasure of the concupiscent act and as such socially unacceptable and reprehensible. Each had declared to the other a determination to follow a barren path into an inextricable jungle of sterile passions without social support or sanction let alone the security that nature's intent would be fulfilled. This was clearly a case of wayward and recalcitrant genitalia. Yet so it was that these two young animals were daily in each other's unsupervised company without any danger that lulled by the gentle summer breezes and seduced by the softly shaded potential bed provided by fallen pine needles on the forest floor they might disrobe and spreading their garments to protect their flesh from any untoward abrasion in their frenzy so commune with each other that the folly of their former proclivities might be made at last manifest.

Instead their walks through the forest along the spring-fed river were confined to the prosaic topics better reserved for people of twice their age. They discussed pedagogy, careers, politics, and even touched upon matters of metaphysics and epistemology. They discovered that they shared many of the same views, had many memories of the same things, and saw their lives terminating at some future date with the same summation as to life's ultimate meaning. In this they were already somewhat estranged from their peers who were too busy living to speculate about life's end. Both confessed to times when the possibility of extinction beckoned as the premature end of unwarranted pain rather than the termination of all prospect of fulfillment and contentment by finding love at last.

Of course it is easy to hold time as cheap when one is burdened by a surfeit of days. Age would no doubt have taught them otherwise. It is trite to say that youth is wasted on the young, but it is only older people who mutter such nonsense, imagining that if they could as if by magic be restored to that era of taut skin and radiant form, of lushness of limb, and charged with an energy that can only be revived at a later date by hormone supplements that they would do better this time, that they would be grateful for each hour rather than callously lavish with that one irretrievable commodity, time.

Bathed in unmerited riches however these two found nothing

odd in the thought that their stories might end in a self-determined manner. Enamored of tragedy from reading various books they did not really know the true cost of anything. Happiness seemed something owed to them so that the only real question was whether any particular happiness would prove adequate to their imagined desserts. They thought it strange that their parents were so obsessed with externals and appearances when they each enjoyed finding ways to give the world the metaphorical finger on the slightest pretext. Everything seemed slightly ridiculous to them. Surely life must be easier than their elders made it out to be.

"I don't know why I can't find anyone to love," Allison confessed to Anthony one day after one of their comfortable silences when walking together along the spring-fed river that wound through the woods near Pinemont.

"Don't be ridiculous," Anthony said, "The only problem is finding someone who is sufficiently hung."

"Don't be crude," Allison remarked.

"Well if you can't stand honesty…"

"Are gay men really that shallow?"

"No, just gay men in their twenties; by forty they would rather gossip about things like opera or *haute cuisine*."

"I think you may have read too many books by Edmund White."

"And what is a lesbian doing reading Edmund White?"

"He functions as a reset button after reading *The Well of Loneliness*."

Anthony reflected. "You should read *Dancer from the Dance* by Andrew Holleran. The period that he deals with is gone forever of course, it is more remote and idealized in its way than *The Great Gatsby*, but it gives one the same feeling of inevitable and pervading doom and loss."

"If you like doom and loss…"

Anthony shrugged, "What else is there really?"

"And I thought I was the morbid one."

"What makes *you* so morbid?"

"Well for one thing I'm in love with the music of Lana Del Rey," Allison confessed.

Anthony considered, "Well I guess that qualifies, at least until you turn eighteen."

Allison bridled. "You're so supercilious, what makes you an expert on everything?"

"Extensive reading."

"Oh really! What have you read?"

"In English or in the original languages."

"Come on."

"I mean it; test me."

"Okay - Lautreamont."

"The Song of Maldoror, a bit affected but graphic. I think he was going for shock value just like *Justine*, horribly boring really, both of them."

"You mean Lawrence Durrell."

"Please! De Sade of course."

"Henry Miller."

"Wishful autobiography, sordid heterosexuality."

"Anais Nin."

"Most of it never happened."

"Who says?"

"Gore Vidal."

Allison objected. "And you think *he* never told any lies?"

"Who cares when he's so witty?"

"And cruel, you must admit that he could be cruel, to poor

Truman for instance."

"Capote deserved it; besides truth is always cruel."

Allison reflected. "Who have you read in the 21st century?"

"Nothing. I only read classics. I am a man born after my time."

Allison mimicked a fit of nausea and said, "You make me so sick."

"Then why do you keep hanging out with me?"

"Deluded Dodo-child, it is you who are hanging out with me I thought you knew."

They both laughed.

Finally Allison said, "You won't ever become an investment banker you know."

"And you won't have any kids," Anthony countered.

"Stop it."

"Oh? I didn't think you wanted any kids."

"Why should you think that?"

"Well don't look at me as a prospect; go and find a doctor with a Petri dish or whatever they use."

"I wouldn't want any sperm from you. It's probably tainted with virus."

"What virus?"

"You have probably found a new one: California Streptococcus Herpes 5."

"I'll have you know that I always play hard to get. I am only an icon for admiration and unfulfilled longing."

"Until your third drink maybe."

"Nasty bitch."

"Easy trollope."

"Don't make me cry."

They both laughed.

Anthony shrugged. "Alright so I won't be an investment

banker so what?"

"Well how will you get money to live?"

"I'll repair to my garage and invent something with popular appeal that will save people money or something."

"Like what for instance?"

"A re-usable condom."

"You just can't be serious can you?"

"Not with you."

"What makes me so special?"

"I don't know. I have been trying to figure that out. If you want to know I find it a little disconcerting."

"Do I remind you of a man?"

"No."

"Then what?"

"I told you. I don't know."

They walked on in silence for a bit.

At last Allison asked, "Are we friends?"

Anthony replied. "I don't like friends; they always make demands ... especially women."

"What do you mean by that?"

"I mean there are only so many hours in the day and I am not interested in spending one or two of them hearing the details about some incident that even the woman in question will have forgotten by the next day."

"You better stay gay then."

"I plan to."

Allison was quiet again before asking, "I am trying to figure you out. What if you are worse than just an unpleasant little twit? What if you are evil?"

"Then go back to the lodge and find another sucker with a cheese tray on whom to exercise your frustrated motherly instincts."

"Remember I have a gun."

Anthony pulled-up short. "I thought you told me that the priest told you to get rid of it."

"I might have bought a new one since."

"Oh."

"I can help you realize your ambition for a tragic and premature end."

"Psycho."

"I can see the headlines now 'Blond Youth Murdered at Cushy Resort\Deranged Lesbian Held in Custody.' Then the copy, 'The distraught mother was quoted as saying "We did everything we could for the poor girl. She was the most beautiful debutante in her season.'"

"Were you?"

"My dad says I was."

"He would have to."

"You *are* evil."

"Artists are dedicated to the truth."

They walked along side by side.

"Your problem Allison is that you are a cliché."

"Me! Well so are you. I bet you've never done anything outside the Castro Street playbook in your life."

"Alright, let's be daring, I'll ask you out on a date, how would that be?"

"Come on."

"No I mean it, a real date. Call it mutual revenge on our parents."

"You might have to kiss me to make it appear authentic," Allison warned him.

Anthony made a wry face. "Very well, I'll think of England and jump, parachute or no parachute."

"You might get to like it."

"Only if you start calling me Foxy Dude instead of Dodo-child."

"But you are a dodo-child the proof is that you don't know that you are."

"You're such a girl."

"Well I suppose at thirty-five that's a compliment."

"Take it any way you want."

So it was then that Anthony and Allison started dating. Their parents were at first skeptical and then cautiously thrilled. It would save so much in expensive conversion therapy and in making lame excuses to friends of the family for their unmarried state. Days passed and the pair became one of the seasonal collective memories at Pinemont that summer. They made a beautiful couple, especially when Anthony kissed her hand or they toasted each other with Shirley Temple's designed to look like pink champagne. Each had an element of untapped theatricality and had watched sufficient movies to recreate classic love scenes in pantomime. Sometimes they didn't even talk but simply engaged in a series of passionate expressions made and exchanged between them to the delight of the surrounding tables. Each tried to top the other in simulating restrained passion so that even older couples seeing them together began to smile with nostalgia and a few reached out and joined hands shyly.

It was all a grand lark but as the days passed Allison would occasionally have to excuse herself. She would go into the ladies room and cry for no reason that she could comprehend. She would splash water in her face and reapply her make-up before returning and going on just as before. Anthony in turn would pose as one who was growing impatient for his beloved's return and light up in simulated delight when she walked up again in her full-length dress to resume her place at the table by his side.

So did the summer days pass and September imperceptibly neared. The wind shook the aspen trees outside the windows of the lodge. Autumn seemed at once infinitely far away and close at hand and the faux-romance became a fixture in both of their lives. Allison thought back to her time with a cousin and her family from some years ago and of how hard it had been for her to bid them goodbye at last and return to her own solitary life again, a life spent without context or meaning.

Perhaps it was natural that she was more preoccupied than Anthony by existential questions; after all she had majored in philosophy. He on the other hand was obsessed with the expressive possibilities of literature rather than whether any particular proposition was true or not. In addition there was always their difference in age, not a particularly large one of course, but a significant one to a woman whose available window for child-bearing is rather narrow. Love and death as ultimate realities are more the concern of the sex that gestates life and thus comprehends its inherent value.

One day Allison asked him. "What's your objection to women anyway Dodo-child?"

Anthony walked on in silence before answering at last. "I suppose the problem is that I see them as competition for what I really want. They have all the advantages, a sort of direct line to most men's libido, breasts and all that. Other than that everything on a woman seems designed with babies in mind. It is all just too physical. I crave sterile refinement punctuated by short bouts of focal passion with no encumbrances attached."

"Selfish through and through," Allison said in disgust.

"Oh I don't know. After all someone must preserve the culture. The Greeks knew that. Children are the death of superfluous leisure and it is leisure alone that creates monuments of culture. Besides, I don't think women like men all that much. Just listen to them when they are meeting in one of their various cabalistic discussions. The primary topic is usually men's shortcomings. Women immediately set about dismantling a man's interests after the marriage ceremony is concluded. Out go the toys, gone are the old drinking buddies, and what is left to him but yards to mow and garage doors to fix. The highpoint is the occasional weekend barbecue with "mutual friends" which means the wife's BGF and her desiccated mate brought along from the mummy case to help carry plates out from the kitchen while she and her hostess sit laughing by the pool asking over their iced-teas if the burgers are ready yet."

"Evidently you've never visualized a relationship of gender-equality between men and women."

"That's the last thing that most women would ever want! Women maintain an icon of the ideal man, a sort of combination of their idealized fathers and some lobotomized stud with an Austrian accent."

"And you men want some endlessly nubile young blond thing to worship you combined with a twenty-four/seven cleaning machine and secretary."

"Thus the whole LGBT movement: everyone is freed to seek their own kind."

Both were silent until Allison asked, "Then why aren't we happy?"

Anthony looked surprised. "I thought it was me who wasn't happy and you were acting the part of the wise older sister and confidant."

"I'm not that old," Allison said defensively.

"Everyone's old after thirty; it's all in the LGBT guidebook and bylaws."

"There isn't any such thing."

"Well then it's an unwritten rule and those are the most binding of all."

Allison was quiet for a time before muttering to herself, "I hate rules."

They walked on in silence. At last Allison stated, "Your problem is that you don't understand love."

"Me?"

"Yes you. You are leading an entirely derivative existence as though everything can be expressed in a book. Henry James! How disgusting!"

"What's disgusting about Henry James?"

"It took him until he wrote *The Ambassadors* to realize that you have to grab life or it escapes you. Besides, it always takes him a whole page to describe the most trivial actions, description run amuck. He dug so deeply into his characters that they became ciphers and not people anymore. It might have worked for that wacky governess at Bly with the two possessed kids but most people just aren't that neurotic."

"So you *have* read Henry James."

"Nobody *reads* Henry James. They labor though him like a particularly painful delivery. He isn't an avocation, he's a punitive sentence imposed on those who want to sound extra sophisticated. I'd rather read Faulkner with all that dust and old Civil War monuments to a vanished age of glory, all the decadent and incestuous families too proud of their heritage to let anyone else in."

"Well I think incest is tacky," Anthony said fastidiously.

"You think everything is tacky unless it happens in a men's room at a bus station."

"And I think you are too into stereotypes, a poor excuse for your poor skills in argument. You better go back and read some more philosophy."

Allison smiled before saying triumphantly, "So! Did I finally get under your skin a little bit? I knew poking critical remarks at Henry James would do it. Maybe now you can understand why I said that you don't understand love."

"I do too."

"You don't. I bet you never even saw *Picnic* with Kim Novak and William Holden."

"Well I haven't, so what."

"So there's something wrong with you if you never saw *Picnic*."

Anthony objected, "How can you make blanket statements like that? Who makes you the almighty film guru?"

Allison turned away. "Well maybe I just want you to know something about love that's all. Love is worth any price you have to pay for it."

"Well *Picnic* as a title sounds pretty trivial."

"It's by William Inge, a gay man who ended up dying by suicide ... interested yet?"

Allison walked ahead of Anthony and ignored him. After several minutes Anthony conceded, "Fine, tell me about your *Picnic*."

"It isn't *my picnic* Dodo-child. In fact love isn't a picnic. Did you ever think that people die over love or better still they realize the full value of living by being in love? You have to take risks to love. Sometimes you even have to endure endless betrayal and cruelty from the one you love. And sometimes for no good reason at all opportunity introduces you to someone who is completely wrong for you and you still love them anyway."

"Tell me about *Picnic*," Anthony said.

Allison looked around for a fallen log by the hiking path. "Alright sit down with me and I'll tell you."

The two walked over to a fallen log covered with a light dusting of dried moss and sat down there side by side.

Allison said, "Okay. *Picnic* is the story of a few short days in little town where everybody is stripped of their illusions."

"Well that sounds fairly typical to any drama."

"Do you want to hear this or not?"

"Yes, I do."

"Then be quiet. The main character, Hal, is an ex athlete, a real jock."

"I think I might like this after all."

"Will you shut up!"

"Okay."

"Anyway, he comes to town to look up an old buddy of his because he's out of work and riding the rails. His buddy comes from a rich family in the grain business. His old buddy is at first really glad at first to see Hal because he can show off his foxy fiancée Madge, the prettiest girl in town."

"So the buddy isn't gay."

"No. Try and pay attention will you."

"Alright."

"So anyway by coming to town Hal ends up stirring up all these hidden feelings among all the other characters and Madge falls for him like a ton of bricks. It all happens at a picnic where the town elects the Queen of Neewollah."

"The what?

"Neewollah, Dodo-child, Halloween spelled backwards, a sort of harvest queen. Madge gets elected of course and through a series of circumstances Madge ends up dancing with Hal and oh my God this music called *Moonglow* starts to play and they dance too and ... oh I guess you have to see it, but it is so beyond sexy ... and then this stupid middle-aged lady school teacher tries to muscle in and dance with Hal too and she ends up tearing his shirt almost off and the buddy thinks that Hal tried to seduce Madge and he claims that Hal stole his car and suddenly Hal is on the run again because he doesn't want to spend a night in jail because his Mom once had him thrown into juvenile detention and he hates jail even if it is just until everything can get straightened out."

"Slow down."

Allison paused to catch her breath. "Anyway Hal is basically suddenly a fugitive with no job, just lost his good buddy, and all he can figure is that he has to get enough cash to split town. But before that he runs into Madge sort of in the woods and he tells her to just leave him alone but Madge starts to tell him how great a dancer he was and what it meant to her when he held her in his arms. And then..."

"What? Did they do it or something?"

"No, disgusting twerp, they didn't *do it*; they didn't have to. She tells him how tired she is of being just told that she's pretty and then she kisses him. I mean she *really* kisses him and, oh my God, there's something there that's ... well it's iconic, it's *love*."

Allison stopped talking and it was quiet in the woods and the dry heat of the day was only softened by the breeze in the high tree-tops.

Anthony said nothing.

Finally Allison continued, "Well Hal can't believe that this beautiful girl loves him but events are moving fast now and he goes to the boyfriend of the dopey teacher lady that ended up tearing his shirt almost off at the picnic to borrow enough money to leave town because the ex-good-buddy said that Hal stole his car and he has to get away. Anyway, the father of the ex-good-buddy doesn't want his precious son to marry Madge anyway because she doesn't come from their social strata."

Anthony interrupted her story, "Is that it then? Does Hal get away?"

"Be quiet. Madge and her sister are talking in their bedroom and Millie, that's the little sort of butch sister, she tells Madge she should go off with Hal, do something smart for once. Madge's mother doesn't want Madge to go. She knows about men, how fickle they can be, how shallow they are, even if they say that they love you. *But Madge doesn't care…*"

She paused.

"Why?" Anthony asked.

"Dodo-child! It's because *she loves Hal.* She'd go anywhere with him now, but even then he has to ask her to go away with him and he does."

"What does he say?"

"He pulls her away from her mother and he tells her that she belongs to him but even more than that he makes her feel like no other woman has ever done before. She makes him feel…"

She paused again.

Anthony showed some interest at last. "What does she make him feel?"

"She makes him feel … *patient.*"

Anthony hesitated and then he blurted out, "What the hell does that mean, she makes him feel patient?"

"Well you wouldn't know Dodo-child. And I thought you were a literature major! Think about it. Hal's problem has always been that he just moves along from flower to flower like a bee and here is this girl who has *brought him down!* Do you see? Now his life has meaning at last. He'll do anything now to keep her; she belongs to him."

Allison stopped talking.

"So how does it end?" Anthony asked at last.

"Hal runs away and hops a train yelling back at Madge to remind her that she loves him. The mother tries everything to keep Madge from going and the old neighbor lady tells her Mom that

Madge has to go out and discover life for herself for better or for worse and then the camera pans back and it shows the train crossing the dry grass plains and Madge is riding on a bus past the high school leaving her little going-nowhere-town to meet up with him and start her new life.”

The two of them walked on together in silence.

Finally Allison spoke up, “So what do you think?”

Anthony thought about it before answering, “I think that girl could use some counseling.”

Allison said, “You’re just lucky that at this moment I am unarmed.”

But later Anthony thought about it and resolved to see the movie at his first opportunity.

“So what are you reading today,” Allison asked Anthony a few days later when she came up to him at the least used pool at Pinemont.

Anthony looked at his faded book-cover. “Oh it’s an old biography of John Galsworthy, you know, the author of *The Forsyte Saga.*”

“There must be something in the gay genes that can only imagine true fulfillment as season tickets to the opera and an upper-middle class existence,” Allison commented.

Anthony ignored the remark. “I am masochistically drawn to family sagas. I guess I always imagined myself the scion of a wealthy family with an elegant family townhouse in London and a great manor house in the country for weekends. The closest I can come to the image of a tolerable old age would be this: me clad in old tweeds grown curmudgeonly with the years and a wife rather like Vita Sackville-West keeping the gardens at the old place in trim, bringing in asters and zinnias from the garden to place in vases hither and yon, and her listening to me complain about the state of the empire. The vicar and his wife would call later and we would discuss the latest poems by Tennyson over tea. Does that sound good to you?"

"Is that an indirect proposal?"

Anthony cringed, "Heavens no, but I thought the image of me in a straight guise for once might please you."

"Well I have my own cherished images," Allison said turning away.

"Would you care to share them with me?"

"No."

"Too personal?"

"Yes … and painful."

"You aren't as tough as I first thought you were," Anthony remarked.

Allison made no comment.

"I think people are buying it," Allison said quietly as they sat in a corner table in the lodge looking out on the lake shore and the mountains beyond.

"And why shouldn't they," Anthony answered. "Aren't we both accomplished performers? Isn't that what we have both been doing all our lives."

"Not I," Allison returned, "I consider myself to be an entirely frank person. It goes with being a philosopher."

"Hah, you are a basket of emotions and secrets," Anthony scoffed.

"I am not."

"You ooze feminine mystique and estrogen from every pore."

"Shush, people might be listening."

"Of course they are listening; we are the hit of the season."

Allison slammed her fork down.

"Is that all that this means to you? You thrive on inauthentic gestures and pretence; you would make Sartre nauseous."

Her outburst of passion disturbed him at first but Anthony tried to pass it off, "Very cute, a play on words. I think I am doing you lots of good. You have moved from being a lunatic spinster to being almost a match for my foil."

"Conceited twit, I let you emerge at times into the footlights because I know that your ego just thrives on any escape from being one of life's little unnamed extra players."

"I caution you not to bandy words with a gay boy; my talons could shred you on the instant."

"Smile Darling, people are watching. You might take my hand you know; you haven't touched me all evening."

"I am a model of strategic restraint. The audience must imagine that I will pounce on you in the backseat the moment we cross the parking lot and reach the comparative solitude of my T-bird."

"Who drives a T-bird? You are so retro."

"You're the one who thrives on a movie made in 1956."

Allison ignored his jibes. "The people can tell that you are all tied up in your Oedipus conflicts and I in turn am terminally frustrated by your male frigidity."

Both of them lapsed into silence to regroup for another assault. Finally Allison said, "We aren't laughing like we did a few weeks ago."

Anthony said tight-lipped, "I'm smiling. It's you that are betraying the game; get with the program."

Allison whispered, "I don't have to follow your orders you little martinet. I'm older than you are."

"It's never out of my mind."

Tears blinded Allison, "That was unnecessarily cruel."

"Love is an anthology of unkind actions."

"Only in your twisted conception of it!" Allison began to dab at her eyes with her napkin.

Anthony protested, "You would hurt me too if you could."

"Stop reading Edward Albee; he's too grown-up for you."

Allison was about to excuse herself and go to the ladies room but Anthony grasped her wrist and said in a voice tinged with desperation, "Why isn't it working for us tonight?"

Allison answered, "You know why. I brought love to close to you and you can't stand it. Human warmth causes you to curl up like the little snail you are. Back into your shell you little escargot!"

She scored with that one.

"Time of the month?" Anthony inquired.

"Trite!"

They both fell silent.

The older couples shook their heads and went back to eating. "Just lover's quarrel," they thought complacently. "Nothing perfect lasts."

Time passed and things returned to normal between them.

One late-August day the two conspirators sat looking out to where little cat's paws played about on the lake. Several small sailboats skimmed over the waves appearing to be destined to collide and then turning away at the last moment. It reminded each of them of when they had been children at Pinemont in days gone by, each entertaining dreams of finding their proper place in a society that has only been preserved in the literature that they both read when they should have been learning the intricate art of mixing, meeting, networking, and of course concealing. Romantic success is the fruit of conformity and duplicity with just a spark of charm or beauty thrown into the mix.

It was strange that being raised at and around Pinemont had

somehow passed over them like a summer wind leaving them tossing about in agitation but still rooted in their native illusions. Each had evolved an armored persona to shield them from an uncomprehending majority to whom same-sex loves will always be disordered and anathema.

Another season in the mountains was ending and already the night temperatures were showing the disturbing alteration that betokened the chill to come when snows would close the passes and the summer houses would groan unheeded through the long winter nights.

Anthony was ineffectively throwing stones into the lake when Allison spoke up.

"You know you can't drive me away," Allison said.

Anthony wearily sighed, "I'm not trying to drive you away; I'm trying to keep you grounded in reality."

"Reality is always a matter of contention," she answered.

"Time resolves all conflicts," Anthony said to console her.

It didn't work.

"You only talk like that because you can't hear it," Allison said.

"Hear what?"

"Time's winged chariot."

"I know: Andrew Marvel, a 17th century poet."

"Someday soon we won't be young anymore," Allison said disconsolately. "We'll be like the people who have watched us all summer."

"I know. It worries me considerably," Anthony answered. "People like us are creatures of a season not tethered to home or family, at least…"

"Yes?"

"Nothing."

"No, what were you going to say?"

Anthony shrugged, "I was going to clarify a point of gay taxonomy, at least in our pure form. I mean all the Castro gays in jeans and with shaved heads trying to look like the kind of guys they hope will be interested in them, these know all about time's chariot."

"Are you one of them?"

"Hardly! I am literary gay through and through; we never get down to actually doing anything. Can you picture me in leathers?"

Allison laughed. "No. it wouldn't work for you. You are pure tenderized chicken through and through. You better find yourself a Gustav Achenbach somewhere out there in Venice Dodo-child. You were born to be admired from afar."

"You promised not to call me that, Dodo-child; I'm not a child."

"I did not promise you that."

"Well you did … and what about you? Where will you look for identity and permanence? You're as lost as me."

Allison tried to sound blasé. "Oh I suppose I'll eventually get to look like Alice B. Toklas and find my own Gertrude Stein."

"Now who's being the drama queen?"

They both fell into silence.

"Actually, I think I will end up permanently single," Allison finally remarked.

"Well with your attitude…" Anthony smiled.

"I like my attitude," Allison said with something of her old anger.

"I remember; it's who you are right?"

"That's right," Allison said quietly.

The wind came up again and shook the leaves on the aspens over their heads turning them into silver hearts.

"I love it here," Allison said softly. "I know that it costs a lot to live here and when my parents die I will have to give it up but it is the same land that the Indians once wandered over, never thinking that anyone would ever land here from Europe and take it all away from them."

"Rich people take what they want," Anthony agreed.

"I was speaking about the original settlers," Allison looked up.

"So was I," Anthony answered. "What is a better example of an invasive species but a settler, a so-called pioneer? What was present is pushed slowly away until there is no place for it anymore. The survival of the fittest is not as violent as it is usually supposed to be, it moves incorrigibly and insidiously into new lands treaty by treaty and suddenly my father is ensconced on Mercer Island and the Suquamish dead are buried on a little reservation next to Agate Pass just west of Seattle."

"Is that where you are from, Mercer Island? You never said."

"Yes."

"I'm from Lake Oswego."

"Right... lots of nice homes there."

"Yes."

The two of them were silent.

The wind continued to blow and the clouds began to drift over the Cascade Range and to fall down the other side like an airy avalanche. The air began gradually to cool and there was a promise of thunderstorms before evening. Behind them the activities of Pinemont continued unabated impervious to the changes in the atmosphere. Love affairs were concluded or broken, deaths occurred, summer residences were sold, new staff was hired, new expansions were planned, yet Pinemont remained Pinemont and the children of Pinemont played on the golf courses and the tennis courts or swam safely in the pools surrounded by parents who knew each other from prior summers.

At last Allison spoke up. "If you weren't gay you could ask me to marry you and if I wasn't lesbian I might accept and our parents would be happy and we would get married down there by the lake and all of our friends from past years would gather to wish us well. We might have to move away for awhile until you found your wings and your business began to grow. I would get pregnant of course in due time and we would come here for summers as our parent's guests and our kids would be able to return to school and tell their friends about how exciting their summer had been in the mountains of Oregon; their friends who had spent their own summers running through sprinklers on the back lawn to cool off, they would envy them. Some of our children's little friends would have packed a tent and a cooler full of soft drinks and stayed in a state park with barking dogs only a few yards away. Others would be trapped in the city and hear only the rap music from next door all summer long. Some of the girls would come back to school pregnant because they let themselves be fucked because their boyfriends got tired of blow jobs..."

"You paint a pretty picture of heterosexuality," Anthony said. "Maybe you should be a publicist for the family-values groups."

"Do you think they would have me?"

"I was speaking ironically."

"You seldom speak in any other way."

The pair was silent again.

"The worst part about heterosexuality is that I wish I could have just a little bit of it just to feel really connected to something..."

The wind in the trees rose again to a wail and the water on the lake shivered.

At last Allison said, "I will miss you when you go Anthony."

Anthony looked up, "I thought you didn't like men."

"Sometimes I don't know what I like."

They were both silent again.

Anthony spoke up suddenly like one who wishes to end a long debate. "Well nobody will stop you now. It's all up to you what you become."

Allison hesitated before blurting out. "So I'm in charge of my life?"

"Yes."

Allison shook her head and said quietly, almost to herself, "If that was true then I would ask you to marry me."

Anthony started as though he had been stabbed with a pin.

"You are a dangerous lady to share a cheese tray with." And then immediately, "You know it wouldn't work."

Allison protested. "It works for other people, why not us."

Anthony turned and gripped Allison by the shoulders before crying out, "I think this is just a game you are playing with me because I am just a dodo-child like you said."

Allison closed her eyes and shook her head violently.

"Tell me it's a game!" he insisted.

"No."

"Tell me."

"No it isn't a game; it would solve all of my problems don't you see? God, my parents, everybody … they would just rejoice. I could dig up the last of my old college classmates and ask them up to Pinemont for the wedding. We could choose any music that you like and you could look just all spiffed up and your father would be able to see you as a proper investment banker at last or at least gainfully employed. There would be a great wedding feast and I would be there all in white, sacramental but sexy, and I could have babies before it's too late for me and you wouldn't have to go off and become some little gay Euro-slut just to pay for room and board in Capri and years later emerge sick and jaded when your beauty fades and die on the streets in Milan or Naples. Don't you see, Anthony?"

Anthony shook her by the shoulders, "Stop it. That isn't the way it is with us."

"What does it take to reach you? Tell me what I have to do!" Allison cried.

Anthony spoke slowly. "It isn't you. Maybe it isn't even me. Maybe we received poor modeling in our youth so that love and sex got separated somehow and death became the uneasy tag-along to both. I don't think either of us expects to be happy or even loved. I'd settle for just a lustful glance from the right guy and you ... Allison you deserve someone who will be for you..."

"What?"

Anthony searched for the right word.

"Allison, you need somebody who will be patient."

Allison was silent as the beautiful vision of sexual complementarity between them faded away. She saw herself, an object of pity and disdain, not all that much different from when pictures of lesbian love appeared on lurid paperback book covers sold in drug stores across America. She did not know how she had come to feel something for the blond youth before her but she felt his fear, not just of her, but of everything that went along with upper-class suburbia where decade was linked to decade as the hard-won promotions succeeded each other in the inevitable march to the possession of a coveted corner office. Had she betrayed their little conspiracy and ruined whatever was between them by popping the question that he had dreaded most to hear because even if it was offered to him by a man it would have meant the surrender of his only real possession: his pretense to the possession of inextinguishable youth?

She felt him fading away from her like the sun that was declining to rest upon the mountains west of them. An unwonted chill was rising from the grass around the lake and she clasped her bare shoulders to ward off the cold. She could feel the full impact of the metaphor of night.

When she spoke again it was with the voice that he had first heard from her earlier that summer. She looked away from him into infinite distance.

"You are right of course. But you can see where and how I might just get thoughts like this from time to time. My mother is thinking again of having me sent into treatment. It's what they do with dangerous maniacs like me who carry guns and threaten priests and propose marriage to little dumb gay boys. The ones like you who had already made up their minds about love and death before we even met."

"It may help that I have not made my mind up about anything. I think you will haunt me Allison for a very long time."

"Well that's something at least."

"It is … and it isn't flattery."

"I wish it was. Flattery my dear Anthony will get you anything, even me."

Alternative Ending...

And that might have ended the story for each of them and they would have parted each to pursue a separate tragic fate according to their original conceptions but Anthony suddenly said, "Unless…"

Allison looked up at him, "Unless what."

"Oh I don't know. I just felt suddenly uncomfortable that's all."

"Why?

"Well, I didn't like that image of you in a lunatic asylum. Do they still have places like that?"

"They do if you can afford them. Otherwise you have to get an old grocery cart and push it around town filled with ugly tops, knit stretch pants, and old yellow bras."

"Disgusting! I'd never allow it."

"Well don't worry about me. My family will find me a nice place with a name like Oakhurst Rehabilitation Center or something."

Anthony thought about it.

"I still don't like it. After all, you are a friend and you sounded so tragic."

"It was just a crazy dream. I mean me, the Lunatic and you, the Dodo-child."

Anthony thought more about it. "Well you sprung it all on me kind of quickly. I mean a girl likes to be prepared."

"I thought you wanted to be a fetching boy chased about Europe by aging noblemen."

"You always made that plan sound so sordid."

"Well it just seems to me that if you want to end up a trollop that you could do better as a girl. I don't think you would have said those awful things about women if you weren't a little bit envious of us."

"Well it does seem a bit much that you can make big money flashing a little leg on camera. If I looked good enough I could be a reporter on Fox News or one of the real housewives of ... someplace. I mean literature doesn't get you very far these days. Nobody can read above a sixth-grade level. I might end up writing nauseating love stories like Nicholas Sparks just to make ends meet."

Allison thought about it. "No, the real money is in televangelism. You can be a complete drag queen as long as you are pushing the prosperity gospel on Christian broadcasting. They love it if you bleed mascara when you cry. How are you at crying on cue?"

"All I have to do is picture myself as an investment banker tied to a desk in some suffocating office building."

Anthony tried to picture himself as a lady televangelist rather than a European Trollope.

"If I'm going to be a televangelist I'll need a partner, couples do better at that kind of work, bleeding the faithful."

"We'd have to be married," Allison said.

"I think it would be the orthodox thing to do," Anthony admitted.

Allison considered the idea, "I'm not that butch."

"Sideburns and some fake facial hair would do the trick," Anthony suggested. "But won't you have trouble promoting generic Christianity as a Catholic, I mean with the Council of Trent and all?"

Allison considered this objection and then her face lit up as though with celestial illumination.

"We'll do a Jonathan Swift on them. Did you ever read Swift's *A Modest Proposal* or Defoe's *The Shortest Way with Dissenters?* No? Well that's your next assignment. Here's how it will work. We'll start our own religion. We'll call it umm, Cosmetology! We'll emphasize the virtues of studied triviality. You'll be the perfect spokesperson Dodo-child; you're half way there already and sculpted eyebrows and a little lip-gloss will do the rest. Our religion will have affirmations instead of commandments. We'll just tell people to do what they are doing already; it's so much easier, the exercise of stoic virtues and discipline are passé."

Anthony considered the idea, "Well you know I'm not as dumb as you are always saying I am."

Allison put her arm around him, "That's alright Sweetie you can be smart, just don't let anyone know that you are; it will spoil the illusion."

Anthony smiled happily before asking, "Alright but what would some of our affirmations be? What is a religion without doctrines?"

Allison though about it and finally replied, "Okay, how about these for starters: 1. be nasty it's the new nice."

"Super!"

"Of course in our religion we'll change and substitute doctrines depending on how well they play with the faithful."

"So it's sort of religion on demand," Anthony said.

"Right," Allison said.

"It might just catch on."

Allison explained, "Well if you've been paying attention everything is moving in that direction anyway from business to education: degrees on demand, studying optional, Presidency on demand knowledge of government optional, faces on demand see your plastic surgeon, nothing just is what it is so why should religion be what it is. Look at the Indian casinos, the Indians finally figured the settlers out: we all want something for nothing."

"It still sounds a little risky."

"Well let's face it Dodo-child does any of your other options sound any better?"

Anthony thought about the summer, its swiftly fading days and the vague and impressionistic sense that he had of his own future. Already prep school seemed a distant memory and he had failed to adjust to the complexities of California's ersatz culture of plastic glamour and dried mesquite hills.

He desired a world of convenience and an ever-ready supply of cash to meet his occasional passions for silver trinkets. He was not extravagant; he preferred zircon, topaz, and amethyst to the sterile glare of diamonds that were said to be a girl's best friend. So far his life had been characterized by a dull sort of resistance to whatever carefully designed and pre-bottled essence his life was to assume.

Allison on the contrary appeared in her daring to possess what he lacked, passion and decision. Surely then any conception that might come from her was at least as likely to lead him to the small measure of freedom that he required, to open a fissure in life's unyielding granite face. He felt words of consent trembling on his pale lips but one last matter troubled him still.

"Alright, suppose we end up being a big success, what about our home life afterward?" Anthony asked. "I could learn to cook but I have to warn you that I might flirt with various tradesmen when I go shopping."

"If you do I'll paddle you," Allison assured him.

"Promise?"

"Yes."

"Will you be quite severe with me?" Anthony asked coyly.

"Yes."

"You'll probably be quite demanding sexually I suppose?"

"I'd consider it my duty" Allison said quietly.

"Very well then," Anthony offered her his hand, "I accept your proposal."

EMERGENCE
BY CARRIE AVERY MORIARTY

I don't understand," he said.

"Come with me and I'll show you," she replied.

"Show me?"

"Just trust me," she implored.

He did trust her. From the moment he placed his hands upon her, she was the only thing that mattered. What she was saying, however, was madness.

"Ready?" she asked.

"Yes," he replied, though he wasn't sure what to expect.

"I promise, it'll be worth it," she said, then let go of his hand.

He could hear her moving away from him slightly, then he was blinded. Not like he was on a daily basis, but a brightness he'd never experienced caused him to shut his eyes and hold his hands over them.

"What is that?" he cried.

"Come with me," she said, grabbing his arm.

He followed her without question, riding in her wake, unable to experience anything around him. Then he began to hear things he'd never heard before. His life had been filled with the sounds of small creatures digging, insects buzzing, and other people breathing and talking in hushed tones. Here, however, he heard sounds he'd never experienced.

Gradually, his eyes became somewhat accustomed to the brightness surrounding him. Blinking, he removed his hand and experienced something new. Color, texture, movement.

"Isn't it amazing?" she asked.

He turned to her voice, and for the first time actually saw Layla. Oh, he'd 'seen' her before, with his hands. But this was a whole new experience, one he simply couldn't describe.

"Where are we?"

"The surface," she beamed.

"Surface," he gasped.

"It's perfectly safe," she said, releasing his hand. "Come and smell this."

He followed her, unable to resist her urging. She picked something from a clump and brought it to his nose. He inhaled and was assaulted with a sweetness he was unaccustomed to.

"I think it's a rose," she said. "That's what Sam said."

"Sam?" he questioned.

"Here he comes," she said, then shouted, "Over here."

Jacob followed her line of sight and saw someone walking toward them. Having never seen any of the others, he was unsure whether this person was larger or smaller than those underground. All he knew was the man was taller than him, and appeared to have more body mass.

"Layla," he said, giving her a hug. "You brought a friend."

"This is Jacob," she said.

"Pleasure to meet you," the man said. "Welcome to the surface."

"Are you sure we're safe up here?" he asked.

"It is perfectly safe," the man said. "But you should stay in the shade until your skin becomes accustomed to the sun."

Jacob looked at Layla, completely confused by what the man was saying.

"You see how parts of the ground are darker than others?" she asked.

He looked at her, still confused. She was using words that had no meaning to him.

She sighed and looked to the other man. "Was I this confused when I first came up?"

"Yes," the man answered. "But you adapted quickly. Each of you will have a different time table when you come up. Some may adapt more quickly, like you did. Others may take a little longer."

"Each of us?" Jacob asked. "You mean more are coming to the surface?"

It seemed impossible that anyone, let alone everyone, would want to chance coming to the surface. The dangers they had been warned about were sure to be up here. It was the reason they'd retreated hundreds of years ago.

"Some may choose to stay below," Layla explained. "But I want to live on the surface full time."

"That will come," Sam said. "But you need to do it gradually. Remember what I said about exposure."

"Where did you come from?" Jacob asked the man.

"Underground, same as you," the man said. "Well, I didn't come from underground. I was born on the surface."

"Your parents came from underground?"

"And their parents before them," the man said. "My family

retreated about the same time as you. By the stories, it was about six hundred years ago. The great war made surface living nearly impossible for everyone."

"Why come back, then?" Jacob asked.

"We're explorers by nature," Sam said. "We like to find things out, see what's on the other side of the wall. It isn't in our nature to hide forever."

"But we weren't hiding," Jacob insisted. "We were staying safe."

"I know," Sam replied. "But it's safe to come back up."

"How can it be?"

"Look around," Layla said. "Trees are growing, plants and animals are thriving. It is just like the stories that we've been told for years. It is the way it was."

"Which means it will end up the way it was, too," Jacob insisted.

"Not necessarily," Sam said. "As long as we remember what happened, and what caused it, we can make this place safe for everyone."

Jacob began to scratch his arm, leaving deep lines on his pale skin.

"I think he's probably had enough," Sam said to Layla.

"Oh, no," she replied. "Come on. We have to go back underground."

She grabbed Jacob's arm and pulled him back where they came from, shoving him through the door before she followed.

"What's happening?" he asked, still clawing at his arms.

"You've never been exposed to the sun," she explained. "It can cause your skin to burn if you aren't careful."

"Why have you done this to me?"

"Because we need to return to the surface," she said. "If we don't, we'll die down here."

"We've lived here for a long time, Layla," he explained. "We haven't died, yet. I don't think we'll die any time soon, either."

"Jacob," she insisted, placing her hands on either side of his face. "We were not created to live underground. We belong up top."

"I'm not sure that's true anymore," he said. "What does your father think about all of this?"

At the mention of her father, Layla sucked in a breath.

"That's what I thought," Jacob said. "You haven't told him, have you?"

"He doesn't understand," she said. "He isn't curious at all."

"Because he knows it's not safe up there," Jacob explained.

"But it is," she insisted. "You saw for yourself. Sam has lived up top for his whole life and he's perfectly fine."

"You don't know he's telling the truth," he cautioned. "He could be trying to get to our supplies."

"Why would he want what we have?" she asked. "He has everything he could ever need up there. More than what we have, that's for sure."

"Have you seen his supply collection?"

"Yes," she insisted. "I've been going up daily for a couple of months now. I can stay in the sun for almost an hour, and the shade for several hours. Didn't you notice that our skin wasn't the same color?"

"The stories from the old days say that there were many different shades of skin before the fall," he argued. "Who's to say that your skin wouldn't naturally be darker than mine?"

"It wasn't," she said. "I don't think anyone who is here has dark skin anymore."

"What makes you say that?"

"Something Sam explained to me," she said.

"And you're going to take it at face value?"

"I actually checked it out," she said. "He has books from before the fall. They explain how the skin of people who were exposed to the sun became darker."

"I don't understand," he said. "What are books?"

"You know how we share stories from long ago?" she asked.

"Yes," he replied.

"Well," she began, "these are those kind of things, only they are put on a surface where you can read them. There are markings on these surfaces, and each marking makes a sound, and when you collect the sounds together, they make words. I've been learning how to use them, and Sam says that I am a natural."

"But what does that have to do with our skin?"

"One of the books I read talked about our bodies," she said. "It explains how our systems work inside and how our skin on the outside was used to protect us. Because we've been down below for so many years, our skin hasn't had to protect us from the sun, so it's changed. Now it's lighter, because it doesn't need mela…I don't remember what it's called, but it's in our skin, and we don't need as much of it now because we don't need its protection."

"I think you're talking too fast," he said. "There's something that used to be in our skin that isn't anymore? And when it was there, we could be on the surface and not have to worry about the sun."

"They still had to worry," she said. "It depended on what kind of skin you had."

"Isn't skin all the same?"

"No," she said. "Some of us have darker skin with more of that mela-whatever in it. Others don't have as much. The mela-whatever helps to protect the skin, but it isn't always safe. They still had to think about the sun and how long they were in it."

"If we stay down here, it doesn't burn," he said. "I don't know why you would want to go up there and risk it."

"Because it's beautiful," she said. "Didn't you see the colors? The textures? All of the animals and the flowers and the sky? It's breathtaking."

"But we have everything we need down here," he tried. "There isn't anything they have up there that we can't find down here."

"Jacob," she said. "You know I love you with all of my heart, but I just don't understand your hesitancy. Why don't you want to go to the surface and live there?"

"Because it's not safe," he insisted. "You saw what happened when I went up there. My skin burned. It still hurts, even though we've been back underground for a while."

"You'll be able to stay above ground longer and longer each time," she said. "The more you go up, the more time you'll be able to spend. It won't be long until your skin will darken like mine. Then you can stay up there for a long time."

"I can't," he said. "I just can't do it. It's not safe, and you'll never convince me it is."

"You're saying that if I decide to move to the surface, you won't go with me?"

The hurt was clear in her voice. She wanted him to come with her, but she was going to go, even if he didn't.

"I don't want you to go," he begged.

"But I can't stay," she replied.

Neither one of them spoke. Both knew the other's mind was made up. She wanted to convince him, but nothing she said was working.

"I will miss you," she finally said, then moved away.

Jacob didn't know how long he stayed there, simply thinking about what she'd shared with him. His curiosity was telling him to follow her up, but the logical side of him knew it wasn't the right thing to do.

Two Months Later

Jacob," Frank said. "Where is Layla?"

He couldn't betray her secret, but he didn't want to lie to her father.

"She said she was going exploring," he finally said.

"I know that," the older man said. "Do you know where?"

Jacob could either tell the truth and out Layla's trips to the surface, or lie and hope the older man couldn't hear it in his voice.

"I can't tell you," he finally said. While it was the truth, it wasn't what Frank wanted to hear.

"You are her partner," he said. "I am her father. You are beholden to me, too."

"She is my first responsibility," Jacob insisted. "I owe you thanks for allowing us to be together, but I am not responsible for telling you everything we share between us."

Jacob could hear the anger in the older man's breathing, but Frank didn't express it in words. Finally, the older man moved away and Jacob was left feeling proud, yet a true disappointment. Seeking Layla out, he found her in their space.

"I need to tell you something," she said when Jacob arrived.

He could hear fear in her voice, something he hadn't ever heard before. He went to her, wrapping her in his arms, and asked, "What is it?"

"I am to have a child," she said.

Jacob's heart filled with joy. "When will the babe be here?"

"In about six months," she replied. "I want to have it on the surface."

"No," Jacob insisted. "I won't let you."

"You can't stop me," she said. "It's my choice, and I want this child to know the beauty of the world above ground."

"How will you survive?" he asked.

"The same way Sam and his people do," she explained. "By working the land. I want you to come with me."

"I can't," he said.

"You can," she replied. "I talked with Sam and he and his family are going to help us build a house where you and I can be out of the sun for long periods of time, gradually giving our skin time to build up resistance to the sun."

"But how will the baby survive?"

"Jacob," she said, caressing his cheek. "Babies were born above ground for hundreds of thousands of years. When we moved underground, we became more fragile. This is why we have such a hard time with babies surviving. We are meant to be on the surface."

"I'm worried," he confessed. "What if something happens?"

"Nothing is going to happen," she assured. "And if it does, we will deal with it. Something could happen whether we are underground or on the surface."

"Some things can only happen on the surface," he insisted.

"Come with me tonight," she said. "I want you to be able to spend more time on the surface. We can do this at night and not risk the burn from the sun."

"Can we tell your father?" he asked.

"I don't want anyone to know," she said. "Least of all him. He doesn't want to return to the surface, doesn't want our people to have the freedom that would allow."

"What do you mean?"

"You didn't grow up with him," she said. "Every day I heard him telling the other men that they needed to ensure that we were unaware of the changes above ground. He knew it was safe to return, but didn't want to lose control of the people. If he let us go up, he wouldn't be able to contain us. We would have the freedom to move away, make our own decisions, do our own thing."

"He wouldn't do that," Jacob insisted.

"He's been doing it for years," she replied. "I remember asking him about it when I was younger. He scolded me for saying such sacrilegious things, saying that the surface is what killed my mother. This is why he can't know."

"Why didn't you tell me this before?" he asked.

"I didn't want you to think less of him," she replied. "He does want to help our people, but he wants to do it his own way. Going to the surface isn't what he wants, and he doesn't think it is best for us. Now that I've been up there, though, I know it is."

"Have you told anyone else about going to the surface?"

"Just Kara," she said. "She has been going with me, and plans to move up there soon as well."

"What does Michael have to say about it?"

"I don't know," she said. "We haven't talked about that, yet."

"Layla," Kara whispered.

"What is it?" Layla replied, concerned with the fear in her friend's voice.

"We have to go now," the other woman said. "Michael is going to tell your father."

"What?" Layla nearly shouted.

"He thinks we're being coerced by the surface people," she said. "I grabbed what I could, but we have to go, now."

"Jacob," Layla said. "Are you coming?"

"Yes," he said. "My place is with you."

Layla sighed in relief, then said, "Grab the bag by the door. It's all we will need."

Doing as she asked, Jacob picked up the bag he found near the door. Even though they had no light, he could sense things without his eyes. It was a skill that they had improved during their time underground. It took them only minutes to make their way to the place where Layla had first brought him to the surface.

"Where do you think you're going?" Frank asked.

"Father," Layla said. "I am an adult. You cannot tell me where to go."

"I am the leader of our people," he insisted. "You will mind me, and the other leaders, or you will pay the consequences."

Before he knew what he was doing, Jacob rushed toward the older man, knocking him off his feet.

"Go now," he shouted to Layla and Kara.

He could hear them moving toward the door, then was blinded by the light coming through it. He released his hold on the older man and moved toward the light, hoping he would be able to get out before Frank could recover. The loud clang of the door shutting behind him made his heart sink. Because he hadn't shielded his eyes, he couldn't see anything around him. Finally, soft hands grabbed his and pulled him away from where he was standing.

"Come on," Layla shouted. "We have to get away from the door."

Following without seeing, Jacob tripped and struggled over the uneven ground beneath his feet. Underground he knew what the floor felt like, where the roots where, what tripping hazards lay in the way. Up here, though, he was not only blind from the light, but also unfamiliar with the land he walked on.

"Over here," he heard Sam shout. "Let's get you out of the sun."

It didn't take long and Jacob found himself feeling cooler, the light dimmer. Blinking, he opened his eyes and saw a structure.

Wooden walls held up the high ceiling.

"You good?" Sam asked him.

"I think so," he replied. "What is this place?"

"This is the barn," Sam said. "It'll be safe for you to stay here until the sun sets. Then you can come outside and see the land. We've been working to build houses for those who might want to come to the surface, and have one ready if you are going to stay."

Jacob looked at Layla and smiled. "We can't really go back," he shrugged. "So I guess we're stuck up here."

"How are you guys doing?" Sam asked.

They had been working at night and had learned to tend the land. It was tough, but Jacob, Layla, and Kara were all getting stronger with the manual labor they were doing.

"I didn't realize it would be this much work," Jacob confessed.

"My grandparents say it is much different than when they were below," Sam agreed.

"When did they come up?"

"My father was very young," Sam said. "Still a child, really. Several families decided to escape the underground. The man in control of the area they lived in was becoming more and more violent. It wasn't safe for them to stay, so they did the only thing they could do."

"Weren't they afraid of what they'd find on the surface?"

"Anything was better than living where they were," he said. "The danger was very real there, and the surface only held mystery. My grandfather had heard some had tried to go to the surface about fifty years earlier, but they were never heard from again. No one knew whether they survived or perished."

"That's still a big risk," Jacob said.

"But completely worth it," Sam replied. "Turns out the people who came up before had found others on the surface who helped them to adapt. Some have been here for almost a hundred years."

"That long?"

"I've met the great-grandchildren of some who were the first to come to the surface," he replied. "They've also told us of some who never went underground."

"How did they survive?"

"Many continued to live on the surface after the great war," Sam explained. "They didn't have anywhere to go, so had to ride out the storms. It wasn't easy, and they lost many in their tribe. But after a while, things began to get better. Three generations after the fall, they were back to living much as they had before, minus all of the technology."

"That's fascinating," Jacob replied. "To think we could have been living on the surface for hundreds of years instead of below."

"Not sure it would have been doable," Sam confessed. "Back then we couldn't agree on anything. It's what caused the great wars to begin with. Having been separated for so long, though, might not work in our favor either. There are some who stayed on the surface who resent those of us who sought shelter, calling us the descendants of cowards."

"That seems harsh," Jacob said. "What we were told was it wasn't safe to remain. That's why we went underground."

"I think it is just a matter of learning to understand each other," Sam said. "Most are fine with us returning, at least in the small numbers so far. When more begin to emerge, though, things might become difficult."

"Staying below may soon become impossible," Jacob said.

"What do you mean?"

"Layla's father was unhappy that she wanted to return to the surface," Jacob began. "She told me he's known it was possible for years, but has refused to allow anyone from our tribe to come up. When Layla brought me up the first time, I was terrified. I think others would be, too. But if what she told me is true, her father may make it unbearable to stay."

"Then we better continue to work on creating more shelters for your families," Sam said. "Those who stayed taught us so much. We need to continue teaching those who decide to come up as well. And we do that by learning."

"It is a process I've been enjoying," Jacob confessed. "Although my body has not enjoyed it nearly as much as my mind."

"Give it time," Sam said. "Before long, you will be able to do things you never thought possible."

"That's already happened," Jacob laughed. "Beginning with being on the surface itself."

"Are you sure?" Jacob asked.

"Everything she's told me fits," Sam replied.

"I don't want to give Layla false hope, but..." Jacob left the sentence unfinished.

"I think we'll have a gathering," Sam decided. "We can invite her to come, then Layla can make her own determination."

"As long as she doesn't upset her," Jacob said. "If it is false, it would crush her."

"But if it's true?" Sam asked.

"Nothing could be better," Jacob said.

"Perfect," Sam said. "I'll ask Penny to get things set up."

"I'll tell Layla that we are helping," Jacob said. "So she doesn't have to feel like she hasn't contributed. She already feels that way as it is, with her limits because of the babe."

"How close is she?"

"Should be within a month," Jacob said.

"Should we wait?"

"No," Jacob replied. "Either way, I think it would be good for this to happen before the wee one arrives."

"As long as it isn't going to be too taxing on her," Sam said.

"If it's true, she will be thrilled," Jacob said.

"I just hope it is," Sam replied.

"Hello, Layla," a woman said.

"I'm sorry," Layla replied. "I don't think we've met, yet. I'm new to the surface, and have met so many new people I have lost track."

"We haven't been introduced," the woman said.

"Layla," Jacob said, coming up to the women. "I'm glad I found you."

"I'm not hard to spot. I'm nearly as big as the barn."

"You are beautiful," the woman said.

"Thank you," Layla replied. "I'm sorry, I don't know your name. This is my partner, Jacob."

"Truly a pleasure," the woman said. "My name is Grace."

"That was my mother's name," Layla said.

"Pleasure to meet you, Grace," Jacob said.

"I'm glad my daughter found someone strong to help her escape," Grace said to Jacob.

"She is the strong one," Jacob replied.

"Did you just say daughter?" Layla asked.

"Yes," Grace said. "I believe you are my daughter."

"But my father said my mother was dead," Layla gasped.

"To him, I was," Grace replied. "When I left the underground, he told me I was never allowed to return. I tried to bring you with me, but he would not hear of it."

"But why didn't you stay, then?"

"I couldn't live under his rule any longer," she said. "Even then, he was beginning to show his need for control over all of us. He never wanted to come up to the surface, even when we'd talked to people who had been here. I begged him to let me bring you up, but he wouldn't hear it. He demanded I leave as soon as he found out I was planning to sneak away with you."

"Why would he do that?"

"Because some men need control," she said. "I have been waiting for you to discover the escape hatch. I knew you were smart, and I planted seeds in your memories, telling you stories of the surface, making sure you knew that it was safe to come up. I'm just glad you made it out before your baby got here."

Layla ran her hand across her stomach, soothing the child that was active inside.

"I only asked father one time about the surface," Layla recalled. "He told me it was too dangerous, that some had tried to come up, only to return sick. That's what he told me about you. You came to the surface and never returned. He said he couldn't risk anyone coming to search for you, even though he wanted desperately to find you. He never let me talk about it again."

"But you found a way," she said.

"Kara's family had talked about coming to the surface," Layla explained. "Her father told her repeatedly that she was not to discuss it with anyone. When we became friends, her father was worried that she would tell me and I would tell father. I asked her to come with me first, so she told me about her family's plan."

"Did they make it up?"

"Kara came with us," Jacob explained. "We don't know what happened to her family."

"She's thinking of going back down to find them," Layla confided.

"Doesn't she know how dangerous that can be?"

"She doesn't care," Layla said. "Her little brother is down there, and she is worried about him, as well as her parents."

"Then we need to send a group with her," Grace said.

"What do you mean?" Jacob asked.

"There have been talks in some of the communities up here," Grace said. "Many of those on the surface left loved ones below. Some know their family will not share in their desire to be surface dwellers, but others know that it is just a matter of time before their families join them."

"When are you planning to go?" Jacob asked. "I'll go with you."

"Sam has been working with the leaders of the other communities to set it up," Grace said. "That's how I heard about you. When he was talking with our leaders, asking if we had loved ones below that we thought might want to come to the surface, I asked about the hatch."

"Why did you leave the area?" Layla whispered.

"I didn't want to see your father again," Grace said.

"What do you mean?" Jacob asked.

"He probably never told you he came to the surface," Grace said. Layla shook her head, and Grace continued. "At first it was nearly every night, but it tapered off gradually. I last saw him twelve years ago. He begged me to return to the bunker, said that I was being selfish staying above ground. I told him that he was the selfish one, not wanting you to grow up in the fresh air of the surface. That last time, he said if I didn't return with him, that I would never see you again."

"And you thought the surface was more important than me?"

"No, darling," Grace said, shushing her daughter. "I begged him again to let me keep you up here. To let you grow up in the wilds

421

of the surface where you had room to run and jump and play. He refused, telling me that I would never see you again, that I was dead to him and he would tell you that I had died because I came to the surface."

"You said to keep her up here," Jacob said. "Did she come to the surface before?"

"Not the first few times I came," Grace explained. "But when I was sure it was safe, I brought her up with me. Oh, how you loved to run in the grass of the meadow. You danced and sang and carried on with such a joy. When I finally decided to leave, I told your father what my plan was. He had his friends escort me to the hatch and throw me out. You sobbed so much, begging him to let you go with me. How you wanted to see the world. He simply held you back and had his men lock the hatch."

"I remember," Layla said. "I remember it like it was a dream. The sunshine and the flowers. How easy it was for me to breathe up here. When father held me back, I think something shut the memories out, like they broke that part of me. Finding the hatch was like opening a piece of my past."

"And now you can live it for real," Grace said. "You and your family."

"You have to rescue her," Layla sobbed.

"We're going tonight," Sam replied.

"I won't leave her there," Jacob insisted.

"I told her not to go alone," Layla continued. "But she insisted she could handle it."

"Why didn't you tell us as soon as she left?" Grace asked.

"She made me promise," Layla said. "Told me to wait two days before I said anything. She knew you would go searching for her."

"They won't hurt her," Jacob said.

"You don't know that," Layla insisted. "Father has become more and more paranoid about anyone who talks about the surface. When we left, he was alone. But if he'd had time, he would have gathered his men to keep us underground."

"He wasn't that bad when I left," Grace said.

"Times have changed him," Layla said. "More and more he's talked about hunters on the surface. People who remained after the wars becoming mutants and eating those who ventured above ground."

"What kind of weapons does he have?" Sam asked.

"I don't know," Layla replied. "There's never been a need for anything underground, so I don't think he has anything."

"Weapons were forbidden," Jacob asserted. "Even the council members were barred from having anything that could cause harm to another."

"Just because it wasn't allowed doesn't mean they don't have something," Sam said.

"I think the most you'll find are some bladed weapons," Grace said. "Your biggest disadvantage will be the darkness. Living underground built up our other senses, so you should plan to take a light source. Just know that if it goes out, you'll be in more danger than them."

"I can lead them," Jacob said. "I know my way around down there and can act as a guide in the dark. Once we find Kara, we can escape without them even knowing we were there. If we use a light source, they'll know we're there and we won't get far."

"You know she's going to be kept in confines," Layla said.

"Exactly," Jacob said. "That gives us the advantage. We know where she will be and can get in and out without being found."

"With the guard?"

"Michael will be there," Jacob said. "I can reason with him."

"He's on my father's side," Layla said.

"But he loves Kara," Jacob insisted. "Love can make you do some pretty crazy things."

"Promise me you'll be careful," Layla said.

"It will be highest on my list," Jacob replied. "Now," he continued, turning to Sam. "Let's get a plan of action in place."

"Stay close," Sam insisted. "Jacob is our guide. He knows where we need to go. Be quiet and follow along. Watch your footing so you don't stumble. You'll be blind down there, but we'll be fine."

After the decision to rescue Kara was made, Sam had asked for volunteers to go on the mission. Five men agreed to go, and they'd spent the day laying out their plan. Jacob had drawn a rough map of what the tunnels were like and which way they would go to get to Kara. Now was the time to put their plan in action.

"I love you," Layla said, hugging her partner. "Be smart and come back to me."

"I'll do my best," Jacob returned. "Ready?" he asked the group of men.

Grace held her daughter as the men grabbed the rope they were using to stay together in the dark. Jacob had worn a cloth across his eyes most of the day to return his vision to what it was before he'd emerged. He hoped it would be enough. With a deep breath he nodded. Philip, one of the men who would be waiting just inside the entrance opened the hatch and stepped inside. He helped Jacob through, then let the others come in to follow. Once the last man was through the portal, he shut it tight.

"And now we wait," Grace said.

"Slow your breathing," Jacob hissed.

The men behind him were so loud, he was sure the entirety of the community could hear them coming. Being thrust back into the dark, he found he easily adapted to the environment he'd grown up in. He didn't need his eyes to see where he needed to go, that was ingrained in his mind. Each curve and dip brought him closer to the confines and closer to his return to his partner.

"Finally," a man said. "I was wondering when my replacement would get here. What took you so long?"

Jacob recognized David's voice in the dark. Why they'd left such a young man in charge at the confines surprised him, so he deepened his voice and replied, hoping to fool the younger man.

"Just overslept," he said.

"I know how that goes," the younger man said. "She's been quiet the whole time. Shouldn't be any trouble."

"No problem," Jacob said.

Jacob heard the younger man leave without noticing the others with him. That would likely get him in trouble, but for now he was thankful for the guard's youth.

"Kara," he said once a sufficient amount of time had passed.

"Jacob?"

"It's me," he said.

"Layla told you," she said. "I didn't want you to risk yourself."

"I've brought help," he said.

"Now?" Sam asked.

"Yes," Jacob said.

The room flooded with light, even though it was a small match. Eyes adjusting quickly, theyworked to free Kara from her cell.

"We need to get Michael," she said.

"He didn't want to come," Jacob insisted. "He's the one who told Frank we were leaving."

"They've disciplined him for allowing me to go," she said. "He won't survive if we don't take him with us now."

"Are you sure?" Sam asked her.

"As sure as I've ever been," she replied.

"Then lead the way," he said, dousing the light and plunging them once again into darkness.

"Michael, please," Kara begged.

"I won't go to the surface," he insisted.

"They'll kill you," she sobbed.

"You know she's right," Jacob said.

"I've done nothing wrong," Michael countered.

"Then why did they punish you?" Kara asked.

"Discipline is mandatory in order to ensure we are safe," Michael repeated the motto they'd been taught from birth.

"Do you hear yourself?" Jacob asked. "There is a bounty of supplies on the surface. We want for nothing. Are you telling me you'd rather survive on scraps and roots and bugs?"

"We do just fine down here," Michael countered, but they could hear the doubt in his voice.

"Michael," Kara said, placing her hands on his cheeks. "I love you. I want you to live a life full of everything that is beautiful, but you can't do that trapped beneath the surface."

"Jacob," Sam said.

"Michael," Jacob said. "We need a decision. Are you going to stay here and face near certain death, or are you willing to risk just a little bit and find a life that is beyond fulfilling on the surface?"

"Please, Michael," Kara begged again.

They could all feel the tension filling the space.

"You're sure it's safe?" Michael finally asked.

"Much safer than staying down here," Jacob said.

"OK," he finally said. "I'm trusting you, Jacob."

"You won't be disappointed," he returned.

"Let's go," Sam said.

"How long have they been gone?" Layla asked.

"They'll be fine," Grace comforted.

Philip opened the hatch and the men tumbled out, blinking even though it was night and the light wasn't too bright. Layla waited in anticipation of seeing her partner emerge. Finally, everyone was out of the door, and Philip stepped out and shut it.

"Where's Jacob?" she asked Sam.

"He's fine," Sam insisted.

"He should be with you," Layla replied. "Why did you leave him there?"

"He and Michael are getting our families," Kara said.

"Why didn't the rest of you stay behind?"

"Michael insisted," Sam said. "Since they are both from below, they felt they would be the best to rescue the remaining members of both Kara's and Michael's family."

"You were a team," Layla insisted. "All in together, and all out together. That was the plan."

"We're going back," Sam said. "Just need to get a few more supplies."

"Going back?" Grace asked. "For what?"

"Layla was right," Sam began. "Her father has changed over the last few months. He's become even more demanding on the community. Michael told us what they did to him, even though he alerted them to your leaving."

"It was horrible," Kara said. "No one is safe down there."

"The plan is to give everyone the opportunity to come up," Sam said.

427

"Will they come?" Grace asked.

"Michael and Jacob are planning on getting their families out," Sam said. "Once they have them to the door, they will rescue as many others as possible. This is why we are getting supplies to go back."

"What are you going to do?"

"Light the underworld," Sam said.

While they talked, the rest of the team had gotten sticks to use as torches. They wrapped some cloth smeared with pitch around the ends. Once they were done, they brought them over, preparing to return underground.

"We're ready," Philip said.

"Bring him home," Layla said to Sam.

"Let's go," Sam said, giving Layla a reassuring smile. "We've got a community to liberate."

"Stop," Frank shouted.

"No," Jacob returned. "You've held us in captivity for far too long. It's time we all saw the light of day and lived a life of freedom."

"Charles," Frank called. "Are you going to let your son get away with this?"

"I'd actually like to find out for myself," Charles replied.

The noise had drawn many in the community to the area near the hatch, and the murmurs were building with many wondering whether what Jacob had said was true. Three loud raps sounded on the hatch, and the group grew quiet.

"I'm going to open it," Jacob said. "There will be light, but it will be minimal. It is night on the surface, so we won't have to deal with the sun. If you want to come, you are all welcome. If you'd like to remain, that is your choice."

With his speech finished, he turned to the hatch and twisted the wheel, unlocking it. It opened and flooded the area with the soft blue light of night. The gasp was nearly deafening as the community as a whole saw for the first time.

"Jacob," Sam said, holding a torch above his head.

"I've got some friends I'd like you to meet," he replied, then stepped back to allow the first of the group to set foot on the surface.

"Welcome," Grace said. "We're happy to see you."

Blinking, men, women, and children stepped through the hatch into the night air, many taking deep breaths of the fresh air that surrounded them. Children stumbled and giggled as they felt the grass beneath their feet for the first time. An owl hooted nearby, and a young woman gasped in fear.

"It's safe," Layla said, holding the woman's hand. "That's a bird. They won't harm you."

The woman blinked and smiled at Layla.

"Come on," Layla said to the group. "Let's find you something to eat."

"Tonight, you'll stay in the barn," Sam said. "Tomorrow we'll show you around and help you get acclimated."

"Come back," Frank shouted from the opening.

"Frank," Grace said. "You need to let them choose. I know you want them to be safe, but that can be provided for them up here, now. Won't you come join us?"

Frank looked at her and blinked.

"Please, father," Layla said. "I want you to be happy."

"I'm staying down here," he said firmly.

"The door is always open," Grace said. "Come up when you're ready."

With that final statement, she turned and began the walk to the barn. Layla watched her father as he silently begged her with his eyes to stay with him.

"I love you, daddy," she said. "But I belong up here, now."

She waited a few minutes longer, then watched as he reached out and pulled the hatch closed. The clank of the locking mechanism broke her heart, knowing that her father would not come up with them.

"He might come around," Jacob said as he hugged his partner.

"I hope so," she said before turning with him to follow the others from their community toward the barn.

Epilogue

25 years later

Granny," Francis said. "What's that?"

The child was pointing to a rusting hunk of metal in the middle of the field.

"That's where we emerged," Layla said. "Back before your daddy was born, we lived underground."

"Why?"

"That is a very good question," she said. "A very long time ago, the people in charge of the government couldn't agree on much of anything. They had some terrible weapons which were unleashed on the world. Our kind scrambled to find someplace safe to live, and underground shelters where the best option we had."

"Why didn't they just talk?" Francis asked. "It's much better to find a way to get along by talking."

Ruffling the child's blonde hair, Layla laughed. "Grown ups aren't nearly as smart as you, my sweet child."

"Are we going to have to live underground?"

"I certainly hope not," Layla said. "It was not a fun place to be. I'm much happier up here on the surface where I can see the sun, smell the flowers, and look at your beautiful face."

"I don't want to live underground," Francis said.

"Then you need to make sure you know how to solve conflicts," Layla said.

FRUIT
BY DAVID MECKLENBURG

It takes a long time and many left turns to get to Orangevale. My mother drove east down El Camino from our apartment and then she turned left on Fair Oaks Boulevard until we reached Sunrise and then another left. When we turned right on Madison, I knew we were sort of close, but there was another left much further on near Hazel. And then I was usually spacing out and lost. But it was pretty out there: with rolling hills and orchards. The one thing I didn't like was the roaring. Even when I learned what it was, it still scared me somewhere deep inside.

My mother and I did not speak. We didn't much by that point. I knew well enough that any lengthy discussion would have included a few examples of me Being Wrong. I knew I was Wrong already. I did not like having my "nose rubbed in it" so the best thing to do was remain quiet. It was more difficult to Be Wrong when you didn't say anything.

I sat in the back seat and thought about the shirts of my mother's boyfriends. For a long time, they wore eagles, Easter Island heads, matadors and sunsets so black and orange that I could only dream of them in sleeping trips to Jupiter. The patterns shifted in the men's shirts, either in the amber light of our foyer or the darker shades of eucalyptus night, because then, green began to disappear in the shining grey of the tree trunks.

Evan, the one she was dating now, wore a polo shirt with a little alligator on the chest and a popped collar. He often wore a blue or white sweater draped over it. He liked to sail. That's where he was taking my mother for the weekend. I don't know if he ever wore one of the poplin long sleeved cowboy shirts; the kind with the gull-shaped piping on the chest pockets and pearl snap buttons. Before Sam and Rick, who wore those and had feathered hair and mustaches, there was Phil. He also had long feathered hair, but he wore a polyester shirt with the amazing designs. I remember him because he took my mother and me to see *Star Wars*.

It was shortly after *Star Wars* when my mother started having bad dreams. Phil had come over for dinner and we watched TV together. Then I went to bed. I woke up and my mother was shouting for Jesus. I got up and called in the hallway: *"mama, are you OK?"* I did not hear anything for a bit. Then her voice: sharp, commanding, mad. "Ada, go to bed. It's just a bad dream." I was eight. The next weekend my mother asked me if I wanted to have a sleepover at Uncle Louis's.

I got to spend the night with Uncle Louis a lot, which was fine with me. He had a couple of changes of clothes for me, some of my toys and dolls also had homes there. He had a funny cat named Mickey who would curl up in the crook of my leg when I went to bed there in my room. We would watch old movies on Channel 40. Or play board games. We always went out to eat. "I'm an engineer, not a chef." He would say. Sometimes he couldn't take care of me because he would be out of town. Then I went to Orangevale and Aunt Katie's.

We drove up the gravel driveway. Only the regular roads had

pavement there. She wasn't my "real" Aunt, but had been a best friend of the family for years, so she was as much an aunt as I knew. Like a lot of people there, Aunt Katie's house had a lot of fruit trees because the whole place had once been nothing but orchards. Hers were peaches and nectarines.

"Come on in! Milly's just over. Would you like a glass of wine or a Tab?" Aunt Katie was friendly, but pretty strict. She believed my mother that I was too smart for my own good and required watching. Like my mother, Aunt Katie was also Always Right. It was stressful being right, I suppose, which is why she always seemed to have a Kool burning in an ashtray somewhere. My Uncle Stan was hardly ever there. He worked at Aerojet nearby along with Milly's husband Paul.

"Hello Ada, I heard you were coming over this weekend. The kids are looking forward to it." Milly was Aunt Katie's neighbor. Aunt Katie was blonde and shaped like a roll of carpet in a blue silk housecoat.

My mother was dressed in a white cotton jumpsuit, platform heels, glossy red lipstick and her hair neatly pulled back in a bun. Her sunglasses were large. The scarf she wore was red and blue with little white anchors on it.

"So, Katie tells me you and Evan are still a thing. Sailing on the Bay. How romantic," Milly said.

"Yes, and there's not enough room on the boat for Ada, and Louis is gone so she gets to spend the weekend with us!" Katie added. I got the weird sense this had already been said before. Milly looked at Aunt Katie with a cocked eye and then said:

"I imagine the Queen Mary wouldn't be big enough, right Maria?"

My mother smirked and then turned to me. She kissed me on the cheek, told me to be good and blah blah. Then she left.

"Ada, Porsche's out back with Corey," Milly said. "Why don't you go outside with them."

Although she was strict, Aunt Katie was OK. She and Uncle Stan liked to fish, sunbathe and play *Password* at friends' houses. But Milly was strange and exotic. Like my mom, Milly was curvy, with big breasts but she didn't keep them in a bra. She usually wore loose brown and purple dresses with long flowery skirts. Her hair was long and parted in the middle. She looked a lot more like my mother and I than Katie. She had dark, smoky eyes and rich brown skin. She had a certain way of moving—like she was always dancing but not like a ballet dancer bobbing and jumping like a bird. She moved like someone trying to be a cat.

"Ada, just first take your bag to your room. Then you can go play."

I was getting a little too old to play. I was going to hang out, but I smiled and did as she said. After I dropped off my bag, I walked through the kitchen and opened the sliding glass door and heard Milly faintly say: "that poor kid."

I didn't want to be that poor kid, but I knew I was that poor kid. I got that look or downturned voice, like a frown in sounds.

The peach and nectarine trees were full of fruit: orange and pink planets almost in a galaxy of leaves and it felt cooler under them even through the smell of rotting fruit, which was like a thick syrup on your skin and nose. There was no fence between the houses. The nectarines were mostly on Milly's side and peaches on Aunt Katie's. The ground simply rolled down to a little hollow and then up again and this was as much a boundary as anything. The trunks were all painted white with something that kept the mold or pests at bay. I remember it looked very pretty against the green grass in the spring, but by now the grass was tan and gold and dead.

And then the roaring started. It came up low and rumbled through my legs, but it also fell down from the air like needles.

Aerojet, the company that made Minuteman missiles, was testing their rocket motors again. Even though I knew it wasn't the end of the world, it felt like it. And then how could I be sure when the end did come?

"Ada! I'm up here!"

"Hi Ada!"

They were shouting over the roar. Milly's daughter Porsche was sitting in the branches just above me and her little five-year-old brother Corey was even higher up. Porsche pronounced it the way many Americans do: with a silent e. She spelled it out the first time I met her. "P-O-R-S-C-H-E but the e is silent."

"No, it isn't."

"It's my name, Ada. I know how to say it."

I stayed quiet. Her mother said it the "right way" according to my Ompa who thought it was funny I had a girlfriend who was named after a Nazi car and tank designer. "But I don't think anyone bothers to think about that anymore," he would say. My Grandfather drove Chevrolets.

Porsche was like her name. She was sleek, powerful, and very beautiful. She had brown eyes and long hair styled like Farrah Fawcett Major's but it was brown with these red highlights you could catch in certain lights. Porsche was very brown in the summer and looked like she had grown out of the earth, took some clothes off a clothesline and knew how to walk the day she was born.

"Hi Ada. Do you want to come up? The peaches are ripe."

"Thanks." I climbed up in the tree and sat next to her. Corey, her little brother was scampering around swinging like a monkey. Porsche ate a peach and the juice was running down her chin and onto her chest.

"What are you doing?" I asked.

"Watching him. Here." She gently touched a couple of

peaches and then found one so eager for her hand that it simply came off the branch without a pull. It bruised in my hands even though I was barely cradling it. Pink, red, fuzzy and perfect, I felt shame to eat it. "There are lots of others. C'mon. It won't eat itself," she said. When I bit into it, I had to lean way out to not get any juice on my shirt. I left a yellow and red wound in the fruit.

"It'll be great when your twelve, Ada."

"Why? I don't want to go to Junior High. It sounds awful."

"Then you can baby sit Corey and I won't have to anymore. My mom will even pay you."

"Really?"

"You're such a nerd. You'll be a perfect babysitter. I mean, your mom drops you off mostly with your uncle, but when will you get to stay by yourself?"

"Never, my mom says I'm irresponsible."

"Ha. I hate to say this, but I am so glad she's your mom and not mine."

"Yeah, your mom's not very strict."

"Sometimes I'd like her to be. But she's kind of off in her own world." She looked at Corey swinging upside down. "Your mom's too strict, though," Porsche continued. "It's funny how nerd-girls parents are some of the worst even though they don't need to be. You're a good kid. I'd trust you with Corey. I don't know if I'd trust him. He's such a little retard." She leaned in close "I think he's an accident. Look at him."

Corey was, in his own way, as attractive as his older sister with a sandy-brown mop of hair that moved around randomly, like a sea creature on some Jacques Yves-Cousteau show. But I noticed Porsche and Corey didn't look all that much alike.

"Ssshhhh. I'll tell you more later. What were you eating before? Your lips are all red," Porsche said.

"A cherry Jolly Rancher."

"You know there's an easier way to do that."

"What?"

"Make your lips red. Corey, come on. Let's go inside for a while. It's too hot out here."

"You go in," he said.

"No, come on. Ada and I want to go inside. I'm thirsty."

I always liked Porsche's house because while it had coasters, books, pillows, boxes of chalk, a roll of cellophane tape, envelopes, a coffee can with a dying fern, a chessboard with the pieces all over the house, it wasn't a dirty house. I like the way it smelled of wood and incense, but not the sharp smoke from Mass. Rather a lingering scent, kind of like Porsche's mom. We walked through the kitchen and jars upon jars stood full of peaches; the big canning pot was still on the stove. It wasn't steaming anymore, but the house still felt heavy and full of sugar.

Last summer I got to help Porsche and her mom can. I remembered her mom showing me how to ladle peaches into the clean jars. I never did that sort of thing with my mother. Porsche's mother even smelled different: like crushed sage, honey and her own body smell. It wasn't gross, just very different.

"Come on. Let's put some make up on you," Porsche said and led me through the hall and into her parents' room. Their huge waterbed lay covered in a mess of sheets and there were clothes on the floor, mostly the tops and shapeless dresses her mom wore. The room had lots of candles and a wooden statue of two naked people holding one another. The floor was wood, but there was a big white shag rug on the floor. There was a painting on the wall, most of it was dark but in the middle was a naked Aztec warrior. I recognized him from the pictures I had seen in my history books. He was kneeling near a naked woman laying down.

"It's a legend. Lost love. They became mountains in Mexico. I'm surprised you didn't know that." I realized she was right but all of the pictures I had seen of Popocatepetel and Iztaccihautl had them in clothes.

We went into the bathroom: a tiled room full of mirrors and oak. Even the toilet seat was oak. Porsche's mom had lots of different kinds of makeup.

"Sit down. Uck. My shirt's all sticky. I'll be right back. And Porsche just took off her shirt right there in front of me and turned around and walked out to go to her bedroom. Even though she was tall and slender, she already had breasts and hips and I felt like I didn't belong anywhere. I was too tall to be a kid and too skinny to be a woman. She came back in another t-shirt and looked at me.

"Hmmmm. We have to figure out how to frame your good features, and make the other ones disappear. We have to be careful with the lipstick. Your mouth's already pretty big, Ada. The wrong lipstick will just make it look bigger."

She got out foundation, powder, some rouge, a few brushes, and mascara. She started with the foundation and powder.

"Not too much. You have nice skin," she said. "I'm already getting acne. It sucks. Did your mom have acne?"

"I don't know"

"Her skin looks pretty smooth. If you look closely at my mom, you can see the scars on her face. She says I won't have to do that. I have an appointment with a dermatologist next week. I just hope they don't give me Accutane. Ginny Bridge's older sister had that, and she lost her hair!"

I wanted to change the subject, but I was a little afraid of Porsche.

"Hold still, Ada." She had started brushing on rouge. "You'll ruin this if you talk. Open your mouth but hold it. It makes your cheeks hollow out."

I gulped hard while she was swirling on rouge. "You're almost there. You know, you might be very pretty one day. People grow at different rates. At least you don't wear glasses. You have pretty hair. You should do something with it though. You always wear it this way. You haven't had your period, have you?"

"No."

"Well, don't believe the stuff in the books about it being a special time for womanhood and all that hippie stuff. Nothing was different the next day, except I had cramps. But it's no big deal. If you wear a tampon you can go swimming, everything. Are your breasts getting bigger?"

"Kind of."

"Hmmm. Well. Your mom's got big boobs. I wonder why you don't show already. Did your Dad's mother... Oh, yeah, I'm sorry, Ada. You're a bastard and all. Oh well, who knows then?! Maybe you'll get Dolly Parton battleships!"

We still used that word then. Bastard. There was a big TV miniseries back then called *The Bastard*. Kids loved it because they could get away with saying *Bastard, like the TV show, duh*. I never heard the end of it because my parents weren't married—I didn't even know who my father was, save for stories my mom told about some guy she dated when she was studying abroad. The stories changed a lot like her other boyfriends changed. My mom liked men. A lot of my friends had single moms, but their parents *had* been married once. But I was her little one-and-only Bastard.

By fifth grade I knew that if you were popular and beautiful you got to have a boyfriend. I didn't. I was still taller than all the boys in my class and I kept growing but not in the ways that got you noticed. Except of course, for the *wrong* way. And then I began to understand Porsche. Boys would always want her.

We heard Corey out in the bedroom making rocket noises.

"Why do you think Joey's an accident?"

"Can't you tell?"

"No, what do you mean?"

"You've seen my dad. Do you think he looks like him?"

Through the door I saw Joey climb up on the bed. He was playing with a silver rocket and I thought about Porsche's Dad. He wasn't very tall, but he was broad and tightly muscled. She was right. Their jaws were different. Her dad had a rounder face and dark hair. Corey's face was thinner, his eyes were light brown. Corey was a bean pole, but he was just a kid.

"See those freckles? Come on, Ada. Can't you see it?" I looked at her and she raised her perfect, long eyebrows and smirked. "Who else around here has freckles like that?"

"Uncle Stan…" and I trailed off and gulped again. Porsche just laughed. "Now you get it."

"But how do you know?"

"Ada, they do it with each other. A lot."

Porsche took out the lipstick, gave it a quick, expert twist and gently put it on my lips. She stood there looking at me and smiled that cat-like way again. "C'mon, do this," she said and rolled and smacked her lips so I would mimic her.

"It's a thing they do. Before Corey, I woke up early on this Sunday. I went to go see if Mom and Dad were asleep so I could play. But it was Stan sleeping in bed with my mom. They weren't wearing any clothes. And who is coming across the back orchard but my dad in a bathrobe. I was seven. I didn't understand. I asked Dad what he was doing, and he said he was looking for Mr. Jaspers."

"The cat?"

"Yeah, I believed him. I still believed in Santa back then. I'd rather believe in Santa."

I thought about walking out and seeing my Uncle Louis and mom piling gifts under the Christmas tree one year. I already had doubts, but my mom was relieved.

"Did you ever catch them?" I asked Porsche.

"Walk in on them? No. I could tell though. It was usually once a month. On a Saturday night after I had gone to bed." She then sat down on the bathtub and frowned. "I finally had to do something. I mean I knew, but they didn't know I knew. For all I knew they'd keep at it. I could hear them you know.

"One time I knew your aunt was over here because I could smell those cigarettes she smokes. So, I got up and loudly went to the kitchen. I acted all sleepy so when my Dad came out, he asked me if I was OK. I said I was thirsty and wanted some water. That was all. I then went back to bed. I think he believed me. I wouldn't have tried that with mom. She's a space case but women are smarter than men. They can figure out that stuff and she always knows when I'm lying. My dad was clueless.

"But then Saturdays stopped for a while. Then my mom had Corey. After that, they started up again and I got to sleep over at friends' houses a lot. Remember when I came over to Uncle Louis's a couple of times?"

"Yes."

She leaned in close to my face and started brushing mascara on my right eye-lashes. And then I knew my mom wasn't having bad dreams. She was having sex and didn't want me around so she could do it as much as she wanted. And I knew she was driving as fast as she could over the Yolo Causeway to Vallejo, Evan, and his boat for two.

"It still happens when I'm not here," Porsche said. "Your Aunt over here. My Dad over there sometimes.

"Oh."

"I guess it's... what grown-ups do sometimes."

443

"I'm sorry."

"It's OK, my mom went on the Pill."

"How do you know?"

"Ha. Oh Ada. Come on, I'll show you."

Corey was out in the living room still making rocket noises, so we figured he was fine. We snuck over to the waterbed. It was huge and had all sorts of drawers tucked into it.

"She keeps them right next to her vibra..." She looked at an open drawer. I saw a packet, a circle of little pills each one separate. I knew what it was. My mom was on the Pill. But something was wrong. Something was missing. I could see it on Porsche's face because her cat-look was gone.

"... Corey!" she yelled.

Porsche ran out of the bedroom and I followed her. Corey saw us and turned to run. It was then the deep roar of the Aerojet plant came again. You could hear the windows rattle. Corey was faster than he looked and had a whole bunch of furniture between us. In his hand he held a long silver rocket and he roared along with the Aerojet motors. But it wasn't a rocket.

He ran out the open door and into the yard and the sunlight glinted off the thing in his hand as it flew over the green grass and beneath the trees so full of those perfect pink peaches. He ran and ran until we saw him head straight to Aunt Katie's back porch.

And there was Aunt Katie, outside smoking one of her Kools and Milly was with her. They were laughing at first. But then my Aunt's face dropped into a frown. Milly's was... flat. She had no expression.

"Oh, where'd you find that, baby?" she asked.

"In your bedroom, the girls were in there playing make up..."

Porsche and I got grounded. Corey didn't get in trouble

because he didn't know what was wrong and if we *"knew what's good for you, you won't ever tell him. Got that?!?!?!?"*

I didn't think it was fair, but the world didn't seem all that fair anyway. I remember Aunt Katie took me in and got out the Noxzema to wash the makeup off my face.

I don't think it ever really came off.

ABOUT THE AUTHORS

JENNIFER DiMARCO

A PNWC and Bumbershoot award-winning poet and Seattle Times bestselling novelist, Jennifer DiMarco first toured nationally as an author when she was nineteen years old. Her resume of publications includes contemporary drama, science fiction, high fantasy, and mystery novels as well as poetry collections and stage plays. For the last ten years, DiMarco has worked as a filmmaker writing and directing more than a dozen feature films, half a dozen mini series, and more than a hundred short films. She lives in the Pacific Northwest with her wife, author and actor Brianne, and their children, author and illustrator Maxwell, and producer and actor Faith. Find out more about DiMarco at www.jenniferdimarco.com.

LAUREN PATZER

Hailing from Tacoma, WA, Lauren has been an information technology guru, actor, writer and film producer among other pursuits. From the earliest days when he could sit up in a chair, he typed happily away at his grandparents IBM Selectric typewriter, writing somewhat less coherent stories than he does now. He feels the best part of writing short stories is the ability to briefly immerse yourself in a brand new world (even if it's modern day America) and tell the reader a complete, entertaining and /or thought-provoking story in just a few short pages. When he's not spending time with his wife, three daughters and grandson, Lauren is pouring over the details of his next pursuit.

HIROMI COTA

Hiromi Cota has been a special operations heavy weapons expert, an adjunct professor, a rave journalist, and the flaming-sword-swinging lead in a heavy metal opera. They (singular) have lived in nations around the world, but have settled down in Seattle with their spouse Randi and their (plural) dog Nasus. Outside of crafting queer science fiction/fantasy, Hiromi writes roleplaying games, produces the inclusive and comedic D&D radio drama podcast "Dear High Elves," programs video games, and gets into sword fights as a member of the Seattle Knights actor-combatant troupe. A reasonably complete list of their work can be found at: HiromiCota.com

AMBER RAINEY

A mom first in all things she does, Amber just happens to also be an author, actor, and award-winning filmmaker. She lives in Texas with her engineer husband, precocious son, and two cats, who vie for her lap while she writes. Amber has yet to find a medium she doesn't enjoy so she writes novels, short stories, and screenplays. Her first novel, *Eternal Willow*, can be found online at Amazon. You can visit www.amberrainey.com and www.tiny.cc/amberrainey for more about Amber and her work.

MARSHALL MILLER

After retiring as a Senior Special Agent/Federal Criminal Investigator, Marshall found a second career in writing and has a published four book series called THE TSCHAAA INFESTATION. These in-depth science fiction/speculative fiction works examine the human condition, and what people would do to survive when threatened with being eaten by an invading intelligent alien species. His thirty years of law enforcement experience and world travel provides him with the basis for the many varied characters which populate his literary works, demonstrating the good, the bad, and the ugly.

ELIZA LOEB

A United States actor, Eliza stepped in to the writing field in 2018, beginning with *Prompt Generation 1*. Originally born on Guam, they had spent their life reading, writing and creating with many artistic influences. Today, Eliza channels their creativity and experiences through their writing and does their best to reach out to their readers with a subtle portrayal of empathy or compassion. Sometimes, by allowing the reader to get close to them through the pages, other times by a means of fiction. Most times with wine that rarely touches the glass. A recently published piece of Eliza Loeb's work can be found on Amazon in the horror anthology *Unnerving*. But for those of you who would like to see the human behind the writer with occasional writing tidbits, feel free to follow Eliza on Tumbler at imelizaloeb.tumblr.com.

SHEILA MENGERT

A transgender novelist, dramatist, and poet, Sheila is also a political commentator. She has a Masters Degree in English Literature from the University of Washington with an emphasis on the works of James Joyce and Virginia Woolf. Her stories in *Prompt Generation 1* are a debut effort for her in a new genre. Her previous books include a non-fiction book on Borderline Personality Disorder and a seven volume epic re-telling of the Sherlock Holmes Saga published under another name. The story of her transition is told in her book *Transsexualism and its Discontents: A Political Profile* available from KitsapPublishing.com under the separate editorial imprint of Trannie-Goddess Press. Sheila is currently at work on an eighth volume sequel to her Sherlock Holmes Saga dealing with The Great European War of 1914-1918 and its critical aftermath in the Peace Conference of 1919 in Paris.

CARRIE AVERY MORIARTY

Born and raised in the Pacific Northwest, Carrie still lives there with the love of her life. She raised two wonderful, if not slightly warped, children who both live close to home. When she's not yelling at her hometown sports teams on the television, she's cheering them on from the stands. She loves nature and spending time enjoying it with her family. And you don't want to attempt to beat her in any board game. They are meant to be played to the death. Find more from Carrie at www.facebook.com/AuthorCarrieAveryMoriarty/ and on Twitter or Instagram @camoriarty13

DAVID MECKLENBURG

Much like his unseen Gemini half/fictional narrator Ada Ludenow, writer & illustrator David Mecklenburg was born in Sacramento, and moved home to Washington to attend the University of Washington. He has worked as a chef, tech support specialist, and capital project manager. You can often find him on the Washington State ferries commuting to and from Bremerton where he now lives. His stories were written "on the water." For more information about David (& Ada) please visit www.hagengard.com.

ABOUT THE EDITOR

BRIANNE DIMARCO

A published short story author, poet, and writer of more than a dozen short films, Brianne has been captivated by the written word from an early age and doesn't even remember when she learned to read. She currently works as a full-time volunteer for Blue Forge Group and is the Senior Editor of their publishing division, Blue Forge Press. Brianne lives with her wife, Jennifer, and their children on the Olympic Peninsula in the Pacific Northwest.